# MOONLIGHT
# & LOVESONGS

# MOONLIGHT & LOVESONGS

*Lilian Harry*

ORION

The right of Lilian Harry to be identified as the author of this work
has been asserted by her in accordance with the
Copyright, Designs and Patents Act 1988.

First published in Great Britain in 1997 by
Orion
An imprint of Orion Books Ltd
Orion House, 5 Upper St Martin's Lane, London WC2H 9EA

A CIP catalogue record for this book is available
from the British Library

ISBN 0 75280 498 7 (hardcover)
ISBN 0 75280 499 5 (trade paperback)

Typeset at The Spartan Press Ltd,
Lymington, Hants
Printed in Great Britain by
Clays Ltd, St Ives plc

*To my brother Alan,*
*with much love*

# ACKNOWLEDGEMENTS

With many thanks to my friends Maurice and Valerie Hutty, who have been of such help and encouragement to me in the writing of the four 'Street At War' books, and especially to Maurice for the very useful research he did for *Moonlight and Lovesongs*.

Thanks also to Jan and Mike Minshull for the story of the boys on the beach.

And most of all, my thanks to the people of Portsmouth and Gosport – especially those members of my own family – for, without them, none of these books would have been possible.

*

'*As Time Goes By*' by Herman Hupfeld, © 1931 Harms, Inc. (now Warner Chappell Music, Inc.) lyric reproduced by kind permission of Redwood Music Ltd.

# CHAPTER ONE

Even in wartime Portsmouth, a wedding could run to a bit of cake. The whole of April Grove had contributed towards Betty Chapman's, and everyone was entitled to a few crumbs to wish the newlyweds well. Right down to Ethel Glaister, who'd handed over a few spoonfuls of dried egg with hardly a grudging look, and old Granny Kinch, Ethel's arch-enemy, who had pressed a sticky paper bag containing a few sultanas, hardened by long incarceration at the back of a cupboard, into Annie Chapman's hand.

'You give the girl a good send-off,' she'd said with a toothless smile. 'She's a good girl, your Betty. Always 'ad a soft spot for 'er, I 'ave.'

There was no icing, of course. It seemed funny to have a cake with no icing, and funny that an iced cake should be against the law, but a lot of things were funny in this war. Not that *funny* was the right word, Annie thought as she cut the cake into small slices and set each in the middle of a square of greaseproof paper. Queer was better. Queer, and sad and downright heartbreaking. And – yes – sometimes funny as well. But, most of all, worrying.

I didn't know what worry was before all this started, she thought. None of us did. We didn't know we were born.

Her mother, Mary, was sitting in the old Windsor armchair she'd brought from the house at North End, after Arthur had died. It hadn't been easy to persuade Mary to come and live with Annie and Ted in April Grove, but she'd agreed at last, quite suddenly, as if she were collapsing. Since then, she'd more or less taken root in that old chair, willing enough to do any little jobs you might give her, like shelling peas or top-and-tailing gooseberries, but otherwise not doing anything except just sit there, staring at nothing, her wrinkled old hands folded in her lap, her lips working as if she were talking silently to someone nobody else could see. When Annie thought of her mother as she used to be, always active, always busy, it brought the tears to her eyes.

There was too much else to cry about these days, though, and once you started you'd never stop. There was Colin, Annie's son, who'd joined the Navy before the war and gone swaggering off in his bell-bottoms. He had been serving on HMS *Exeter* when she'd chased the *Graf Spee* all over the world back in 1940, and was still serving on her when she'd been sunk in the Java Sea over a year ago. It was only yesterday – at Betty and Dennis's wedding reception – that they'd heard he was a Japanese prisoner of war, and Annie still felt weak at the knees as she relived the moment when she'd read the telegram. Colin, alive. Colin, safe. A prisoner of war, it was true, and they were starting to say some funny – no, *queer* – things about the Japanese, but alive and safe all the same.

This time, the tears did come and she brushed her hand across her eyes hastily, not wanting them to drop on a bit of cake.

'They made a lovely couple,' Mary said suddenly, breaking into Annie's thoughts with a voice as dry and dusty as Granny Kinch's sultanas. 'I still don't know why Betty couldn't 'ave wore a white frock. You don't think they'd bin – well, you know . . . ?'

'I don't think any such thing, Mum,' Annie said sharply. 'Betty's a good girl, you know that, and young Dennis is religious. It's because he's a Quaker that she never wore white. They don't believe in it.'

She folded greaseproof paper over a piece of cake with exaggerated care. In her mind, she wasn't nearly as sure as she'd have liked to believe about Betty and Dennis. They'd been walking out together a long time, and who knew what could have gone on at that farm where Betty was a Land Girl, what with all the haystacks and long grass and that, and no mother to keep an eye on them? The Spencers were a decent enough couple, it was true, but they couldn't be expected to take the same care as if Betty'd been their own daughter, and maybe things were different out in the country.

Religious though Dennis might be, it was a queer sort of religion, when all was said and done. Wouldn't fight for his country – and what a to-do that had created in the family! She still went hot and cold when she thought of that speech Ted had made at the wedding, even though it had turned out all right in the end. Wouldn't argue the point, which exasperated Ted nearly as much when all he wanted was a good set-to, with Dennis ending up by seeing it Ted's way. Wouldn't take his hat off to any man, not even the King himself, nor call anyone 'sir' which was their right and proper entitlement. Yet a quieter or more respectful young man you'd go a long day's march to meet, and he'd risked his life time and time again in bomb disposal. It didn't add up, somehow, and when things didn't add up ordinary folk like Annie and Ted felt uneasy.

'He'll make Betty a good husband, all the same,' she said aloud, to herself as much as to her mother. 'Even though he's blind and lost a couple of fingers in that explosion. You can tell they think the world of each other. He's learning to do things round the farm already, so that Mr Spencer was telling me.' She laughed suddenly. 'Even if he did creosote the same bit of fence twice and leave the next bit bare!'

She finished packing up the cake and put it all in her basket. 'There, that's done. Our Olive can take those bits and pieces round the neighbours when she comes in. She's just gone up the road to see Florrie Harker.' Florrie Harker was Olive's mother-in-law.

The back door opened and Olive came into the kitchen. Gladys Shaw was with her. Annie smiled. She'd always got on well with Peggy Shaw, Gladys's mother, although before the war she'd not had a lot of time for Gladys, nor her younger sister Diane – a pair of flighty pieces, she'd thought them. But Gladys had proved what stuff she was made of when she'd driven an ambulance all through the Blitz, saving goodness knows how many lives, and finally been presented with a medal by the King – not that the King himself had actually pinned it on her chest, but the Chief Constable had and that was nearly as good. Now she was nursing at the Royal Hospital.

'Those the pieces of cake?' Olive asked, seeing the basket on the table. 'I hope you left a bit for tea, and I wouldn't mind some to take back to camp with me.'

'Go on, there's not enough to feed half the Army,' Annie said. 'You take those bits round and then I'll see what we can spare . . . You'll take a bit for your Bob, won't you, Gladys? He'll appreciate that, out in the desert.'

'That's if it gets past the censor,' Gladys said with a grin. 'If they don't eat it, they'll blow it up. I was ever so pleased to hear about Colin,' she added, rather shyly. She'd been carrying a torch for him ever since before he joined up, Annie thought, feeling sorry for the girl. She was sure Colin had never done anything to encourage her. 'D'you know an address I could write to? I know they like getting letters from home,' she added, turning pink.

'I'm sure he'd like to hear from you,' Annie said, 'but we don't know any details yet. Just the telegram that said he'd been reported as a prisoner of war. I'll let you know as soon as we hear anything more.'

'Trust our Col to fall on his feet,' Olive remarked carelessly. 'I never did believe he was lost. Take more than a ship sinking to get rid of him. You'll see, soon as the war's over he'll be back, strutting about pretending he's cock of the walk and shooting old man Jones's cats with a bow and arrow from the turret.'

3

Gladys laughed, but Annie's mouth twisted a little as she smiled. Her emotions were too near the surface to let her take it as lightly as Olive seemed to. They'd waited for news of Colin for a whole year, never knowing whether he was alive or dead, and she still hadn't properly taken it in.

'He can shoot all the cats in the street,' she said, 'as long as he comes home safe and sound,' and her eyes filled with sudden tears.

Olive made a face, annoyed with herself for being so tactless. 'I'm sorry, Ma. I didn't mean to upset you. We'll all be glad to have Colin back. And I'm as thankful as you that he's safe. You know, I reckon they're better off as POWs. At least you know they're not having to fight any more.'

Annie nodded, determinedly pushing away the rumours about what the Japanese were doing. She got up and laid a clean tea towel over the small greaseproof packets in the basket.

'There you are. You take those round while I get the tea ready. How's your Diane?' she asked Gladys. 'I hear she's going in the WAAF.'

Gladys nodded. 'She's hoping to hear any day. She's just about old enough; they're taking them at seventeen and a half now. Dad's not too pleased – he says she could get exemption, with working at Airspeed – but nothing'll satisfy her except getting into uniform.' She sighed and looked disparagingly at her own grey dress. 'Wish I could. I reckon they've forgotten me, it's been so long since I applied. The Wrens are the most popular, see, with Pompey being a Naval town, and they had thousands right at the beginning.'

'Nursing's just as good war work,' Annie said. 'You know that.'

Gladys and Olive went out and strolled along the pavement. April Grove ran alongside a large area of allotments which stretched away almost like a little bit of countryside, with plots freshly dug and sown. Broad beans were poking their green leaves an inch or so above ground now, and the potatoes weren't far behind. Anyone who was able to do a bit of gardening had an allotment and grew their own vegetables, and a lot of them grew soft fruit as well. The homes of April Grove and the other streets round about were as well stocked with jams and bottled fruit as sugar rationing would allow.

'Mum and Dad are thinking of keeping hens,' Olive remarked. 'Uncle Frank's getting some. Rhode Island Reds, he's going in for. And a couple of cockerels – he says they'll be ready for the table by Christmas.'

'I know.' Gladys lived next door to Frank and Jess Budd and had seen the coop being built. With Frank's shed at the bottom of the garden and the Anderson shelter in between, it took up most of the space that was

4

left. There was just room for the tomatoes to be planted in the square bit left at the top, and Jess's washing line to be strung along the path. 'I hope they don't crow too much, specially when I'm on night shift.'

Olive laughed. 'After four years of air-raid sirens, a few cocks crowing won't make much difference.' She stopped. 'Here, isn't that Carol Glaister coming down March Street with her mum?'

Gladys stopped too and they watched the pair walking rather self-consciously down the street. Ethel Glaister looked much as usual, in her powder-blue costume that she'd had since before the war started, with a bit of frilly veiling that was supposed to be a hat. She wore high-heeled shoes, white gloves and a dainty brooch on the lapel of her jacket, and all she needed was a flower in her buttonhole to look as if she was going to a wedding.

Carol, however, looked as if she'd just got out of bed after a night spent in her clothes. She was wearing an ill-fitting skirt, bunched around her waist, with a grubby white blouse and an old winter coat in brown herringbone tweed which she'd left unbuttoned. Her shoes were scuffed and hadn't seen a brush or a bit of polish in weeks. She looked tired, her skin muddy and her hair lank, in contrast to her mother's brightly made-up face and Marcel-waved hair.

Ethel Glaister looked vexed at seeing Olive and Gladys. She hesitated briefly, then walked on, looking as if she meant to march past them with no more than a nod, but Gladys stood in her way and she was forced to stop.

'Hello, Mrs Glaister. Hello, Carol. It's a long time since we saw you – how did you like Devon, then?'

The story Ethel had given out was that Carol had gone down to Devon to help look after her sister Shirley, who was staying with relatives there, but everyone knew Carol had been in a home for unmarried mothers, having a baby. The baby had been adopted and the whole thing had caused a lot of talk in April Grove, with the older people sniffing their disapproval and the younger ones half inclined to stand up for Carol. Most of them were well aware that there, by the grace of God, went they, although some of them, like Diane Shaw, scoffed at Carol for 'getting caught'.

What must it be like to give your baby away? Olive thought now, staring at the younger girl. She thought of the one she'd lost before it could even be born, and the one she and Derek had tried for before he went away. Her disappointment when she discovered a couple of weeks later that they'd failed had been nearly as great as when she'd had the miscarriage.

5

But Carol had actually given birth to a live baby, a little boy, and had looked after it for six weeks in the home before it went to new parents. How had she felt about that?

'Devon was all right,' Carol said in a dreary voice. She had gone to her relatives there for a few weeks after leaving the home, but there wasn't really room for her and in the end Ethel had agreed to have her back home again. Neither of them relished the prospect much. 'Plymouth's much the same as Pompey, really.'

'Go on, don't they get lots of cream and stuff there?' Gladys asked. 'I thought you'd come back as fat as butter.' Olive nudged her sharply, and Gladys blushed. 'Well, you know what I mean . . . So what are you going to do now, get a job? Or join up?'

'Carol's not old enough to join up,' Ethel said sharply. 'Anyway, I want her at home to give me a hand. It's time she did a bit to help out.'

She jerked at Carol's arm and turned away, clacking down the pavement in her high heels. Carol shrugged, gave the two girls an apathetic glance, and followed her.

'She looks really fed up,' Gladys said. 'And that coat! It looks like one old Granny Kinch might have thrown out. Well, I wouldn't want to be her, stuck in that house with a cat like Mrs Glaister.'

'I wonder what happened to her baby,' Olive said. 'I wonder if she knows where he's gone. They take them miles away sometimes, and don't tell you who's got them, or anything. One of the girls on the gun was telling me about it.'

'I suppose they think it's better that way. Gives you a chance to forget about it. I mean, there's no good hankering after it once you've made up your mind, is there? You've just got to put it behind you and start again.'

Olive couldn't see how that would be possible. Forget you'd had a baby? When you'd carried it in your body for nine months, given birth to it, held it in your arms and fed it? When you'd looked after it for six weeks — bathed it, cuddled it, seen its first smile? She shuddered, feeling the pain as sharply as if she'd shared Carol's experience. That poor kid, she thought. No wonder she looks so awful. But you couldn't expect Gladys to understand that.

'Come on, she said, 'let's get rid of this cake. Mum's packed up enough slices for the whole street.' She sighed. 'I ought to have given Mrs Glaister and Carol a bit, I suppose. That means I'll have to knock on their door. I just hope it doesn't upset that poor girl too much.'

There was no need to call at number 14 with wedding cake. Jess Budd was Annie's sister and Betty and Olive's aunt, and she had helped with the wedding, using her dressmaking skills to make the grey frock that had given Annie such heartache, and saving lard and margarine for sausage rolls for the reception. She and the rest of the family had had their share of cake, though she knew the boys, Tim and Keith, would have eagerly accepted more if they'd had the chance.

'That's to go round everyone,' she'd told them sternly when they'd looked askance at the minute portions they'd been given on Saturday. 'It's a token, that's all. It's not meant to keep you from death's door.'

'It wouldn't keep a mouse from death's door, a tiny piece like that,' Tim had grumbled. 'I don't see the point of little bits of cake. I'm going to have doughnuts at my wedding.'

'Who will you marry?' Keith asked with interest. 'Wendy Atkinson? She's about the right age. Or maybe Stella, or Muriel. They need a husband, now they've got no mum or dad.'

Tim scowled. The thought of a wedding, at some distant point in the future, was one thing – actually considering any of the girls he knew as a bride was quite another. 'I shan't marry any of them. Actually, I probably won't get married at all. Wives aren't much use to explorers.'

'They can help them pack, and have tea ready for them when they get home,' Keith pointed out. 'It's like the Home Front. There has to be someone to do all the work while the men are away.'

The boys were out now, roaming around some of their old haunts. Keith would be going back to Bridge End later this afternoon, to the old vicarage where he'd been staying as an evacuee. Tim had been there too, until a few weeks ago, and he'd been happy enough until he'd had to leave the village primary school and go to the secondary school at Winchester. It was the Portsmouth school really, but like a lot of other schools they'd had to try to fit two lots of pupils into one space, taking turns with the classrooms and playing fields. After the muddle over his scholarship exam, Tim had never settled down again and in the end it had been decided he would be better off at home, where he was working for the local chemist as a delivery boy and waiting for an apprenticeship to come up.

The boys' elder sister Rose was indoors with Jess and Maureen, who was nearly four. Maureen was playing on the floor with a set of old wooden building bricks and a bag of coloured marbles. She spent hours like this, arranging the bricks in enclosures and shifting the marbles around between them, sometimes one or two at a time, sometimes in clusters. Sometimes Tim would let her play with a couple of old Dinky toys he had – a car with an open top and a Pickfords furniture van with a rear door that really opened – and she would settle some of the marbles in the car seats

7

for all the world as if they were people, and push them around on the rag rug.

'There's something wrong with her,' Rose said. 'Why doesn't she play with dolls, like other little girls?'

'Well, there aren't many dolls around for her to play with, are there?' Jess said. 'Only that old one of yours with the china head, and she don't seem to like that one all that much. And the rag doll I made her that she takes to bed, and the golliwog Cherry knitted for her.'

'That's three. That's as many as I ever had,' Rose said with a touch of resentment. Rose was almost sixteen now and she'd grown out of the novelty of having a baby sister. It had been all right when Maureen *was* a baby, she thought, a real one in a pram you could push around the streets. It had been nice having her to cuddle and play with and feed with a spoon, though she hadn't been so keen on the nappy-changing part. But a four-year-old was a very different matter, always wanting to poke her fingers in where they weren't wanted, and forever asking questions. Maybe it was as well to leave her quietly playing on the rug with her bricks and marbles.

'I wonder sometimes what's going on in that little head,' Jess observed. 'I mean, look how she's got them all arranged. It's almost as if she's making up a story with them. She's in a world of her own half the time.'

There was a knock on the door and a moment later they heard Peggy Shaw's voice calling. The door was never locked during the day and Peggy, who lived next door in number 13, was a close enough friend to just pop in, but she always called out first. That was only polite. She came in now, thin and wiry, bristling with energy as usual, her eyes snapping, and behind her, scarlet with excitement, came her daughter Diane.

'Guess what! Our Di's got her papers from the WAAF. Came this morning. She's tickled pink but my Bert's proper upset. Says he'll go along and try to get her out of it—'

Diane butted in. 'He can't do that. It's the law now, girls of seventeen and a half—'

'Yes, but you don't really have to go, not when you're already doing important war work, making planes,' Peggy said, clearly continuing an argument which had been going on for some time. She turned back to Jess. 'I'm not even sure they'll let her go from Airspeed, but she's so mad about flying, she won't take no for an answer. Not that she'll ever get the chance to *fly*. Well, it stands to reason she won't, doesn't it, a bit of a girl, not when there's all those chaps—'

'They're letting women fly,' Rose interrupted. Jess frowned at her, but she continued, 'I read about it the other day. They're building so many planes, there just aren't enough men to take them to the airfields. They need the RAF pilots for bombing and fighting anyway, so they're letting women do it. They wouldn't be able to manage without the women.'

Diane looked pleased. 'See, that's just what I told you,' she said to her mother, and then to Rose, 'You'll be able to volunteer yourself soon, won't you? Why don't you try the WAAF as well? We might get posted together.'

'Rose has got a long time before she needs think about that,' Jess said sharply. The thought of any of her children having to go to war filled her with terror. It was bad enough having the boys evacuated, so that they'd never been able to be a proper family, all together, since Maureen was a few weeks old. 'She's nearly two years younger than you, Diane.'

'Oh, that doesn't matter,' Diane said offhandedly. 'You don't have to show your birth certificate. I don't reckon they ever check up: they're too glad to get people. And Rose looks older than fifteen when she does her hair up. I bet she'd pass all right.'

'Well, she's not going to try,' Jess said, annoyed. 'She's all right at home, learning shorthand and typing. That'll be a lot more use to her after the war than flying an aeroplane.'

Diane shrugged. She was too excited at having got her own way to bother about what other people said, and she was looking forward to leaving home and getting some independence. Her father's insistence that she should be home by ten-thirty at night was getting beyond a joke.

'Have you heard about the Americans?' she asked Rose now. 'They're coming to Pompey soon – soldiers, sailors, airmen, the lot. That'll brighten the place up a bit.'

'Well, you needn't think you'll be mixing with them,' Peggy said. 'It's best to keep with your own sort. They're different from us, Americans, you don't know what their standards are.'

'Go on, they're all right,' Rose said. 'I've seen them on films. They're just like us, except they talk with American accents and live in big houses. I think it'd be smashing to have a Yankee boyfriend, don't you, Diane?'

Jess pursed her lips. Rose hadn't had a boyfriend at all yet, and she agreed with Peggy that the girls should stay with their own kind. She didn't want Rose influenced by Diane, either. Peggy was a good friend, but there was no doubt that her younger daughter was flighty, always had been.

'You'd better get back indoors,' Peggy said severely to Diane. 'And if you think you're going to join the WAAF just so you can stay out late and get up to goodness knows what with Americans, you can think again, young lady. You're still under your father's and my control till you're twenty-one, war or no war, and don't you forget it.'

9

Diane rolled her eyes towards Rose and pulled a comical face. Rose giggled and the two older women sighed. There was just no telling young people these days, and they both knew that Peggy's words were empty really. How *could* you control a girl once she was away from home? You just had to hope and pray they'd remember all they'd been taught. And some of them forgot even before they'd left their own front rooms. Like Carol Glaister, next door.

I don't know what I'd do if our Rose got into that sort of a mess, Jess thought as Diane whispered something that made both girls go off into fits of giggles. I just don't know what I'd do. You can't feel safe with any of them now, till they're decently married off like Olive and Betty.

'Here,' she said to Peggy. 'Have a cup of tea. The kettle's boiled five minutes ago, and I've got a nice piece of wedding cake here, that Annie gave me. I reckon we deserve a treat.'

Receiving a piece of Betty Chapman's wedding cake almost as soon as she'd got inside the door of number 15, was something Carol Glaister could have done without. Coming home for the first time for nearly a year was bad enough, especially considering all the things that had happened during that year, and walking back into her mother's front room, with its fussy little knick-knacks and antimacassars on the chairs, felt like walking back into a trap.

'You needn't think you're going to be Lady Muck here,' Ethel said sharply as Carol put down her shabby cardboard suitcase. 'You might have bin living in a big house all this time, with bathrooms and inside lavatories, but we don't run to that kind of thing in April Grove. Not but what we couldn't have had a bath put in the scullery with a lid over it, like Mrs Hawkins has got round Carlisle Crescent, if your father had put his mind to it,' she added bitterly.

'I wasn't exactly waited on hand and foot in the home,' Carol answered. 'We had to do all the cooking and cleaning. Like slaves, we were.'

'And quite right too. Teach you a few home truths. I reckon I always did too much for you. Why, you couldn't even knit before you went away.'

'I can now.' Carol thought of all the tiny garments she had knitted during the past year. There hadn't been a moment when you could sit down with your hands idle. You had to be doing something all the time – knitting, sewing, hemming and stitching, for the babies that were expected. And if it wasn't that, it was socks for the Army, or balaclava helmets. There seemed to be no end to the socks and balaclava helmets soldiers could get through.

'Anyway,' she said, reverting to her mother's earlier remark, 'you can't say I was living in a big house down in Devon. Ten of us there was in that little cottage. We had to take turns to breathe.'

'You needn't be clever with me, miss,' her mother retorted. 'I had enough of that before. Too easy with you, I was, and look where that got us. Now you're back, we'll have things a bit different. You'll do as you're told and you'll do some work around the place. I've had enough of being a skivvy.'

Carol gazed at her. Like all the other houses in April Grove, except for the Chapmans' at the far end, number 15 had only two rooms downstairs and two bedrooms above, with a lean-to scullery and an outside lavatory. Some years before, Ethel had bullied her husband George into glassing over the area between the scullery and the wall between them and number 14, turning it into what Ethel grandly called 'the conservatory'. It made more room and meant you didn't have to put on your mac to go to the lav, but the house was still really just a two-up, two-down, and with only Ethel living there it couldn't have made much work.

'I don't see how you can call yourself a skivvy,' Carol said. 'With Dad away in the Army, and our Joe at sea, and Shirl down in Devon still—'

'Well, *you'll* make more work, won't you, just being here. There'll be your bed to make and sheets and clothes to wash, and your meals to get, not to mention all the dust and dirt you'll drag in on your shoes.' Ethel slammed the door of the front room. 'Come on. We'll keep at least one room decent.'

What does she think I'm going to do, keep pigs in there? Carol thought as she followed her mother into the back room, where the family spent most of their time. But Ethel had always been proud of her front room. She'd tried to make them call it the 'parlour' and all her best ornaments were in there, together with the bone china tea set with roses on which was displayed in a glass-fronted cupboard, and the cushions she'd embroidered herself, as plump and untouched as the day she'd first set them carefully in position, balanced on their points, in the two armchairs. Small though the house was, the room was only used at Christmas or if there were visitors for tea on Sunday afternoons, and the rest of the family had always preferred the back room, which was as shabby as any room could be that Ethel had anything to do with, and comfortably cluttered.

However, there wasn't much sign of a family now. Since Joe had joined the Royal Navy, Ethel had put away all the clutter of model aeroplanes and ships which he'd made, all the cigarette cards and copies of *Hotspur* and *Wizard* which he'd left piled up in a corner, and all the Joe Loss records he'd saved up for. They were all in a box on top of the wardrobe, waiting for him to come back again. She'd thrown out all her husband George's stuff – the pokerwork pipe-holder Joe had made him, the pictures of himself as part of a local cricket team years ago, the books about woodwork and the old tobacco pouch that he'd kept loose change in, which had sat on the corner of the mantelpiece for as long as Carol could remember.

There was only Ethel in the room now: Ethel's mirror with its fancy shape over the fireplace; Ethel's frilly pink curtains hanging at the window; Ethel's lace edging fixed all the way along the mantelpiece. The wedding photo of her and George had disappeared, replaced by one of herself in her best summer frock and a large straw hat with flowers on its brim, taken in a studio by a local photographer, and on the shelf where George had kept his books and Joe had piled up his records were half a dozen romantic novels. Ethel always had liked a good love story.

'You can take your case straight upstairs,' Ethel commanded, sinking into an overstuffed chair with embroidered covers on its arms. She took off her shoes and held them up to examine the heels. 'Those pavements are getting worse every day. Look at the marks on these, and I've only had them a month . . . Well, go on,' she added sharply, 'and I'll have a cup of tea when you come down. Kettle's in the same place as it always was.'

It's about the only thing that is, Carol thought as she climbed the narrow staircase. She didn't recognise any of the furniture in the room. Mum must have got rid of all the old stuff and bought new during the year Carol had been away. She wondered where she'd got the money.

Carol knew that her father had walked out on Ethel some time before his unit had been sent to North Africa. He'd been under Ethel's thumb for years, keeping his head down under her tirades, retreating to his shed and his own thoughts as often as he dared, but once war had been declared, he'd been off, reporting to his Territorial Army unit and getting sent off straight away. After that, he'd seemed to change and finally he'd told Ethel just where she got off, and marched out. Ethel had never admitted it to anyone, just as she'd never admitted that Carol had had a baby, but the whole of April Grove knew. Enough of them had heard that last row as George and Ethel shouted and yelled at each other, and Ethel's screeching as he'd walked away up the street.

George had continued to pay Ethel her allowance, so she hadn't gone short, but he'd taken off enough to send Carol a few bob as well, to help with her expenses. I suppose I'll have to give that to Mum now, she thought, hauling her case into the little back bedroom and staring round at the dreary mud-coloured distemper on the walls ('a nice fawn', Ethel had called it) and the brown curtains. She won't want me having money of my own. She won't want me having any independence at all.

The shrill ring on the doorbell interrupted her thoughts, just as they were beginning to circle back again, as they so often did, to Roddy and the baby. She heard Ethel shuffle along the passage in the pink slippers with the bit of fluff on the front she always wore indoors. There was a murmur of voices, then the front door closed again and Ethel came to the foot of the stairs to yell up at her.

'That was young Olive Harker, Chapman as was. She's just passed on a bit of her sister's wedding cake. I must say, it's nice to know *some* people still do things the right way round . . .'

Carol sat down on the narrow bed and closed her eyes. She and Roddy would have done things the right way round, if only they could have. *They* would have got married and had a little home and started their family, like Betty Chapman, like Roddy's sister Moira in Scotland that he was always talking about, like the people in the books Mum was always reading. But they hadn't had a chance, had they? There'd been a war to drag them apart. And there'd been Ethel herself, the sort of mother any girl would want to get away from.

'Well, what are you doing up there?' Ethel demanded shrilly from the bottom of the stairs. 'I thought I told you to come down and make me a cup of tea. I'm parched, after all that long wait at the bus station. Come on now, you can do your bit of unpacking later on when I'm out.'

She must have walked right past the kettle to shout up the stairs, Carol thought, dragging herself to her feet, and she only had to stretch her arm out across the tiny scullery to turn on the tap. But that was the way it was going to be, from now on.

Ethel had been made to look a fool in front of the neighbours. Her husband had left her and her daughter had got herself 'into trouble'. George was thousands of miles away in North Africa, but Carol was here on the spot, and Carol could be punished for everything.

# CHAPTER TWO

Four years of war. Why, that was as long as the Great War of 1914–18 had lasted – the First World War, people were now calling it, and this was the second, and no end in sight. Twice in less than thirty years, and almost every country in the world at each others' throats.

'We never thought we'd be doing this sort of thing, did we?' Olive remarked to Claudia Stannard as they took their positions on the anti-aircraft gun emplacement. 'I mean, four years ago I was only just walking out with my Derek, thinking about nothing more than his new sports car and whether to have my hair cut, and whether he might kiss me goodnight. We used to come out here to Southsea Common all the time, and walk along the front and look at the Island. Now we're married and I could count the nights we've had together on my fingers. He's thousands of miles away in Africa and I'm here firing guns at aeroplanes. Me! I never thought I'd do anything but work in his dad's office.'

'I never thought I'd do anything, full stop,' Claudia said. 'My mother was all set to have me at home when I left finishing school, arranging flowers and helping Dad a bit in his surgery. And paying calls. *Paying calls!*' She snorted. 'D'you have any idea what that means, Livvy? Dressing up in a pretty frock and white gloves and sitting down with a lot of twittery women who've got nothing to do but eat cucumber sandwiches and gossip. In the most ladylike way, of course. We were never anything but ladylike.'

'I bet she thinks you've changed,' Olive said with a grin. 'The only gloves I've seen you wear are khaki, and your language would get you drummed out of the sergeant-major's tea party, let alone your mum's.'

'I can tell you which I'd rather be invited to, anyway,' Claudia said, smiling. ''Specially that new sergeant-major in F-block. He's got a definite touch of the film star about him.'

'Has he?' Olive said off-handedly, and Claudia smiled again.

'Go on, Livvy, I know you're married and there isn't a man in the world to touch your Derek, but you can't tell me you haven't noticed. I mean, being married doesn't mean you switch everything off. It's not natural.'

'I don't see why not,' Olive said a little stiffly. 'I'm just not bothered about other men. I haven't ever fancied anyone else, not since I first went out with Derek.'

'Well, you will one day, especially if he's away a long time. It's biology, isn't it?' Claudia's father was a doctor in Fareham and there were times when she had a strangely clinical attitude towards love. 'It's the perpetuation of the species and all that.'

'You don't have to tell me that,' Olive said, more sharply than she'd intended. 'There's nothing Derek and me would like more than to do our bit towards perpetuating the species. Trouble is, the government seems to be doing its best to kill it off.'

Claudia bit her lip and reached over to touch Olive's hand. 'I'm sorry, Livvy. I shouldn't have said that. I just – well, you know what it's like for women who are left at home while their chaps go off to fight. They're lonely. Nobody can be blamed if they go off the rails a bit. It's just human nature.'

'Well, it's not mine,' Olive said positively. 'Me and Derek don't mess about. We think too much of each other – never mind *how* lonely we might get.'

The sergeant in charge of the gun poked his head round the turret. He was a regular soldier who had been in the Army for twenty years, and to start with he'd been suspicious of bringing women into the Service. It had taken Olive and Claudia and the rest months to get him to admit that they were among the best crews he'd ever worked with.

'Stop nattering, you two. There's blokes trying to sleep round 'ere.' The girls giggled and he lifted his eyes skywards. 'I dunno what it's comin' to, I really don't. Bits of girls in Army uniform, chatterin' on about their boyfriends all the time. 'Ow're we supposed to win a war with this lot, eh? Nothin' but perms and nail varnish and what was on at the pictures last night.' He leered. 'I s'pose you bin canoodlin' in the back seat, droolin' over that Leslie 'Oward again.'

'Certainly not,' Claudia said with dignity. 'If you must know, I went to see *The Chocolate Soldier* at the King's. And Olive's a married woman. She doesn't canoodle.'

'Whoo!' he said. '*The Chocolate Soldier*, eh! Sounds like summat we used ter get in our Christmas stockin's.'

'He was a lot sweeter than you, that's for sure,' Claudia retorted, and the sergeant retreated round the turret, chuckling. The girls grinned at each other.

'He's all bark and rubber teeth,' Olive said. 'Quite cuddly, actually, in a teddy-bear sort of way. But that doesn't mean I *want* to cuddle him – or anyone else,' she added fiercely, and leaned against the turret, gazing out across the sparkling sea.

The sun was glinting off the water, and the Isle of Wight was very clear. There was a saying in Portsmouth: that if the Island was clear it was going to rain; if it wasn't, it was raining already. Today, you could see the buildings in Ryde and the church tower poking above the skyline, and you could almost believe that you could see trees coming into leaf in the woods that clothed the hills.

The Island was only a few miles away and a part of Hampshire, but it was somehow different. Like a tiny bit of foreign country, with queer names for its little towns and villages: Ryde where you had to walk; Cowes you couldn't milk; Newport you couldn't bottle; Freshwater you couldn't drink; Needles you couldn't thread . . . Going to the Island on one of the paddle steamers from Portsmouth Harbour station was a treat, a real day out.

We were going to go to the Island for our honeymoon, she thought. We were going to Ventnor and Blackgang Chine, right round the back looking towards France, and Freshwater. I was going to collect some of that coloured sand in Alum Bay and put it in a bottle in a pattern, like Auntie Jess had got on her mantelpiece. We were going to go all over the place. And instead of that we never got any honeymoon at all, just a couple of nights in Mum and Dad's old double bed that me and Betty used to share, and then Derek was off back down to Wiltshire.

But at least he was still alive, at least they still had a future to look forward to, when the war was over. Some girls were widows before they were twenty. Some girls had never got as far as a wedding ring.

Go off the rails? she thought. Me and Derek? Never in all this world.

There was a new announcer reading the news on the wireless. His name was Wilfred Pickles and he spoke with a northern accent. Apparently, it was thought that this would be difficult for a foreigner to impersonate.

'It would be, too,' Jess Budd said. 'I can hardly understand it myself. Anyway, why would a foreigner want to read the news on the wireless?'

'It's in case they start up a wireless station and make up lies,' Frank said. 'Propaganda.' He frowned at the big map on the living-room wall. 'I'm running out of pins for this lot. You got any to spare, Jess?'

'No, I haven't, and don't you go looking in my sewing box neither. I need the ones I've got for making Rose's new frock. You can't get pins for love nor money these days.'

'I suppose if you could, it'd be called pin money,' Tim remarked without looking up from his comic, and his parents groaned. Tim's jokes got cornier every day, and Rose was beginning to ask him when he was going to start harvesting. She liked having Tim home, though. They all did.

'They're advising us to start stocking up with coal for the winter,' Jess said, turning over the pages of the *Evening News*. 'We'll get a ton for each household between now and June and a ton of coke or anthracite for each month. I can't ever get coke to burn properly. It's no good unless you mix it with coal.'

'Well, you'd better get whatever we can afford,' Frank said, 'and what we've got room for. Four tons between now and June! They must think people have got mines in their back gardens. I think the paper must have got it wrong, we can't possibly be getting that much.'

'Well, it's what it says, look, in black and white.' Jess showed him the paper. 'I suppose the thing is there might not be any more, and that'll have to last us all winter. They need it for ships and trains and factories, don't they?' She read on for a few moments. 'It says here that charcoal burners are making silk for parachutes. I thought silk came from silkworms.'

'So did I.' Frank came over and took the paper from her. The article had a picture of women working as charcoal burners in the woods. 'I don't see how they can make silk out of that. I reckon that's a bit more propaganda.'

'Why would they say that?' Jess reached for the paper but he was still reading. 'I mean, what's the point of telling us stories like that?'

'It's not us, it's the enemy. If we can make them think we know how to make silk out of charcoal, they might try too and waste a lot of time and money. Or maybe it'll put them off looking for wherever we do get silk from.' Frank had an image of a huge factory, filled with fat silkworms busily spinning, and felt a twinge of doubt. It seemed almost as unlikely as the charcoal burners.

Jess had almost given up hope of getting the paper back and picked up one of the sailors' collars she was forever stitching as her war effort, but Frank dropped it on the arm of her chair and she glanced at it again. 'Look, there's a bit in here about the *Ranpura*. Isn't that the old P&O liner that's being converted to a depot ship? It says here they've put a lot of the women on board, as dilutie tradesmen. What's a dilutie tradesman?'

Frank worked as a boilermaker in Portsmouth dockyard. He'd never actually worked aboard a ship but most of what he made was destined for one of the Navy warships. Since the beginning of the war, a lot of merchant ships had come in for refitting and conversion.

'Well, it's just a mate really. They help the fitters and shipwrights and that. They can't be proper tradesmen without serving their five years' apprenticeship, not even in wartime. Not that any woman would ever want to – it's not a woman's job, shipwork.'

'I don't know,' Jess said. 'Cherry seems to enjoy it all right.'

'Cherry's different.'

Cherry was one of the women who had been drafted into the yard to take the place of the many men who had been called up. Frank had talked a lot about her when she first came and eventually Jess had invited her to Sunday dinner, just to see what she was like. She'd been half expecting a flirty little baggage with saucy eyes, but to her surprise Cherry had turned out to be a dumpy little doughnut of a woman with a beaming round face and a strong Birmingham accent. She was very forthright and a great favourite with the children; she had become almost a member of the family and spent a lot of time knitting toy animals for Maureen, out of old cardigans and jumpers.

'If it's an old liner it must be a big ship,' Jess said. 'You could get lost on a thing like that. How do they ever keep track of them all?'

'They don't,' Frank said, and Jess glanced up at his tone. He was looking disapproving and she guessed that he knew more about the *Ranpura* than he wanted to let on. Probably the men and women working on it knew plenty of places where they could sneak away and have a bit of fun together without being caught. It was human nature.

'Isn't it awful about that woman who was machine-gunned in the street by a sneak raider?' she remarked, threading her needle with strong black cotton. 'It makes you feel you're not safe stepping outside your own front door. Annie was saying there are smoke machines out at Southsea. Lorries with long funnels pointing up to the sky, putting out black smoke.'

'That's to confuse the enemy too, like Wilfred Pickles and the charcoal burners,' Frank said, but Jess snorted.

'Seems to me it just makes things more miserable for us. It leaves oily filth everywhere – people have to seal their doors and windows with wet sheets to keep it out. Just as if they hadn't got enough to put up with.'

'I've seen 'em up Cosham,' Tim put in. 'And I saw another lorry with a huge gun on it. It fired at a plane and smashed half the windows in the street.'

'You see?' Jess said. 'What good does that do? It's enough to scare people to death. Strikes me the Germans might as well pack up and go home, leave us to do our own damage.'

She sighed. You weren't supposed to talk like this, but everyone had to let off steam with a bit of a grumble sometimes. Some people grumbled more than others, mind – Bert Shaw next door, for instance, and Ethel Glaister on the other side – and some people didn't grumble enough, like her mother Mary and poor old Dad, who'd let it all get on top of him until he couldn't stand it any longer and did away with himself. That had been one of the worst shocks of the war, especially for poor Mum, who'd found him, and none of the family had properly got over it yet. It wasn't healthy to keep it all bottled up, and who else could you talk to if it wasn't your own husband?

'That nephew of Tommy Vickers has come back,' she said after a moment. 'You know the one. Clifford Weeks, his name is. Got flaming red hair and a temper to match. Used to knock about with our Colin and Bob Shaw when he came to stay with Tommy and Freda. There was a time when Peggy thought he was sweet on Gladys. He's in the Army now, got wounded and been sent home for a bit of leave till he's fit to go back.'

'Why hasn't he gone to his own home?' Frank asked. 'Don't his parents live up Basingstoke way?'

'They got bombed,' Jess said, and her eyes filled with tears. 'Don't you remember me telling you? His mum was Tommy Vickers's sister, and Tommy was really upset about it. Killed outright, both of them, and the house completely destroyed. Poor Clifford hasn't got a home any more, nor no family except for Freda and Tommy.' She shook her head, trying to peer through the tears at her work. 'I'm sorry, Frank. It just seems all too much, sometimes. Jenny Weeks was such a quiet, nice little woman, she never hurt a fly. It isn't fair.' She sniffed and found a handkerchief. 'I know we mustn't give in, but I just can't help it sometimes.'

Frank patted her shoulder awkwardly. If they'd been on their own, he could have offered more comfort, but he felt inhibited about even kissing his wife in front of Tim. 'You need an afternoon out,' he said. 'Why don't you get Annie to go to the pictures with you? There must be something on that'd take your mind off things.'

'I might.' Jess would rather have gone with Frank, but she knew it was impossible. He was home too late in the evenings to think of going to the pictures, and Saturday afternoons were reserved for gardening or doing things round the house. The only exception he made was when Elsie and Doris Waters came to the King's: he would always make time to go and laugh at them, just as he always listened to their comic chats on the wireless. He liked programmes like *ITMA* and *Stand Easy* as well, but it was Elsie and Doris who were his favourites. He'd even wanted to call Maureen after one of them, until Jess had put her foot down.

'There's people getting into trouble all over Pompey,' he said, still reading the paper. 'Bloke here from Gieves – you know, that Naval shop in Arundel Street – fined thirty bob for "emitting a light". Blimey, that's a bit steep. Thirty bob – that's nearly a week's wage to some people. And one here was allocated petrol to take his wife to the doctor, and they copped him at a pub! Serve him right. Twenty pounds, they fined him, for misuse of petrol. *Twenty pounds!* And there's someone else stung for five quid for selling sausages with not enough meat in them, and a woman got caught writing details of a bombing raid in a letter to her mum. "Information that may be useful to the enemy." It just goes to show, they do think it's important to keep things quiet.'

'You can get into trouble for just walking down the street,' Tim said with some feeling, recalling his own court appearance. 'I heard about someone who got sent to prison just for not having their identity cards on them.'

'Well, they could have been spies, see,' Frank said. 'How are the police supposed to know? Some of these Germans can speak English as good as you and me.'

'P'raps we'd all better practise talking like Wilfred Pickles,' Tim suggested, and his parents looked at him with mild exasperation. Trust Tim to have the last word, and trust Tim to make a joke of it.

All the same, Jess thought, smiling as she threaded her needle again, it's nice to have his cheery face and silly jokes about the place again. She'd missed her boys when they'd been out in the country. Families should be together.

All she wanted now was for Keith to come home as well, and she'd be happy.

Keith wanted to be back at home too. He'd enjoyed being in the country with Tim when they'd first arrived, though at only nine years old he'd missed his mother a lot to begin with. But Reg and Edna Corner had treated them like their own boys, playing games with them and teaching them about country life. He remembered going to collect blackberries and sweet chestnuts with Reg, and Reg telling them about how babies were born. Neither he nor Tim had believed it for a long while, but by now they'd seen enough going on in the fields and farmyards to accept that it must be true. They still didn't fancy it much for themselves, though.

It would have been nice if they could have stayed with Reg and Edna right through the war, but Reg had got called up and Edna had gone to live with her mum and have a baby of her own. (Neither Tim nor Keith had quite dared to ask all the questions about this that they would have liked.)

After that, the two boys had gone to live with Mr Beckett, the local vicar, and his housekeeper Mrs Mudge, and after a while Stella and Muriel Simmons had come to live with them.

Stella and Muriel had been bombed out of their house in October Street, the road that led up from April Grove to September Street, where the shops were. Before that, they'd been bombed out of Porchester Road, where some of the first bombs of the war had fallen, but the second time had been the worst because their mother Kathy and baby brother had been killed. Now their father Mike, who had been in the Merchant Navy, was dead as well, and Stella and Muriel were supposed to be leaving the vicarage and going into an orphanage.

'I really don't see the need,' Mr Beckett said to anyone who would listen. 'The girls are happy here – as happy as they can be anywhere, given their tragic circumstances – they consider this their home. Mrs Mudge and I are more than willing to take care of them. Why, I'd adopt them myself if I could.'

However, the authorities had shaken their heads and said that the Simmons girls were no longer evacuees but came into a different category, and places had been found for them at two very nice children's homes, one near Winchester and the other at Basingstoke. At this, the vicar became even more upset.

'You're not going to separate them! They're sisters, they depend on each other. They have no other relatives. It's inhumane. It's *cruel*.'

The authorities were deeply offended by this. They knew best, the vicar was told. It was often better for children to be separated. It helped them to make other friends. In any case, there was no room for two more children at either of the homes.

'Then leave them with me,' he begged, but on the appointed day a large black car drew up outside and a woman in a brown suit that looked as stiff and hard as a suit of armour, with a felt hat that came down low over her forehead, stepped out and marched up to the vicarage door. She carried a briefcase in one hand and a rolled-up umbrella in the other, holding it like a weapon, and Keith, who was peering out of the shrubbery, noticed stiff, bristly hairs growing on her chin, and remembered Miss Woddis who lived at the other end of the village and had shut her evacuees in the hall cupboard. He shuddered and retreated into the undergrowth.

'I've come for the gels,' she announced in clear, commanding tones when Mrs Mudge opened the door. The housekeeper hesitated briefly, then let her in and Keith could hear voices through the open window of the vicar's study. At first they were quite low, but soon they began to rise, and Keith could hear Mr Beckett shouting. He drew back, startled, from his planned skulk through the bushes to get close to the window. He had never heard Mr Beckett shout before.

'The sisters need to be together. They've suffered enough in this terrible war. Separation would be the last straw for them – I couldn't answer for the consequences.'

'You won't have to,' the woman said. She had a dull, flat voice, as hard as a paving slab. 'The gels are not your responsibility. They've been Taken Over.'

'But there's no need!' Mr Beckett cried. 'They're settled here. They're welcome. Mrs Mudge and I are fond of them – we want to help them to forget their troubles.'

'They'll forget much more quickly when they're away from here,' she stated. 'In any case, that's not the point. The point is that the authorities—'

'It *is* the point! It's the whole point. I want these children to grow up in an atmosphere of security, where they know they can rely on things being the same, where they can be sure that they won't be touched any more by all the terrible things that are going on in the world. I want to give them their childhood.' He gazed helplessly at the woman, whose face was as flat and hard as her voice. 'It was here they last saw their father,' he said desperately. 'It's their last link—'

'A link that's better broken. We find such memories are best ignored. They're unsettling to the children and do them no good. As for security, I'm afraid you're living in a world of fantasy, Mr Beckett. No doubt it's due to your calling.' He gasped, but she went on, talking over him like a steamroller. 'There *is* no security these days, only the security that the authorities can provide in homes that are specially staffed to look after these orphans. I'm afraid such attitudes as yours, well meaning though they may be, can be downright harmful.' She gathered up the papers she had spread on the table and folded them back into her briefcase. 'I see no point in continuing this discussion. If you'll just have your housekeeper call the gels and see that they're ready . . .'

'Please,' he said, his voice low. 'Let them stay a little while longer. Let me have a word with the authorities myself.'

'That's impossible.' She spoke curtly. 'I can assure you, Mr Beckett, they'll be better off in homes. There will be other children for them to play with. Young, trained staff. Surely you can see that this would be better for them than living in a rambling old house with two elderly people?'

'But they already have other children to play with. They have the village children – the other evacuees. Their *friends*. They have Keith Budd, who lives here too—'

'Ah yes,' the woman said. 'A boy. *Quite* unsuitable,' and she shut her briefcase with a snap. 'Call the gels in, please, Mr Beckett. I have another appointment in half an hour and can't afford to waste any more time here.' She stood with her feet planted slightly apart, as solid as a tree, and he knew that nothing would move her until she had Stella and Muriel in front of her with their outdoors clothes on and their small suitcases packed.

He sighed, a sigh that seemed to come from some deep, deep recess in his heart. There was an ache in his body that started somewhere in his chest and spread down his sides, along his arms. The grief that he had known ever since the war began – a grief that had begun years before, during the First World War, when he'd been a chaplain ministering to the gassed and wounded who were dragged from the trenches of Flanders – swept over him in a cloud of blackness that he could no longer ward off. And all his efforts to give the children what he considered the birthright of every child – a few, short years free of sorrow, pain, and a despair they could not comprehend – seemed to shrivel away to nothing.

He turned away and rang the little bell he kept on his desk. A few moments later, Mrs Mudge tramped along the passage and opened the door. She stood there, breathing heavily, her homely face creased with anxiety.

'Tell Stella and Muriel to put on their coats,' the vicar said dully, 'and make sure they have everything they need – everything they want.' He turned back from the window, and the housekeeper flinched at the shadows in his eyes. 'Give them something – anything they want – from me, as a token to keep and remember us by. And then bring them in to say goodbye.'

The pain of bidding them goodbye would be almost more than he could bear, but bear it he must, for the sake of the memories that he knew would forever endure.

Betty and Dennis were back with the Spencers, but there was no more creeping downstairs in the middle of the night to be together. They shared, legitimately, the long, low-ceilinged attic that had been given over to the three land girls when they had first arrived on the farm. One of the narrow single beds had been removed and the other two were pushed together to make a large double.

Erica, who had come to work on the farm at the same time as Betty and had married the Spencers' son Gerald, slept in his room, and Yvonne, the third land girl, found herself, for the first time in her life, with a bedroom of her own. She hardly knew whether she enjoyed the privacy or felt lonely.

'I'm the only one here who's got no one to sleep with,' she complained once, and blushed as everyone else laughed. 'Well, you know what I mean. Erica's got the baby, and Betty and Dennis have got each other. I mean, who am I supposed to talk to in the middle of the night?'

'You're supposed to be asleep,' Mr Spencer said. 'Maybe I'm not working you hard enough.'

Yvonne made a face at him. 'It's not that. It's just that it's so light in the evenings, with this Double Summer Time. I dunno what it's going to be like in a month or so when it's light till nearly midnight. I suppose you'll have us working out in the fields till gone eleven.'

'Well, that's what they've done it for,' the farmer said. 'Give us a few more hours' daylight to get the harvest in. Anyway, it's going back to ordinary Summer Time in August, so it won't be so bad.'

'If you're lonely in the night,' his wife said to Yvonne, 'why not take one of the cats up with you? Or one of Fly's puppies? That'd be company.'

Yvonne thought this was a good idea. She had taken a fancy to the smallest of the sheepdog's pups, which she called Gnat – 'It was too small to be a Fly,' she had said with a grin – and taken it over as her own. Mr Spencer shook his head and said it was the runt of the litter and he'd have drowned it in a bucket of water if he'd had his way, but Yvonne defended it.

'He only needs a bit of feeding up. It's those other bullies, never letting him get near his mum.'

She borrowed one of the bottles used to feed orphan lambs and gave the puppy extra feeds. Sure enough, it began to put on weight and gain strength. It adored Yvonne and followed her everywhere.

'Spoilt, that's what that animal'll be,' old Jonas said in disgust. 'Never be any bloody use for work.'

Jonas was the ancient ploughman who had come out of retirement to help on the farm when Gerald and Dick and the two young farmhands had been called up. He took a disapproving stance on everything, especially land girls, and was never afraid to let his opinions be known, usually in the coarsest language. But over the years since they had first come here, the girls had learned to take his grumbling with a pinch of salt, and he had even been known – albeit grudgingly – to admit that they were 'not bad workers, get 'em on a good day'.

Jonas had given Dennis the benefit of his opinions, too, when he'd discovered that the healthy, able-bodied young man who had come to work on the farm was a conscientious objector. This repugnance was the one thing he and Erica had had in common, and had caused a good deal

24

of friction on the farm before Dennis decided to join the Pioneers and go into bomb disposal.

However, that was all over for Dennis now, and he was learning to adapt himself to being sightless and without two fingers on his left hand. He spent his first few weeks learning to find his way about, then he began to take over some of the work.

'I can do the milking,' he said one morning. 'I've got enough fingers left for that, and I don't need to be able to see to squeeze a pair of teats. And the cows all know me.'

Jonas had snorted, but within a week he was forced to admit that Dennis was as efficient as he had ever been in the byre. He had always enjoyed milking, and the cows seemed to relax with him and let down their milk more easily. He moved confidently from one to the other, settling the bucket beneath each full udder and sitting on his three-legged stool, his cheek pressed into the cow's flank, listening to the steady spurt of the milk.

'If he just does that twice a day, it's a big help,' Mr Spencer said, and Betty squeezed Dennis's arm, her face flushed with pride.

Betty had never been so happy. She had been in love with Dennis ever since the early days, when she had still been half engaged to Graham Philpotts, but for much of the time they had had to keep their feelings secret. There was too much prejudice towards COs, and Dennis was reluctant to draw Betty into the intolerance he sometimes had to endure. After he had volunteered for bomb disposal the unpleasantness diminished, but they still had to overcome Ted Chapman's disapproval before they could marry. And all the while, Betty had suffered the knowledge that at any moment, day or night, Dennis might be blown up by one of the bombs he worked on.

'I know you're safe now, that's all that matters,' she said as he tried to decide what else he could do on the farm. 'You don't have to work all the hours there are. Milking's enough, you heard Mr Spencer say so.'

'I'm still idle a lot of the day,' he said. 'I don't want to be a passenger, Betty.'

'You're not.' She wouldn't have cared if he never lifted a finger, but she knew that wasn't Dennis's style. He needed to feel he was making a proper contribution, despite his disabilities. 'There'll be plenty of other things you can do.'

'You can look after Michael if you like, while I drive the tractor,' Erica said with what Betty thought was a complete lack of tact, but to her surprise Dennis didn't seem to think there was anything wrong in looking after the baby while its mother worked in the fields. There was no getting away from it, she thought: being a Quaker did make you different from other people. And it had to be said that most of the time it seemed to be no more than a matter of common sense.

'Looking after a baby is a privilege,' Dennis said when she tried to express these feelings. 'I'm surprised more women don't realise it. You're actually having an influence on how a human being will behave for the rest of its life – what more important work can there be than that? Anyway, if it sets Erica free to do something I can't do, it counts as war work, doesn't it?'

Betty supposed that it did. She watched Dennis handling the baby with a confidence few men seemed to possess, and realised what a good father he would make. Her body grew warm at the thought, although she wasn't desperate to have a baby, as her sister Olive was. There'd be plenty of time for that later. Just for now, she was happy to have Dennis, and happy to be here on the farm where they had first met and fallen in love.

Even in wartime, she thought, life could be good.

# CHAPTER THREE

Easter came at the end of April, about the latest it could be. That meant it was warm enough for picnics and days out, though – according to the *Evening News* afterwards – it was the quietest Easter on record. There was no petrol allowance for pleasure, so even those who had cars or motorcycles were unable to use them, but for those who had pushbikes or were willing to catch a bus into the countryside and then walk, it was possible to get away and forget the war for a few hours.

On Easter Monday, a gymkhana was held in Horndean, a few miles beyond Portsdown Hill. Jess and Frank Budd took Rose and Maureen out on the bus to see it, and then went for a walk in some nearby woods. The bluebells made an azure mist over the thick brown carpet of last year's leaves, and deep amongst the trees they could hear the rustle of squirrels and the note of the cuckoo. Cushions of primroses were like splashes of fallen sunshine on the dappled ground, and Jess and Rose gathered a basketful to take home. They sat on the grass, looking up at the blue sky through the tracery of fresh new leaves, and tried to believe there was no war.

'Where did you say Tim was off to?' Frank asked, lying back with his hands behind his head.

Jess smiled. She had told him at least three times, but it was so good to see Frank relax for once, she didn't have the heart to say so. She hardly ever saw him like this nowadays, just resting with nothing to do. The war had changed him, she thought a little sadly. He had always been on the serious side, but now he was weighed down by responsibility and care, and sometimes he seemed to have lost all pleasure in life.

But not today. He was looking just like he used to, the lines smoothed away from his forehead, his skin already tanned from working in the garden. He'd carried Maureen almost all the way here from the gymkhana, pretending to be a horse as she shouted 'Gee-up, Dobbin!' and 'Whoa there!' It had been a good idea, this day out, and Jess made up her mind there would be more of them.

She suddenly remembered that he'd asked her about Tim. 'He's gone off on his bike with Dave Willis. They were talking about making a fire somewhere and cooking their dinner. I gave them some sausages and a few potatoes. I hope they'll be all right.'

'Well, Tim ought to know how to carry on in the country,' Frank said easily. 'He won't go setting the woods on fire. And Dave Willis is a sensible sort of boy. I know his dad in the yard.' He lay with his eyes shut for a few minutes, then said dreamily, 'I like this, Jess. Getting out into the country of an afternoon. I reckon when all this lot's over we ought to get ourselves a tandem. We could go out every weekend.'

'A tandem! But I can't even ride a bike. I could never get the hang of how to balance.'

'You don't have to. I can do all the balancing, and steering and that. You just sit on the back and pedal.' He sat up. 'We could go all over the place, Jess. Down the New Forest – out the back of the Hill – into Sussex. You can do forty or fifty miles on a tandem in a day. Think of it!'

Jess thought of it. Forty or fifty miles. She had hardly ever been so far, except for charabanc outings or days out on the train before the war. Her mother had had relatives in London and used to take her and Annie to see them when they were little, and apart from that and the honeymoon she and Frank had had in Devon, she'd hardly been anywhere. But on a tandem . . . ?

She looked at his face and saw the youthful eagerness that had attracted her when they'd first met. It had almost disappeared under the weight of family responsibilities and the grinding effort of the war, but for a moment the old Frank was there, the one who never let anything get him down, and she felt a rush of affection.

'But what about the family? I mean, how could we go off for a whole day every weekend?'

'They're growing up,' he said. 'They won't want to come with us. Rose is getting on for sixteen, and boys want to be off by themselves. Look at Tim this weekend. And we can take Maureen with us. You can get little seats to put on the back. She'd enjoy it.'

'It sounds lovely,' Jess said. 'Oh Frank, won't it be nice when the war's over and we can do things like that again – do just what we like.' She lay back beside him in the grass. 'To be able to come out like this every weekend – it sounds just like a little bit of heaven.' She was silent for a moment or two, then added very quietly, 'I wonder if it'll ever really happen . . .'

Jess and Frank were not the only ones to be planning for when the war ended. Portsmouth City Council was making plans too. They formed a committee to discuss how to attract new industry to the city, and they talked of grand new developments: a large concert and conference hall at Southsea with a winter garden, and a pleasure garden at Lumps Fort with bathing and boating facilities, a small harbour, sports stadium and theatre and numerous other attractions. They also suggested either reconstructing the gutted Guildhall, in the centre of Portsmouth, or building a new civic centre, to be used as a social centre, with a good dance floor.

'Sounds like Pompey's going to be a real posh place,' Diane commented when Gladys read this out of the paper. 'I'll go to the dances! And the pleasure gardens. What d'you think goes on there, eh? I mean, most gardens are just a bit of grass and some flowers, but *pleasure* gardens – well . . .'

'Not the sort of pleasure *you* think,' her sister said tartly, and Diane giggled. 'Well, that's not what they're meant for, anyway. And I don't suppose you'll be invited to the dances they'll have at the Guildhall, anyway. They'll be for the high-ups. The mayor and all that sort.'

Diane screwed up her face. 'I wouldn't want to go to those anyway. No fun at all. I like a bit of jitterbugging.' She jumped up and began to dance jerkily round the room, shrugging her shoulders and flinging out her arms. Her father came through from the scullery and stared at her.

'What on earth are you doing, our Di? Got St Vitus's Dance, or something?'

'No, I don't know that one,' Diane said innocently. 'How d'you do it?'

Gladys gave a snort of laughter and Bert raised his eyes to the ceiling. 'I don't know what's got into you just lately, I really don't. Where do you get all these ideas?'

'She goes to the pictures too much,' Gladys said. 'She don't think of anything else but Clark Gable and Leslie Howard.'

'Go on, they didn't do any jitterbugging in *Gone With The Wind*,' Diane said. 'Mind you, I reckon that's the best film I've ever seen. The way he said, "Frankly, my dear, I don't give a damn . . ." It made goose-pimples come up all over my arms. And when he carried her upstairs . . .' She sighed and rolled her eyes. 'I wish it could've been me he was carrying upstairs.'

'Yes, and that's what's wrong with all these films,' Bert grumbled. 'It gives young girls a lot of ideas they shouldn't be having. Jitterbugging! Americans! They're talking about sending 'em over in thousands, you know. It'll be a black day for Pompey when they arrive, you mark my words. Too much money and too much – well, never mind.' He turned away, and the girls looked at each other and giggled.

'Well, I shan't mind them spending their money on me,' Diane said, 'but they can keep their "never mind". I haven't got no time for the Yanks. They took all that time to come into the war and help our lads out, and now they act like they're saving the world.'

The front door opened and Peggy came in with a half-full basket of shopping. She had spent the night at the first aid post and half the morning standing in queues, but her wiry body still quivered with energy. She dumped the basket on the table and started to unpack it.

'I just saw young Clifford Weeks up the street, with Tommy Vickers. Been wounded, he was telling me, and sent back to Tommy and Freda for a bit of leave to get over it. He was asking after you, Gladys.'

'Well, he knows where I am if he wants to see for himself,' Gladys said, picking up the balaclava helmet she was knitting. 'Mind, I don't suppose I'd know him now, it's years since I saw him. He hasn't been round here since before the war started.'

'Oh, you'd know him all right. He's got hair like a bunch of carrots. Not unlike that young Graham—' Peggy stopped abruptly. She gave Gladys a swift glance, but her daughter's eyes were fixed firmly on her work.

Diane looked from one to the other, and spoke a shade too loudly. 'What if he does have red hair? So do lots of other people. You can't pretend they don't exist, our Glad.'

'I'm not pretending anyone doesn't exist. If Clifford Weeks wants to come round here, he's welcome to. He was never too shy to knock on the door before. Only don't expect me to jump for joy, that's all. I'm not interested.'

'That's just stupid,' Diane said scornfully. 'He can't help it if he looks like Graham Philpotts, and you think it's your fault Graham got kill—'

'Shut up!' Gladys jumped to her feet, the knitting clutched in her hands. 'Shut up! I never said anything about it being my fault. I never said anything about Graham. And I don't see why you have to bring him up.' She turned her back on Diane and looked at her mother. 'Graham wasn't my boyfriend,' she said rapidly. 'He was just helping out that night. He didn't have to, it was my job. How do you think I feel about that, how would *anyone* feel?'

'I know, I know,' Peggy said soothingly. 'It wasn't your fault and you know it, but you can't help going over and over it in your mind. It's all right, Glad. It'll get better with time, really it will.' She looked at her younger daughter. 'And it'll get better a lot quicker if *some other* people had a bit of sense and let the whole thing drop.' There was a short silence, then Peggy went on in a different tone, 'I saw that Ethel Glaister out in the street too. Carrying on at Nancy Baxter like nobody's business, she was. I

30

dunno what the row's about this time – you'd think they'd have learned to ignore each other by now.'

'They're like a pair of cats tied together over a washing-line,' Bert said. 'Can't leave each other alone, got to scratch each other's eyes out. I don't have no time for them meself.'

'Nobody's got much time for them,' Peggy said. 'There's Nancy no better than she should be, and Ethel thinks she's better than anyone. I reckon if push came to shove, it'd be Nancy most folk'd choose though. At least she's not spiteful.'

Ethel Glaister wouldn't have agreed with her. She had always felt affronted by Nancy's presence in the street, and when young Micky Baxter had broken into Ethel's house and left it in such a mess, she'd raged straight round to the police station, expecting him to be sent to prison at once. It was only the fact that he hadn't actually taken anything that had saved him. His sins had caught up with him in the end, of course, and now he was at the approved school at Drayton, but Nancy was still in April Grove to ply her trade, and her mother, old Granny Kinch, still sat in her doorway morning, noon and night, ready to make a sarcastic comment every time Ethel stalked past.

''Ow's your Carol, then? Lost a bit of weight while she was away, I see. Getting quite chubby she was, before 'er 'oliday in *Devon*.'

Ethel knew she should ignore the jibes, but she couldn't do it. She stopped and glared at the old woman.

'How my Carol is, is nothing to do with you, you nosy old baggage. We'd rather keep ourselves to ourselves, if you don't mind.'

Granny Kinch put her finger on her top lip and tilted her head upwards. 'Hoity-toity! *I* don't mind, I'm sure. It's no skin off my nose what you and your kids get up to. It's just the way you parades around the streets, pretending you're so high and mighty when you're no better than the rest of us, that sticks in my craw, that's all.'

Ethel turned red. 'Pretending! It don't take much pretending to be better than you and your Nancy. We all know what *she* is. How much are they paying her now – is it by the hour or by the minute? Beats me how anyone can fancy her at all, but there, I suppose all cats are grey in the dark, as they say.'

Granny Kinch took a step forward and raised her hand as if to hit Ethel, who jerked backwards and collided with Nancy herself, standing right behind her. Ethel stumbled, and only saved herself from falling by grabbing at Nancy's arm. Furious and humiliated, she snatched her hand away, while the other two women laughed.

31

'You'll 'ave to go 'ome and give yourself a good scrub now, won'cher?' Nancy said. 'Lord knows what you might 'ave caught, touchin' me like that.'

'Get out of my way,' Ethel hissed, but Nancy stood her ground.

'It's not your pavement. Belongs to us all, this does. And this bit's right in front of our door, so if it's anyone's it's ours.'

'That's right,' her mother chimed in. 'Nobody arst you to stand 'ere. Go an' stand on your own bit of pavement.' She looked at Nancy. 'That's what comes of givin' someone like Lady Muck the time of day. All I did was arsk after 'er Carol, an' she give me a mouthful. No good tryin' to be neighbourly with some people. I shan't bother again.'

'Nah, she's not worth wastin' breath on,' Nancy agreed. 'Mind you, Ma, there's a lot of us got quite worried about Carol at one time. When she disappeared like that, I mean. It was a funny do all round, wasn't it, and then when she come back lookin' like—'

'Stop it!' Ethel screeched. Peggy Shaw was just coming down the road, and although Ethel had realised by now that most people probably had a good idea what had happened to Carol, she was still determined to keep up the pretence. 'Stop your filthy lies! I won't have it – I won't have you saying such things about my daughter. She's a good girl, Carol is. She's been brought up respectable and decent, which is more than anyone can say about you, Nancy Baxter, or that hooligan of a son of yours. *In approved school* – he'd be in jail if I had my way, and the key thrown down a drain. It's people like you that brings the tone of a street right down. April Grove wouldn't be a bad place if it wasn't for you turning it into a slum, sitting out here all day in your curlers, letting your kids run wild.'

At that moment, as if responding to a cue, Nancy's four-year-old daughter Vera appeared behind her grandmother, dressed in a torn and dirty pinafore, with a grimy thumb stuck into her mouth. She stared up at Ethel from under a fringe of hair matted with what looked like stale jam.

'And I suppose this one'll go the same way, soon as she's old enough. She's out in the street half the time already, messing about with stones and tar and rubbish – she'll get run over one of these days, mark my words, and we'll all know who to blame.'

Ethel paused for breath. Peggy Shaw had gone past and into her own house. Nancy and her mother were sniggering and she felt a surge of pure rage. She stared at them, longing to punch their grinning faces, and then she turned abruptly and marched down the street to her own front door. It opened just as she arrived and Carol appeared with a bucket of water, ready to wash the step.

'Get inside,' Ethel snapped, pushing her out of the way. 'I don't want you out there, displaying yourself for all to see and sneer at. Find yourself something to do indoors.' She slammed the front door and leaned against it for a moment. 'I don't know what I done to deserve all the trouble you've brought on me, I really don't, but I can tell you this, my girl: you put one foot wrong – just one, just for a second – and you're out on your ear. And next time I *won't* have you back!'

For many of the young people in Portsmouth, April was marked by the presence of Joe Loss and his band at South Parade Pier. The dance hall was packed every night: nearly everyone tuned in to Joe Loss on the wireless and possessed some of his records. His signature tune, 'In the Mood' was played over and over again, and when he stood on the platform and asked half seriously for 'any *other* requests, please', the dancers stamped and shouted until he shrugged and smilingly gave in, and let the band play it yet again.

Claudia persuaded Olive to go along with her and the rest of the gun-crew one evening when they were off duty. 'Your Derek wouldn't mind, I'm sure. It's only a dance. They put on dances for the soldiers in the camps, don't they?'

'Ye-es.' Olive preferred not to think about Derek taking another girl in his arms, even for a dance. 'But that's different.'

'Of course it's not. It's exactly the same. Anyway, we're really going to listen to the music, aren't we? You don't have to dance if you don't want to.' Claudia gave her a critical look. 'You need a bit of fun, Olive. You're looking washed out these days. You've got to keep yourself beautiful for when he comes home, you know.'

Olive smiled. 'It'd help if I was beautiful to start with!' But Derek had often told her she was beautiful, and she thought that, in his eyes, perhaps she was.

The next time Olive was in the women's lavatories, she glanced at herself in the speckled mirror. Claudia was right: she was looking a bit pale. But would going to a dance make all that much difference?

'I don't see why you shouldn't go,' Gladys said when they talked about it later. 'Nobody can expect you to let the best years of your life go by without a bit of fun. The way this war's dragging on, we'll all be old and grey before we get the chance of anything else.'

The fighting hadn't ceased. Day after day, night after night, the planes of Bomber Command flew over the south coast on their way to Germany. The *blitzkrieg* with which Hitler had tried to crush Britain was now turned upon his own cities. Hamburg, Berlin, Wilhelmshaven and the Ruhr were all attacked with huge concentrations of bombs. The city centres were devastated, but the RAF did not rest on its laurels: it returned again and again, pounding away at the stricken cities and salving its conscience by reminding everyone what the Luftwaffe had done to London and Coventry and Plymouth.

Olive had agreed at last to go to the dance and was now busy preparing. Uniform would be worn, of course, so there was no pretty frock to make or mend, but it must be immaculate, with each brass button polished till it gleamed like gold, and shoes you could see your face in. She spent hours curling and setting her chestnut hair, and bought a new lipstick. Gladys lent her her small, precious bottle of perfume. 'Only two drops, mind,' she warned. 'One behind each ear.'

I wonder if you can split drops of perfume in half, Olive thought as she got ready on the night. I'd like some on my wrists as well. In the end, she put a drop on each wrist and then rubbed them behind her ears. The scent was strong and rose around her in a cloud.

'Well, don't we all look glamorous?' Claudia remarked as they set out across the Common. 'That's the worst of the Army uniform: it's not exactly alluring. Rough brown khaki – it's a real passion-killer.'

'It's all right when it's on a chap,' one of the other girls said, and they all laughed. 'Mind you, the buttons do get a bit caught up – me and Bri couldn't make out which were whose the other night. We had to take our battledress off to sort it out.'

'Oh, yeah,' Claudia mocked. 'We'll believe you, thousands wouldn't.'

They arrived at the pier. It stretched out into the sea and you could walk round the outside and look down through the planks at the water. There were funfair machines on the wooden decking: a black-haired gypsy manikin which would tell your fortune, and huge claws with which you could – if you were very lucky – pick up a watch or a necklace from the display strewn on a tray inside the Perspex dome. More often, you got nothing at all, or the time would run out just as you were getting the claw over the item you wanted. There were a good few Servicemen and girls playing on the machines, but most people were making their way inside. Everyone wanted a good position near the band.

'They say he's looking for a new singer,' Claudia whispered as she and Olive squirmed their way to the front. 'Suppose he picked one of us?'

'He'd soon unpick, if it was me. I can't sing a note.'

'You're not that bad,' but Claudia spoke absently. She had a very good singing voice and knew all the latest hits. 'It could happen, you know. I mean, he could just pick someone here. That girl that sings with Ambrose, Anne Shelton, they say she's only fifteen, and she started singing with him when she was twelve. She looks older in her pictures, doesn't she?'

'She's got a lovely voice,' Olive said. 'I like the way she sings "You'll Never Know" and "As Time Goes By". It must be nice to be called the Forces' Favourite.'

'Even better to be their sweetheart, like Vera Lynn,' Claudia murmured wickedly, and then the band came on stage and everyone applauded enthusiastically.

At first, Olive felt awkward being at a dance without Derek. In fact, when she came to think of it they hadn't been to all that many dances together – they'd gone for walks, or drives in his sports car. They'd had too little time together to want to spend it with a crowd of other people. But she missed him desperately as she hesitated on the fringe of the crowd, trying to look as if it were indeed only the music she had come for.

That's funny, she thought. It *is* the music – but all the same, it doesn't feel right not to be dancing.

A corporal came up to her. He was short and rather stout, with sallow skin and oily dark hair. He looked a bit foreign but when he spoke his voice was broad Yorkshire, like the newsreader Wilfred Pickles.

''Ave a dance, lass?' he asked. He had thick slobbery lips and Olive cringed at the thought of being held in his arms, but she knew that some men got quite abusive if you refused them. She glanced round a little desperately for Claudia, but her friend had gone, whirled on to the floor by a pilot with smooth yellow hair.

The corporal's hand was on her arm and she found herself following him on to the floor. It was a quickstep, which most people could manage, but he seemed to have feet about six sizes larger than anyone Olive had ever danced with, and she kept tripping over them as he pushed her round the floor. Instead of saying 'sorry', he turned his head each time to look at her with accusation. He held her uncomfortably close with his warm, moist hands and she was thankful when the dance came to an end.

'I'll stop with you, shall I?' he suggested, lumbering along beside her as she walked back to her place. 'Do the next dance, eh?'

Olive shook her head, hardly caring now whether she offended him. 'I don't expect I'll dance again for a while. I'm with a friend.'

'I could find her a partner too,' he offered, but at that moment Claudia reappeared with the young pilot. The corporal gave them a glance of disfavour and turned away. 'Didn't know you were with the toffee-nosed lot. I'll make meself scarce.'

Claudia raised her eyebrows. 'Was he annoying you? He looks horrible. Like a plate of cold fish and chips.'

Olive smiled, feeling better. 'He wasn't all that bad, but I don't think I'll dance again, Claud. It doesn't feel right. I'll just find somewhere in a corner and listen to the band.'

Claudia nodded. The band was striking up with the dramatic notes of 'Jealousy' now and she turned, her eyes alight, to the pilot. 'Can you do this? It's ages since I did a tango . . .' They steamed on to the floor, arms held rigidly before them, heads jerking stiffly and bodies turning with all the abrupt, staccato movements of the music.

Olive listened. It's a gorgeous tune, she thought – but does he know what he's doing, playing that? How many people here are dancing with people they don't really know? And what would their husbands and wives and sweethearts think if they could see them?

She watched the dancers for a while and then noticed a soldier standing nearby. He was watching them too, and there was an odd expression on his face – sadness, she thought, mixed with something else. A sort of longing . . . He was probably thinking of his sweetheart, just like she was thinking of Derek, and wishing she was here too. He looked lonely.

As if he'd felt her eyes on his face, the soldier turned suddenly and looked straight at her. Olive felt her cheeks flush, but she couldn't look away at once and for a moment their gaze held. Then she turned her head. To her surprise, her heart was thumping a little and there was an odd tingling sensation running up her arms.

'Don't you want to dance?' a quiet voice said in her ear. 'I can't believe nobody's asked a lovely girl like you.'

Olive turned again. He had come over to her and was standing quite close. He was only a few inches taller than she, and rather craggily built, with a friendly face that looked a bit like a brown paper bag that had been crumpled and then smoothed out again. There were little crinkles at the corners of his mouth and round his dark brown eyes. He had brown hair combed back from his forehead in small, crisp waves. He looked clean and pleasant and reassuringly ordinary.

'I danced just now,' she said, stammering a little, 'but I'm not really here to – I mean, I came just to listen to the music. It's good, isn't it? I like Joe Loss, don't you? He's always been one of my favourites.'

'He's one of the best. But you get more out of the music if you dance to it.' The tango came to an end and people came off the floor, laughing and chatting. Olive looked for Claudia and her pilot, but they were nowhere in sight. Probably they'd gone for a drink.

'I'm not a very good dancer,' she said. 'I haven't had all that much practice.' She glanced down at the wedding ring on her left hand. 'Actually, my husband and I don't go to all that many dances.'

His expression didn't change. He was still looking at her with the same friendliness, as if mention of a husband didn't just not put him off, it didn't matter.

'I'm married too,' he said. 'My wife's up in Doncaster.'

'Oh.' Olive looked at him again. So she'd been right about his expression. He'd probably come here like herself, talked into it by his mates, and seeing all these people having fun together had made him realise just how lonely he was. Well, at least he wasn't one of those who pretended they were single in order to lead a girl on.

'Look,' he said, 'it seems to me we're both the same – on our own, and feeling a bit out of it. Why don't we have a few dances together? No strings attached.' He grinned at her. 'I won't ask you to come outside with me!'

Olive laughed. She felt suddenly comfortable with him. He's more like a brother, she thought. Dancing with him won't matter, because he's not interested in me in that way. Any more than I'm interested in him.

'Yes, all right.' The band had started playing again. 'It's a foxtrot. Can you do that?'

'Can I do the foxtrot!' he exclaimed, and drew her into his arms. They swept on to the floor and Olive discovered that he could indeed do the foxtrot. She felt a sudden wave of exhilaration. He was right. It *was* better to dance to the music. It was better to let your body answer to the rhythms being created by the band, to let yourself be caught up in the release of flowing movement – and it was better, too, to do this in company with another person, a man whose body seemed so perfectly in tune, whose feet were swift and nimble, whose arms were firm, who could guide and lead her in all the twists and turns of the dance without once treading on her toes, or letting her collide with another dancer.

'Oh, that was nice!' she exclaimed as the dance came to an end and they stood in the middle of the floor. 'I really enjoyed it.'

'Let's do the next one too,' he said. 'Don't go and sit down. They'll be starting again in a moment.'

This time it was a samba. Olive had only ever done this at home, giggling in the front room with Betty to the gramophone, but she found that the rhythm from a live band made it easy to follow the exotic movements. Feeling very daring, she wriggled her shoulders and moved her hips and arms in imitation of her partner. He encouraged her with his eyes, smiling and nodding at her, and when the music stopped he caught her in his arms.

'You're terrific! You're a natural dancer! Let's spend the rest of the evening together, shall we? This is much more fun than I expected.'

Olive, slightly startled by his enthusiastic hug, nodded breathlessly. She still felt comfortable with him. Comfortable and safe, she thought. There had been nothing threatening in his touch – no sense that he was 'pawing' her, as some men were liable to do. Nothing that Derek could have objected to.

'It's nice,' she said. 'I'm enjoying it too. You're a really good dancer.'

'Oh well,' he said, 'we used to do a lot of it back in Doncaster, before the war.' His smile faded for a moment, leaving him looking sad, even a little lost, as he had been looking when Olive had first noticed him. Then he shrugged slightly and turned to her, his grin once more crinkling his brown paper-bag face. 'That sounds like a quickstep. Come on, and I'll show you my fancy turns!'

Olive could scarcely believe it when the band started to play the National Anthem, signifying that the evening was at an end. She stood to attention beside the soldier, her body still caught in the music of the last waltz, dazed and happy. I don't know when I last enjoyed myself so much, she thought, and felt immediately guilty. Of course I do – it was last time Derek was home and I enjoyed myself *much* more!

However, she couldn't dim the light from her eyes or prevent her mouth from smiling as the last strains of 'God Save The King' died away and people began to move again. Dancers began to leave the floor, coats were collected, groups of friends regathered, and Olive could see Claudia and the yellow-haired pilot across the hall, talking animatedly. She felt suddenly awkward, wondering what to do. We were supposed to be going back to camp together, she thought; but Claudia looked so engrossed that it seemed unlikely she would even remember that she and Olive had come together.

'Is your friend about?' the soldier asked. He had told her that his name was Ray and he was in one of the other ack-ack teams on the Common. She must have seen him around the camp, but she didn't take much notice of the other soldiers, and if they didn't share the same mess you didn't really run into each other a lot. 'Are you supposed to be meeting her?'

'Well, that was the idea, but it looks as if she's forgotten.' Olive watched Claudia leave the floor and felt annoyed. 'It doesn't matter. It's only a few minutes' walk back across the Common.'

'I'll walk with you, if you like. I don't think it's a good idea to go on your own. I won't try anything on,' he added without looking at her.

Olive hesitated. If a chap walked a girl home, he normally expected a kiss at the end of it – if nothing else – but this wasn't the same. Ray had only offered because Claudia had let her down, and they'd danced together for the fun of dancing – not because they were going out together or anything like that.

'I'm going that way, after all,' he pointed out with a grin, and she made up her mind and smiled at him.

'All right. Thanks.'

They made their way out of the crowded hall and along the pier. The crowd streamed out with them, laughing and chattering, lots of couples with their arms round each other's waist or holding hands, a few already embracing in hidden corners. Olive looked at them a little enviously. It would be so nice to have someone – Derek – to cuddle up with after an evening's dancing to one of the best bands in the country. It would be so good to have a night's lovemaking and warm, shared sleep to look forward to when they got home.

She and Ray walked decorously a foot apart, not touching. Once again, Olive wondered if she should be feeling guilty at having come out this evening. I only came to listen to the music, she reminded herself. I didn't mean to dance, although – with Ray – there surely wasn't any harm in it. He never held me too close, or let his hands wander where they shouldn't. I'm sure Derek wouldn't have minded.

However, later on, after their polite parting at the camp gate, and when she was lying in bed in the hut, listening to the breathing of the other girls – including Claudia, who had come in a few minutes after Olive, declaring that she'd 'looked everywhere, honestly', but looking remarkably flushed and excited – Olive remembered the feel of being in Ray's arms as they danced. It had felt warm and companionable. Not exciting, as she was excited when Derek held and caressed her, but . . . nice.

Nothing that Derek could possibly object to, but very, very nice.

'If only we could hear from them,' Mr Beckett said miserably. 'Just to know that they're all right. They've been gone almost two months now.' He stirred his tea, not even bothering to put in any sugar, and Keith watched, remembering how the vicar had got them all to sell him their own sugar ration at a halfpenny a teaspoonful when they had first arrived here. Tim and Keith had thought it an excellent idea but Mrs Mudge had been outraged, and only the vicar's assurance that sugar was bad for their teeth had mollified her. The boys, not caring about their teeth, went straight out and spent their halfpennies on the few sweets that could be bought off ration.

Now it seemed as if Mr Beckett had forgotten how to be a sort of elderly boy. His long, thin face was sad, and although he still smiled at Keith whenever they met, his mouth would droop again almost at once. He still rode his creaking old bicycle round the parish, his spidery legs sticking out sideways because it was really too small for him, but he no longer suggested games of cricket or football in the overgrown garden. Instead, he sat indoors and showed Keith how to play patience and gin rummy, and even then he would sit for long minutes with his cards in his hands, forgetting when it was his turn and getting the score all wrong.

'No news is good news,' Mrs Mudge said in an unconvinced tone. 'I'm sure they'd let us know if the girls weren't all right.'

The vicar shook his head. 'You heard what that woman said. They think it's better to break all links.' A spasm of pain crossed his face. 'I could accept that – though I don't believe for one moment that they're right – if only they hadn't separated them. That's what I think is so cruel. Poor little Muriel – she needs her big sister. And Stella needs someone to love and look after. You know how she's been since their father was killed. She's too quiet, Mrs Mudge. It's as if she'd gone away somewhere inside where she couldn't be reached, and only her sister could find the way in.'

'Well, there's nothing we can do about it,' the housekeeper said. 'All we can do is carry on, same as we've always done, and look after the souls who are still with us.' She glanced at Keith, who was sitting silently at the table, trying to let the talk flow over his head but unable to escape the heavy sadness that lay over the vicarage these days.

'You're quite right.' Mr Beckett gave her a crooked smile. 'Sometimes, Mrs Mudge, I think you would be better at this job than I am. I'm getting old, that's the trouble. Too old . . .' He rose from his chair and Keith noticed how stooped he had become lately, his thin body bent over almost as if he had an ache somewhere. 'I'll go into my study and make a start on Sunday's sermon. It's Ascension Day next week. Perhaps a few words on hope and renewal will help us all.'

He went slowly from the room, and Mrs Mudge looked at Keith. He had hardly touched the toast she had put on his plate, and his breakfast cocoa had an unappetising skin on its surface.

'And what's the matter with you?' she said, more sharply than she'd meant to. 'Lost your appetite?'

Keith looked at her without speaking. He could not have begun to explain the tumble of emotions he felt inside: missing Tim; missing his family; missing Stella and Muriel. The sensation that everything was changing, changing beyond his control, that nothing would ever again be as it was. He couldn't even remember how it should be. He had had so many changes already in his life, that he no longer knew what he wanted.

'There, it doesn't matter,' she said, her tone softening. 'I'll make you some more cocoa, and you can have some puffed wheat if you like.'

Puffed wheat was a treat kept normally for Sundays. Keith loved it and would have bought the girls' share with his sugar halfpennies if Mrs Mudge had allowed it, but now he shook his head.

'I'm not hungry.'

Mrs Mudge mixed cocoa and a few spoonfuls of milk into a thin paste and poured hot water on to it. She set it in front of him.

'All right. Drink that, and then you can go out to play. Oh – no, before you go, the vicar wanted something from the village shop. You can slip down and get it for him, can't you? Just go and see what it is, and I'll give you the money.'

Keith nodded. He sipped his cocoa, the heat warming his chilled body. He didn't know why he felt so cold this morning. Perhaps it was because the weather was grey and dull, the late May sunshine hidden behind clouds, but the range was alight, and the kitchen – the only really warm room in the house – as cosy as ever. He wondered if Mr Beckett was cold in his study.

A few minutes later, he went along the passage to the room the vicar used to write his sermons and see parishioners who called for his help or advice. It was a room that Keith rather liked. He liked the big desk with its shabby green baize top, and the shelves of books that lined the walls. He liked the picture of a huge stag, standing amongst mountains with its front feet placed on a rock, that Tim had told him was somewhere in Scotland.

The children had been taught not to burst into the study as they would into any other room in the house. They had to knock and wait for the vicar to tell them to come in. Keith did this. He waited for several minutes. Then he knocked again.

Perhaps Mr Beckett had gone to sleep. He had seemed very tired at breakfast time. He did sometimes go to sleep in the study in the afternoons, and if he didn't answer Mrs Mudge's knock then, she would go in anyway, taking him a cup of tea.

Keith hesitated. He didn't like to break the rule, but he wanted to be outside, even though it wasn't a particularly nice day. He wanted to be away from the gloom that had settled like a dark, clammy cloud over the vicarage just lately.

He knocked for a third time and then made up his mind and opened the door, just enough to poke his head around.

There. Mr Beckett was asleep. He was sitting behind the desk as usual, his head resting on the green baize and his arms flung out across the top. He must have been really tired, Keith thought.

All the same, there was something a bit queer about the way he was sitting there. Normally, if he wanted to sleep, he would tilt back his chair and put his feet on the desk, and sometimes he laid a handkerchief over his face to keep the light out of his eyes. Keith had never seen him like this, lying there as if he'd been knocked over.

He went forward softly, still not quite liking to disturb the old man. Then he saw Mr Beckett's face, and caught his breath. It was white, a strange, ashen white, and there was a blueness, almost like a bruise, around his lips and nose.

Someone's hit him, Keith thought, outraged. Someone's come in here and punched Mr Beckett in the face. Why, they've knocked him out. He reached out and touched the old man's shoulder, half to awaken him, half to offer comfort.

'Mr Beckett!' His voice came out in a squeak. 'Mr Beckett, wake up. It's me, Keith – I've come to ask what you want at the shop.'

But the old man's face didn't change. Instead his body slipped a little under Keith's touch. And as Keith watched, paralysed with horror, he crumpled on his chair and slid sideways, slowly at first and then in an uncontrollable heap, bringing half the contents of the desk with him, to the threadbare carpet that covered the floor.

# CHAPTER FOUR

Nobody had broken into the vicarage and hit Mr Beckett. He had died of a heart attack. The doctor said so when he came, summoned hurriedly by Mrs Mudge, who was now sitting in the kitchen crying and blaming herself.

'I should have known he was ill,' she wept. 'I knew he'd been having pains but he said it was just indigestion. He looked proper screwed up with them sometimes. I told him to come and see you, but he wouldn't. I should have *made* him go.'

'You couldn't make the vicar take care of himself,' the doctor said. He was also churchwarden and had known Mr Beckett well. 'He was too busy taking care of other people. And he was old, Mrs Mudge, and tired. I'm just as much to blame as you: I've been thinking for a long time, when I saw him in church and around the village, that he wasn't looking well.'

'It was the little girls was the last straw,' she said, sniffing and blowing her nose. 'Being took away like that. He took that very hard. And their father being killed – and all the worry over half the village. Reg Corner's been posted missing now too, you know, and poor Edna left with the baby and all. I don't know what the world's coming to.'

'None of us does,' the doctor said, closing his bag. 'Well, I'll see that everything gets done as it should, Mrs Mudge. I'll notify the undertakers and they'll do what's necessary. And I'll see to the funeral arrangements and let the Church authorities know. There's nothing for you to worry about.'

'There'll be funeral meats though, won't there?' she said. 'I mean, everyone will come back here, after – after . . .'

'I'm sure there will,' he said, laying his hand on her shoulder. 'I know you'll want to look after all that side of things, but it's my duty to see to everything else. You must let me know what help you need. For the moment, though, I don't think there's anything else that anyone can do.'

She looked up at him. 'What about Keith?'

'Keith!' The doctor looked disconcerted. 'I'd forgotten all about him. He's your evacuee, isn't he?'

'Yes. He . . . found Mr Beckett. I put him to bed – he seemed sort of dazed. I think he's all right, but what should I do about him, Doctor? I suppose I ought to let his parents know, and the billeting officer. I mean, I don't see why he shouldn't stay on here afterwards, but it don't seem right to have a little boy in the house now, not with the – the – Mr Beckett here, like, and a funeral and all that. I don't know what I ought to do.'

'Certainly his parents will have to know, and the billeting officer. I agree that somewhere else will have to be found for him, for the time being at any rate.' The doctor frowned. Mrs Mudge was no spring chicken herself. She was looking exhausted, and no wonder. She'd been the vicar's housekeeper for upwards of twenty years, ever since her husband had died, and she'd had a lot to put up with lately. But then, so had everybody.

'Write to his parents now and they'll get the letter tomorrow,' he said. 'I'll see the billeting officer. It's Mrs Tupper, isn't it? She'll know what to do. I daresay there'll be a home in the village where they can place him until it's decided what to do with him. Meanwhile, I don't see what harm there is in leaving him here with you. He's in bed, did you say?'

Mrs Mudge nodded. 'He was upset, you see. I thought it was the best thing for him: bed and a drop of hot milk. I daresay he'd never seen a – anyone passed away before.'

'A lot of children are having to see things like that, and worse . . .' the doctor said a little grimly. 'Well, I'll leave you now, Mrs Mudge, but I'll be in touch again soon. And if you'll take my advice, you'll have a rest yourself, with a cup of tea. It's been a shock for you too.'

He left the house and Mrs Mudge heard his car start up outside. A moment or two later, the kitchen door opened and Keith's head appeared. He looked round to make sure she was alone, then crept in and sat down beside her.

'Mr Beckett is dead, isn't he?' he said, as if there had been some doubt on the matter. 'I mean, he wasn't just asleep or knocked out.'

'No, lovey,' she said, and put her arm around his shoulders. 'He wasn't asleep.'

'So we won't be seeing him any more,' Keith went on. He knew perfectly well that this was the case, but somehow he needed to say it, to hear the words in the air, before he could quite believe it.

'No, lovey.' Mrs Mudge gripped him tightly against her side. Keith saw a large tear fall on to the surface of the kitchen table and spread out in a splash. He felt dangerously close to crying himself, but his father got cross if he saw him or Tim crying, and anyway Keith was the man of the house now and men definitely didn't cry.

'It's all right,' he said, his voice wavering. 'I'll look after you.'

At this, Mrs Mudge wept harder than ever. Keith sat nonplussed and a little hurt. 'I can do the fireplace,' he went on defensively, 'and bring in coke for the range, and clear out the ashes. And I can . . .' He racked his brains for other jobs the vicar used to do. 'I can unlock the church in the mornings. I don't know about the service,' he added with a twinge of doubt. 'I don't think I can remember the words. Me and Tim didn't used to listen much.'

Mrs Mudge made a hiccuping noise, half laugh, half sob. 'Bless you, lovey, no one's going to expect you to do any of those things. Why, you're just a little boy. In any case, I don't suppose you'll be here.'

'Not be here?' Keith stared at her. 'Why not? Why won't I be here?' His voice rose.

'Why, because I expect they'll bring in another vicar, of course, and he might not have room. Lots of vicars have got their own families, you know, four or five children quite often. That's why they have these big houses for them. I don't even know if they'll want me.' Her voice was suddenly bleak.

'But what will happen to us?' Keith asked. 'Where shall we go?'

Mrs Mudge, who had drifted away for a moment into another world, a lonely, frightening world where she had no home and no way of earning her living, looked at him unseeingly for a moment. Then her eyes came back into focus and she hugged him close again.

'You'll be all right, lovey, don't you fret. The billeting officer will find you a nice place to go to. And I daresay there's someone somewhere who wants a housekeeper . . . With all these young women going into the Forces, there must be someone.'

'The billeting officer? You mean that big lady who looks like a leather settee?' Keith's face paled. 'I'm not going with her. She took Stella and Muriel away and now we don't know where they are. I won't go with her.'

'No, that's not Mrs Tupper. You're getting them mixed up.' She knew that in Keith's eyes there must be very little difference between the two women. Mrs Tupper bore a distinct resemblance to the woman who had come for the girls, and it wasn't just in looks. Their manner was the same: commanding, officious, implacable. They carried briefcases and had the authorities on their side.

'I'm not going to a home,' Keith stated, his voice edged with panic. 'I *won't*.'

'Nobody's taking you to a home, Keith,' the housekeeper said, but he twisted away as if he suspected her of being about to hand him over, and backed away to the kitchen door. Distressed, she saw that he was really frightened. Poor little boy, she thought. It's the shock. It's like when his brother found that hand, up in the woods. Little boys shouldn't have to go through all this.

'Keith, listen to me. I shouldn't have said all that about a new vicar and a big family, I don't know what I was thinking about. It's all right. Nobody's going to take you away. Go back to bed and I'll bring you up some more hot milk.'

'I don't want hot milk,' he said. 'I don't want anything. I just want it to be yesterday again. I want Mr Beckett here, and Stella and Muriel, and our Tim. I want everything to be the *same* again.' He stared at her and then added in a voice that rose higher with every word, 'He still owes me tuppence for my *sugar* . . .'

'Oh, Keith,' she said, 'how can you think about sugar at a time like this?' Even as she said it, though, she knew that he could not be reproached. He was only a little boy and he'd had a bad shock. Tears and laughter bubbled within her, threatening to escape, but she caught at the hysteria and held it firmly down. It would not do to give way in front of the child; it wouldn't do at all.

'It's all right,' she said gently. 'It doesn't matter about the sugar. I'll give you the tuppence – Mr Beckett would want me to, I know. Or perhaps you'd rather have the sugar back?'

She saw his expression change and knew at once that she had said the wrong thing again, reminding him that Mr Beckett had gone for ever, that there was no one left who would want his sugar.

She pressed her hands on the table, levering herself to her feet. A small part of her noted that everything seemed more difficult this morning, as if she had got heavier in the night, or weaker. I suppose that's shock as well, she thought as she reached her hands out to the boy. She had often reached out to him in this way, and he had always come to her, leaning into her broad cushion of a bosom, resting against her, but now he refused to come. Instead, he retreated, keeping his eyes on her, and twisted the doorknob behind his back.

'Keith . . .' she said pleadingly, but he shook his head. His lips were wobbling and his large brown eyes filled with tears. He drew in a sudden long, sobbing breath, dragged open the door and ran from the kitchen. She heard his feet pounding up the stairs and the distant slam of a door, and then all was quiet.

It was only just noon, but Mrs Mudge was exhausted. Suddenly overcome, she turned back and took one of the tablets the doctor had given her, with the cup of tea that was now almost stone cold. She sat there, her arms on the table, the tears trickling down her cheeks, and then slowly she drooped her head forward until it was resting on her arms, and gave herself over to a steady, quiet, heartbroken sobbing.

Keith did not go back to bed. Instead, he collected up his most treasured belongings – his squirrel's tail, the horseshoe he had discovered in the woods, a sheep's horn he had broken from the animal's head when he had found it dead in a field, his collection of cigarette cards of footballers, a wooden model aeroplane he had made himself and a picture of Princess Margaret Rose that even Tim didn't know he had – and stowed them all in an old haversack that Reg Corner had given him for picnics. He then emptied out his money box and counted his money.

Keith was never very good at saving money. He had never had much to save, of course, but whereas Tim could sometimes keep his threepence from one week till the next before spending it, Keith was always down at the sweet shop almost before the coin had left Mr Beckett's hand. However, it happencd that he had been given some sweets a week or two ago by the father of one of the village children, who was home on leave, and he also had nearly five shillings that had been given him by various people for passing the scholarship examination. He would be going to the grammar school in the autumn, and he was pleased about that, but he'd been more pleased to have the five shillings and had decided to save up for a bike.

Now he was going to have to use his bike money for something else, but it was better than being taken away from all his friends and family and disappearing for ever into a home.

Jess was just putting a plate of bread and margarine on the table when the knock came at the door. She clicked her tongue in annoyance. More than likely it would be someone who'd come collecting old clothes for the Lady Mayoress's Appeal – though why anyone should think there were clothes to spare in a place like April Grove, she couldn't imagine – or wanting the last saucepan they had in the place to build a Spitfire with, or some new idea that would make her feel both guilty, because there just *wasn't* anything else she could give up, and despairing, because how *could* you win a war on old pullovers and burnt-out saucepans?

'You see who that is, Tim,' she said, making the tea. 'Whatever it is they want, I don't suppose we've got any. Rose, put Maureen's bib on, will you? She's had that frock clean on this afternoon and I don't want her getting jam all down the front.'

'Don't want my bib on,' Maureen announced rebelliously, but Rose pinned the child's arms to her sides and tied it round her neck. She was still dragging at the strings when Tim came back, grinning.

'Says he wants to see you, Mum.'

'Who is it?' Jess asked crossly. She stood undecided for a moment, aware of her own pinafore which ought to have gone into the wash yesterday. 'What are you looking like that for, Tim? Take that silly expression off your face.'

Tim sniggered and she flung him a glance of exasperation before marching to the door. Whoever it was would just have to put up with her pinafore, and anyway it couldn't be anyone important, not to make Tim behave like that. Besides, she—

'*Keith!*'

He stood on the doorstep, his face smudged with flecks of soot from the train, one sock held up by an elastic garter, the other wrinkled around his ankle. His grey school pullover was coming unravelled on one sleeve and he trailed a bulging canvas haversack from one hand. His hair didn't look as if it had been combed in a fortnight.

'Hullo, Mum,' he said, and his mouth wobbled into a grin. 'I've come home.' And then, as she stared at him, she saw his grin disintegrate and his face crumple as the tears came instead. 'Don't let them send me away, Mum,' he begged piteously. 'I don't want to go away. I don't want to go into a home . . .'

'I couldn't make out what he was on about,' Jess told Frank later, when all the children were in bed at last. 'He was crying that hard . . . I thought he'd got himself into some awful trouble, like our Tim last year. Then it came out that Mr Beckett was dead and – well, I didn't know *what* to think. Of course Keith hadn't done anything – I *knew* he couldn't have really, but he was so upset, and no wonder. He found him, you see. Found Mr Beckett dead in that room he called his study. He went in and thought he was asleep, but when he touched him the old man just fell over. It must have been an awful shock.'

'But why did he come home?' Frank asked. 'Why didn't he wait till we could go and fetch him?'

'He didn't know we'd do that. He thought he was going to be sent away. He'd got it into his head he'd be sent to an orphanage, like Stella and Muriel. He was terrified, Frank. I've never seen him in such a state.'

'Daft kid,' Frank said. 'I'm sorry he's had a fright, of course, but he didn't need to go thinking things like that. He's not an orphan. He's got a mum and dad and a proper home.'

48

'I don't think he knows what he's got, not really,' Jess said. 'He was only nine when they were first evacuated. He's like a lot of children who were sent away at the beginning of the war. They don't know when they'll ever come to live at home again. Some of them must wonder whether they ever will. They're all muddled up.'

Frank turned his head and stared at her. 'D'you really think that?'

'Yes,' she said, 'I do.'

There was a moment's silence. Then he said, 'What d'you think they'll do? I mean, what'll happen to the vicarage and that housekeeper woman?'

Jess shook her head. 'I don't know. Keith said something about a new vicar with a big family. It seemed a bit quick, but maybe he's right. They'll have to do something like that, won't they? And Mrs Mudge is getting on – I doubt if she'd be staying there. I think she's got a married son in the Army, so perhaps she'd go and live with her daughter-in-law. I don't really know what will happen.'

'And what about Keith?'

'Another billet somewhere – I don't know,' she said again. 'Frank . . .'

'I know what you're going to say,' he said quickly. 'You're going to say we ought to have him back here. Well, we've talked about this a lot, on and off. You were all evacuated at the start of the war – you and the baby, our Rose, and both the boys. You've all come back, and none of us has been killed yet. What I've got to say is – yes, I reckon you're right. Keith might as well be here with the rest of us. I'm as tired of having the family split up as you are, and I don't want him having to go and stay with someone he doesn't know. He's had enough changes and he needs his family round him.'

Jess gazed at him. Then her lips began to tremble. She reached out and he took her in his arms and held her head against his shoulder as she wept.

'Oh, Frank. I thought it was never going to happen. All of us together at last, a proper family. I feel awful, being so happy when poor Mr Beckett's dead. I mean, if it wasn't for that, you wouldn't have said all that and Keith would still be away, and – oh, I'm sorry, going on like this, and I'm making your shirt all wet too and—'

'It's all right,' he said, patting her back with his big hands. 'It's all right, Jess. We're both sorry about Mr Beckett. He was a good man. But he was old, and you can't ask for a much better way to go than just sitting down in a chair and falling asleep. It's brought Keith home to us, and I don't see anything wrong with being glad about that . . . but I reckon we'd better write and tell that poor woman out at Bridge End first thing

49

in the morning. She'll be worrying herself sick about where Keith's got to.'

Jess raised her head. 'Mrs Mudge! I hadn't thought a word about her, in all the upset. And she's been so kind to the boys too.'

'Well, perhaps Keith left her a note,' Frank said, rather sorry that he'd spoken, 'or she'd have been in touch with us by now. Anyway, there's nothing we can do about it till morning. Unless – isn't the vicarage on the telephone? I could go up the street to the telephone box and ring up.'

'Yes, it is. I've got the number written down.' Jess fetched the tin box where they kept all their papers. 'Here it is. I hope she won't have gone to bed.'

'Well, if she's asleep she probably won't hear it ring anyway.' Frank fished in his pocket for a couple of pennies. 'I won't be long.'

He came back five minutes later, looking relieved. 'Yes, she thought Keith would be here. He never thought to leave a note, but someone saw him at the railway station. She's written to tell us about the vicar, but she doesn't know what'll happen about the house or anything.' He paused. 'I told her we were thinking of keeping Keith at home.'

'What did she say?'

'She said she thought it was the best thing that could happen. Keith's been miserable lately, she said, missing Tim, and then the girls. Mr Beckett had been worrying over him.' He stopped, not wanting to add that the housekeeper had hinted that this might have had something to do with the vicar's heart attack. It was no use making Jess feel bad about that too. 'So – that's that. It's a sad ending, but we've got our family back together again and I know that's what we've both been wanting. All the rest of it – what school he's going to go to, and so on – we'll get sorted out as and when the time comes. And now we'd better go to bed. I've got to be up early in the morning.'

They went upstairs and undressed. Jess lay down in the big feather bed, conscious of a warmth that she had felt on only a few occasions since the day the war had started, nearly four long years ago. A warmth that came from knowing that the little terraced house was filled with her family, the children she and Frank had made through loving each other; that every member was safe under the same roof and that they would be here, under her care, until their natural growing-up took them away, as was only right and proper.

It's never felt right, having them sent away, she thought. I've never been able to be happy while any one of them's been living with other people, no matter how kind they might be. But now they're all home again, and I can rest easy.

With only four rooms, number 14 was a tiny house for a family of six people, but until tonight, it had always felt strangely empty.

'Shirkers!' Ethel Glaister exclaimed indignantly. 'D'you see what they're calling us now? *Shirkers!* The cheek of it.'

'Well, I wouldn't mind working.' Carol's old boss hadn't wanted her back – he'd taken on other staff while she'd been away – and she hadn't been able to get another job yet. 'I could do with some money to go to the pictures with.'

'You're better off at home, I've told you that. You're not like a young girl any more, not now that you've had – well, you know.' Ethel never allowed the word 'baby' to pass her lips if she could help it. 'Not that I wouldn't like a bit more to help pay your keep. But I don't see why *I* should have to go and slave to keep you.' She looked back at the newspaper in disgust. 'That Mr Bevin wants to wash his mouth out, using language like that about respectable, hardworking women.'

'Go on, he's not using "language",' Carol said. 'Just saying what he thinks.' She took the newspaper. '"Women between eighteen and forty-five can now be directed into part-time work." I think you ought to think yourself lucky you haven't been told to work fulltime. It's only because of me that you haven't.' She sniggered. 'Pity it wasn't you had a baby, then you'd have been exempt. You ought to have done something about it last time Dad was here.'

'*Carol!*' Ethel raised her hand, but Carol dodged smartly out of reach. 'Don't you *dare* talk like that. You've got really coarse since all this happened. I suppose it comes from mixing with all those other sluts in that home.'

'Well, you made me go there,' Carol retorted. 'Didn't want the shame of the neighbours all seeing me with a fat belly. Not that they don't all know about it anyway,' she added. She knew very well why a lot of the people in April Grove, and March and October Streets, turned their heads away and pretended not to see her when she walked past. Some of them, like Jess Budd and Annie Chapman, were all right, but even they looked a bit embarrassed and didn't know quite what to say. Nancy Baxter was the only one who'd give her a grin and a friendly wink, but Carol didn't altogether like that either. There was something in Nancy's look that made her feel the older woman was saying they were two of a kind. And I'm not, Carol thought. Me and Roddy loved each other – we still do. At least, I hope he does . . .

She had never heard from Roddy since the day he'd been arrested down in Bournemouth. She had written to tell him what was happening to her and to their baby, but he'd never answered. Probably, she thought, he hadn't been allowed to. And she hadn't written to his mother, though she still had her address on the letter that Roddy had given her.

She looked at the paper again. There was another piece of news in there. Leslie Howard, the film star she had seen the first time she and Roddy had gone out together to the pictures, had been shot down and was presumed dead. He'd been to Spain to tell people about his films, *Pimpernel Smith* – the one she and Roddy had seen – and *The First of the Few*, and they were going to be shown in cinemas there. He'd been in *Gone With The Wind* too, with Clark Gable and Vivien Leigh. Clark Gable was flying with the United States Army Air Force now. If the film stars weren't in the war, they were making films about it. *Casablanca* was another one she and Roddy had seen, with Humphrey Bogart and Ingrid Bergman. Carol had gone round singing 'As Time Goes By' for days after seeing that film.

Ethel changed the subject back to the new order about women working part time. 'I suppose you think this lets you out, not being eighteen yet, but I reckon there's plenty of jobs about, and it's time you found yourself one. They're asking for women up the aeroplane factory, I saw a notice yesterday.'

'What, making planes like Diane Shaw? I wouldn't mind that.'

'No,' Ethel said scornfully. 'They'd never have you for important work like that. This is sweeping the floors to collect all the rivets and things that have been dropped, so they can be used. They used to get chucked away with the rubbish. Save thousands of pounds, they reckon.' She glanced disparagingly at her daughter. 'I reckon you could just about manage that.'

'Well, I reckon I'll apply, an' all. At least it'd get me out of this house,' Carol retorted. She grinned with sudden malice. 'Be a laugh if they put you on the same job. Mother and daughter working together – brings the tears to your eyes, don't it?'

'*I'll* bring tears to your eyes if you give me any more lip,' Ethel said savagely. 'I dunno what I'm going to do with you, Carol. It was a poor day for me when they said I had to have you back here. Pity it can't be our Joe what's left at home, that's all I can say.' She glanced at the mantelpiece where she kept Joe's photograph, in his bell-bottoms and square rig. 'At least I can be proud of one of my children,' she added, and then, with bitterness in her voice, 'As long as he's left to me, anyway.'

Carol stared at her mother and caught a flicker of real feeling in the hard blue eyes. She had a sudden insight into what lay behind the façade, and for a moment she could feel a touch of empathy, of woman-to-woman closeness, the sharing of a mother's feelings about her son. She thought about her own baby, the little boy she had called Roderick after his father and had loved and cared for during the six weeks he had been hers, before he was taken away for adoption. She thought of him grown up, a boy on the verge of manhood, sent away from her protection to face dangers she could only imagine. And then the moment passed. I had to give my baby away, she thought angrily. I'll never know what he'll be like when he's grown up. I don't even know his name.

Worse still, she wouldn't even know if he was still alive. There'd been a report in the paper only the other day about a harbour boatman who had found a suitcase floating in the water and opened it to discover a dead baby inside. It was about four or five months old and well nourished. Suppose it had been little Roderick? No one would ever tell her. She had lain awake all night, unable to get the story out of her mind.

'I bet our Joe's as glad to get away as I'd be,' she said, turning away so that her mother would not see her tears. 'I bet he's really enjoying himself out there at sea.'

Peggy Shaw was walking back from church with her daughter Gladys, who had met her on the way home from the hospital. Peggy had gone on to church from her duty at the first aid post. There wasn't so much to do these days, now that the bombing raids seemed almost over, but you still got the sneak raiders who dashed in past the defences and swooped low over the city, dropping small bombs or machine-gunning people in the streets. And you never knew when it was all going to start again, that was the problem. At any time, Hitler might send his aircraft over and rain death from the sky once more, as he'd done in that terrible winter of 1941.

'They say he's working on a secret weapon,' Peggy said. 'Worse than anything we've had up till now. I can't imagine it, can you?'

Gladys remembered the nights she had spent driving an old van done up as an ambulance through the blazing streets, and shook her head. 'I don't think there *could* be anything worse.'

'At least we're getting better prepared all the time. I mean, these static water tanks they put up on the bomb sites – they make it easier to put out the fires, having water handy. There's one going where Kathy Simmons's house was, in October Street, so Tommy Vickers told me. Trust him to know everything that's going on!' Peggy laughed.

'Mm.' Gladys didn't seem to be listening. She glanced at her mother and then said, 'I've got something to tell you, Mum.'

'Oh?' Peggy said with mild interest, and then stopped dead and stared at her. 'What? What's happened?' And then, 'You've got your papers, haven't you?'

Gladys nodded. 'I'm off in two weeks' time. It's just local, to begin with.' She gave her mother a grin. 'That's the advantage of living in a Naval town! I wouldn't be surprised if I'm posted locally too, so it won't be like I'm going away, not really. Just changing my job.'

'Oh,' Peggy said again, on a different note. She stopped for a moment, staring across a garden fence at a small patch of garden with some pansies growing in it. It had just been raining and they looked as if their velvet faces were wet with tears. 'Oh, Glad. Our Diane going into the WAAF, and Bob away in the Army . . . There'll be only me and your dad left in the house.'

'That's right,' Gladys said, still trying to cheer her up. 'Just like honeymooners, you'll be. Darby and Joan.'

Peggy gave her a weak smile and moved on. After a pause, she said, 'I knew it was going to come, but somehow I sort of hoped – well, I know you've been wanting it a long time, Glad, but I wouldn't have been heartbroken if they'd never called you up. I mean, you're doing just as good work nursing at the Royal.'

'I know. I've thought of that myself, but it's like it's something I've got to do, Mum. You know, I keep seeing that recruiting poster – "Free A Man For the Fleet". I feel like I owe it, somehow.'

'Because of Graham,' Peggy said, and Gladys nodded. 'Glad, that wasn't your fault. You know that. You were dead beat that night, and he helped you with the ambulance—'

'And got killed. You don't have to remind me, Mum.' Gladys looked at her. 'I know in my head it wasn't my fault, but I *feel* as if it was. And it don't matter how many times I tell myself that, I still go on feeling.'

Peggy sighed and nodded. 'I know. It goes against all common sense, but if that's the way you feel, there ain't nothing to be done about it. And his poor mum must appreciate the way you go over to Gosport to see her every couple of weeks. Well, you'll have a nice smart uniform, anyway. Dark blue always did suit you, though it's a devil to keep clean. I often wonder why they make so many uniforms dark blue – policemen, firemen, they're all in it and it shows every mark. I reckon the Army have got it right, using mud colour – the only trouble is it's downright ugly.'

Gladys laughed. 'I don't think Olive Harker would like to hear you call it "mud colour". She's proud of her khaki.'

'Well, and so she should be. I admire her for joining up and I admire you too, Gladys. And our Diane. I might be upset to see you go, but I wouldn't have it any other way. I'm proud of you, and that's the truth of it.'

'Oh, Mum . . .'

'Yes, well, no need to go piping your eye,' Peggy said, not far from tears herself. She stepped out briskly along the pavement. 'We'd better be getting a move on. Your dad'll be hungry after his gardening, expects his dinner on the table the minute he walks in. Not that he won't turn his nose up at whatever I provide. He's never got used to making do.'

'What is it today, then? A proper roast dinner for Sunday, like we used to have?' Gladys sighed. 'I can hardly remember what a joint of meat looks like when it comes out of the oven.'

'You'll be lucky. It was going to be that Lord Woolton pie again, but I've got a bit of pig's fry, and some onions and a bit of bacon to go with it. And treacle pudding for afters.'

'Sounds all right to me. We can always pretend it's pork – same animal, after all.'

They were just passing Wesley Avenue now. It wouldn't be long before they were home and Gladys knew she would be thankful to sit down. She'd been on her feet all night in the ward before going on to meet her mother from church, and her legs ached. I wonder if I'll get a sit-down job when I'm in the Wrens, she thought. I wouldn't mind a bit of a rest, to start with anyway.

She became aware of a low, throbbing hum coming from somewhere behind her. It wasn't like a sound at first, more a deep vibration in the air. It grew and seemed to gather, like a cloud spreading over the sky until it was coming from all around. Gladys and Peggy stopped and looked at each other and then up at the sky.

'It's a plane,' Gladys said, but she couldn't hear her own voice and she raised it to a shout. 'Mum, it's a plane, flying low. It's a *German* plane.' It was almost overhead now, the throb grown into a steady, roaring thunder. Other people were stopping and looking up too, screaming and running backwards and forwards, like ants whose nest had been suddenly uncovered. The street was suddenly in pandemonium.

The plane was huge. It came swooping over the rooftops, almost at chimney height. It was dark grey, a gigantic, solid shadow that seemed to fill the sky and obscure the sun, blotting out all light. Rigid with fear, Gladys stared up at it. She saw the swastika painted on its wings and fuselage; she saw the gleam of the cockpit, and later she swore that she had seen the pilot bent over his controls, his eyes hidden behind black goggles, his lips drawn back over his teeth. And she heard the harsh, staccato rattle of the gunfire.

'Lie down!' Peggy was screaming in her ear, dragging at her arm. 'Lie down, for God's sake. We're going to be strafed!'

What difference will it make whether I'm lying down or not? Gladys wondered, but already she was on the pavement, curling herself up into a ball, her arms wrapped about her head. She felt her mother beside her, and heard the scream of bullets, the sharp crack as they hit the road. For what seemed to be an eternity, the noise was deafening: the plane, the shrill whine of the bullets, the clatter of the gun. And then, abruptly, it was over and the roar of the engines receded as the plane swept on towards Portsdown Hill.

Gladys lay quite still on the pavement, trembling with shock, not even certain whether or not she had been hit. She heard people running, felt hands on her body and heard voices asking questions. 'Are you all right, duck? Are you hurt? Didn't get you, did he, the bastard?' Someone turned her over and stared anxiously into her eyes.

A tremendous explosion shook the ground. Gladys felt it rock the pavement beneath her and she cried out and tried to curl up again, but the hands went on holding her firmly, and the eyes that looked into hers took on an expression of satisfaction.

'That got 'im. '*E* won't come botherin' about us no more,' and the man jerked his head towards the Hill.

Gladys sat up gingerly, and followed his gaze. Something had caught fire on the Hill and was sending up plumes of orange flame and thick, black smoke. She stared at it, still dazed.

'That's the bugger what shot at you, girl. Bin shot down hisself by the ack-ack guns, and serve 'im right. Cowardly, that's what it is, shooting at women in the street. Downright cowardly. Now, then, love, what about you? All right, are yer? I don't see no blood, you don't seem to 'ave bin 'it.'

'No,' she said shakily, 'I don't think I was. I'm all right.'

'This one ain't though, Charlie,' said someone else, just out of Gladys's sight. 'Copped a right packet, she 'as. 'Ad it, I reckon.' The crowd that had gathered gave a collective sigh of horror and dismay.

This one . . . ? Gladys's senses reeled again. Mum was with me, she thought. She pulled me down. *Mum* . . .

She turned her head with difficulty and saw Peggy lying there in her black coat, the one she'd always worn to go to church. She looked smaller than ever, huddled there with the black fabric draped around her like a shroud. One arm was flung out, and her bag of shopping was scattered all around.

Peggy lay quite still, despite the noise and the people who were now examining her, moving her gently, parting the torn material of her best coat and the skirt and blouse she had on underneath. She took no notice of any of them, and then someone touched her face and her head rolled

56

sideways. Gladys saw her eyes, wide open, staring from a bloody face towards the sky.

A dark red stain spread slowly across the pavement.

# CHAPTER FIVE

'You'll never go off and join up now, Glad,' Bert Shaw said heavily. He was sitting in his armchair by the empty fireplace, a cup of tea beside him. His face was pasty and he hadn't shaved for two days. His eyes were blank and empty.

Gladys sat on the other side of the little living-room. She couldn't bring herself to sit opposite him, in her mother's chair; nobody had sat there yet. She still felt ill and shaky, and she didn't want to think about things like joining up, or making funeral arrangements, or even what to have for tea tonight. It all seemed too complicated, too difficult. I just want to crawl away into a corner and curl up in a ball, she thought. Let someone else do it all.

However, you couldn't just leave things. Decisions had to be made, people notified, ration books handed in – it seemed the cruellest thing of all, somehow, that her mother's ration book mustn't be used now, that it seemed to have died with her. It wasn't that Gladys wanted the rations themselves, it was the thought that it had suddenly become illegal. If someone – she, or Diane, or Bert – had been using the ration book while Peggy was lying there being peppered with machine-gun bullets, there would have been a moment when they'd have been breaking the law. It seemed inhuman.

There were Gladys's papers too, her joining-up papers for the Wrens. She'd signed on, committed herself, but with her dad sitting over there, all shrunken into his old jumper that he normally wore for gardening, how could she go off and leave him? He couldn't even boil himself an egg.

'I don't know,' she said. 'I don't know if I can get out of it.'

'What d'you mean, get out of it? 'Course you can get out of it. I'm your father, ain't I? I need you here. All you got to do is tell 'em.' He stared at her with red, puffy eyes. '*I'll* go and tell 'em if you want me to.'

'No – don't do that, Dad.' Gladys didn't feel ready to make any decision herself, but she knew she didn't want one made for her. 'I've got a couple of weeks. We can get something sorted out in that time.'

'What? What d'you mean, get something sorted out? There's only one thing to sort out and that's getting those papers cancelled. And the sooner the better. You know what these offices are like.'

I ought to, Gladys thought. I'd have been in the Wrens a year ago if I'd had my way, but what with them stopping recruiting for a while saying they'd got enough, and then me breaking my arm, and then starting nursing and still the papers never came through . . . If I'd gone into the Wrens when I first wanted to, me and Mum might never have been walking down the street just then. She'd be alive now and getting Dad's tea ready.

She'd said something like that to Elsie Philpotts, Graham's mum, when she'd gone over to Gosport on her regular fortnightly visit. Elsie Philpotts was a fat, blowsy woman, who had always been full of bawdy good humour and ready to squawk with laughter at the slightest thing, until her son had been killed. Now some of the flippancy had left her, though she still tried to keep a smile on her face, and teased her thin wisp of a husband, Charlie, just as much as ever. But it didn't sound quite so real any more, Gladys thought.

Elsie had been quite sharp with her when she'd said that about Mum being still alive, if it hadn't been for her.

'Look, you can't take responsibility for everyone that gets killed in this war,' she said. 'I know how you feel about my Graham: if he hadn't bin helping you with the ambulance that night, he'd still be alive. But who's to say that's true? He might just as easy have got killed the next day, walking under a bus. Or on his ship. Or *anywhere*. And so could your mum. There might even have bin times before that day, when she might've got killed if you *hadn't* bin with her. It's no good even thinking about it. We just has to carry on.'

'Elsie's right,' Charlie Philpotts piped up. 'I reckon when your number's up, it's up, and there ain't nothing you can do about it. That mine had our Graham's name on it, not yours, and it wasn't nothing to do with you.'

Perhaps they were right, Gladys thought now, pouring her dad another cup of tea, but that didn't help her decide what she ought to do about the Wrens.

The back door opened and Diane came in. She had joined the WAAF a fortnight ago and wore the Air Force blue uniform and cap. It suits her, Gladys thought enviously, shows up her yellow hair and blue eyes. I bet the erks really go for her.

59

Two weeks, that was all the difference there was. Two weeks since Diane had joined up, and two weeks before Gladys was due to go. That two weeks had set Di free, while it looked as though Gladys was caught once more in a trap.

'I just met Ernie Barrow, from the undertaker's,' Diane said. She looked tired and her eyes had dark shadows under them. She'd been given leave to come home until after the funeral. 'He said he'd be round this evening, to see what service we want. Choose the hymns and that. I don't know, do you? What sort of hymns do you have at funerals?'

'Don't ask me,' Bert said. 'It was your mum went to church.'

'I suppose there's special hymns,' Gladys said doubtfully. 'They'd be in the hymn book.'

They found Peggy's hymn book, which had been rescued, unstained, from her handbag, and thumbed through it until they came to 'Burial of the Dead'. There were three. One was for a child. Gladys read out some of the verses from the others.

'"Often were they wounded, In the deadly strife . . ."' Her eyes filled with tears. 'We can't sing that. I'll never be able to sing that.'

'What's the other one like?' Diane asked.

'It's not quite as bad. It's all about eternal light and rest, and green pastures and sheep.'

'What have sheep got to do with it?' Bert asked in astonishment. 'Peggy and me never had no sheep.'

'It's a thing they say in hymns, Dad. Sheep and lambs and that, they're all religious. There's a lot about them in the Bible too.'

'Well, I dunno about that. It's a long time since I went to Sunday school. Anyway, I always fancied a bit of pork meself, or some beef. Lamb's a bit tasteless to my way of thinking.'

'Well, we've got to choose something,' Gladys said.

They were still sitting there, gazing at the book, when Jess Budd came in from next door. She took one look at the despondent little group, and went through to the scullery to put on the kettle. They heard her getting out cups and saucers, and presently she came back with the tea on an old tin tray.

'What are you doing? Choosing hymns?'

'We don't know what to have,' Gladys said. 'There's only two for funerals and we don't really like either of them.'

'Well, why not have a couple of your mum's own favourites? I reckon that'd be what she'd have liked you to do.'

'We don't know what they are,' Gladys confessed. Peggy had been unable to persuade any of her children to accompany her to church since they were twelve years old. 'I mean, she used to sing them round the house sometimes but I couldn't tell you which ones.'

'No, but I can,' Jess said. 'I stood beside her often enough on Sunday mornings. I'll tell you what she liked best. "All Things Bright and Beautiful", that was one of her favourites. And "He Who Would Valiant Be". I reckon both those would be nice. Peggy was always bright, and she was pretty too, when she was a girl. And nobody could say she wasn't valiant.'

Gladys gazed at her. 'You think it'd be all right to have those? I mean – "All Things Bright and Beautiful" . . . It doesn't sound much like a funeral.'

'Well, you'd have to ask the vicar,' Jess said. 'He might have other ideas, but I don't see why not. Remember your mum as she was: always busy, always cheerful and singing. Let's be glad she was alive.' Her voice trembled a little. She had wept for Peggy almost all night and knew she would miss her sorely, but the main thing now was to help her friend's family. The two girls, and poor Bert.

'"All Things Bright and Beautiful,"' Bert said suddenly. 'You're right, Jess. That was her favourite, and it's all about her, too. We'll have that one. And that other one you mentioned.'

'"He Who Would Valiant Be,"' Jess said. 'I don't think the vicar would have any objection to that. Anyway, they're all hymns, aren't they? I don't see how he can object to any of them really.'

After they had drunk their tea, Gladys saw Jess to the door and stood talking to her for a few minutes. 'I don't know what to do about Dad. He's taken it really hard. I don't reckon he knew how much he depended on her. He's sort of folded up on himself now, don't seem able to do a thing.'

'It's shock,' Jess said. 'He'll be better after the funeral.' She sighed. The last few weeks seemed to be nothing but funerals: first Mr Beckett's, and now Peggy's. There had been three others in the streets near by, as well: an old woman who had fallen over and broken her hip and never got over it, a dockyardman who had had an accident in the yard, and a little boy of three who had crawled under a milkman's van and got crushed by a wheel. And Jess and Annie were getting increasingly worried about their mother, who seemed to have retreated into herself and hardly spoke or ate a thing these days.

'The thing is,' Gladys said, 'I don't know what to do – about the Wrens, I mean. I got my papers the day before – before Mum . . . And now Dad don't want me to go. Well, you can't blame him, I suppose, not with our Diane only just gone into the WAAF. I mean, how would he manage? I don't think he's ever cooked a meal in his life.'

Jess looked at her thoughtfully. 'What do you feel about it? Do you want to go?'

'Well, I've been waiting for a long time,' Gladys said, not quite answering the question, 'and I probably wouldn't have to go *away*, exactly. Specially not now. There must be plenty of posts round Pompey. But I couldn't be here all the time, not regular. He'd have to do a lot for himself.' She looked unhappy. 'I suppose I'll have to see if I can be let off. I'd feel guilty all the time.'

Jess frowned. Then she shook her head. 'Don't decide anything in a hurry, Gladys. Take your time. Wait till after the funeral, at least – things'll seem different then. You've got too many other things to think about to decide all at once.'


Jess went back indoors. Rose was laying the table while Maureen played one of her interminable games on the hearthrug with the coloured bricks and the bag of marbles. Tim was reading *Hotspur* and Keith was chipping away at a bit of wood with a penknife.

She and Frank had thought it was safer in Portsmouth now that the bombing had stopped. Yet this horrible thing had happened, if not in April Grove itself, just a few streets away, to the person she was closest to apart from her sister Annie. Who would be next? Yet you couldn't keep the family indoors. Everyone had to be allowed out to take their own risks. You could do nothing but hope and pray they'd be safe.

She went out to the scullery and looked with disfavour at the tart she'd made for tea. It was another idea cooked up (that was a joke!) by the food people. Parsnips, sliced up and sprinkled with banana essence and covered with custard made from household dried milk.

'Nobody's going to think they're bananas, not in a month of Sundays,' she said, sliding the dish into the gas oven, and yet – it was so long since any of them had tasted a real banana. Maureen had never even seen one. What did it really matter?

You had to keep trying. There wasn't anything else to do, really.


After the funeral, everyone came back to number 13 for a cup of tea or a glass of sherry or beer. Frank Budd, who was practically teetotal, sipped his sherry as if he was afraid it might bite him. He only ever drank at Christmas, weddings and funerals.

'I'm going to miss her something awful,' Jess said to her sister. 'We were real pals. Nothing was ever too much trouble for her, always ready to lend a helping hand, she was, and we used to have a cup of tea and a natter most days. It's what keeps you going, a good old chinwag with a real friend.'

'I know.' Annie was friendly in the same way with her own next-door neighbour, Milly Mace. Although the sisters lived at opposite ends of the same short street and saw each other regularly, you still needed a friend who was outside the family, and Jess wasn't likely to get on the same terms with Ethel Glaister, on her other side.

Ethel was here now, of course, looking stiff and self-conscious in her powder-blue costume. She'd always managed to dress it up a bit with a glittery brooch or a bit of lace at the neck, but today it was looking its age. A bit grubby and worn around the cuffs, Annie noticed, and the collar not as smartly pressed as it might be. Ethel herself was looking a bit the worse for wear too – powder clogged around her nostrils and her lipstick smudged.

'You all right, Ethel?' Annie asked when she got a chance. 'You're looking tired.'

'So I might be,' came the sharp rejoinder, 'working all the hours God sends at that aircraft factory. Making us sweep up all the mess, they are, and then sort through it like a lot of scavengers for rivets. Me! What's always been so careful to keep meself nice. It's worse than being a skivvy.' Her hard blue eyes snapped with anger. 'And that girl of mine, that Carol, what d'you think they've given *her* to do? Up Eastney Barracks, that's where she is, doing tailoring for the Marines. Sitting at a sewing machine all day working on nice material. D'you think that's fair? *Do* you?'

Annie took a step back. Ethel was glaring at her as if it was all her fault, and one of her hands was clenched and half raised, almost as if she meant to hit out. For a moment, Annie really thought the other woman was going to strike her.

'I'm sorry, Ethel,' she began, 'but it's not my doing. There's no call to go on at me about it.'

'No, but you're not going to have to do it, are you? You managed to get out of it, you and that sister of yours with her family all back at home. I told her, I'd have done the same as her if I'd seen this lot coming – had a baby. But me and my George, we were too responsible. We didn't want to bring children we couldn't afford to keep into the world, cramming them into little houses and making them wear hand-me-downs.' Her lip curled as she glanced across the room at Jess. 'If you ask me, the evacuation came at just the right time for them, what with Maureen being born a few weeks before. And that coat her Rose is wearing this summer's been on two other girls in the street, to my knowledge.'

'I don't see as that's any of your business,' Annie retorted. 'And since Jess made it in the first place, I should think she could feel proud of her workmanship. It looks as good now as the day she finished sewing it. You ought to be glad your Carol's been given something to do that'll teach her a bit of a trade too. At least if she can sew, she'll never be reduced to scrabbling on the floor for a few rivets!'

Ethel gasped, but Annie turned away before she could say any more. I shouldn't have done that, she thought guiltily, not at poor Peg's funeral, but that woman gets my goat, always has done. Peg didn't like her no more than I do, nor does anyone else, neither. She's got a nasty, vicious tongue on her, and that's the truth of it.

Annie found Jess again, out in the scullery washing some cups and making another pot of tea.

'I'll have to be going now. I left Mum all on her own, and you know what she's like these days, gets frightened if there's no one within call. Milly said she'd keep an ear open, but I promised I wouldn't be too long.' She hesitated, wanting to say something to comfort her sister, but what could you say when a woman's best friend had been strafed and shot to pieces in the street? 'You'll come up whenever you want to. There's always a kettle on the go.'

'Thanks, Annie.' Jess paused for a moment with her hands in tepid water only slightly softened by the small lump of washing soda she'd put in. 'Don't worry about me, I've got Frank and the kids. It's Bert I worry about, and those two girls. Specially Gladys.' They could see Gladys through the half open door, sitting in a corner with Olive. 'She looks dead beat, and Bert's no help. He seems to think she's just here for his convenience. You know he's trying to stop her going in the Wrens?'

Annie nodded. 'Olive told me. She thinks Gladys should go, but that'll leave him all on his own, won't it? How would he manage?'

Jess shook her head. 'There's plenty of others having to. It's not as if he's all that old. I've said I'll help out with his bit of washing, and pass him in a bit of Sunday dinner, and his sister says she'll come down from Cosham once a week to flick round with a duster, keep him tidy.' She sighed. 'Gladys asked me what she ought to do, but I just don't know what I ought to say. I mean, a few years ago it was all cut and dried, wasn't it? A girl would stay home automatically to help her dad. But now, with the war effort and all – well, you don't feel you can say that any more. Gladys thinks she's more use to the country in the Wrens, and who am I to say she shouldn't go?'

Olive came out to the scullery. 'Is there any more tea going, Mum? Poor Gladys has just about had it. She did all those sandwiches on her own, and put everything out ready, and she hasn't had a bit herself. I think it's time all these people went and left her in peace.'

'Here.' Annie poured her a cup of tea. 'It's hardly got the strength to struggle out of the pot, but it's hot. Put some saccharin in it, sweet tea's good for you after a shock. I know it happened last week, but she's still suffering from it, if you ask me.'

Olive took the cup and tipped in two small tablets from the little bottle. Nearly everyone took saccharin in their tea now that sugar was so severely rationed. 'It'll be a good thing for her when she can get out of this house. That Mr Shaw's enough to drive anyone to drink, he's so miserable. I never noticed he was all that fond of Mrs Shaw when she was alive!'

'Go on, he thought the world of her,' Jess said. 'He just didn't show it much, that's all. There's a lot of men like that, hardly give their wives the time of day, and then the world collapses round 'em when they haven't got 'em any more.'

'Well, that don't do the wives much good, does it?' Olive said, stirring the tea briskly. 'I'm thankful my Derek's not like that. He knows how to show his appreciation – when he's here.' She blushed as her mother and aunt laughed, and went quickly back into the other room to give Gladys her tea.

'When he's here,' Annie said, her smile fading, 'and that's little enough. Goodness knows when she'll see him again. But she's right, he's a good chap and a good husband, and once this lot's over they'll be able to settle down and have as good a life together as you and me have had with our chaps, Jess.'

'I hope so,' Jess said, smiling as Frank finally finished his glass of sherry. 'I really do hope so.'

When the house was finally silent again, Gladys went out for a walk. Her father was sitting in his armchair as she put her head round the door to say cheerio, and she felt a pang of guilt. He looked so crumpled, somehow, with his best trousers still on but his braces dangling and the collar off his shirt because it had been starched too stiffly and cut into his neck. He'd put up with it all through the service and the get-together afterwards, but as soon as his sister Jean, who'd been the last to leave, had shut the door behind her, he'd ripped it off and chucked it on the sideboard. After that, he'd seemed to lose his energy, and just sagged.

In a way, Gladys didn't want to leave him. She wanted to give him comfort; she wanted to put her arms round him and tell him not to look so sad, it was all right, everything was all right. But it wasn't, and she couldn't make it so. Nobody could.

She desperately needed to get away. To be by herself, with the fresh air blowing away the misery which hung about the little house like a sticky web, clinging to everything in it. She needed some time on her own, to work out her own ideas with no one telling her what they thought.

She walked up April Grove, hoping she wouldn't meet anyone who'd want to stop and talk, but most of the neighbours had been at the funeral, and now they were all indoors. If anyone saw her walk by they realised that she wanted to be alone, and respected it.

Except for one. As she passed the last house in April Grove, the one that was better than the rest because it was on the end of the terrace, so had a side wall and a garden with a hedge all the way along, the garden gate opened and a young man stepped out.

He had flaming red hair, and wore soldier's khaki, and Gladys didn't have to look at him more than once to know that he was Clifford Weeks, Tommy and Freda Vickers's nephew.

'Hullo, Glad.' His face was thick with freckles but his eyes were very blue. He stood still for a moment, hesitating, and then said, 'Mind if I walk along with you for a bit?'

Gladys shrugged. His hair was even redder than Graham's, she thought. Graham's had been just ginger, but Clifford's was as bright as a traffic light. 'Can't stop you walking. It's a free country.'

He fell into step beside her. He was taller than she remembered, and walked very upright in his uniform. For few minutes, neither spoke, and then he said quietly, 'I was really sorry to hear about your mum, Glad. That was a rotten thing to happen. She was a smasher.'

Gladys felt the tears well up. She kept her eyes down and said in a low voice, 'I know. Thanks.'

They came to the top of October Street. Gladys paused, undecided. She wanted to walk beside the sea, but that meant turning towards Langstone, or else getting on a bus and going all the way out to Southsea, and she didn't feel like buses just now. She gave Clifford a swift glance, wondering what he was going to do, and found him watching her intently. To her annoyance, a blush spread warmly over her cheeks.

'Look, Glad,' he said, 'I don't think you ought to be on your own just now. I think you need someone to be with you. You don't have to say anything. You don't have to talk to me at all, but I'd like to walk along with you. Where were you thinking of going?'

She shrugged again. 'Nowhere special. I just – I just wanted to be out somewhere.' She looked at him again, at the bright red hair and the intense blue eyes. 'Yes, all right, I'd like you to walk with me. It would be nice.'

He grinned suddenly and she blinked, dazzled by the sudden warmth of his smile. 'OK. Let's go down by Langstone Harbour. I want to smell the seaweed!'

Gladys laughed. 'You'll smell plenty there.' Her awkwardness had disappeared, melted by that sudden smile, and she felt her spirits lift. What did she have against him, after all? She'd liked him well enough when he'd come and played with Bob, and Colin Chapman, when they'd all been kids. In fact, now she came to think about it, they'd been pretty good friends . . . but that was years ago, she reminded herself. They were grown up now and a lot had changed. For one thing, she was still writing pretty often to Colin, in the Japanese prisoner-of-war camp, and she didn't really want to get involved with anyone else – especially since Graham's death.

Perhaps Diane was right, though, and she was holding it against Clifford that his hair was ginger, like Graham's. That was daft. He was an old friend, a boy she'd knocked about with as a child, and nothing more. There was no reason at all why she shouldn't be friendly towards him.

They walked together without speaking. Feeling easier than she had since her mother had died, Gladys found her mind going back to the problem of whether or not she should go ahead with her intention to join the Wrens. She'd been accepted, and she was supposed to be reporting for duty in less than a fortnight. She wanted to do it – but still she was haunted by the thought of her father, crumpled like a heap of washing in his chair.

She was so absorbed in her thoughts that when Clifford spoke again, she jumped, almost forgetting that he was there.

'Uncle Tommy told me about you going into the Wrens. He said he reckoned your dad wasn't too keen – thought you ought to be stopping home to look after him.'

'Maybe I should.'

He was silent again for a few moments. Then he said, quietly, 'I felt pretty rotten after my mum and dad died. I was their only one. They didn't want me to join up – I volunteered, before the call-up started – but they told me I had to do whatever I thought was right, and they knew the country needed us young men. They gave me a good send-off, and that was the last time I saw them.' He paused again. 'They were standing at the corner of the road, waving goodbye, and Mum was crying into her hanky, but they never said a word to stop me going.'

Gladys couldn't speak. She dashed a hand across her eyes and waited. They turned a corner and came within sight of the harbour. All her life, Gladys had known it as a quiet place, where the waves washed a deserted beach and nobody but a few fishermen waded in the sea or put out in small boats, but now it was littered with barbed wire and there were strange structures taking shape along the shore, hidden by a web of scaffolding. She looked at them without much interest. There was so much going on that you couldn't understand, that in general you just turned a blind eye.

'My mum wouldn't have stopped me going,' she said. 'She was all for it, but Dad never reckoned us girls should do anything, and now Diane's gone in the WAAF—'

'I don't see as that's got anything to do with it,' he said. 'You're not Diane. You've got your own life to live. And it's *your* life, Glad. Not his. Just because he and your mum – well, you know what I mean. He's done his bit by you, he's worked to give you a home and all that, but you're not a kid any more. You've got to decide for yourself.'

'I know, but it's not that easy. He'll be on his own—'

'*I'm* on my own,' Clifford said. 'One day this war'll be over, and my home's not there any more, but I'm not going to come back to Uncle Tommy and expect him and Auntie Freda to take me in. Why should they? I'm big enough and ugly enough to look after myself. If I can fight Germans, I reckon I can learn to boil myself an egg. Matter of fact, I already have.' He grinned. 'They don't mollycoddle us in the Army, you know. We've got to be able to do all our own jobs – washing, ironing, mending, the lot. And cook a meal, with any bits and bobs we can scrounge, because that's what we'll be doing when we get over there.' He jerked his head towards the Solent and the Channel that lay beyond.

Gladys looked at him. 'You think you'll be going soon? To Germany?'

'Bound to be, aren't we? France first, and then Germany. That's what all that's about.' He jerked his head again, this time at the network of scaffolding surrounding the strange edifice on the beach. 'I dunno what it is, but it's something big, you can see that, and they're not just playing with their Meccano. There'll be an invasion one day – a really big one – and this time we'll win.' He turned suddenly and put his hands on her shoulders. 'It's people like you and me who'll win it, Glad. It's people like us they need. Young people, who are strong and got plenty of guts. Girls like you who've already won a medal, and blokes like me who've been wounded and still can't wait to get back and have a crack at Jerry.' He stopped, and then said, 'You want to know what I think?'

Gladys nodded. He was already telling her what he thought, and pretty forcibly, but she was mesmerised by that intent blue gaze and couldn't have stopped him if she'd tried. His words were filling her with an exhilaration that she hadn't felt for months.

'I think you ought to go ahead and join up,' he said. 'Remember the old poster? "Your Country Needs You." It needs you a hell of a sight more than your dad does, right now. He'll survive, Glad. He'll learn to look after himself, and it won't do him any harm either. But the rest of us – well, you know what they say. We've all got to do our bit, and your bit's as important as mine. *Everyone*'s important in this war, Gladys.'

Gladys stared at him, and suddenly her mind was made up. I will go, she thought. Cliff's right: Dad's got to learn to look after himself. It's hard on him, but the war's hard on everyone and I can't put his Sunday dinner before my war work.

They turned and walked back. At the top of April Grove, Tommy Vickers was out working in his garden, and they stopped just out of earshot. Gladys saw Tommy glance up and then turn his attention back to his work. She looked up into Clifford's eyes.

'Thanks, Cliff,' she said quietly. 'I feel a lot better for that. It was nice to have you to talk to. And—' She stopped, her heart beating a little more quickly. If I say this, she thought, it'll change things. I don't know exactly how, but it will. I can't *not* say it, though: he's going away tomorrow. He might never come back. It's the least I can do.

'If you want me to write to you while you're away,' she said rapidly, 'I will. If it helps . . .'

Once again she saw his eyes change, the pupils widening so that his eyes looked almost black, with only a rim of brilliant blue. A grin split his freckled face and he took a step towards her. Gladys glanced quickly round at Tommy Vickers, still bent with concentration over his gardening, and backed hastily away. 'I only said I'd write to you . . .'

'I know. That'll be smashing, Gladys. Really smashing.' He stared at her with a look of almost idiot delight. 'And I'll write back. Tell you all about things – you know, little things, the things we don't know about each other. And you'll tell me things, won't you?'

She hadn't meant to write that sort of letter at all, just the sort of chatty daily news that she wrote to Colin Chapman, but she found herself nodding dumbly.

'If I don't get sent away straight off – if I get leave again – I'll come and see you, shall I? We'll go for a walk again.' It was as though she'd promised him the moon, she thought dazedly.

'It's just friends,' she said warningly. 'I'm not promising any more than that.'

'I know. It's all right. I won't expect any more. It'll just be smashing to get letters. You'll write a lot, won't you? I mean, every week at least. It won't just be now and then?'

Poor Cliff, she thought, staring at him. He must be really lonely when he's away. No mum and dad to write to, no brothers or sisters – just Mr and Mrs Vickers. 'I'll write a lot,' she promised.

Mrs Vickers came out of the house to speak to Tommy, and saw them standing there. She called out to Clifford, and Gladys muttered a hasty goodbye. She turned and walked back down April Grove to number 13, where her father was still sitting in his chair and staring morosely at the empty fireplace.

Just what have you got yourself into now, Gladys Shaw? she asked herself ruefully.


'You don't have to salute me,' a voice remarked as Olive walked past one of the huts in camp. 'Just say hello.'

She turned quickly. The soldier she'd met at the dance was leaning against the corner of the hut, grinning, and she smiled back.

'Hello, Ray.'

'Hello, Olive,' he answered gravely. 'How have you been keeping? Pleasant weather for the time of year, isn't it? What are you paying for cauliflowers these days?' And in the same tone, as Olive laughed at him, 'I see that *No, No, Nanette* is going to be on at the King's next week. How about coming with me?'

Olive stopped laughing and looked at him uncertainly. Since they had met, they had been dancing at South Parade Pier twice – once to the Squadronnaires, and once to Oscar Rabin and his band. Both times, Olive had gone with Claudia and the other girls and met Ray inside, and she'd salved her conscience by telling herself it was by accident. But going to the theatre with him, deliberately – well, that was something else.

'I don't think—' she began, but he raised a hand to stop her.

'No strings, Livvy. We'll ask your friend along as well. She's going out regular now with that pilot, isn't she? We'll make up a foursome.'

'I still don't—'

'Look,' he said, 'we both know we're married and there's nothing in it, but it's lonely being miles away from home. I'd like to go and see the show but I don't fancy going on my own.' He tilted his head to one side and looked at her with those crinkly eyes. 'How about it? Just for the company, eh?'

Olive hesitated for a few seconds more, then made up her mind. 'All right. So long as it's understood that's all it is.'

'Cross my heart,' he said solemnly, and then his grin broke out again. 'Oh, that's marvellous. And you'll get your friend to come as well? Just to make it all honest and so on?'

70

'Yes, I'll get Claudia and Mark to come,' Olive said, laughing.

'I'll get the tickets, then,' he said eagerly. 'Which night? Where d'you want to sit? Stalls? Gallery? A *box*?' He flashed his eyes a little and leered like a comic film star.

'Don't be daft. The dress circle's the best place, and Tuesday'll be best for me. I don't know about Claud. I'll ask her and let you know.'

However, Claudia could not come on Tuesday, or any other night. She was seeing her pilot seriously now, and they had already arranged all their off-duty time together. 'I'm taking him home to meet the parents,' she told Olive. 'I wouldn't be surprised if he pops the question soon. He's got that look in his eye!'

'Not really!' Olive was diverted. 'What'll you do, Claud? Will you say yes?'

'After a bit of prevaricating.' Claudia grinned. 'You don't want to give in too quickly, gives 'em ideas above their station, but he hasn't got a chance of getting away. I've been reeling him in like Daddy reels in a fish. He's *hooked*.'

'You're awful!' Olive exclaimed, but Claudia shook her head.

'If I didn't do it, some other girl would, and he'll be better off with me! Men shouldn't look like that if they want to stay bachelors.' She gave Olive a thoughtful look. 'So what's all this about the theatre, then? Bit of hand-holding in the back row?'

'No! It's nothing like that.' Olive could feel her cheeks grow warm and knew that Claudia had noticed. 'He just wants someone to go with, that's all. You know there's nothing going on. He's married as well.'

'Not that that always makes any difference,' Claudia murmured. 'Well, if you're sure . . . You could always ask one of the others.'

'I know.' But somehow Olive didn't feel like doing that. Claudia was her real friend, the one she was close to. 'No, I expect we'll just go on our own. After all, as Ray said, there's nothing in it. It's just for company.'

'Hmm.' Claudia pursed her lips. 'Make sure you keep it that way, then. I know these platonic friendships. They're fine until something goes wrong for one of you and you need a shoulder to cry on – and then, wham! You're off down the slippery slope before you've got time to say "Jack Robinson".'

'Not that I *would* say Jack Robinson,' Olive commented. 'More likely "Ray Whitaker" . . .' and they nudged each other and roared with laughter.

Olive went to bed that night feeling pleasantly excited and a little daring. Fancy going out with another chap! She looked at Derek's photograph on her locker and gave him a wry little grin of apology. There really isn't anything in it, she told him silently. And anyway, how do I know what you're getting up to, under the desert stars?

Immediately, she scolded herself for thinking such a thing. Derek was as straight and true as a blade. He wouldn't be getting up to anything under the desert stars. And nor will I, she told herself firmly. This isn't any different to going out with a girl. Its just company, someone to stand with in the queue and sit with and talk to in the interval. Nothing more than that.

It seemed that Ray felt exactly the same way. On Tuesday evening, they met at the camp gate, each feeling a bit self-conscious under the eye of the guard, and walked off together down the road. Olive had put on a new lipstick, and she noticed that Ray looked very smart, with his buttons shining brightly and his belt freshly blanco-ed. He glanced sideways and caught her look, and they both grinned awkwardly.

'Honestly, this is daft,' he exclaimed. 'I feel like a kid out on his first date.'

'I know. And it isn't even like that – a date, I mean. We're just going—'

'—for company,' he finished. 'I did mean that, Olive. No funny business. You really don't have to worry.'

She looked at him and then laughed. 'We're a couple of twerps! There's hundreds and thousands of people doing what we're doing – just spending a bit of time together – and we're making it seem like the crime of the century. There really isn't anything to feel guilty about, is there?'

'Nothing at all,' he said gravely, and took her hand in his.

Olive let him hold it for a moment or two, then she slid it away from his fingers and smiled into his eyes. 'It's all right, Ray,' she said. 'I feel happy about it now.'

'Yes,' he said, 'so do I.'

They walked on down the street towards the theatre. They stood in the queue together; they sat together in the dress circle, watching the story being played out on the brightly lit stage, wafted away for a while into a different world where problems could be resolved with a song, where lovers came together with a dance; and when it was over, they came out together, humming the tunes they had heard, laughing, feeling the closeness and the intimacy that comes from a shared experience.

'That was lovely,' Olive said as they walked slowly back to the camp. 'I really enjoyed it, Ray. Thank you.'

They stood together for a moment in a shadow, and he took her hand. For a moment, she thought he was about to kiss her, but instead he just gave her fingers a squeeze and then let go.

'I enjoyed it too, Livvy,' he said. 'Let's do it again some time, shall we?'

and then he turned and walked away, leaving her to return to her hut and slip into the narrow bed that stood beside Claudia's.

Her friend was still out, staying the night with her parents after introducing them to her pilot, and Olive lay gazing through the uncurtained window at the starlit sky.

It had been a lovely evening. The colour and gaiety of the stage, the romance of the story, the music and the laughter, had lifted her out of her sadness and reminded her what it was to enjoy life.

The moonlight, stretching in through the window, touched Derek's photograph with light and she saw the glint of his eyes and the shine of his teeth, almost as if he were really there. Reaching out her hand, she laid her fingertips lightly across the smooth, flat surface of his face.

'I love you, Derek,' she whispered softly. 'And there's no harm in it. I promise you. No harm at all.'

# CHAPTER SIX

The war dragged slowly on. The RAF, aided by the American Forces, seemed intent on reducing the whole of Germany to rubble. Night after night, waves of aircraft – Halifaxes, Stirlings, Flying Fortresses – departed in a black cloud to blitz major cities such as Stuttgart, Hamburg and Kiel, sometimes dropping so many bombs that they created a firestorm – a wave of flame that brought its own rush of air and fanned itself into an inferno. The Germans defended their skies as best they could, and each dawn brought news of the loss of a few more young pilots.

People at home followed the battles from the news that was released. German place-names became as familiar to the tongue as those in England. Housewives, who had previously known nothing of the shores beyond the Channel and whose conversation in the streets had been confined to local gossip and the price of vegetables, now talked about the Battle of the Ruhr. Men, who until four years ago had concerned themselves more with football than politics, exulted over news of the daring raids that had destroyed the great Mohne and Eder dams so vital to the heavily industrialised valley.

'That'll hit 'em where it hurts,' Bert Shaw said with vicious satisfaction. Since Peggy had been killed, he had nursed a bitter grievance against the enemy, and had joined Ethel Glaister in avoiding the shop in September Street where Heinrich Brunner and his wife Alice sold newspapers and sweets. It wasn't reasonable – Heinrich had lived in Portsmouth for almost twenty-five years and although he'd been interned at the beginning of the war, he was now back in the shop. Alice was as English as could be and had grown up with all the other kids around September Street – why, she and Peggy had been friends, and Peggy had stuck up for her and Heinrich when Ethel had been nasty about them.

'I can't help it, Jess,' Bert had said when Jess tried to point out how unfair he was being. 'It's knowing he's German. If he'd even *tried* to be English – changed his name, got rid of his accent – well, maybe I'd feel different. As it is, every time I see him I think of that swine that shot my Peg, and there ain't nothing I can do about it.'

Bert was on his own now, for Diane was back at the RAF station and Gladys had gone into the Wrens after all. Gladys still didn't feel happy about it, and lay awake at night, remembering how Bert had sat in his chair, staring with empty eyes at the cold fireplace. He hadn't been able to take it in at all at first, looking up every time there was a sound at the door, as if he was expecting Peggy to walk in, brisk and wiry with her shopping basket, ready to recount a tale of how long she'd had to stand in the latest queue, or the bit of cheek she'd had from the fishmonger and what she'd told him in reply. But of course it never was Peggy, and he'd turn away again, sinking back into himself and not even bothering to hide the water that seeped from his eyes.

He'd got through the funeral better than they'd expected, as if he was glad to have something to do, somewhere to go, but after that he'd sunk back again, and looked at Diane like a hurt dog when she'd told him she was going back to camp.

'It's no good,' she'd said to Gladys, 'I can't stop here and look after him. It'd drive me crackers. He'd be on at me all the time, you know what he's like: "Be in by ten o'clock, my girl, or you'll feel the flat of my hand." I've had enough of that, and he'll be worse now Mum's not here any more.'

'So I've got to stop here, is that it?' Gladys said. 'Just when I thought I was going to get away, too. My papers have come through, you know, I've signed on. I don't even know as I *could* get out of it.'

'I don't see why you should,' Diane said. 'Dad's not a baby. He can manage on his own. Mum'd have to, if it had been him that had gone.'

'That's different. Women can manage better than men. How would he manage with his washing and cooking? He's never had to do a thing for himself at home, you know that.'

'Well, it's time he learned, then. *We're* doing things we never had to do before, aren't we? Look at you, driving an ambulance through all those air raids, and me, doing mechanic's work. And Betty Chapman out on a farm, and Olive working a gun. Girls never used to do that sort of thing, but we're managing. If you ask me, it's a pretty poor show if a bloke Dad's age can't learn to put on the kettle for a cup of tea and boil an egg.'

'He can't live on boiled eggs and cups of tea—' Gladys began, but Diane broke in impatiently.

'Well, he can learn to cook whatever he does want to eat, can't he? It don't take much skill to fry a few sausages and boil up some spuds. I tell you what, Glad; if you stop on now you'll never get away. He's never going to learn to manage for himself, is he? And what's going to happen when you want to

75

get married? Going to take him with you, are you? On your honeymoon and all? You'll have a job finding a bloke what'll put up with that.'

'The way things are going, there's not going to be anyone left for me to marry,' Gladys said bitterly.

A few days later, however, she announced that she was going ahead with her plans to join the Wrens. 'I've got to go, Dad. I'll never feel right if I don't.'

She listened dutifully to his grumbles, steeling herself against being dissuaded, but was surprised when he suddenly gave in and turned away, saying that if she was determined to go, that was all there was to it. 'You're your mother's daughter, and nothing could shift her once she'd made up her mind. I just hope you'll be able to spare a minute to come back and see your old dad once in a while.'

'Oh Dad, of course I will.' She flung her arms around his neck and hugged him, a thing she hadn't done since she was a little girl. He flushed red, and she laughed, feeling almost as embarrassed. 'I'll be back so often you'll hardly know I've gone,' although they both knew that couldn't be true. Once she had signed on, her life wouldn't be her own any more, and she would need someone else's permission for what she did.

She had written to tell Clifford of her decision, and he'd answered that he couldn't wait to see her in her Wren's uniform. Clifford's unit was camped in a field somewhere in north Hampshire now and they wrote to each other two or three times a week. Cliff's letters were so open and so trusting that Gladys gradually found herself, rather to her surprise, pouring out all the small thoughts and fears and pleasures that until now hadn't been shared with anyone.

Swinging wildly between grief over her mother, worry over her father and an odd sensation, almost excitement, that she couldn't quite identify, she went through the first bewildering days of her initiation as a Wren almost without noticing, and was rebuked several times for inattention and sloppiness.

'Don't imagine you can act like Lady Muck just because you've got a medal,' the Leading Wren told her sharply. 'We all start equal here, and you're no better than anyone else.'

The rebuke stung, and Gladys concentrated hard on the drill they did each morning, determined to make the most of being in the Wrens after the long wait she'd endured.

In Cliff's letters, she found the kind of encouragement and pride in her achievements that her mother would have given her. He's a good friend, she thought. I don't really know what I'd have done without him.

*

The Ruhr valley continued to be a major objective for Bomber Command. There was so much industry there, that almost every bomb dropped found a target. In July, for the first time, Rome was bombed, with the pilots and navigators briefed to take every possible care not to damage cultural and religious buildings. A few days later Mussolini was deposed and there were riots and demonstrations for peace in Italy. At the end of the month, British and American planes attacked Hamburg and created a firestorm, killing forty thousand people. It was almost unimaginable that so many could have died in one night.

Jess lay awake thinking of the children and babies who must have died in that terrible inferno. I know they did it to us, she thought, remembering the Blitz, and the nights of terror she and so many others had endured as the air-raid warnings wailed and the Luftwaffe droned overhead, but does that make it right? Little, innocent children having to suffer like that . . . At such times she sympathised with Betty's Quaker husband, Dennis, who had refused point-blank to kill anyone, and been sent to prison for his beliefs.

'Stay-at-home holidays' were all the rage that summer. As Tommy Vickers remarked, they had to be – there was no other option. Anyway, for most of the folk of April Grove, any other sort of holiday was an undreamed-of treat, unless you had relatives somewhere nice, like George Glaister's family in Devon.

Quite a lot of people went out into the countryside to work on the farms. This wasn't like the evacuation – whole families went, and slept under canvas or in huts, while toiling for ten or twelve hours a day in the fields, hoeing or making hay. Others gathered strawberries and raspberries, slipping the odd one into their mouths when nobody was looking, returning to camp in the evening, stained with the juice, tired and with aching backs – yet ready, after a shower and a hearty meal, to sing and dance the night away. It was hard work, but they were determined that it was still to be a holiday. And while their parents worked, even small children could help by gathering coltsfoot, or foxglove seeds at four shillings a pound, for medicines.

'That sort of idea's good for people who never get out into the fresh air,' Frank said, 'but for people like us who've got an allotment to look after, as long as we can go to the beach, there's no need for anything else.'

You couldn't always go to the beach these days, though. Every so often, the authorities took it into their heads to close long stretches, and nobody knew what went on there. The children who would normally have been sent off to spend every day racing in and out of the waves or playing ducks and drakes with flat pebbles, found themselves wandering around the streets in frustration, with only the static water tanks to provide them with a bit of fun. And you had only to climb up the outside of one of those to have a warden or a copper yelling the odds at you, telling you to get away.

Still, this year the beaches were open and the Council did put itself out to organise quite a few events. They spent over a thousand pounds on concert parties, bands, open-air dancing, regattas, and a gymkhana which was held at Wymering racecourse on August Bank Holiday.

It began in the morning, with all the trade turn-outs showing off their paces – carts specially scrubbed and polished, horses' brasses gleaming against their shining coats, the drivers sitting proudly up top in their best suits. Then there were all the usual riding and driving classes, and in the afternoon a series of competitions for children. The Royal Marine band from HMS *Excellent* played patriotic tunes, which pleased Frank enormously – his mother's father and his uncles had all been Marines, and he still possessed a watch given him by his grandfather many years ago, presented to him when he'd left the Service.

Best of all, for Jess and the children, were the donkey races. They came away aching with laughter.

'Half of them wouldn't go at all,' Jess said, wiping her eyes, 'and the rest got halfway and then stopped to eat grass. There was only that one kept going at all, and he threw the little boy off when he stopped at the finishing post. And that one who just stood there refusing to budge, while all those people pushed and shoved and pulled – he was a real scream.'

'He'll still be there this time next year,' agreed Cherry, who had come with them. Cherry spent most of her spare time with the Budds, helping Jess and entertaining the children with her forthright tongue and fund of stories. 'I reckon he'd taken root.'

Ray and Olive went to some of the events. They saw George Formby and Ronald Shiner in *Get Cracking* at the Royal Theatre, and *Chu Chin Chow* at the King's. They went out to South Parade Pier again and danced to Jack Payne and his Orchestra, with Carole Carr singing. But best of all, they agreed, was the Services Tattoo, which was held at Fratton Park on 14 August.

With a crowd of others from the camp, they watched critically as each contingent marched past, comparing their smartness and marching ability. The Marines were far and away the best, they conceded, though the Navy were a pretty good second.

'Our lot are almost as good, all the same,' Olive said. 'They just don't have the time to practise, that's all. I reckon the Marines do nothing but march about playing trumpets.'

78

'Don't say that too loud,' Ray warned her. 'There's a crowd of 'em close behind us. I don't want to find myself on the end of a bayonet.'

'Go on, they wouldn't do more than give you a nasty poke with their trombones,' Olive said.

They turned and wandered away from the main arena. It was still light, for Double Summer Time wasn't due to end till next day, and they strolled slowly through the quiet, twilit streets.

Olive and Ray had grown closer during the past few weeks. Soon after their visit to King's, the sergeant on Olive's gun-crew had been taken ill with appendicitis and rushed off to the Army hospital. Olive had arrived on duty next evening to find Ray sitting at the foot of the turret, grinning at her. She had stopped dead.

'Whatever are you doing here?'

'Waiting for enemy raiders, of course,' he had answered cheekily. 'What else? You didn't think I was waiting for *you*, did you?'

'You? You'd wait for a blue moon if you thought it'd do you any good,' Olive had retorted, dumping her knapsack. 'How'd you wangle that, then?'

Ray had raised his eyebrows. 'Wangle? As if I'd do a thing like that!' He grinned again. 'Here, it's all right, though, ain't it! We can have some fun here.'

Olive had given him a severe look. 'We're not here to have fun. There's a war on, remember?'

She had taken her place, trying to keep her hands steady. Ray was the last person she'd expected to find here, but she couldn't say she was annoyed. Disturbed, in a funny sort of way – almost excited. But that was daft. There was nothing to get excited about. Ray was a friend, that was all.

I hope he's not going to come over all soppy, she had thought. That's the last thing we need.

But instead Ray remained friendly, warm, slightly detached – just as a friend should. More like a brother than anything else. Olive relaxed again and began to look forward to seeing his funny, crinkly face grinning at her when she came on duty. And as often as not, Claudia by now firmly engaged, with a diamond ring to show for it, and spending every spare minute with her pilot, Olive and Ray would finish their duty with a walk along the sea front, or meet in a pub half an hour before, with the rest of the crew.

More and more, they found themselves alone. Drinking and laughing, chaffing the others and joining in the sing-songs, was all very well, but they wanted to talk. Both married, both lonely, they had a bond that drew them together, and they both wanted someone to share and sympathise with their loneliness.

It wasn't long before they were telling each other details they would not normally have dreamed of talking about.

'We were too young, that's what it was really,' Ray said to Olive. 'We shouldn't ever have got married. I mean, she was only seventeen and I was nineteen – just kids.'

'I wasn't much older,' Olive said. 'A few months short of twenty-one. I don't reckon I was too young.'

Ray shook his head. They were sitting on the gun emplacement, sharing a flask of cocoa. It had been a quiet night and so far there had been no planes over. The rest of the crew were on the other side, smoking. Claudia was keeping lookout.

'There's a lot of difference between seventeen and twenty-one. And blokes don't grow up as quick as girls. We didn't know what life was all about.'

'So why did you get married?'

He gave her a wry look. 'Why d'you think? Shotgun wedding. We got a bit carried away one night and she fell for our Dorothy. Wasn't nothing else we could do, was there?'

Olive remembered when she had been afraid of pregnancy, the first time she'd stayed with Derek. It had been a false alarm but she still sweated at the thought of her parents' reaction if it had been real. 'What happened? Did her mum and dad turn her out?'

'They nearly turned me inside out,' he said. 'Whipped us round to the priest and he read the riot act over us and then read the banns. We were married three weeks later, all quiet on a weekday morning. They're Roman Catholics, see. Joan had to go to confession and everything. I had to say I'd be a Catholic too, and bring up Dorothy the same.'

'So how old's the baby now?'

'Four,' he said. 'Pretty as a picture and sweet as a nut. Not that I see much of her.'

'Oh, Ray. That's sad.'

He shrugged. 'Well, I hardly ever get home, do I? And when I do, Joan's mum looks at me as if I'm something the cat's dragged in.'

'Are you living with your in-laws, then?'

'She is,' he said. 'I reckon I live here.'

Olive was silent. Impulsively, she put her hand over his.

'I'm really sorry, Ray. It must be ever so miserable for you.'

'Not much fun for any of us, I suppose,' he said wryly. 'And the war doesn't help. If we'd been able to start off right, got a place of our own, even rooms with someone else. But as it is . . . I do get fed up sometimes, though.'

'Well,' Olive said, 'you know there's always a shoulder here for you to cry on if you want it.'

He looked at her and turned his hand over to squeeze her fingers.

'Thanks, Olive.' He hesitated, then said, 'You know, if I'd met you first, I reckon things could've been a lot different.'

Olive felt her face grow hot. She looked down at their hands.

'Ray,' she said in a low voice, 'don't say things like that. I'm married, and I love my husband. I can't – I don't *want*—'

'It's all right.' He took his hand away. 'I don't mean we ought to do anything about it – Christ, there's nothing we *can* do – but it's a bugger, the way life turns out, isn't it?'

Far away in the distance, they heard the mutter of an approaching aircraft. They leaped to their feet, and at the same moment Claudia and the others shot into their positions.

Olive trained her binoculars on the sky, trying to pick out the shape of the enemy plane in the beam of the searchlight. She thrust their conversation firmly from her mind.

This was war, and war must always come first.

That had been in June, almost eight weeks ago. It had been the first real raid for quite a long time and four houses had been demolished and quite a few others damaged. There hadn't been another since, but that didn't mean the gun-crews could relax. You always had to be vigilant in case another sudden attack was made, or a sneak raider slipped in, like the one which had shot and killed Peggy Shaw. But time off was more of a pleasure when you could enjoy yourself without the shadow of a raid hanging over you all the time, and these stay-at-home holidays had made it a much better summer than they'd expected, with all the things going on all over Pompey.

There was a band playing out on the Common now. Olive and the rest of the gun-crew wandered along to listen before going on watch for the night. They enjoyed the music, which was a mixture of patriotic tunes such as 'Rule, Britannia!' and 'Land of Hope and Glory', and the popular dance music of bandleaders like Glenn Miller and Joe Loss, whose band Olive and Ray had been dancing to when they first met. They all linked arms and formed a line to dance back to the gun emplacement, singing 'In the Mood' and 'Pennsylvania 65000'.

'Feeling better now?' Ray murmured to Olive, squeezing her arm against his side. 'You were pretty miserable for a time after that woman down your street died, weren't you?'

'I know. She was my best friend's mum. It was so awful, the way she went. She'd always been such a cheerful sort of person, and then to be just mown down like that on her way home from church. It seems so sad.'

'It's happening all the time,' Ray said. 'We can't let it upset us every time, or we'd go mad.'

'I know.' Olive was silent for a few moments, then she said, 'It wasn't just that, though. It was not having Derek here to talk to about it. I ought to be used to it by now, but it just seems to get worse all the time. D'you know, there are times when I almost wish he wouldn't come home any more till it's all over, so that we wouldn't have to keep parting.' She glanced up at Ray's face. 'That's an awful thing to say, isn't it?'

'It is, but not in the way you mean. It's awful that you have to feel that way. And there's another thing that's awful about it too, something you haven't thought of.'

'What's that?'

'It's awful that some people don't feel that way,' he said in a low voice. 'I just wish I had someone who felt like that about me, Olive. Joan – well, she's glad to see the back of me and she doesn't trouble to hide it.'

'Oh, Ray. Yes, that is worse. Everyone ought to have someone who really cares about them. But your little girl – she loves you, doesn't she? You're her daddy, after all.'

'I doubt if she even knows it,' he said bitterly. 'I hardly ever go back there now, and when I do they keep her away from me. "Don't go near the soldier, Dorothy, you'll mark his nice uniform" – as if they cared! And calling me "the soldier" as if I was a stranger. Or else she's in bed and fast asleep. Or gone out with her auntie. She hasn't sat on my lap for more than five minutes in the past six weeks, and I haven't had any time at all with her on my own.' He gave Olive a twisted smile. 'Sometimes I reckon it'd be better all round if I just stopped going there – sent the money and forgot about them.'

'But she's your daughter! I thought you said they were Roman Catholics. Surely they don't believe in marriages breaking up.'

'They don't believe in divorce. They don't mind so much if a bloke just keeps out of the way, so long as there's still a marriage certificate and the money keeps coming through. Anyway, I reckon she could have the marriage annulled – say it had never been a proper marriage – but she won't do that, not unless she meets some other bloke with a good pay packet.'

Olive shook her head. She hated to hear the bitter tone in Ray's voice, yet she couldn't blame him. She contrasted his unhappiness with the love between herself and Derek, and felt overwhelmingly sorry for him. He was lonely and unhappy, and he needed some friendship and comfort.

She realised suddenly that the line of laughing dancers had broken up and that she and Ray were the only two still walking arm-in-arm. She looked up at him, instinctively drawing away, but he tightened his elbow against hers and she hesitated only for a second before relaxing against him.

'Don't pull away from me, Olive,' he said quietly. 'Let's walk like this, just for a little while. I don't mind if you pretend I'm someone else. I just want to feel for a few minutes that I've got someone who cares, as well.'

Olive closed her eyes. She felt his warmth against her side, and the strength of his muscular body. She smelt the tang of masculinity and felt an unexpected tingle low down in her body.

For a moment or two, she tried to pretend that he was Derek, but her senses would not be deceived. It was not Derek by her side, holding her close against him, but Ray Whitaker. As they walked together through the twilight, she was shaken by a deep, yearning loneliness.

There must be thousands of us all over the world doing this, she thought. Trying to pretend we're with someone else. And it doesn't work. It just doesn't work.

However, she could not pull away from Ray now. For her, there was someone else, someone who would come back to her with a heart full of love. For Ray, there was only a cold, unloving wife, and even his little girl would hardly know him.

Derek, she thought. Oh, Derek, I miss you so much.

The raiders came again the very next day. It was almost as if they'd been waiting, like a cat waiting to pounce on a mouse. Letting them have their fun with their stay-at-home holidays and the gymkhanas and tattoos, letting them relax and think perhaps things were going to get better after all – letting them have just a taste, a fleeting memory of what it had been like before the war. And then leaping.

The planes swept in almost before anyone had time to know they were on their way, a black, menacing cloud no bigger than a cloud of flies approaching over the Isle of Wight. Olive, on watch on the gun turret, saw them first in the clear moonlit sky, and yelped a warning just as the rising note of the siren began to scream across the air. The gun-crew was in action straight away and worked smoothly together, keeping their eyes fixed on the sky, sighting the guns and firing the instant an aircraft was caught in the beam of the searchlight. The hard work that Olive and Claudia had put into their aircraft recognition paid off as they snapped out swiftly calculated heights and distances to the gunners. They cheered as the deafening rattle of firing resulted in a shell-burst high above them and they watched their target spiral in flames into the sea.

'That's it! We got him!' Olive shouted, leaping up and down with jubilation. 'Oh, well done, well done!' She turned to Ray and flung her arms around him, laughing. 'Another hit. You're wonderful!'

'So are you.' He caught her hard against him and kissed her fiercely. 'Oh, Olive, so are you . . .'

'Ray . . .' She clung to him, too dazed to stand alone, knowing that if he released her now she would fall. She could not let him go.

'Olive.' Gently, he held her away from him, and she felt the cool night air brush against her cheeks. 'Olive, the planes . . .'

She put her hand to her head, feeling the sudden nausea of returning consciousness. It was as if for a few moments they had both been transported to another world, and now they were jerked crudely and roughly back into reality. The reality of a darkness pierced by the white swords of searchlights, a silence split by the drone of enemy aircraft.

Claudia was at her side, looking at her curiously. Olive shook her head to clear it, and picked up her binoculars. The blood was still roaring in her ears, her heart still kicking in her breast, but she ignored the tumult and trained her glasses on the sky.

It didn't mean a thing. It was no more than the reaction of the moment, the sudden triumph, that had swept them off their feet. It was to be forgotten and never permitted to happen again.

# CHAPTER SEVEN

It was as if 14 August, that last day of the stay-at-home holidays with its spectacular tattoo, had been marked by everyone as the beginning of a new stage in the war. The entertainments arranged by the City Council were over, Double Summer Time had come to an end, and the Germans were back in force with their sixty-second raid on the city of Portsmouth.

It was like the Blitz all over again. Once again, phosphorus and high-explosive bombs had devastated the streets. Houses, shops and offices lay in ruins. A boathouse and timber-stack in Langstone Harbour was destroyed. Gas and water mains were fractured, and over five hundred people were made homeless. Twenty-one were killed and more than three times as many injured.

'We're off again,' Frank said grimly as he prepared to go to the dockyard as usual at six o'clock, not knowing what he might find on his way. 'I suppose they thought we ought to have a few fireworks to round off the tattoo.'

As if in swift response, the government began to announce new orders. A notice in the *Evening News* reminded people to sign their identity cards. The police were going to check all the population of south coast towns, and all members of the Armed Forces were authorised to demand to see the cards of civilians whenever they wished. Not producing your card at any time carried heavy penalties: two women visiting Portsmouth from Exeter were sentenced to several months' hard labour for the offence.

Police vehicles began to tour the streets of the city to announce new restrictions. From noon on 17 August, all members of the public must leave the sea front and immediate vicinity at once. Nobody without a special permit was to pass the barriers. Hotels and boarding-houses within the restricted area had already been warned that guests who were not in the area for an approved purpose must be told to leave, and no more visitors were to be accepted. The road that ran along the front at Southsea was barricaded off, the shore out of reach, and the wide, grassy Common that had given Portsmouth people so much pleasure was now frequented only by the soldiers and ATS girls who manned the anti-aircraft guns.

'D'you think we're planning to invade?' Jess asked Frank. 'I mean, the government's got to do it some time, hasn't it? They've been talking about it long enough.'

'If they do, we'll know all about it,' he said. 'They'll have to go from the south coast. It'll be like a huge Army camp right the way along . . . You could be right, Jess. This could be the beginning.'

Children, frustrated by not being able to go to the beach on the summer days, turned again to the static water tanks that had been erected on bomb sites and other patches of waste ground. A toddler of three was rescued from one by a seventy-nine-year-old man who had heard his screams as he struggled in the six-foot-deep water. The old man had climbed on some bricks that children had piled against the tank, and managed to drag the little boy out. The incident was reported in the *Evening News*, with yet another warning to parents of the dangers of the tanks.

'It's bound to happen,' Frank said. 'Boys get larking about in them and the little ones follow. I'm surprised there haven't been more getting drowned. There's always ways for kids to get themselves into trouble and you're going to get drownings in a place like this. I mean, Pompey's an island when all's said and done, and what with all those little creeks, and the moats around the old forts, it's sure to happen. You can't have your eye on them all the time.'

On the eighteenth, Bomber Command carried out a massive daylight raid over Germany. There was a tremendous battle, and thirty-six planes out of the three hundred and seventy-six which had gone did not return. This was considered to be an unacceptable number of losses, and the heads of the combined air forces conceded that the RAF had been right in warning that daylight raids were impossible for unescorted bombers. There was still a place for the fighter aircraft, the Hurricane and – everyone's darling – the Spitfire, to escort the heavier planes across the Channel.

Dramatic news like this was interspersed with announcements of a more domestic kind. A couple of days later, Frank was exclaiming over an item about paint. He and Jess had been wanting to redecorate the living-room for the past eighteen months; it hadn't been done since before Maureen was born, and looked faded and tired, the wallpaper scuffed all along the skirting-board by the boys' boots, and a patch in one corner scratched and torn by Henry when he'd been a kitten.

'Looks as if you'll have to wait a bit longer to freshen things up,' he told Jess. 'They're letting us have what they call "a limited quantity of wartime emergency paint". It's going to be dark brown and it'll cost ninepence a pint. We can't use it for anything but patching.'

'I wouldn't want to use it for anything else,' Jess said. 'I mean, I like a nice dark brown skirting-board, but you don't want it on the walls, do you? It'd be like living in a cave. Why does it have to be dark brown, anyway? Couldn't it be a nice fresh cream? Colour don't make it more expensive, does it?'

'I wouldn't have thought so. I suppose they think it's more service-able.'

'Well, so it would be if everything was already dark brown. You don't want to use that for patching white or cream though.' Jess shook her head. 'I reckon we'll wait till the war's over and then do everything fresh. A nice cream and green, that's what I fancy.'

'An ice-cream?' Tim said, coming into the room. 'I fancy one of them too! A Wall's ice-cream cornet – I haven't seen one of them for years. D'you think they'll ever make ice-cream again, Mum?'

Frank grinned and Jess laughed. Trust Tim to find a joke in it all. She remembered the day Cherry had told Tim it was patriotic to make jokes so that people laughed and felt better. He'd certainly taken that bit of advice to heart.

Tim had left Mr Driver and started as an apprentice on the Gosport ferry. He worked down in the engine-room of his Uncle Ted's boat, and spent a lot of his time shovelling coke into the boiler. The little *Ferry King* chugged across the harbour turn and turn about with the others – the *Ferry Queen*, the *Ferry Princess*, the *Ferry Prince* and two or three more – transporting people between the two towns. Most passengers were people who lived in Gosport but worked in Portsmouth – dockyardmen, who filled the boats almost to sinking point in the morning and evening; servicemen who had homes there; clerks and civil servants who worked in the big offices and shops. Some of the dockyardmen were friends of Frank's and knew Tim. They would poke their heads down over the skylights above the engine-room and give him a shout, and he would wave back, his grinning face smeared with oil and a lump of greasy cotton-waste in his hand.

'He gets filthy just for the fun of it,' Jess said when faced with his overalls to wash. 'Thinks it makes him look grown up.'

'Well, so he is growing up,' her sister Annie said. 'Anyway, they're not that bad.' You couldn't tell Annie anything about washing a ferryman's overalls, not when she'd been doing Ted's for the past thirty years. Annie sat down at the living-room table and laid a creased and dirty envelope on the table. 'We've had a letter from our Colin.'

'Colin! Oh, Annie, I am glad.' Jess dried her hands hastily on the roller-towel and came to look. 'How is he?'

'It's hard to know.' Annie looked at the crumpled bit of paper, covered with a few scrawled words. 'He says he's all right, he says they're treated well and fed properly – but how do you know it's true? I mean, I daresay they censor the letters just like we do here, and you hear such awful stories about what's going on in those camps. What would they do to anyone that told the truth?' She shook her head. 'You know, when we first heard he'd been taken prisoner I was so relieved he was still alive, I never gave a thought to anything else. But now – Jess, I can't bear to think of my Colin being knocked about and tortured.' Her eyes filled with tears.

'Of course you can't.' Jess came swiftly across to wrap her arms around her sister. 'None of us can. It's awful, Annie, but – well, we don't know there's anything bad happening to him, do we? Perhaps the camp he's in is better. They can't all be bad. I mean, we know the Germans are pretty rough in some of their camps, yet there's chaps writing home to say they're having quite a good time, playing football, getting up concert parties, studying to improve themselves for when they come home . . . I bet it's the same there, and if Colin says he's all right, then so he is.'

'I know. I hope so.' Annie looked at the letter again. 'There's nothing we can do about it anyway. If only I knew he was getting enough to eat.'

'How's Mum today?' Jess asked, seeing her eyes fill again. Not that it was a very cheerful change of subject, but at least it got Annie's thoughts off Colin for a few minutes.

Annie sighed. 'Oh, same as usual only a bit worse, if you know what I mean. She perks up every now and then, but she's going downhill, there's no doubt about it. Sits in her chair just staring at the fireplace. If it's sunny I put a chair out in the garden for her, but I'm half afraid she'll blow away in the wind, she's getting so frail.'

Jess nodded. She walked up to Annie's every day to visit their mother and had seen the old woman age before her eyes. Well, she was in her mid-seventies so it was no wonder, but until Dad had died last year she'd been spry as could be, always busy about the place, with more energy than Jess herself had at times. She'd never got over her loss, that was the truth of it.

Jess turned her mind away from the manner of her father's death. She tried never to think about it – but for her mother, it was an ever-present memory, a ghost that wouldn't let her go.

Something else you just couldn't do anything about. That was one of the worst things about this war. Everyone felt so helpless, as if they were being swept along on a huge flood from which there was no escape. You could reach out and grab at something as you went past, but you could never really drag yourself out, and you certainly couldn't do much to help anyone else . . .

With an effort, she dragged her mind away from those thoughts too. Frank often told her she was too imaginative and she supposed he was right, but you couldn't help what your mind thought of, could you? You could try to stop it, but the pictures that came into her mind sometimes were there before she had a chance to stop them. Some of them were too awful to forget, and the feelings they brought with them just wouldn't go away.

It was worse when she thought of other people than when she thought about herself. People like her own family and friends – Annie, worrying about Colin; Colin himself, perhaps going through things she couldn't imagine and didn't want to; Peggy Shaw, gunned down in the street, and poor Bert not knowing what to do with himself without her. And people she didn't know, never would know, but felt for all the same. Soldiers and sailors battling on land and sea, airmen in the sky, and the millions of people who didn't fight at all but had their homes and countries invaded and taken from them, who were herded and driven from place to place, who were shot and bombed and killed in so many, such unimaginable ways.

And the children. Most of all, she thought and dreamed and worried about the unknowing, the *innocent* children.

Carol Glaister was thinking about children too, but her thoughts were concerned mostly with babies. She didn't seem able to get them off her mind these days.

Some of the young women she worked with at the barracks had children. They didn't have to work, but they were glad of the extra money and left them with their mothers. They talked about them, swapping stories about the things they'd done and said, and sometimes they discussed their pregnancies and births.

Carol listened. She wanted to join in and share her own experiences, to be part of the group, but she knew that if she admitted to having had an illegitimate child the others would look down on her as if she were dirty. Never mind that half of them had been lucky to get to the altar before their first kid was born, she thought resentfully. That was all glossed over and forgotten. All that mattered was getting your marriage lines before the birth certificate, and no questions asked about whether your husband was really the father . . .

'I sweated top line before my Sidney was born,' one girl confessed with a giggle. 'I thought, if the baby's got red hair Tom'll know straight off it's not his . . . but luckily he's the spitting image of me, so who's to tell?'

'Not even you, by all accounts,' the overseer said sourly, coming up behind them unexpectedly. 'There's more than one bloke been doing a spot of overtime behind the sheds with you. If you don't stop chinwagging and get on with your work, it'll be the office for you, so mind your p's and q's, see?'

The girl bent her head over her sewing machine, but as soon as the overseer had passed on along the line she looked up again and winked at Carol. 'Nasty old cow. She's only jealous 'cause she's never had it herself. Well, nobody'd want to take her round the sheds, would they? She's got a face like the back of a bus.' She looked at Carol. 'You keep pretty quiet. Don't you have no boyfriend?'

Carol hesitated. To say no seemed disloyal to Roddy, but to say yes invited a lot of questions she couldn't answer. Before she could say anything, one of the older women chipped in from across the long bench.

'Leave the kid alone, Eileen. Not everyone's like you, off after the boys the minute you got out of your pram. Don't you take no notice,' she added to Carol. 'You bin brought up decent, anyone can see that. There's plenty of time for that sort of thing, and you don't want to go looking for trouble.'

Carol turned hastily back to her work. It would be impossible to say anything now, and if they ever found out the truth . . . She longed to join in with the banter and gossip that flew across the sewing machines whenever the overseer was out of the way, but she dared not give herself away. So she stayed quiet, getting a reputation for being 'shy' with those who liked her, and 'stuck-up' with those who didn't. She didn't even take part in the bawdy sing-songs the girls sometimes indulged in on a Friday afternoon, especially if someone were getting married the next day.

> Dave and Sandra, on the sofa,
> All through the night.
> First he's on her, then he's off her,
> All through the night.
> Ooh, said Sandra, what a whopper,
> Let's lay down and do it proper . . .

She didn't really like it anyway. Her memories of making love with Roddy were too precious to be the subject of a rude song. Instead, she concentrated on her work, and when the hooter blew to tell them it was time to go home, she packed up quickly and slipped away as soon as she could.

'Lives with her mum,' she heard Eileen whisper to another girl. 'Proper tied to Mummy's apron strings, she is. Can't wait to get home for a bit of spoiling, that's what it is.'

Carol walked out, pretending not to have heard. If only you knew, she thought, if only you knew.

She walked most of the way home. It was a long way and she could have taken a bus but, contrary to Eileen's belief, she was in no hurry to get there. Instead, she dawdled, looking in shop windows and thinking of Roddy and their baby.

There seemed to be a lot of babies around these days. Carol had never noticed so many before, perhaps because a lot of them had been evacuated at the beginning of the war. It was funny really, when you knew that so many men were away in the Forces, but she'd heard that one of the reasons they sent the Servicemen home on leave whenever they could was so that they could get their wives pregnant. Leave a bun in the oven, as the women at work would have put it. It was to do with the population. With the war dragging on so long and so many people being killed, there was a danger that there wouldn't be enough people to keep the country going later on.

It sounded a bit far-fetched to Carol. There was no shortage of men, with all the Americans that had come over just recently. Soldiers, sailors, airmen, they were everywhere, grinning, chewing gum, tossing pennies to the kids. And the presents they gave the girls! Chocolate – they didn't seem to have any rations at all – and nylon stockings. Carol had seen a pair, brought in by one of the girls who had a Yankee boyfriend. They'd been as fine and sheer as silk, and the rest of the girls, accustomed to going bare-legged in summer and wearing thick lisle stockings that had to be darned in winter, had almost drooled over them. I bet there'll be a lot of babies around with Yankee accents in a few months' time, she thought cynically, and where will the girls find the blokes to marry them then, I wonder?

There was a woman in front of her, pushing a pram. Carol trailed along behind, looking at the baby. It was sitting up, grinning toothlessly at its mother, who was chattering to it, telling it what she was going to cook for supper and all sorts of nonsense. It couldn't have understood – and wouldn't have cared if it did, Carol thought – but it seemed to like being talked to, and every now and then it chuckled, as if its mother had made a huge joke.

Little Roderick would be about that age now. Sitting up, laughing and grabbing at his toys with fat fingers. She wondered what sort of toys he'd been given, and if he liked them. Did he have a teddy bear? Or a golliwog?

It wasn't easy to get soft toys, or any sort of toys, these days. Perhaps the woman who'd taken him made his toys, knitted ones like that Cherry who came to see Jess Budd made for Maureen.

The mother leaned forward suddenly and poked the baby in the stomach. It twisted and squirmed and roared with laughter, and Carol felt her eyes sting. I bet Roderick likes being tickled too, she thought. I bet he laughs just like that. And she stopped for a moment or two, unable to look at the baby any more.

That could just be my little Roddy, she thought. It could be him. Any one of these babies I keep seeing could be him, and I wouldn't know. I could pass my own baby in the street and I just wouldn't know.

Jess passed Carol on her way up April Grove to see her mother. She gave the girl a smile, but Carol's lips hardly twitched in return. She's getting as sour as her mother, Jess thought, and then scolded herself. Carol had done wrong, but she'd suffered for it and it didn't matter who you were or what you'd done, it must be awful to have to give up your own baby. She'd heard Carol sobbing in the night, through the wall between the two houses, and felt a sharp pang of pity. There was never any sound of comfort coming from Ethel – no more than a voice snapping at her to give over. It was a shame.

I hope neither of my girls ever gets into trouble like that, she thought, but if they do I'll stand by them. I couldn't treat them the way Ethel Glaister's treated that poor girl.

She went round the side of Annie's house to the back door. It stood open and her mother was sitting on her chair outside. She looked up and gave Jess a weary little smile.

'Our Jess. It's nice to see you, dear. Annie's just popped up to Atkinson's to see if they've got any oranges in. She heard there'd been a delivery.'

'I know. I got mine this morning. One each. We're going to have them after tea tonight.'

'What I'd like is a banana. I ain't seen a banana for years.'

'You won't, neither, not till it's all over.' Jess fetched another chair and sat down beside her mother. 'Be worth waiting for though, won't they?'

Mary shook her head. 'I dunno, love. I don't know as I want to go on hanging about, the way things are. I mean, look at the world, it's just going to rack and ruin. Last time was bad enough, but at least the men thought they were fighting to make a world fit for heroes to live in. Now you got to be a hero to live in it! Your dad used to say that, remember? He got fed up with it too.'

'I know, Mum, but—'

'And look what it did for him,' Mary went on. 'I never thought to see him so miserable as he was those last few months. I never want to see anyone get like that again.'

'I know.' Jess couldn't think what to say. Surely her mother wasn't thinking of following his example? 'He was ill, Mum. Not just miserable.'

'And what made him ill, eh? Tell me that.' Mary gestured with a wrinkled hand, the veins standing out like blue knots. 'It was all this, that's what. War. Four years of his life in the trenches in the 'fourteen to 'eighteen lot, not to mention the Boer War. Seeing his mates killed before his eyes – always scared he was going to be next, but having to go over the top just the same. Mud and bullets and all the rest of it – and what for? So he could end his days jumping out of his skin if someone slammed a door.' She turned her head and looked into her daughter's eyes. 'They got no right, you know, Jess. They got no right to mess up people's lives like that.'

'Mum, he had a good life. He had you, and us – we had some good times, you know we did. He was always cheerful, always on the go, up till those last few months. Why, he was famous for his smile, you know he was.'

'And how d'you know what he was really thinking?' Mary asked quietly. 'How d'you know what he was feeling, deep down inside?'

Jess was silent. She had many memories of her father as a younger man, playing with her and Annie, laughing and joking, but she could also remember times when she'd noticed him being very still, looking at nothing in particular, with an expression on his face she didn't recognise, couldn't understand.

She understood it now. She'd seen that same expression on Ted's face, when he had his breakdown after Dunkirk. And on Heinrich Brunner's face when he'd come home from his internment after being torpedoed on the *Arandora Star*. And on Gladys Shaw's, and Peggy's, and the faces of countless other men and women who had encountered terrible danger and seen terrible sights.

'I know, Mum,' she said. 'You think you've got over these things and they come back years later, like ghosts, to haunt you. There's some things you can't ever forget, but we can't give in to them. We've got to think of the good things, the things we've had and enjoyed. And we've got to look ahead – think of the future.'

'What future?' her mother asked. 'Jess, you don't know that there *is* a future. You know as well as I do, we might all be blown up in the night, before we've even had our tea. Waiting – waiting for bananas, waiting for oranges, waiting for peace – it's our lives disappearing while we wait, that's what it is. And what's past *is* past – we can't enjoy it all over again.' She shook her head. 'It's *now* that's important, Jess, and *now* don't seem very good to me, just at present. I reckon your dad's well out of it.'

Jess gazed at her. But not the way he went, she wanted to cry, not doing what he did. She reached out blindly and touched her mother's hand. Mary's fingers were hard and bony with big, knobbly knuckles, not the soft, comforting hands Jess remembered as a child.

'Mum . . .'

'It's all right,' Mary said in her cracked, old voice. 'I ain't thinking of doing what he done, but I just don't see no point in hanging around much longer, getting in Annie's way and making a nuisance of meself. There's times when you do have a choice, you know. I wake up in the night sometimes and I lay there awake and I think – why bother waking up at all? Why not just slip away, nice and quiet, in me sleep? I'm old enough, I done enough, I seen enough. What's to stop me?'

'Mum, don't talk like that,' Jess begged, tears in her eyes. 'You know we don't want to lose you.'

'You got to some time, girl,' Mary said, and fell silent.

Jess sat very still, fighting the tears, then looked at her mother again. She felt a sudden jolt of fear. Mary's eyes were closed. As Jess stared, she realised how very thin and pale her mother had become. Almost transparent . . . Then panic gripped her and she shook her mother's arm and patted her cheek. 'Mum! *Mum* . . .'

Mary's eyes opened again and she frowned a little, staring at Jess as if she weren't quite sure who she might be. Then her rheumy eyes cleared and she smiled, a weary little smile.

'Our Jess. It's nice to see you, dear. Annie's just popped up to Atkinson's, they've got some oranges in . . .'

'I can't,' Olive said, looking at her hands. Derek's wedding ring gleamed in the sunshine. She twisted her fingers together. 'I'm sorry, Ray, I just can't.'

They were sitting on a bench outside the NAAFI hut. Around them, soldiers and ATS girls came and went, but they took little notice.

'But don't you want to see *No Orchids For Miss Blandish*? Everyone's talking about it. It's supposed to be really good.' Ray tilted his head, trying to see her face. 'Is there something else you'd rather do?'

'It isn't that. I just can't come out with you any more.' She raised her eyes and looked at him at last. 'Not to the theatre nor to anywhere else.'

'But why not? What have I done? Have I upset you?'

'No,' she said, 'no, you haven't upset me. At least . . .' She hesitated, trying to find the right words, the words that would tell him what she meant without hurting him. 'Look, Ray, you know I like you – I like you very much – but . . .'

'That's the trouble, isn't it?' he said after a moment or two. 'We like each other, and you're scared it's going to lead on to something more. It doesn't have to, Olive. We agreed that it wouldn't, remember? You don't have to worry about that.'

'Don't I?' she said, holding his gaze. 'Don't I really?'

Ray bit his lip and reddened a little. 'Look, if you're thinking of what happened the other night . . . It was just a kiss, that's all. We were excited, we were pleased at what we'd done. It didn't have to mean anything else.'

'No,' she said in a low voice, 'it didn't have to mean anything else at all.'

There was a long pause. Olive had returned her gaze to her hands, still twisted together in her lap. At last she looked up again and found Ray's eyes on her, and she knew that he had understood.

'All right, Livvy,' he said heavily. 'If that's the way you want it . . .'

'It is. I'm sorry, Ray.'

'I'm sorry, too,' he said quietly. 'It's come to mean a lot to me, seeing you, but I suppose you're right – that's the moment when it ought to stop.' He turned away and she saw his fist clench. He beat it softly but violently into the palm of his other hand. 'My God, if I'd only known – if someone had only *told* me . . .'

'Told you what?' She knew she shouldn't ask. She should just say goodbye and walk away, as she'd intended, but seeing him so frustrated, so bitterly hopeless . . . He's my friend, she told herself. Friends don't just walk away. 'What should you have been told, Ray?'

'Oh, a thousand things,' he said with a gesture of helplessness. 'Like not to get involved with the wrong girl just because she had pretty eyes and a baby voice. Like not to go walking down Lovers' Lane . . . and not to get carried away just because the moon was shining and somebody'd been singing love songs. Like how a few minutes can change your whole life . . .'

'It wouldn't have made any difference to us,' she pointed out. 'I'd still be married to Derek. And I'd still love him just the same,' she added more strongly. 'Ray, I'm sorry, it's nothing against you. Like you said once, if we'd met years ago, things might have been different, we might have – well, you know . . . But it was Derek I met and fell in love with, and it's Derek I'm married to, and that's the way I want it to stay. I really do.'

'I know,' he said sadly. 'And I don't want to mess up your life as well as my own. If I hadn't gone with Joan – well, at least there might be someone else for me, someone like you who'd love me and want me . . . I'd give my right arm to have someone think about me the way you think about your Derek, Livvy.'

'Oh, Ray,' she said, and her eyes filled with tears.

For a long moment, they sat gazing at each other, not quite touching. Olive's heart thumped in her breast. She felt both glad and sorry that she'd chosen this place, which was so public, to tell him she wouldn't go out with him again. Glad because she was afraid that if there hadn't been so many people about, he might have taken her in his arms and kissed her again – a kiss that wasn't 'just a kiss'. And sorry . . . for the same reason.

And I'd have let him, she thought. I know I would have let him.

She looked into his eyes and saw the sadness there, the loneliness. The loneliness of a man whose marriage had already turned cold, whose daughter hardly knew him. There would be no loving home for Ray to return to when the war was over, no happy family life to build up. None of the plans that she and Derek could still make and hope for, even through their long separation. She couldn't even picture the life that lay ahead for Ray, could not begin to imagine it.

However, she knew that these thoughts must be pushed away. The feeling she had for Ray could not be allowed to continue. I was right, she thought. It was getting dangerous, this friendship. It's time it stopped.

Maybe it should never have started.

'Well, then,' he said at last, 'I suppose I'd better apply for a transfer. Ask for another gun.'

She looked at him in distress. She had not even considered this.

'Oh, Ray, no! Why? I've only said I can't go out with you any more.'

'I know that's all you've said, but we can't go on seeing each other every day – every night – not now things have changed.'

'They haven't changed!' she cried. 'Nothing's any different. We can still be friends. I just – look, I know Derek wouldn't like it if he knew I was going out regular with someone else. I know there's nothing in it, but that'd be hard for him to understand. I mean, wouldn't you feel the same? If you were away and your wife . . .' She floundered to a stop, knowing that the situation between Ray and his wife was very different from that between herself and Derek. 'I mean, if – if – well, you know what I mean . . .'

'If I was married to you,' he said, with the same soft violence with which he had punched his fist into his palm, 'and I knew you were going out with some other bloke, I'd want to come home and kill him. Yes, I know what you mean, Olive, but I wonder if *you* know what *I* mean.' He stood up abruptly. 'Look, it's no use going on about it. You've told me the score and I'm not going to make a pest of myself. It's up to me what I do, right? And if

I reckon it's best to get moved away, that's what I'll do.' He turned away and she stared at him, afraid that he was going to march out of her life without another word. Then he turned back and stared down into her face.

She gazed up at him, mute. Very slowly he reached out and touched her cheek. She felt his fingertips move very softly over her skin, and she closed her eyes, unprepared for the surge of emotion, the rush of longing that swept her body. It was all she could do not to put up her own hand and clasp his, hold it against her face.

'Thanks for everything, Livvy,' he said, so quietly that she barely heard him. 'Thanks for being a pal.'

She opened her mouth, but could find no words to answer him. By the time she knew what she wanted to say, he had turned away and she knew that this time he was indeed walking out of her life.

The tears were sudden and hot. She bent her head again, desperate to hide them from the passing men and women. She knew that it was as well that Ray had gone then, before she could say the words that had come to her mind, because they were words that must never, ever, be spoken.

# CHAPTER EIGHT

After a few weeks in the Women's Auxiliary Air Force, Diane decided that it was all that she had expected, and a good deal that she had not.

Coming straight from an aircraft factory, she had taken a rather lofty attitude with her fellow recruits. How many of them, after all, had already spent months actually assembling aeroplanes, knew their parts, had even had a snatched lesson or two on flying in the cockpit when nobody was looking? The recruiting procedure would be no more than a formality during which her talents would be recognised. She looked up at the sky and hugged herself at the thought of piloting planes to different airfields all over the country.

'Worked at Airspeed? Well, you can forget all that for a few weeks,' the sergeant told her as she reached the head of the first of many queues she was to join in those first days. 'You've got to learn to be a WAAF first. You're just a rookie here, and don't you forget it.'

Diane left the queue, furious and humiliated. She had been best on the production line at Airspeed and had taken the trouble to learn all the tasks she could. She'd been a 'key girl', able to take over from anyone who was missing. It was ridiculous to tell her that she had to start all over again, at the bottom.

And the bottom was even lower than she had expected. For weeks, the only planes she saw were those in the sky. The 'rookies' weren't allowed near them. There were other things to be done first. Things like being inspected for 'babies, scabies and rabies' – something nobody had told them about. And if Diane had felt humiliated by being told she was 'just a rookie', she felt even worse when ordered to strip off all her clothes and stand to be inspected.

She glanced quickly at the other girls. They were all looking as stunned as she was. The corporal in charge saw their expressions and sighed, then snapped out her order again.

'I told you, strip. We ain't got all day.'

'Don't we get any privacy?' one of the girls, braver than the others, asked a little desperately.

'Privacy? 'Oo d'you think you are, Greta Garbo? Anyway, what you got to be private about? Same as the rest of us, ain'tcher? Get 'em off, and look sharp about it.'

It was bad enough having to comply, but at least they were all in the same boat and tried not to look at each other. Worse was having to endure the none-too-gentle inspection of their bodies, which included being picked over for lice and nits as well as studied for signs of pregnancy or venereal disease.

'Sorry, that's not necessary,' said a tall, fair-haired girl who had a very upper-class accent. 'I don't understand why I'm being put with all these girls anyway. I expected to become an office-ah.'

'Sorry, but we think it is,' the corporal said smartly, and a few minutes later the girl was led away to another room, looking shocked and ready to cry.

'Wonder what she's got?' Diane whispered to her neighbour, but there was no response and she glanced at her face and saw the terror there. Sure enough, the little dark-haired girl soon followed the tall fair one, and then it was Diane's turn.

'What d'you think you'll find?' she asked the WAAF orderly assisting the doctor, and the woman gave her a cynical glance.

'If you don't know, you've probably got it.' She led Diane behind a curtain. 'Lie down there on your back, knees up . . .'

Then there was the business of amassing all the bits and pieces of uniform. Like the others, Diane had looked forward to the smartness of the Air Force blue tunic and cap, but she hadn't reckoned with the underclothes – the boned corsets, the thick winter bloomers, the vests with their fiddly tapes. The new recruits carried their burdens back from the depot to their hut and laid them out on their beds.

'My gran wears things like this,' one girl said. 'Look at these – proper passion-killers. We won't get off with many airmen in this lot, they'll never find their way past the armour.'

'I shan't wear 'em at all,' Diane said with decision. 'I don't need corsets, with my figure. No one's going to tell me what to wear under my clothes.'

There were other girls in the hut who had been in the WAAF for some time and knew all the ropes. They laughed and one of them said, 'You'll soon learn to toe the line. If old Hatchet-face thinks you're improperly dressed, she'll have you stripped off on the parade ground in front of everyone. You'll wear chainmail and hair shirts after that, if she tells you to.'

Diane made a face. 'I don't care. I shan't be here for long, anyway. I'm volunteering to be a transport pilot.'

'Hark at her,' the girl jeered. 'God's gift to the RAF! You can volunteer till you're blue in the face, it don't mean you'll be taken. You've got to be pretty special to fly, you know.'

'She thinks she is pretty special,' one of the other rookies said. They had all heard about Diane's skills and ambitions as they stood in the various queues. 'I should think Airspeed's just about closed down without her to tell 'em what to do.'

They all laughed, and Diane turned away, her face reddening. She made up her mind to take no notice. She'd never been all that bothered about girls, anyway. It was men's company she liked, and there ought to be plenty of that available.

However, there was little time even for that in those first weeks. From the first day, the girls were drilled in a large, empty hangar, until they were too exhausted to do anything more at night than eat their supper (sometimes they were too tired even for that) and fall into bed. Some of them, who had been accustomed to having a bathroom at home (the ultimate in luxury to Diane and others like her, who had been used to helping drag the tin bath into the scullery on Saturday nights), said they were longing for a good, hot soak and went off the first night to the ablutions hut, carrying towels and soap, only to return a short time later shivering and with disappointed faces.

'It's nothing but a tin shack with a bit of dirty concrete on the floor,' the girl who had the next bed to Diane reported in disgust. 'The baths look as if they came out of the Ark, all stained and chipped. The water's almost cold, and you get so muddy drying yourself you might as well not bother.'

'I was expecting them to come and inspect us in the bath any minute,' another girl remarked. 'See if we had more than five inches of water.' She sat down suddenly, looking ready to cry. 'I want to go home. I wish I hadn't never volunteered.'

'Well, if you hadn't you'd have got called up.' The others gathered up their towels ready for their turn. Tin hut or not, it was all there was and had to be made the best of. However, there was more than one bed shaking that night to the sobs of its occupant, and more than one red-eyed rookie reporting for drill next morning.

The two weeks of basic training seemed endless, but their trials served to break down the reserve and shyness that had made the initiation so painful. When the day of their passing-out parade arrived, the girls knew each other better than sisters. They linked arms and danced round the camp that night, celebrating their triumph.

Only Diane did not celebrate, for that was the evening she heard about her mother's death, and the next morning she was packing to go home on compassionate leave. By the time she went back to camp, it would be to start her trade training and, because she would by then be behind the others, she would probably be with strangers.

Not that I care, she thought, sitting in the train as she returned to camp after Peggy's funeral. They were a lot of cats anyway. I'll be glad to get to a decent station and do some proper work instead of all this marching about to a tin whistle.

Flying still seemed to be out of reach. The best Diane could achieve was training as a flight mechanic. Once again she paraded her previous experience and knowledge, only to be severely cut down to size by her instructors.

'I don't care what they did at Airspeed,' the sergeant told her curtly when she dared to correct him over a minor point. 'This is the way we do it here, all right?'

'But nobody does it that way any more,' she argued. 'Look, I'll show you – it's much quicker the way we did it at—'

'I *said*, this is the way we do it here. Never mind quicker and better. This is the RAF, understand? If you don't like it, you shouldn't have joined.'

'I thought there was a war on,' Diane retorted. 'I thought the WAAF needed people like me. Seems to me all it's done so far is waste time. I could've built half a dozen Spitfires single-handed while I've been messing about learning to walk in step and scrubbing out ablution huts.'

'Listen,' he said heavily, 'any more lip from you and you'll go back to Basic, see? Maybe a couple more weeks' square-bashing might give you a bit of respect for your betters.'

'He means it, you know,' one of the other girls muttered when he'd moved on along the bench to pull another girl's work to pieces. 'He sent a girl back a fortnight ago. And they don't give you such soft treatment the second time around.'

'Soft? I thought I'd ended up in a POW camp by mistake!' Diane said. 'Look, Miriam, I wouldn't mind, but it really is better the way I learned. I mean, *Airspeed* – they're one of the best aircraft factories in the country.'

'There was a girl here from down your way a month or two back,' Miriam observed. 'Been working at Supermarine, near Southampton. She *was* building Spitfires. Think it made any difference? They put her through basic training twice and then she went through the mill when she got back here. "Go and bring me the golden rivet." That's the last one to go on the plane, in case they didn't teach you that at Airspeed. "Hang it on a skyhook." They had her on the go all the time, made a right fool of her. She never said a word about Supermarine after that.'

'But that's daft,' Diane said. 'If we've got the experience, why not use it? I mean, what's the point of making us start all over again just as if we'd never seen an aeroplane in our lives?'

'It's all got to be done the same way,' Miriam said. 'It's no good us all using different methods, is it? Suppose you were off sick one day and someone else had to take over your job, and it's all different from what she's used to? They're not going to change everything to a different way just for one girl, are they? You're the one that's got to fit in.'

Diane scowled but it was clear that there was nothing she could do about it. Being in the Services was different from civvy street. You couldn't go home to Mum at the end of the day for a good moan, and be given a cup of cocoa and a bit of sympathy. And if the corporal took a dislike to you, there was no escape. She could follow you anywhere and make your life a misery.

Not that I can go home to Mum anyway, she thought with a wave of misery as she remembered that her mother was dead. It was like this all the time – she'd almost forget for anything from a few minutes to a few hours, and then the memory would come rushing back and fill her with grief. And not just grief: she felt guilty too, at having forgotten, and guilty at having come back to the station and left her dad and Gladys to manage on their own.

It hadn't been too bad, though – Jess Budd next door, and some of the other women, said they'd look out for him, and the day before Diane returned to camp he'd actually cooked some sausages for tea. They were a bit burned on the outside and still pink in the middle, but it was a start.

Diane had thought it wouldn't worry her, thinking of her dad on his own, but now she was back she was haunted by visions of him struggling to find his clean underpants, standing at the sink with the washboard and scrubbing ineffectually at his overalls, and sitting down to meals of half-raw meat and overcooked vegetables. All on his own, without Mum to brighten him up with a flash of quick wit, or give him a caustic answer when he got grumpy.

Maybe I should have stopped at home after all, she thought. It's no great shakes being here, with that sergeant carping at me worse than Dad ever did, and that cow of a WAAF corporal treating us all like dirt.

Still, there were advantages. The flight mechanics did a lot of different jobs, once they were trained. You could find yourself working on the Rolls-Royce engines that powered the planes, on Lancasters or Wellingtons as well as Spitfires and Hurricanes, or you might be out on the airfield guiding the planes in to land as they arrived. You might even be part of the duty crew whose task it was to whip away the chocks from under the wheels of a plane as it took off.

Diane found this more unnerving than she'd expected, as she stood beneath the wing of a huge Lancaster bomber, waiting for the command. She heard the engines splutter and then rev into life, watching as Miriam and the other girls turned the propellers before stepping quickly out of the way. There was that odd moment as the vanes seemed to hesitate, then whir so swiftly that they became invisible, and then it was her turn. Already crouching, she jerked the wedge from under the wheel, ducked out of the way, and was almost tugged off her feet by the sudden fierce slipstream as the plane roared away above her. Diane squealed. Her arms covering her head, she crouched on the ground and then heard Miriam's voice in her ear.

'It's all right, kid. He's gone.'

Diane unwrapped her arms and looked up, Miriam was grinning down at her. She got to her feet, still feeling shaky.

'I suppose you think that's funny,' she said crossly. 'I thought I was going to get sucked up with it. You never told me it would be like that.'

'Nobody ever told me either,' the other girl retorted cheerfully. 'And you won't tell the next rookie that comes along . . . It's a perk of the job, Di, seeing the new girls do it. It's worst of all with the Lancasters, for some reason.' She laughed. 'At least nobody could say your reactions aren't quick – you dropped so flat I thought you'd become part of the tarmac!'

'Ha ha,' Diane said, still feeling cross. She dusted herself down. 'If I get caught for having a dirty uniform, you can take the rap.'

You had to get used to the ribbing that went on, though. It was part of Service life. Still, of all the compensations, Diane reckoned that the best was the number of airmen.

They were all over the place. Young, strong, ranging from handsome to not bad, most of them single – or as good as – and all ready with a grin and a bit of cheek.

Diane liked that. She liked a chap who could eye a girl up and down and look as if he was enjoying it. She liked a bloke who was smart and saucy with his answers, just as she was herself. She didn't go much on the quiet ones. You never knew what they were thinking, and some of them looked so shy they'd never get as far as even putting their arm round a girl's waist, let alone kissing her in the back row of the pictures.

Diane liked kissing. She'd had her first kiss at fourteen and she'd first gone 'all the way' when she was seventeen. Her mum would have gone mad if she'd known, and Dad would have chucked her out of the house –

they'd threatened often enough that they'd do that if she or Gladys ever 'got into trouble', but Diane had made sure she never did. She never went with a boy unless he promised to use a French letter, and she insisted on a new one each time, no matter what they cost.

'I'm not having one *you've* washed out and poked your dirty fingernails through,' she'd say, and the boys had to do what she asked, if they wanted what she had to give.

Generally, they did. And generally, Diane was more than happy to give it.

What Diane was enjoying with such carefree abandon, Olive was missing desperately.

She and Derek had always enjoyed their lovemaking. It had begun on a snowy night, right at the beginning of the war, and continued whenever they could be together. Since their marriage, apart from a short time while the regiment was stationed in its home camp at Eastney, their times together had been too infrequent and too brief. Always, the shadow of separation had loomed over them.

'I'm fed up with this war,' Olive told Gladys moodily.

Gladys had completed her initial training and come home on a forty-eight-hour pass. She looked smart in her navy-blue tunic and skirt, with a white blouse and black tie just like a Naval officer. Although the training had been – as all Service training seemed to be – hard and often humiliating, she had enjoyed it because she had waited for so long.

'I'm not. I feel as if I'm doing something at last. I can't wait to get going on a proper job.'

'Doing something?' Olive echoed. 'I should have thought you'd done enough. You've been wounded – that broken arm – you've had a medal from the King himself—'

'Not himself. The Chief Constable it was that gave it to me.'

'Well, it was the King said you had to have it. You can't say you haven't done anything.'

Gladys bit her lip. She knew Olive was right, but she'd never been able to get rid of the memory of that sudden blast at the very door of the Royal Hospital. She'd always felt that joining the Wrens might help, even though she knew she couldn't really take Graham's place. But I can do *something*, she would argue with herself as she lay awake during the long nights that followed his death. Whatever I can do, it'll be something. And now here she was, and here was Olive, both in uniform, doing things they'd never have dreamed of doing a few years ago.

She had Cliff to think about now too. They still wrote to each other several times a week and had managed to meet a few times. He'd come down to see her whenever he could get away from camp, and they'd gone for a walk or to the pictures. She had told him about Colin Chapman. He knew Colin, of course, and reckoned he was a good bloke, and it was a shame he was caught in a Japanese POW camp.

'How's your Derek?' she asked Olive. 'We had a letter from our Bob a couple of days ago – Dad showed it to me. He says they might be moving on soon.'

Olive turned down the corners of her mouth. 'Yes, that's all they can ever say, isn't it? Moving on *where*? That's what I'd like to know. I want to be able to look at a map and think, that's where my Derek is. Instead of that, we're just left to wonder. Don't the high-ups realise what it's like for us, left at home?'

'We know they're in Africa,' Gladys said a little feebly, and Olive gave her a withering look.

'Africa! They might as well be on the moon, for all the good that does. Africa's a huge place.'

'I know.' They sat silent for a moment, thinking of the regiment moving about over a continent the girls could only vaguely visualise. There were elephants there, Gladys supposed, and lions and giraffes. Her brother Bob had never mentioned such things near the camp but there must be some somewhere. Perhaps the censor forbade them to talk of such things in case the letters got into the wrong hands and gave away clues. There were so many things the men weren't allowed to write about.

There were a lot of Pompey men in the 628. So many of them were local it was more like a family. You got that kind of feeling much more in the Army than you did in the Navy or Air Force. The regiment looked after its men, took an interest in their families. Olive had been to Wiltshire when the unit had been based there and had actually talked to some of the officers. Derek's captain had been really nice to her, especially after she'd lost the baby.

She went back to camp that evening feeling more lonely than ever. Derek's letter had come in the same batch as Bob's and he'd written about how lonely he was without her. 'I think about you all the time,' his letter had said. 'I keep remembering that first night, when it snowed so hard you couldn't go home. Well, we *pretended* you couldn't go home! And the night we got married – only, I felt we were married already. Oh, Olive, you're so lovely and I miss you so much it hurts . . .'

There was lots more like that, and Olive's letters back were just the same. We could almost just write them down and keep them, without bothering to put them in the post, she thought, her fingers stroking the envelope in her pocket, but that wouldn't be the same at all. I need to know Derek wrote this. I need to know he held the pen in his own hands and folded the paper up and kissed it just like I do, and licked the envelope with his own tongue. It's the nearest we can get to a real kiss . . .

She took the envelope from her pocket and held it against her lips. Derek's lips had touched this paper – but Derek was thousands of miles away, and the longing that rose in her was a physical pain, a jagged mass that centred somewhere deep inside and reached its prickly tendrils to every part of her body.

I feel as if I've swallowed a bunch of stinging nettles, she thought, rubbing her arms. Oh Derek, why can't you get sent home? Why can't you get wounded – nothing much, just a little wound, but something that would mean you couldn't be in the Army any more . . . Immediately, she felt guilty at thinking such a thing. How could she want her Derek hurt, even a little, even for the sake of having him home again? She sent up a swift prayer of contradiction. Oh God, no, please don't let him get hurt, please keep him safe till the end of the war and then bring him home to me . . .

It seemed so long, so very long, since they had been together. So long since she had lain in his arms and felt his kisses on her lips and skin instead of imagining them on a piece of paper. So long since their bodies had joined in the deep, flowing happiness that she ached for every night.

In bed, she held herself and tried to pretend that it was Derek who caressed her. But it was an empty pretence and she abandoned the attempt and lay still, letting the tears flow silently into her pillow, aware that there were other girls around her who were probably also weeping and for the same reason.

We're all so lonely, she thought, and our lives are just going by. When is it ever going to end?

Carol came home from the barracks, her fingers sore from working with needles and thread all day. The serge used for making the uniforms was rough – goodness knows what it does to the men's skin, she thought – and she didn't really like any sort of needlework, but anything was better than scavenging about on the floor sifting for rivets, as her mother had to do. And never stops reminding me, Carol thought bitterly, though she'd like to pretend to everyone else she's got a better job.

The depression that had crept like a dank grey mist over her life ever since she had come home, was deepening. She felt isolated from the other girls by her secret. She couldn't join in with their jokes and chatter for fear of giving herself away, and she was always aware that she had had experiences they didn't share. There must have been some who were in the same boat, she thought sometimes, watching them as they worked, but if there were you couldn't tell. None of them seemed to have any worries at all, beyond what their boyfriends were doing overseas, or whether they could find some tall, gum-chewing Yank to take them out that evening.

'Aren't you interested in blokes, Carol?' one of the girls asked her in a friendly enough fashion as they put on their coats to go home. 'I can introduce you to a few if you want. You could come out with us of an evening, we have a smashing time.'

Carol shook her head. She was anxious to get home before Ethel, just in case there was a letter from Roddy – not that there ever was, but surely he'd be allowed to write one day. Anyway, she didn't particularly want to go out with a chap she didn't know – a blind date, they called it, out of the American magazines some of the GIs had brought with them. She didn't want some Yankee soldier pawing her and trying to get off with her.

She walked down October Street. Granny Kinch was at the door of number 10 as usual, sitting on an old kitchen chair in her brown herringbone tweed coat and steel curlers. She was hardly ever seen without them – Tommy Vickers, from the end of April Grove, had once suggested that they had grown into her scalp and couldn't be removed without an operation – although nobody knew why she was so anxious to have her hair curled at all. She was nothing to look at, old and a bit fat with a wrinkled face and her mouth drawn in because she never wore her false teeth. She was nosy and liked to see everything that was going on, but she wasn't a bad old soul and even nowadays she still had a few sweets to give to the kids.

Granny Kinch had had a couple of bust-ups with Carol's mum, but that counted in her favour as far as Carol was concerned. Now she grinned her toothless grin at Carol and said, ''Ow are you gettin' along, then, ducks? Got over yer trouble, 'ave yer?'

Carol stopped. Ethel would go mad if she saw her daughter talking to Granny Kinch, but when you never got anything but grumbles and carping at home, you were glad of a kind word, wherever it came from. And Granny Kinch and her daughter Nancy had never made any bones about the fact that they knew just what Carol's 'trouble' was. It made it easier to talk to them, knowing that there were no secrets to guard.

'I'm all right,' she said, her voice dreary. 'A bit fed up, but everyone is these days. I don't suppose it's really any worse for me than it is for anyone else.'

Granny Kinch eyed her. 'You don't look all right. You look proper done in. You wants a nice cup of tea and a sit-down.'

'I've been sitting down all day,' Carol said, 'but it doesn't seem to make any difference. I still feel tired. I feel tired all the time, even when I get up in the morning.'

'Well, yer bound to, after what you bin through. I know my Nance—' Granny Kinch stopped abruptly. 'It's someone to talk to you wants, someone to pour yer heart out to. 'Ere, why don't you come in along of us for a bit? Nancy's indoors, she'll make us a cuppa. Ain't no sense goin' indoors on yer own, and yer mum won't be back for a couple of hours yet.'

How on earth does she know that? Carol marvelled as, after a moment's hesitation, she followed the old woman along the dark, narrow passage to the back room. It was true enough that Mum was on late shift this week, but she'd never have told Granny Kinch or Nancy that, not in a month of Sundays. It must be sitting at the door all those hours that gave her such a good idea of everyone's movements. You couldn't go up or down April Grove or October Street without Granny Kinch's little black eyes fixed on you.

Nancy Baxter was occupying a shabby armchair by the fireplace. The fire hadn't been lit yet – although it was October and the weather had been rough, nobody lit their fire before teatime – but a wisp of smoke curled up from her cigarette. She looked up from a cheap magazine and nodded as Carol came in.

''Ere's young Carol Glaister,' her mother said unnecessarily. 'Come in for a cuppa. Put the kettle on, Nance, there's a good girl.'

Nancy Baxter wasn't a girl, she must be getting on for forty, and she was thin and scraggy, with dark hair that looked as if it had been cut with a knife and fork, and sallow skin, but she nodded amiably and got up to do as her mother asked. She went out to the little scullery and Carol looked around her.

It was the first time she had been into number 10. Like all the houses in April Grove, it consisted of two small rooms and a scullery and outside lavatory downstairs, and two bedrooms upstairs. The back room was distempered in cream, with dark brown below the dado that ran round the walls at waist height, but the cream had long been discoloured to a murky khaki by cigarette smoke, and there were scuff marks where people had leaned against the walls. The floor was covered in dark brown linoleum, and there was a table with green American cloth on top, and a few chairs as old as the one Granny Kinch used at the front door.

'You don't mind if we don't ask yer in the posh room, do yer?' Granny Kinch said with a wink. 'Only Nancy's very particular about who goes in the parlour, ain't yer, Nance?'

'Seein' as we got no furniture in there anyway, apart from a bed, I don't s'pose Carol'd want to be asked in,' Nancy said over her shoulder. 'There's some fags in that packet on the mantelpiece, Ma,' she added, as Granny Kinch picked up an empty Woodbine packet from the table. 'An' it's your turn to buy the next lot. Get out from under me feet, Vera,' she added, coming in with a teapot and three cups on an old tin tray.

Nancy's daughter Vera was the same age as Maureen Budd, but she didn't look as rosy or healthy as Maureen. She was a thin, pale child with the remains of her last meal – and quite possibly the two or three before that, Carol thought – smeared on her pasty face. She was playing on the floor with an old cardboard box and some clothes pegs which she was fixing around the top.

'She's a good little thing,' Granny Kinch said fondly. 'Plays for hours, quiet as a mouse. Not like 'er big brother, eh? He was a little tartar, into everything. You 'ad to 'ave eyes in the back of yer 'ead when Micky was about.'

He hadn't changed, then, Carol thought. Micky had spent his first fourteen years being blamed – usually with justification – for everything that went wrong in April Grove. She wondered how he was getting on in the approved school up at Drayton.

'So 'ow're things with you?' Nancy asked, handing Carol a cup of tea. The cup was chipped and Ethel wouldn't have given it houseroom, but Carol accepted it and sipped gratefully. She shrugged in answer to Nancy's question, and repeated what she had told Mrs Kinch.

'All right. A bit fed up.'

'I daresay you are.' Nancy eyed her, much as her mother had done. 'Takes a bit of time to get over, what you bin through.'

'I don't suppose you gets much sympathy at 'ome, neither,' Granny Kinch said. 'I mean, I don't want to speak ill of your ma, but she ain't exactly the sort to give yer a cuddle and tell yer everything's all right, is she?'

'Well, it ain't all right, is it?' Nancy said. 'Lost yer kid, aincher? It don't matter what anyone says, nothing can make that all right.'

Carol stared at them both. Nancy had spoken bluntly, almost brutally, yet she sensed the real sympathy that lay behind her words. She knows what it's like, she thought suddenly. She really knows what it's like. She understands . . .

The tears came hot to her eyes. 'It's just that I don't know where he is,' she burst out. 'I mean, it's months now since I saw him – he'll be crawling now, he might even be walking. He's got *teeth*. And I don't know. I don't know as I'd even recognise him if I saw him again.' She turned her eyes from one face to the other. 'I might be walking past him every day and not know it's my own baby.'

Granny Kinch and Nancy gazed at her. Their black eyes, so alike, were like the black button-eyes on the teddy bear Carol had once had. She longed suddenly for her bear, for the warm comfort of being able to hug his furry body. Like hugging a baby . . .

'I only had him for six weeks,' she said, her voice breaking. 'My own baby . . . mine and Roddy's . . . and I only had him for six weeks . . .'

The two women glanced at each other, then Granny Kinch reached out and gathered the girl into her arms, drawing her against her grubby pinafore.

'There, there, my duck,' she murmured, patting Carol's heaving shoulders. 'You 'ave a good cry, then. It's what you need. You let it all out. Don't mind me. Granny Kinch understands. There, there . . . Let it out . . . Granny understands . . . Granny understands . . .'

The cracked old voice mumbled on and Carol leaned her head against the warm, softly upholstered bosom and allowed the tears to flow as she had never dared allow them before. She could not have prevented them. The sobs dragged themselves up from deep inside – ragged, gasping, hiccuping sobs that threatened to wrench her body apart, forcing their way through airways that were half-closed with the tension that had been building up, almost vomiting from her open mouth. Within seconds, her face was wet, the tears soaking down her neck into her jumper, running down the cleft between her breasts – breasts that had never quite stopped being sore since the baby had been born. She still saw drops of milk sometimes, squeezing themselves from her nipples, and she touched them with her fingertips, smelling the warm, milky smell, and even tasting the sweetness that should have belonged to her baby.

'They made me give him away,' she gasped at last. 'I never wanted to . . . I wanted to keep him. He was mine and Roddy's. They made me give him away, and I don't know who's got him now. I don't know where he is.' Her eyes were huge as she stared at the two women. '*I don't know where my baby is . . .*'

Granny Kinch hugged her again, looking over her head at Nancy. The younger woman's face was hard and bitter. She turned away with a gesture of rejection and lit another cigarette, but her fingers were trembling and her eyes shone as if with her own tears.

'That's summat you got to get used to,' Nancy said harshly. 'And it don't get no easier, neither. Thinkin' about 'em on their birthdays – wonderin' what sort of Christmas present they bin given – knowin' they're startin' school. Or work.' She crushed the cigarette between her fingers suddenly. 'And then it's are they gettin' married, 'avin' their own kids? Makin' you a gran? There ain't no end to it – specially these days, when there's a war ter worry about an' all.'

Carol lifted her head, staring at her. 'You . . . *you* . . . ?'

'Thass right,' Nancy said abruptly. 'I know just what it's like, 'cause I bin there too. I 'ad a baby when I wasn't no older'n what you are now. Only my feller didn't go to jail for it. 'E was an officer, see – an' 'e never run away with me, neither. 'E just did what 'e wanted with me an' then turned 'is back an' swore 'e'd never seen me before in 'is life. An' 'oo was goin' ter believe me before 'im, eh?' She snorted. 'The kid was the spittin' image of 'im 'an all, but there weren't nothin' we could do about it. There never is when you monkey about with that sort.'

'But – *Micky* . . . ?'

'Nah,' Nancy said, 'it weren't Micky. It was two years before I fell for Mick. 'E give me a bit of money, see, to shut me up – but when that run out, there wasn't nothin' else I could do, was there? I didn't have no other trade.' She gave a bitter little laugh. 'I was a bit better lookin' in those days. I didn't 'ave much trouble gettin' the custom. An' after I 'ad Mick I was a bit more careful – knew a few of the tricks of the trade then, see.' She glanced down at the toddler playing at her feet. 'Till I slipped up again with this one, anyway.'

Carol was silent. She looked down at Vera. There was nothing very appealing about the grimy little face that looked back at her, and Micky Baxter had been nothing but trouble for his mother, but she hadn't given either of them away. Losing one baby had evidently been enough for her.

'How old would he be now?' she asked. 'Your first baby?'

'It was a she,' Nancy said briefly. 'Little girl. Yellow hair – you could see already it was going to be curly – big blue eyes . . . My little fairy, I called 'er. She'd be sixteen now. Gettin' on for seventeen.' She looked at the cigarette crushed between her fingers. 'I just 'ope 'ooever's got 'er brought 'er up right. Taught 'er right from wrong. Makes 'er come 'ome at a decent time at night.'

It seemed funny to hear Nancy talking like that, when Carol knew that she let Micky roam about at all hours, and even little Vera was allowed out into the street with no one to keep much of an eye on her. Maybe she'd have been different if she hadn't been let down so badly.

'What was her name?' she asked, thinking it would probably be something like Joan or Doris or Beryl. Something plain, the sort of name people like Nancy Baxter usually chose.

'Amelia,' Nancy said, sounding the name proudly as she relit the cigarette. 'I always liked that name. I 'ad a dolly once, called Amelia.'

Carol stared at her. She thought of a little girl with yellow hair and blue eyes called Amelia, playing in the gutter of April Grove, and wanted to laugh. But at the same time, she wanted to cry.

'Did you love him?' Carol asked diffidently. 'The man – you know . . .'

Nancy gave a hoot of bitter laughter. '*Love* 'im? Look 'ere, kid, I never even *saw* 'im! Not before'and, anyway. I knew 'oo 'e was after, all right, 'cause of the black eye I give 'im.' She caught Carol's uncomprehending eye. 'Copped 'old of me one night, 'e did, when I was walkin' back 'ome in the dark. That's 'ow I knew 'e was an officer – smelt the whisky on 'is breath. If it'd bin a Tommy, it'd 'ave been beer, wouldn't it?' She drew on the cigarette. 'I went back next day, told 'em what 'ad 'appened, and they tried to pin it on a bloke I'd bin knockin' about with. I could see if I took it any further 'e'd be fer the 'igh jump, so I let it go. I didn't know I was in the family way then, see, but I knew who it was. I knew the minute I laid eyes on 'im. A proper shiner, I'd give 'im, and scratched all down 'is face an' all.'

'You *saw* him?' Carol said, fascinated. 'You saw him, and never said?'

'I told yer, it wouldn't 'ave done no good.' Nancy puffed again. ''E was one of the 'igh-ups. 'E could've swore black was white and they'd 'ave took his word for it.' She leaned forwards and stubbed her cigarette viciously in a saucer. 'Look, they *knew*. They knew 'ow 'e'd got that black eye an' those scratches. They was laughin' be'ind their 'ands, the lot of 'em. If I'd kept on with it, they'd 'ave took it out on my bloke, so I shut me mouth an' went away. By the time I found out I was caught, the whole bleedin' lot of 'em 'ad bin posted, so there weren't nothin' I could do. The doctor an' everyone said I'd better give the baby away, said I'd never be able to keep it meself, so that's what I done.'

Carol could find nothing to say. She thought of Nancy, only sixteen or seventeen years old, finding she was pregnant by an Army officer who had raped her and then denied it. Well, he would, wouldn't he? And then he'd gone off with his regiment and never even known about the baby. Probably he'd forgotten about Nancy almost as soon as his eye and his scratches had healed.

'They're buggers,' Granny Kinch said, 'the lot of them.'

Carol could see she had good reason to say that, but she shook her head and said firmly, 'Not my Roddy. He really loved me, Roddy did. And I loved him. I still do.'

'Love,' Nancy said sardonically. 'It don't seem to make much difference, to me. You're still in the same bloody boat, aincher?' She gave a sudden, small, wry laugh. 'Tell yer what I did – I got out my old dolly, the one I called Amelia. Took 'er to bed with me for years. It wasn't the same, a dolly, but I reckon it kept me from goin' bonkers. Till I 'ad my Mick, anyway, an' 'ad a proper baby to cuddle again.'

'You could do that too,' Granny Kinch said to Carol. 'I don't reckon you get much cuddlin' off your ma. It's what a girl in your position needs, a baby in 'er arms, an' even an old dolly's better than nothin'.'

Carol went home, feeling better for having had a real talk with people who understood. It was funny it should be Granny Kinch and Nancy, she thought, unlocking the front door of number 15, but it didn't matter who it was: it helped, and it made her see too that life hadn't always been easy for the scraggy-looking woman that the rest of the street turned their noses up at.

There's nothing wrong with Nancy Baxter and her mum, she thought, going upstairs to her bedroom. They're good, kind people at heart, and that's the best thing anyone could be.

She opened the cupboard that her father had built over the top of the stairwell to make a bit of a wardrobe in her room. A few old toys had been pushed on to the top shelf, and she reached up and dragged them down. A battered teddy bear. A wooden horse. And a doll with a rag body and a pink china face, rather chipped and with a lot of the roses scratched from its cheeks, but still with a few scraps of dark hair clinging to its scalp and its painted eyes still blue.

It didn't look much like little Roderick, but it was about the same size as he had been when Carol had handed him over on that last day, and if she closed her eyes she could pretend.

She sat on the bed, rocking backwards and forwards, cradling the doll in her arms as she pretended.

# CHAPTER NINE

'D'you know what our Annie told me today,' Jess said. The whole family was sitting down to tea. It was a Friday evening and Frank was home early for once, because tomorrow and Sunday he would be doing overtime. 'Two Pompey chaps in the Army, different units, were in Tripoli, got talking somehow or other, and one said your surname's the same as my pal's, and it turned out it was his brother!'

'Whose brother?' Tim asked. 'I mean, if it was the man he was talking to's brother, how could he have had the same surname?'

'No, it was the man's brother's surname he was talking to,' Jess began, and then caught the twitch of his lips. 'Oh, go on, Tim, you know very well what I mean.'

The three older children laughed, as they often did when Jess got muddled with her stories. Maureen, chewing bread and margarine with home-made blackberry and apple jam spread thinly on top, looked round at them.

'I've got two brothers,' she announced, and pointed at Tim and Keith in turn. Then she frowned. 'What she?'

'*She's* got a name,' Jess said tartly. 'And she's your sister.'

'Sister,' Maureen repeated. 'Rose is my sister.'

'That's right. And you're Tim's sister, and Keith's sister.'

'*I'm* a sister?' Maureen echoed in a tone of astonishment. 'When did I be a sister?'

'The minute you were born.' Tim told her. He had endless patience with Maureen, looking for her the minute he came home from work on the ferry, playing with her and teaching her songs, taking her about with him. 'And Rose is my sister too.'

Maureen frowned again. 'No. Rose isn't your sister. *I* your sister.'

'Oh, for goodness' sake,' Rose said crossly. 'She seems to think Tim's her own special property. I was his sister for twelve years before you came along,' she told the little girl.

'Eleven,' Tim said. 'You were only just over one when I was born, so you've only been my sister for eleven years longer than Maureen.'

'And mine only nine years longer,' Keith added.

Jess sighed. Rose had been so good when Maureen was born, almost taking the baby over as her own, wheeling her pram out in the morning and taking her to the shops, helping about the house – she really didn't know what she'd have done without her. But now she seemed to have lost interest and treated her rather like an irritating puppy. It's not Rose's fault, Jess thought a little guiltily. She shouldn't have to share a room with her little sister, not at her age. At sixteen, she needed a bit of privacy, and if it hadn't been for the war Jess and Frank might have moved to a bigger house, but Hitler had put a stop to anything like that.

'Leave her alone, Rose,' she said. 'She doesn't understand. People can have more than one sister,' she explained to Maureen. 'They can have lots. Like you've got two brothers, you see.'

Maureen furrowed her brow. You could see her brain working, Jess thought, as she tried to understand. 'Tim and Keith are my brothers.'

'That's right, they are. And they're Rose's brothers too.'

'Who else?' Maureen demanded. She finished her bread. 'Who else's brothers?'

'Nobody else's. Just yours and Rose's.'

Maureen put her arms around one of Tim's arms and hugged it against her.

'But Tim's *my* brother, really,' She stared defiantly at Rose. 'Mine.'

Jess saw Rose draw in her breath and intervened hastily. 'Have some more bread, Maureen. You like blackberry and apple jam, don't you? You helped Mummy make it.'

'That yarn about the bloke in Tripoli,' Frank said. 'One of the men in the yard told me almost the same thing happened to his cousin, up in Petersfield. Walked into the works canteen, spotted a chap in Canadian uniform and went to speak to him, and found it was his own son. You wouldn't credit a coincidence like that, would you? His son had gone over to Canada to work before the war started and enlisted. He'd been shipped over before he could even let his family know. He'd only been in Petersfield half a day, and in walks his dad.' Frank shook his head. 'Well, they say it's a small world.'

'I bet his mum's pleased,' Jess said. She always related news of the war to families rather than the political situation. That was why she worried so much about young soldiers being killed, sailors drowned and airmen shot out of the sky. It didn't matter to her what nationality they were, they were somebody's son and at home there would be mothers and fathers, wives and children, grieving for them. 'Though I don't suppose he'll stay in Petersfield for long.'

'I've seen Canadian soldiers,' Tim said. 'When me and Keith rode our bikes out to see our Betty last week we could see their camps in some of the fields. And tanks and big lorries.'

'There's sailors too,' Keith added. 'D'you know, Mum, they've turned a hotel down in Southsea into a ship? HMS *Grasshopper*, it's called, and there's a White Ensign flying from the chimney-pots. That means there's an Admiral there, and—'

'Yes, and Joy told me they're building something out on the beach,' Rose said eagerly. 'What d'you think it is? Huge concrete—'

Frank butted in, his voice angry. 'That's enough! It doesn't matter to you what they're doing. And if Joy says anything about it, you can tell her you don't want to listen. You know we're not supposed to talk about things like that.'

Rose looked injured. 'I don't see what harm there is talking about it at home. None of us are spies.'

'It's not just at home, though, is it?' Frank said. 'You've been talking about it to Joy Brunner and goodness knows who else. You don't know who might be listening.'

'"Walls have ears,"' Tim said, quoting one of the government posters that adorned walls or appeared in newspapers. Frank gave him a quelling look.

'And *you* needn't be so cocky. It wouldn't do you any harm to keep a quiet tongue in your head once in a while.'

'I haven't been saying anything,' Tim began righteously, but was silenced by looks from both his parents.

Frank leaned his elbows on the table, rested his chin on his hands and looked round the table at them all. 'You've all been told this before, but I'll tell you again. There's a lot going on in Pompey these days, what with all these Canadians and Americans and soldiers in the place, not to mention the Navy that's always in and out of harbour, but whatever they're doing, whatever you see and hear, you don't talk about it, see? Not to *anyone*. Not even at home. Then there's no chance you'll give things away to the wrong people. Those posters are right. Walls have ears – you don't know who might be listening, and once information starts getting passed around it's bound to end up in the wrong hands. And—'

'Walls don't have ears, Daddy,' Maureen broke in. She had been getting increasingly agitated ever since Tim had first quoted it. 'They *don't*. Only people have ears, and dogs and cats and—'

'*Be quiet!*' Frank's voice was so sharp that everyone jumped and Maureen began to cry. 'You're just like your brothers, got too much to say about everything. And that's another reason not to talk about what the military are doing,' he went on to the others. 'If anyone's got ears, that child has, like a donkey's they are, and she chatters away to everyone she meets. You might think it's safe to say whatever you like at home, but it's not, not when you've got an information service here that's better than the BBC.'

Tim and Keith giggled, then straightened their faces hastily. That was the trouble with Dad: he said things that sounded like jokes and then you found he was serious. 'Maureen doesn't know any spies,' Tim said, hoping to rectify the situation.

'You don't know who's a spy,' his father told him. 'That's the whole point of spies, isn't it? They keep it to themselves. They don't go round wearing badges. The government's right. Don't talk at all, and then you don't take any risks. And you can tell Joy Brunner I said so,' he added to Rose.

Rose continued to look sulky, but Tim was ready with another quotation. He nudged Keith and grinned.

'"Be Like Dad,"' he whispered. '"Keep Mum!"' And the two boys fell against each other in a heap of giggles.

Maureen, the tears still on her cheeks, stared at them. Then she reached out to her mother.

'Daddy's not going to give you away,' she said in a wobbly voice. 'He's *not* going to give you away . . .'

Jess put out her hand automatically to soothe her, and looked anxiously at her husband. Frank had never been the most patient of men but just lately his temper seemed shorter than ever. He snapped the children's heads off for no reason and was often short with her too. She knew that there was a lot of work on in the dockyard, work he wasn't allowed to talk about, and she knew he was desperately anxious about the war, but she'd hoped that it would make him feel better, having the children all at home, having a proper family life. She'd hoped that coming home of an evening would be like coming into a haven.

'Don't be hard on them, Frank,' she said in a quiet voice as they got ready for bed a few hours later. 'It's awful for them to have to spend their growing-up years like this, scared to open their mouths, scared of being bombed to bits or machine-gunned in the street. They're bound to break out a bit sometimes.'

He turned in the act of shrugging on his pyjama jacket and put his arms around her. He was a huge bear of a man, and Jess was small and slight, but for once she had the feeling that he was leaning against her rather than the other way about, that he was drawing strength from her embrace. She felt his head heavy on her shoulder, and put up her hands to stroke his neck and shoulders.

'Come to bed, Frank,' she murmured, knowing how difficult it was for him to tell her what was in his heart. 'Come to bed and let me love you. Let's forget about the war for a few hours and just be us. Let's pretend everything's just the same as it used to be.'

'Oh, Jess,' he said hoarsely, 'if only we could. If only it *was* like it used to be.' He paused for a moment, then said, 'You know, I always thought we had pretty bad worries, what with never having enough money and not being able to do the sort of work I'd really like – but now, looking back, it seems like we had nothing to worry about at all. It seems like we lived in sunshine all the time.'

'Perhaps we still do,' she said. 'Perhaps one day we'll look back at this and think how lucky we were. We've got a lot to be thankful for, Frank. We've got our family around us, safe and sound, and none of them old enough to be taken away from us. I reckon the sun's still shining on us really, however bad things might seem.'

She slipped into the wide bed, drawing Frank with her, holding his head against her breast and whispering to him. But later, when he had fallen asleep beside her, she lay with her head on his outflung arm staring into the darkness, knowing that nothing would ever be just as it used to be. Even if the war were to end tomorrow, they could never go back entirely to the way they had been before.

The world had changed, and they had changed with it.

Next door, on the other side of the wall that separated the two houses, Carol Glaister sat on her bed with her doll in her arms. She stared at the unblinking eyes, trying to do as Nancy Baxter had suggested and pretend it was her baby, but instead her mind went back to the months she had spent in the home, waiting for him to be born. And the few weeks afterwards, when she had held him in her arms and felt warm, living flesh instead of hard china and rag.

The people at the home for unmarried mothers hadn't exactly been unkind, but they hadn't gone out of their way to make the girls feel better. It was a bit like being in hospital, only you were patient, nurse, cook and charlady all rolled into one. The girls were expected to help the ones who were poorly – not that being poorly was encouraged, you had to be on your knees before the matron let you off duties – and do all the cleaning, washing and cooking. The only staff kept were a housekeeper who had a face like the back of a bus, two maids who did the really hard scrubbing and scouring, and a gnarled and ancient man who looked after the garden. The girls were expected to help out there as well, hoeing and weeding, and staggering into the kitchen laden with baskets of vegetables.

It wasn't too bad, most of the time. They had a few laughs, and in the evenings they were allowed to sit in the big common-room and do their knitting or sewing. They had to make every item of clothing for their babies, unless they were lucky enough to have relatives who would do some, but the girls who found themselves in homes didn't often have that kind of relative. Mostly, they'd been sent there because their families were ashamed to have them at home, and hadn't admitted to the neighbours – and sometimes even the rest of the family – that there was a baby on the way. Nobody was going to be seen knitting tiny garments for a baby which wasn't supposed to exist.

The girls stayed in the home for six weeks after their babies had been born. They were kept in bed for the first fortnight, not allowed to put a foot to the floor, even though after the first day or two – sooner than that in some cases – they felt as fit as ever, their suddenly lightened bodies full of energy. However, there was milk coming through, making their breasts sore and swollen, and bleeding worse than the longest and heaviest period anyone had ever had, which more than made up for the nine months free of the 'curse', and after the months of toil and anxiety it was a nice change to lie back for a bit and let someone else do the scrubbing and cooking.

Not that they were allowed to be idle. There was still plenty of sewing and knitting to be done. Where the wool and materials came from, Carol never knew, but there seemed to be an endless supply, some of it from old garments that had to be unravelled and the crinkled wool washed before being wound into balls ready for use. Babies seemed to need more clothes than adults, and each one went out with a full layette, even if it was going to a new home where it would have new parents who had been getting ready for it and, presumably, doing their own knitting and sewing.

'Have you decided what to do with yours yet?' Pearl, in the next bed to Carol, asked as they fed the babies one afternoon.

Carol shrugged her free shoulder. 'Don't have no choice. Mum won't have the baby at home and I don't have nowhere else to go. Only to my auntie in Devon for a bit, and she don't even know I've had a baby.' A tear dropped on to the baby's hair as he nuzzled and sucked on her breast. The midwife said she'd never seen a baby with so much hair. It was brown like Roddy's, and ruffled in just the same way. The nurse said it would all rub off, but it hadn't done so far.

The other girl eyed her. 'Don't you want to give him away?'

Carol flushed. ''Course not. He's mine, isn't he? Mine and Roddy's. We're a *family*.'

'Go on, how can you be a family when you're not married? You don't even see the bloke any more, do you?'

'Well, he's away, isn't he? In the Navy.' Carol had never told anyone that Roddy was in prison. 'There's lots of blokes haven't seen their kids yet. They're still a family.'

'And they're married,' Pearl pointed out. She glanced down at the bald head of her own little girl. 'I tell you what, I'll be glad to see the back of this one. I wouldn't want a kid round *my* neck. I want a bit of life.'

Carol thought Pearl had already had quite a bit of 'life'. This was her second pregnancy – the first had ended in a miscarriage – and by Pearl's own account she was lucky not to have had more, and all by different men. Carol didn't think she was all that different from Nancy Baxter, although Pearl denied hotly that she was a tart, saying she never took money.

'Only presents and booze,' someone else had said caustically. 'They don't count, of course.'

'I can't help it if blokes want to give me nice things,' Pearl said, tossing her head, and flushed when the others laughed.

'The last one give you something a bit too nice, didn't he, Pearl! What you going to do about that, then?'

'Go on,' someone else said, 'she's got more French letters than the Paris Post Office. Bet you won't let this happen again, will you? There ain't much trade in a mother and baby home, apart from old Wilkins and the boy what comes with the meat.'

Again, they hooted with laughter. 'That's good, that is! The boy what comes with the meat! He can bring his meat round my way any day. I like a nice fat sausage, I do.'

Carol had never joined in their ribaldry. It was like the girls in the factory now, making a joke of something she still felt was precious. They don't none of them know what it's like to love a bloke, she thought. Really love him. And none of them really cares about their kid.

Afterwards, she'd suspected that a lot of them did care about the babies they'd borne and looked after for six weeks before having to give them away. Nearly everyone was red eyed afterwards, and quieter than usual. Even Pearl's bluster was dimmed. But there was never time to talk much, because as soon as the baby had gone the mother would be packing her own bags, for there was no place for her any more in a home for unmarried mothers.

Sitting on her bed in number 15, April Grove and rocking her doll, Carol's mind went back to the day when she had last seen her son.

The rule was that on that last day you gave your baby a special bath and dressed it in the best of the clothes you'd been so busy making all these months. Until then, you wouldn't have used any of them, only the plain white nightgowns that were worn by all the home babies. So that was the first time you saw your baby in a proper frock with a little cardigan on. You brushed the newly washed hair – if the baby had any – and then you put on your own best clothes and waited in the matron's room for the new parents to arrive.

Carol had had to wait a bit longer than usual because her 'people' were late. There'd been an air-raid warning, she heard later, and they'd had to take shelter at the railway station. She'd sat alone, with Roderick in her arms, gazing down at his face and trying to memorise every tiny particle.

He was awake, looking up at her with his dark eyes. People said that all babies had blue eyes, but Carol was convinced that Roderick's were brown, like his father's. He looked just like Roddy at times, just the same expression crossed his tiny face, so that she could almost swear she knew what he was thinking.

Oh my baby, she thought, my little Roddy, how am I going to be able to give you to someone else?

He was just six weeks old. They said that babies started to smile properly at six weeks, not just a windy grin but a proper smile. Carol had searched his face every day for a real smile, and had almost convinced herself that he'd done it, but in her heart she knew he hadn't. She watched him now, stretching her own quivering lips into a smile in the hope that he would copy her. It seemed the worst thing of all, to have to give your baby away before he'd even managed to smile at you.

I know he wants to, she thought. I know he does. He's trying – he just can't get the knack of it yet.

She wondered what the new people would be like. People who wanted a baby but hadn't been able to have one of their own, so they must really want one, to come and take on someone else's.

They must be nice people. They've *got* to be nice people, she thought with sudden passion. I can't give my baby to people who aren't going to be nice to him. I won't. He's got to have a good mum, someone who'll look after him and love him, and kiss him when he hurts himself and when he can't sleep. He's got to have a good dad like Roddy would have been. A dad who'll take him out and teach him to swim and play football and ride a bike.

Roddy would have done those things, and so would I. We'd have been a real family.

She heard footsteps outside, voices talking. Mrs Whiting's posh, commanding tones, and two others. A man and a woman.

They were here.

Carol's arms tightened a little round Roderick's small, warm body. She was trembling. She looked down at him again, barely able to see his face through the blur of sudden tears. I can't, she thought, I can't give him away, it doesn't matter how nice they are, he's mine, he's my baby, I can't . . .

The door opened. Mrs Whiting looked at her, her eyes moving over her critically. The girls were expected to look neat and tidy, to give the visitors a good impression of the home. She appeared reasonably satisfied with Carol's appearance and stood back to allow the couple to enter.

They had seen Roderick already, when they came to the home to register for a baby. They came forward eagerly, the woman already stretching out her arms.

'We like to let our young mothers say goodbye to their babies before letting them go,' Mrs Whiting said, a little repressively. 'We find it helps the babies to settle better in their new homes if the mother hasn't been upset. After that, it's best if you leave as quickly as possible.'

The woman held back, but her eyes were on Roderick. She looked as if she couldn't wait to take him away. She didn't even glance at Carol, who was standing up now, holding him close against her as if defending him against maurauders.

'There's just this last document to sign,' Mrs Whiting said, indicating her desk where a single sheet of paper lay.

The couple moved across to it. Their impatience filled the room, so that even the furniture seemed to quiver with it. Carol watched them and then looked down again at her baby's face.

He was still gazing up at her. His eyes *are* brown, she thought, they're definitely brown. And he was looking at her just as Roddy had looked at her, when he was loving her most.

Dimly, she heard Mrs Whiting's voice. 'Thank you, Mrs Sutcliffe. That's all that's needed.' A short pause, and then, 'The baby's yours now.'

He's not, Carol thought. He's not theirs. He's mine. She held him a little more tightly and shut her eyes so that the tears would not fall.

'Carol. Give Mrs Sutcliffe the baby now, please. They're sometimes a little difficult at this stage,' she added quietly to the couple, and then again, a little more loudly, 'Carol. Did you hear me? Give the Sutcliffes their baby now.'

Their baby. *Their* baby. She shook her head blindly. I can't. I can't.

She felt Mrs Whiting's hands on her arms. She was pulling them, quite gently but very firmly. She would take Roderick away, and Carol would have no choice, because she'd already signed her part of the document with Mrs Whiting standing over her, and Roderick didn't belong to her any more, he was Mr and Mrs Sutcliffe's and Carol had no right to be even standing here holding him, no right to look down into his face and call him hers . . .

She opened her eyes and took one last, despairing look.

The baby gazed at her. And then his face broke into a wide, beaming smile. A real smile.

Roddy's smile.

# CHAPTER TEN

Annie and Ted were just sitting down to their supper of sausages and chips when Olive walked in through the back door. They looked up in surprise. It was nine o'clock in the evening and, with a dense November fog as well as the blackout covering Pompey like a thick eiderdown, not a time for visiting.

'What is it?' Annie said at once. 'What's up?'

Olive tried to smile. 'Can't a girl pop in to say hullo to her mum and dad without there being something up?' But the smile twisted itself around her mouth and pulled the corners down so that she looked more as if she were about to cry. She sat down rather suddenly in Ted's armchair and pushed a piece of paper towards them. 'Read that.'

Annie took it slowly. Pieces of paper generally brought bad news these days, starting with the 'piece of paper' Mr Chamberlain had brought home from Munich in 1938. That had been supposed at the time to be good news, but look what had happened . . . She smoothed out the slip Olive had given her and looked at it.

'It's from Derek,' Olive said, as if her mother couldn't read it for herself. 'He's being posted again. Can't tell me where, of course, I'm only his wife, but you can bet your boots it's not back to Pompey.' She lifted her hands and dropped them helplessly back on to her knees. 'I'm just about fed up with it, I am – just about fed up.'

'Oh, Livvy, I am sorry.' Annie got up and fetched her a cup and saucer from the dresser. 'Here, have a cup of tea, you must be shrammed. It's raw cold out there tonight.'

'I know. I had to walk most of the way. The buses are crawling along, can't hardly see the kerbs.' Olive looked at her parents, her eyes like bruises in her white face. 'I had to come. I just felt so sick of it all.'

'I know.' Annie glanced at Ted, who was reading the scrap of paper that Olive had given them. It was just part of a letter from Derek, and Annie guessed that the rest of it had been intimate, full of love and longing, a real love letter. Love letters! When Olive and Derek had been married for over three years. It was daft, they ought to have got past that stage and been settled down now, raising a family, never parted for long enough to write more than the odd note to say they'd gone up the street or over to the allotment . . . It wasn't right.

'When are we ever going to get a chance to live a proper life?' Olive demanded, thumping her fist on the arm of Ted's chair. 'I mean, I'm twenty-four now – I ought to have kids. I'll be old enough to be a granny before I even get to push a pram at this rate. I tell you, it isn't fair and I'm sick of it!'

'Ssh, I know, I know.' Annie set the cup down beside her, soothing her as if she were a baby. 'It's the same for a lot of people, Livvy. There's lots like you, missing their chaps, and there's plenty who'll never see them again. Think of poor—'

'I know all about them and I *don't care!*' The tears sprang from Olive's eyes and coursed fiercely down her cheeks. 'I'm sorry if that sounds selfish, Mum, but just at the moment I can't think of anything but Derek and me. I'm fed up with it. I'm fed up with him being away, I'm fed up with having to write letters and only getting letters back, I'm fed up with having to sleep in a hut with a lot of other girls instead of in a nice double bed with my own husband, I'm fed up with the war. Derek's fed up too – he's fed up with the Army, and sand, and building endless huts and airstrips. And shall I tell you what I'm fed up with more than anything else?' She banged her fist again. 'I'm fed up with having to pretend everything's *all right*! I'm fed up with having to *smile* about it all!'

'Livvy, don't. You'll upset your gran.' Annie glanced anxiously towards the front room, which had been turned into a bedroom for her mother. 'Don't wake her up when she's just got off to sleep. You'll only frighten her . . .' She looked at her daughter's pale, tear-streaked face. 'Oh, Livvy, I know it's awful for you, but I just don't know what else to say. What can we do? We've just got to put up with it.'

'Just say you know how awful it is,' Olive said with a weak attempt at a grin. 'That's all anyone can do – just sort of feel it with me. I'm sorry, Mum. I just wanted to come and have a cry, I suppose. I can't do it in the mess, not properly – there's so many of us in the same boat, and that helps for a bit, but then there's always someone who's worse off and you have to feel sorry for them, and – oh, I just wanted to forget all that and be sorry for *myself* for a while. Selfish, isn't it?'

'No,' Annie said, 'it's not selfish. You're having just as hard a time of it as anyone else. You deserve a bit of sympathy too. We all need it now and then, don't we, Ted?'

Ted nodded. He wondered if Annie was taking a sly dig at him for the nervous breakdown he'd had, but he didn't think she was. Annie wasn't like that. She'd taken care of him all through it, been really patient with him, and all she meant now was that he was more likely to understand Olive's unhappiness. Which he was.

'You have a good cry, girl,' he said, patting Olive awkwardly on the shoulder. 'It'll do you good. It's bottling things up that does the harm. Like letting a boil fester. You let it out.'

Olive laughed a little shakily. 'It's all right, Dad. I don't think I'm going to flood the place out. It's helped just coming and telling you about it.' She glanced at the clock that ticked on the mantelpiece, and sighed. 'I'll have to be going back anyway. I didn't know it'd take me so long to get here. I don't suppose there'll be any buses running at all now.'

Annie pursed her lips. 'You're never going to walk all the way back to Southsea on your own, at this time of night. Ted, you'd better go with her. It's not right, a young woman out by herself.'

Ted started to get to his feet. He'd been working all day, standing up on the bridge of the *Ferry King*, steering the little boat across the fog-shrouded harbour, and he was dead tired. Annie was right, though, Olive never ought to have walked all the way here and she certainly couldn't go all the way back on her own. He reached for his boots which had been stood in the corner of the hearth to dry out for tomorrow.

'No, it's all right, Dad.' Olive laid her hand on his arm. 'I'll be all right, honest. I don't need no one to see me back.'

'Don't be daft, girl. It's getting on for five miles. I'm not letting you go by yourself.'

'If you come, it'll be gone midnight before you're home again,' she retorted, and then, seeing that he intended to come anyway, added a little awkwardly, 'Anyway, I won't be going on my own.'

Ted lowered the boot he had just lifted, and stared at her.

Annie said, 'Not on your own? Why, who'll be with you?'

'A friend,' Olive said evasively. 'Someone walked up with me – kept me company. They – they're waiting up at the corner.'

*'Waiting up at the corner?'* Annie was scandalised. 'Olive, whatever are you thinking of? Why didn't you bring this friend in? What's her name?'

'It's not a her,' Olive said, mumbling a little, and then, a little more loudly, 'It's a him. A man. He – he used to work on the same gun as me.'

'A *man*?' She might as well have said he was a gorilla, from the look on Annie's face. 'Olive . . .'

'There's nothing wrong in it,' Olive said defensively. 'We're just friends, that's all. People can be friends, can't they? I just happened to be

126

telling him about Derek, and I said I was coming up here to see you and he said he'd walk with me.' She caught her mother's eye and flushed. 'Well, you said I shouldn't have come on my own. I'd have thought you'd be glad I had someone to see me here and back to camp safely.'

'Well, so I am, so long as you *are* safe.' Annie's tone made her doubts clear. 'What bothers me is why you didn't bring him in to meet us, and why you never said nothing about him. As if you're ashamed of him.'

'What would you have thought if I had brought him in? All the things you're thinking now. And don't say you're not.' Olive stared at her mother with indignation. 'He's just a friend, that's all, and when I said I was coming up to see you he offered to walk with me. Nothing more than that. I should have thought you'd be glad,' she repeated.

Annie shook her head. 'Don't get all het up about it, Olive. All I said was I was surprised you never brought him in. Leaving him standing round outside on a night like this! I mean, why be so secretive about it if it's all above board? That's what seems funny to me.'

'There's nothing funny about it at all,' Olive said wearily. 'I just didn't want this sort of inquisition, that's all. I knew you'd look down your noses if I came in with a chap. I'm not being secretive – there's nothing to be secretive about. Ray's a decent bloke and he wouldn't ever try to take advantage of me.'

Annie gave her a long look and Olive was reminded suddenly of the night Annie had got the whole family playing cards because she was afraid of what Betty and her boyfriend might get up to if they were allowed to go in the front room on their own. I'm not a kid! she thought indignantly. I'm a married woman of twenty-four and I'm in the Army – I don't even live at home any more. She's got no right to call me to order like that.

'All right,' Annie said after a pause. 'I know things are different these days, what with the war and all. Maybe I'm old-fashioned, but I just don't like the idea of you walking around in the dark with another man, and I don't think Derek would like it either.'

Olive shrugged. 'It's either that or not come to see you at all.' Her lip quivered again. 'I just wanted to come and tell you about Derek's posting, Mum. Would I have done that if there'd been anything going on between me and Ray? I wouldn't have dragged him all the way up here, now would I? We'd have spent the evening somewhere else – together.'

'That's true,' Ted said. 'You can't say it's not, Annie. All the same –' he turned to his daughter – 'I reckon your mum's right. It's not what your Derek would like, and I don't care how decent this bloke is, he's a man and you're a very nice-looking young woman. Walking five miles with you in the dark is bound to give him ideas, and I think it'd be just as well if I came with you. If there's nothing wrong in it, he won't object, will he?'

'Dad, for goodness' sake! There's no need. He'll think you're daft, and what's more he'll think *I'm* daft. He might even think I've asked you to come because I don't trust him!'

'It'll show him you're a decent young woman who knows what's what,' Ted said, putting on his boots. 'Anyway, the longer you stand here arguing the point, the colder he's going to get out there, have you thought about that? Where's my coat gone, Annie?'

'Where d'you think it's gone? It's on the staircase door, where it always is.' Annie sounded upset. She looked at Olive. 'I dunno what to say. I don't want your dad walking all that way at this time of night, not when he's got to get up in the morning. Why don't you just bring this chap in so we can have a look at him? If he's as decent as you say, he won't mind that. Go to the door and give him a shout.'

'He won't hear me,' Olive said sullenly. 'He'll be in the pub.'

'In the *pub*?'

'Well, why not? You said yourself I shouldn't have left him out there in the cold. There's a pub at the top of the street so he went in there to keep warm and have a drink while he waits. And you needn't look like that,' she said furiously to her mother. 'He's not going to come out roaring drunk. I don't suppose he'll have more than a pint.'

'It's not that,' Annie said. 'I've no objection to pubs, not that we've ever been a family that's gone into them much. It's you having to go in after him that bothers me. What are people going to say?'

'They can say what they like. It doesn't matter a tinker's cuss to me.' Olive got up and pulled on her greatcoat. 'You don't have to come, Dad. I'm old enough to make up my own mind who I go around with, and if I want to be friends with the men I work with, that's my business, see? If people have got such mean, dirty little minds that they have to see something in it that's not there, well, I can't help it, but I'm not letting it stop me having what friends I want, and you can tell 'em that, if anyone passes any remarks to you. And now I'm off.'

She stalked to the door, then paused and looked back at her mother, who was sitting quite still in her chair, her colour high and her lips bitten tightly together.

'Mum,' she said more gently, 'don't look like that, You know how much I think of Derek. You know I'd never do anything to hurt him.'

Annie nodded and sniffed. Her eyes were very bright. She felt for a hankie and dabbed it on her nose. 'I know that, Livvy. I'm not accusing you of anything, but – well, things are all so different these days. Everything's upside down, and sometimes I just don't know where I am any more. I mean, a few years ago a young woman like you wouldn't have dreamed of walking in the dark with a man not her husband, and as for going into pubs – well, it's not our way, never has been. Say what you will, your dad's right: men are men and they don't always know when to stop. I don't mean you'd encourage him, but – you might be putting yourself in an awkward position, that's all.'

'Not with Ray,' Olive said. 'We're friends, that's all. We've talked about it, Mum, and we've agreed that there won't be any funny business.' She looked at Ted. 'Why don't you come up with me and say hello, seeing as you've got your coat on? Maybe that'll put your mind at rest.'

Ted looked at Annie, who nodded. 'Yes, you go on, Ted. It'll look better, you going into the pub with Livvy. And tell him that I said next time he walks Olive up here she's to ask him in. Then it'll be all above board and we won't get no funny remarks from cats like Ethel Glaister.' She turned her eyes to Olive. 'It's not so much a matter of what you do, as what people *say* you do. That's what causes half the trouble in this world.'

'And Hitler causes the other half,' Olive said, and kissed her mother goodbye.

As she walked up the street with Ted in the blackout, her mind was seething with resentment. Mum ought to *know* I'd never let Derek down, she thought. She ought to know there'll never be anyone else for me. And what does it matter what other people say? A lot of snooping old busybodies whispering over garden fences, eyes out on stalks to see if a girl's belly is full every time she walks down the street. Don't they know there's a war on?

If it hadn't been for the war, Derek would never have been sent away to Africa. If it hadn't been for the war, Olive would never have met Ray Whitaker.

'There's no sense in us pretending we don't know each other,' Ray had said to her a few days earlier. He had met her coming from the NAAFI and turned to walk with her, ignoring her reluctance. 'We've got to work together – we can't help it. And we're friends. Even if you never spoke to me again in our entire lives, that wouldn't stop me being your friend. I don't think it'd stop you being mine, either.'

Olive had sighed. 'I know it wouldn't, but I really don't want—'

'You don't want to hurt Derek. I know.' His eyes were very serious. 'I don't want to spoil that, Livvy. I just want us to be friends, like we were before. Where's the harm in it, if we both agree it'll be no more than that?'

Olive hadn't answered at first. Ray had got transferred to another gun, but after only two or three weeks their sergeant had gone sick with appendicitis and Ray had been brought back. The appendicitis had turned to peritonitis and the sergeant had nearly died. It looked as if it would be quite a long time before he came back, and meanwhile Ray stayed.

'I can't stand it,' he had said to Olive, 'working with you and pretending we don't even know each other, let alone like each other. It's daft – Claudia knows we've been out together. She must think we've had a row.'

'She hasn't said anything.'

'Well, no, she probably wouldn't, but I bet she's thinking it. It's making the others feel uncomfortable too, and that's bad for the job.' He had stopped, and Olive stopped too. 'We've got to be on our toes all the time on an ack-ack gun, you know that. If people aren't working properly together they make mistakes, and you know what that could mean.'

An enemy aircraft getting through, Olive had thought. Bombing Pompey. Or machine-gunning people in the streets, like poor Mrs Shaw had been machine-gunned.

'Well, all right, we can talk to each other on the gun,' she had said. 'But—'

'But nothing. We're friends. We can talk to each other about anything. You tell me about Derek, and I tell you about Dorothy. We spend some of our off-duty time together. We help each other get through.' His eyes were very dark. 'Livvy, I need you for my friend. It won't be any more than that. I *promise* you it won't be any more, but I need you.'

She had stared at him for a few moments. The last few weeks, since they had agreed to stop seeing each other, had been as lonely for her as for him. She had filled her time with writing letters to Derek, visiting her family, going to the cinema with other girls, but a part of her had remained unsatisfied, the part that needed male company. Not sex, she thought, not lovemaking, just company. A friend – a male friend.

'I've really missed you, Ray,' she had said suddenly, and taken half a step forwards, 'but I can't—'

'I know.' He had seen that small movement and she could tell that he knew what it meant. 'It'll be all right. So long as we know where the limits are. So long as we don't . . . touch each other.'

Olive had nodded, smiling a little tremulously. 'That's it. So long as we don't touch each other. Then there can't be any harm in it at all. Can there?'

So that was the bargain, and as they walked back to camp from April Grove through the darkened streets of Portsmouth, each was scrupulous about keeping the right amount of distance between them, so that their arms should not touch, their swinging hands not meet.

Nobody could say there was any harm in that.

Gladys had been home too. She had cooked her father a good dinner and it was ready on the table when he came in from work. His heavy face lightened at the smell of meat and onions that greeted him as he came through the door.

'That's a bit more like home. It's a treat to come in to the house with the lights on and a bit of fire in the grate, and the smell of something cooking.' He sat down in his sagging armchair and pulled off his boots. 'It's what a bloke needs after a hard day's work.'

'I know, Dad.' Gladys thought of his life as it was now: setting out in the morning with no more than a bit of bread inside him, eating his dinner in the factory canteen, and then arriving back to a cold house and having to get his own supper ready. There was all the shopping to do too – which meant standing in queues for hours on end, as likely as not – and his clothes to wash and the place to be kept clean and tidy. Though it looked as though that went by the board a bit, she thought, noticing the dust lying thickly on the sideboard that her mother had always kept so brightly polished, and the grubby shirts hung round the fireplace. It was a good scrub and a boil they needed, not the half-hearted swish round in the sink that was probably all that Bert gave them.

It *is* hard on him, she thought, feeling the familiar guilt creep over her, but what can I do? It's a wife he needs, someone who'll be happy to stay at home and do everything for him. It's Mum he needs.

She told Cliff about it the next day as they went for a walk around the streets. He listened and nodded.

'I know, Glad, but we've been all over this before. You can't spend your life dancing attendance on your dad. It'd make life easier for him – and harder for you. You're worth more than just being a skivvy.'

'I suppose so, but Mum never thought she was a skivvy. She did all sorts of things – worked at the first aid post, helped with the church, gave other people a hand.' They stopped beside a bomb site and stared at the broken ground which had been covered by weeds and flowers all summer and was now a dismal tangle of dead foliage. 'If I was at home, I could do those things too. I wouldn't have to stay indoors all the time.'

'You could,' he said. 'You're like your mum – you like to keep busy and you like to be doing something worthwhile. What you've got to decide is what's most worthwhile – serving your country or looking after your dad.'

'I know,' she said uncertainly 'but he needs me . . .'

'So do the rest of us,' he said, and then stopped suddenly and stared at her. He put out his hands and touched her arms, lightly at first, and then gripped them with sudden strength. Startled, she looked up into his eyes and saw their expression darken and change. He's looking at me as if he's never seen me before, she thought a little nervously, and remembered stories of men going 'funny' after having been in action. Shellshock, they'd called it in the last war, and it could come on months after they'd returned home.

She opened her mouth and tried to draw away, but Clifford was already speaking again, his voice quiet and trembling a little. 'The rest of us need you too. Gladys – *I* need you.'

Before she knew what was happening, he had caught her against him and kissed her parted lips. For a moment, she was too surprised to resist but then an unexpected thrill of sensation ran through her body and she jerked herself free.

*'Clifford . . . '*

'Oh, God, Gladys, I'm sorry. I never meant to do that. I just – it just came over me.'

He took a step towards her but she backed away. I ought to slap his face, she thought, but she couldn't bring herself to do it. He'd been so nice to her, so understanding . . . It's just a kiss, she told herself, it doesn't mean he's going to throw me down on the ground and jump on me. It doesn't mean *anything*. She watched him warily, though, and took another step back.

Clifford stopped and stood still, his hands hanging at his sides. There was such a look of abject apology on his face, that she almost relented, but you couldn't afford to take chances, not with a young chap who thought he was going to be sent to France any day and likely to be killed. She remembered Graham Philpotts telling her once what it was like to go away, never having known what sex was like, and thinking you were never going to get the chance to find out. She didn't know what experience Clifford Weeks might have had, but she didn't want him finding out with her.

'Don't think bad of me, Gladys.' His voice was desperate. 'I really am sorry – I never meant it to happen. But it's not just all of a sudden. It started that time I stayed at Uncle Tommy's. I saw you going up and down the street, and – I dunno, I just couldn't stop thinking about you. I couldn't get your face out of my mind. I was going to come and see you, ask you out, but I didn't have the nerve. And then your mum – I couldn't, not after that. That afternoon, when I saw you go by the window and I knew you'd just had the funeral and all, I thought I can't come out and speak to you, it's not the right time – but I had to. You looked so miserable, I just wanted to put my arms round you and hug you. And when we went for that walk and you said you'd write to me – well, I knew it could never be any more than that, but I thought, if we can just be friends . . . I thought, maybe it'll go away, maybe I won't want anything more. But all those letters we've written, and the times we've seen each other, have just made it worse. I'm in love with you, Gladys,' he finished. 'I can't help it. I think you're the most wonderful girl in the world.'

Gladys stared at him. To think that he had been watching her, longing for her . . . It was flattering, exciting – but even as she admitted that, she felt herself withdraw. I don't want to get involved, she thought. Not with him, not with anyone.

'D'you reckon there's any chance for me?' he asked humbly. 'I mean, d'you think you could ever – well, *like* me?'

'I do like you,' Gladys said before she could stop herself, 'but not in that way, Cliff. How could I? I know we were kids together, kicking a ball about out in the street when you came to stay with your auntie and uncle, but we're grown up now, we're different.'

'I don't know,' he said. 'I don't think I've changed all that much, and you still seem the same old Glad to me. I always did like you, you know.'

'We *are* different,' she insisted. 'We're bound to be. Look at all the things that have happened to us.' She lifted her hands. 'Look, I like being with you, I like writing to you and getting your letters. I like being friends with you, but that doesn't mean any more than that.'

'It does to me,' he said. 'Glad, I've never felt this way about anyone. I've had girlfriends but I've never felt I was in love with any of them. I'm in love with you, and nothing you can say will alter that.'

Gladys gazed at him helplessly. He was still standing quite separate from her, but the look in his eyes was so intense that it was almost as though he held her in his arms. She felt a small thrill of fear, and he saw the change in her expression and took another step away.

'Gladys, I'm sorry. I don't want to upset you. I didn't mean to say anything – I knew there couldn't be any chance for me, a girl like you's bound to have all sorts of blokes after her – but I just couldn't help it.' He held out his hands, palms upwards. 'Forget I said anything, can you? I'll walk you home.'

'Oh, Cliff,' she said, near to tears. 'It isn't that I don't like you. And you know I don't have any other boyfriends. I write to Colin Chapman in the Japanese POW camp, but I don't think he's really interested in me. It's just that – well, you took me by surprise.'

'I know. I'm sorry. I couldn't help it.' Tentatively, he reached out one hand, not quite touching her. 'Friends?'

'Of course we're friends,' she said, relief washing over her. She took his hand and held it firmly. 'And I'm sorry too.'

They turned and began to walk slowly back. After a few minutes, he said quietly, 'I won't give up hoping, Glad. I shan't keep on about it – but as long as we keep writing to each other, as long as we're friends, I'll always keep hoping.'

'It won't do any good,' she said. 'It really won't. Not while this war's on, anyway.'

'We'll just have to wait till it's over, then,' he said, and stopped again, still holding her hand so that she had to stop too. He looked down at her. 'I'll wait as long as you want, Gladys,' he said. 'As long as there's hope for me, I'm ready to wait.'

It was baby Roderick's first birthday.

Carol woke early that morning. She sat up and reached, as always, for the doll.

'A year old,' she said softly. She cradled it in her arms and stared down at its scratched, painted face. 'My little Roderick would be a year old today.'

She'd slept badly, her dreams filled with memories of a year ago: the long wait over at last, the first dull ache of labour spreading to become a vicious cramping pain, the sudden deluge of her waters breaking. The terror as she waited to die, convinced that no one could experience such agony and live. And the first bewildered, angry cry of her baby, breaking into her pain, and flooding her with totally unexpected emotion.

'My baby,' she had whispered, half sitting up and reaching out. 'My baby . . . '

They hadn't given him to her at once. He'd had to be washed and weighed and examined, and wrapped tightly in a bundle of napkin and vest and nightgown. It was two days before Carol saw him naked, but she'd held him in her arms at last, and looked down at the tiny, crumpled red face and seen Roddy. She'd known then what it meant to be a mother, and she'd understood already what it was going to mean to lose him.

He'd looked so nice that last day, waiting in Mrs Whiting's office, dressed in his little frock and cardigan that she'd made for him, but it was the way he'd smiled at her, a real smile full of love, that had struck her at the heart. He knew me, she thought. He knew I was his mother. And then I gave him away . . .

Mrs Whiting had taken him out of her arms and held him for a moment or two before giving him to the other woman. Carol didn't want to look, didn't want to see someone else take him and hold him, as if he was theirs – and he *was* theirs now – but she couldn't help it.

'He's called Roderick,' she said. They hadn't even looked at her until now, but the woman glanced up and met her eyes.

'We're not going to call him that. We're going to call him Christopher. Christopher Mark.'

Christopher Mark. They were two nice names, but now Carol hated them. 'Roderick's his daddy's name.'

The woman's face grew cold. 'No. Mark is his daddy's name.' She cradled Roderick in one arm and took her husband's arm with her free hand. 'And we both like Christopher.'

'But he's *used* to Roderick. He'll get muddled up – he'll miss me . . . ' Her voice was rising and Mrs Whiting stepped forwards. She was accustomed to dealing with girls who grew hysterical at this moment. It didn't matter how eager they'd been to give their babies away, they all seemed to want to make a fuss when it came to the point.

'Don't be ridiculous, Carol. The baby can't possibly be used to a name, he's only six weeks old. It doesn't matter to him what he's called, or who looks after him.'

'It does. It *does*. He knows me. He knows his name . . . '

It hadn't been any good. The couple had taken Roderick away, and by now he must be used to being called Christopher. By now, he had forgotten all about her.

She felt sick. Her baby had forgotten all about her. He'd smiled at her once and then forgotten. He thought that other woman was his mother. Perhaps he would always think so. She wondered if they would ever tell him the truth.

'Well, that's that,' Mrs Whiting had said, watching the couple walk away down the path that day, the woman carrying Roderick – *Christopher Mark* – in her arms. 'I'm sure they'll bring him up very nicely too, far better than you could have managed. Now then, Carol, it's no use mooning about the place like a wet weekend. You'd better go up to your bedroom and get your things packed, ready for tomorrow. You're going to Devon, to your auntie's, I believe. What a lucky girl.'

What a lucky girl. Carol had just been forced to give her baby away and this stupid woman, this *cow*, called her a lucky girl, to be able to go to her auntie in Devon.

Carol had said nothing. She'd just stared at Mrs Whiting and then walked out of the room.

The door snapped open and Ethel stared in. Her hard blue eyes looked small and mean. Her lip curled in a sneer.

'A great girl like you, playing with a doll! Whatever next? You'll be sucking your dummy at this rate.'

'Go away, Mum,' Carol said. 'Go away and leave me alone.'

Ethel bridled angrily. 'Go away? That's a fine way to talk to your mother, I must say. After all I've done for you: standing by you when you brought all that trouble on yourself, seeing to it that the neighbours didn't know, till that woman sent a telegram saying you'd had the baby – it wouldn't never have leaked out if she hadn't done that – letting you go down to Devon for a holiday, and then having you back here at home. There's many a mother would have just washed their hands of you at the outset, I'll have you know. And now *you've* got a nice clean job sitting on your backside doing sewing, with a proper machine, while *I* have to scrape about on the floor like some guttersnipe.' She stood in Carol's doorway, arms akimbo, glowering. 'You haven't even got the common decency to do a hand's turn when you come home. Make your mother a cup of tea of a morning? Oh no! Stop in bed, laying about playing with a *doll*! Just as if I hadn't got enough to put up with . . .'

Her voice went on and on, railing at Carol like she used to rail at George. Suddenly, Carol had had enough. She got up and pushed past her mother, almost falling downstairs in her desperation to escape, and then dragged her old coat from its hook and pulled it over her nightie as she ran out of the back door, through the 'conservatory' and down the garden to the back alley.

She walked blindly for miles through the dark, cold streets. Slowly, the sky grew lighter and people began to hurry past, on their way to work or coming home from a night shift. Occasionally, she saw a baby in a pram or in its mother's arms. She saw her own baby over and over again, lying in her arms and smiling up at her.

Roderick. Roderick. A year old today. Crawling. Walking. Talking. Laughing and chuckling, playing with his toys.

She did not even know what toys he had.

A wave of panic swept over her. Suppose the Sutcliffes were being unkind to him. Suppose they were being *cruel*. Suppose the old cow at the home, Mrs Whiting, was wrong, and he did know Carol was his mother, suppose he was still missing her, crying for her. Suppose he actually lived in one of the houses she was passing now, sensing that she was there, screaming for her to hold him in her arms again . . .

Her grip on reality shifted and blurred. Her memory of the months since she had handed him over faded, and her steps quickened as she began to search for him. She had left him somewhere – given him away – lost him. He was in danger without her.

And she was in danger, without him.

There were more people on the streets now. The seeping grey light showed their faces, tired and lined with care, most of them too intent on their own concerns to bother with a young girl running along the pavement with an old coat thrown over her nightdress, but a few glanced at her with more interest, and one or two men called or whistled after her as she ran.

'Bin on night shift, girl?'

'Go on, 'urry up, e'll never know you bin out if you gets 'ome quick.'

And, from one who barred her way with outstretched arms and leered at her, 'Give us a kiss, then. I bet you bin at it all night, aincher? You can spare another one.'

Carol stopped. Her mind shifted again, and she stared wildly at him, and then around her at the grey streets, at the boarded windows of shops that had been bombed, at the roughly filled-in craters in the road. She remembered handing Roderick to the Sutcliffes, remembered coming home without him, remembered the doll.

'Let go of me,' she whispered, and twisted her arms away from the man's big, dirty hands. *'Let go of me!'*

She turned and ran again, ran through endless streets of torn and broken houses, ran past gaping holes where once there had been people's homes, ran through a city that had become a nightmare of destruction yet seemed no more than an echo of her own despair.

At last, cold, weary and conscious of a gnawing hollowness deep inside her, she turned and retraced her steps for home. Her mother had already left for work. Carol knew that if she did not report to the barracks, she would be in trouble.

She let herself into the silent house and dragged slowly upstairs. The doll lay like an abandoned baby in the middle of the bedroom floor.

# CHAPTER ELEVEN

'They say turkeys are going to be short this Christmas,' Jess said as the Budd family sat down to shepherd's pie. Annie and Ted had come down too, with Olive who had the afternoon off.

'Why, how tall are they usually?' Tim asked, and fell against his brother, both giggling.

Frank smiled and Cherry, who was spending Saturday with the family, pointed her fork at Tim and chuckled, her cottage-loaf body shaking. 'My godfathers, you're a star turn, you are. Always got an answer for everything, you have.'

Maureen frowned and rubbed her chin, as she often did when about to ask a question. 'What answer? Tim didn't answer. He went up at the end.'

'There isn't an answer,' Jess said. 'Eat your dinner, Maureen.'

'But Tim said, how tall are they?' Her face creased with the frustration of not being able to understand. 'I want to know how tall they are.'

'They're not tall,' Jess said. 'Nobody said anything about them being tall.'

'Tim did. He *did*.'

'No, he asked—' Jess stopped, remembering Tim's words. 'Well, he didn't mean that. It was a joke. Now be quiet and eat—'

'*What* joke?' Maureen's face was reddening ominously. 'I didn't hear a joke.'

'You wouldn't know what a joke was if it hit you on the nose,' Rose observed, and Maureen turned towards her at once.

'It's *not* to hit me on the nose! Mummy, Rose said—'

'I know what she said. She didn't mean it.' Maureen's voice was rising and Jess knew that if she were not pacified quickly there would be uproar. 'Don't tease, her, Rose. It's all right, Maureen,' she went on, ignoring her elder daughter's indignation, 'nobody's going to hit anyone on the nose.

Tim just made a silly joke, that's all, and it's not your fault you can't understand it. Come on now, take that look off your face and eat up your dinner.'

Maureen looked round the table. Everyone was watching her, a situation she half enjoyed and half hated. She hesitated, her fork hovering over the mound of meat and potato. It was touch and go, Jess thought, whether she laughed or cried.

Cherry smiled broadly at her, then wiped her hand across her mouth and made a throwing motion. 'See if you can catch my smile! Look, it's landed right on your face.' Usually this worked and Maureen grinned involuntarily, but today the corners of her mouth remained turned down. 'Come on,' Cherry encouraged her, 'let it land properly.'

'It's upside down,' Maureen said, half in tears still, and stared as the whole family roared with laughter. She turned to Jess, stretching out her arms. *'Mummy . . . '*

'It's all right.' Jess, laughing herself, drew her close. 'It's all right. They're laughing because it was a joke. You made a joke.'

'*I* made a joke? My very own self? Like Tim?'

'Yes,' Jess nodded, 'a very good joke too. See, it's made everyone laugh. So now you can smile and eat up your dinner, all right? And not another word.'

Maureen, dazed by her success, returned her attention to her plate. Jess went on talking.

'There's going to be a quota. One in every ten families will get a turkey this Christmas. The government's promised that all the American troops stationed over here will get a turkey for Christmas dinner, to make up for being away from their homes.'

'And what about our chaps?' Olive said indignantly. 'Most of them are away from home, and *they* won't be getting turkeys.'

'I reckon the Yanks get well enough served anyway,' Annie agreed. 'More chocolate than they know what to do with, and plenty of money in their pockets. I saw a bunch of 'em down in Commercial Road the other day, chucking pennies at a crowd of nippers that was following them about. You should have heard the children: "Got any gum, chum?" I mean, it's no better than begging.'

'It's no different from what the mudlarks used to do,' Tim said, a little enviously. Jess and Frank had always forbidden the two boys to go 'mudlarking' – wading in the harbour mud down by the Hard at low tide, calling up to passers-by who were using the slipway up from the ferry pontoon and asking for pennies. They'd been one of the sights of Pompey, scrabbling down there in the black mire. The war had put a stop to that, as it had to so many other things, and there weren't so many ways a boy could cadge himself a few coppers to spend.

'That doesn't make it right,' Jess told him severely. 'You know what your father always says. Any money that comes into this house has to be earned.'

'So spend it before you come home,' Tim whispered to Keith, but Frank heard him and his face darkened.

'*Tim!* You'll apologise to your mother at once. Don't let me hear you talk like that again.' His voice was like thunder, and Maureen shrank in her chair and began to cry. Frank ignored her and glowered at Tim. 'You're getting above yourself just lately. Just because you're out at work, you think you're grown up. Let me tell you, you'll be under my control for another seven years yet, and if it had been left to me you'd still be at school. I never was in favour of him leaving so soon,' he added to Jess.

'Ssh, ssh, it's all right,' Jess murmured to the sobbing Maureen. 'Frank, there's no need to shout like that, frightening the baby. You know what Tim's like, he can't help making jokes, it's like a sort of twitch. He's not so very different from what you used to be yourself, you know. I know we wanted him to have more education, but that was before the war started and we could see a different future. At least he's got a good apprenticeship, you've always said it's a good apprenticeship on the ferries. He'll have a trade, isn't that right, Ted?'

'That's right,' Ted affirmed. 'He don't need to stop on the ferry all his life. Once he's got his papers he can go anywhere, and there's always night school.'

Frank grunted. He knew all about night school. He had been forced to leave school himself at the age of twelve, when his own father had died, and there'd been no one else to help his mother support the family. He had done errands for a local chemist, just like Tim had done last summer, and when he'd got his apprenticeship to old Sam Barnes, the blacksmith, he'd gone to night school three or four nights a week, learning maths and English till he could have passed the exams the other children had been able to do at schools like Portsmouth Grammar. However, he'd never taken the exams. It had been more important to finish his apprenticeship and get a tradesman's wage in the dockyard, while his younger brother Howard stayed on at school and enjoyed all the advantages Frank had missed.

'That's all very well,' he said to Jess. 'I don't say the boy's not doing well enough at work. It's his behaviour at home that I don't like. He's getting cheeky and big headed, and it's time he remembered his place. He's lucky he's not getting called up for this ballot for the coal mines that Mr Bevin announced. Thirty thousand lads there's going to be, picked out by ballot. He could just as easy have been one of them. I don't want to hear you answering your mother back again, d'you hear me?' he said to Tim. 'And if you've finished your dinner you can come and help me over the allotment. There's plenty to do there for idle hands. You as well, Keith.' He got up from the table and walked out. They heard him in the scullery, putting on his boots and collecting his gardening jacket from the hook inside the staircase door. The boys glanced at each other and grimaced before going out after him.

Ted wiped his mouth and got up too. 'I'd better go and do a bit on me own patch.' He nodded at Jess. 'That was a nice dinner, Jess. I always did like your shepherd's pie. See you at home later on, Annie.' He followed Frank outside.

Rose went out too, saying she was going up to see Joy Brunner, and Jess looked at the other women and turned the corners of her mouth down a little.

'I don't know what's got into Frank lately. He's never been the most patient of men but the least little thing seems to set him off these days. I mean, Tim wasn't really being cheeky or answering back, he was just being – well, Tim. He's always been one for a joke. Boys are.'

'It's the war,' Annie said. 'It's getting on everyone's nerves. We've all had just about enough, with no sign of it coming to an end. And all these restrictions they're putting on. You can't hardly move these days without someone telling you you shouldn't have. We're all fed up with it.'

Cherry nodded her round little head. 'It's hard work in the yard, too. You wouldn't believe how men like Frank have to keep at it, all day long, with hardly a break. They only get half an hour for their dinner, you know, and no fresh air. That boiler shop where me and Frank work, it's like a steam oven, and the draughts that come in from outside cut through you like knives, they're that cold. It's no wonder he gets tired to death.'

Jess looked at her. She could never quite get used to the fact that Cherry worked alongside Frank, that she spent more daytime hours with him than Jess herself had ever done, that she knew things about him Jess would probably never know. She remembered how Frank had first told her that they were bringing in women to work in the dockyard, how he'd disliked the idea and how he'd slowly thawed towards this 'Cherry', talking about her until Jess – thinking all the time she was no more than a girl – had begun to get quite worried. She'd realised the minute she'd met Cherry that there was nothing whatsoever to worry about, and now the two women were fast friends, but it still seemed queer that Frank should have a woman friend. And queerer still that Cherry could tease him and even tell him off a bit, not in the least afraid of him. Most people found Frank a bit intimidating.

'I know he gets tired,' Jess said thoughtfully, 'and he worries about it all, too. But he works so hard, he won't let us see how tired and worried he is most of the time. He keeps it all to himself. I suppose most men are like that.'

'It don't do 'em no good, though,' Annie said. 'Look how my Ted cracked up that time. The doctor said that came from keeping it all bottled up, but you can't tell men that. They're used to being the strong ones, can't understand that everyone's got to give way sometimes.'

Cherry nodded again. 'Even Mr Churchill. They say he's poorly again – got a chest infection. I wouldn't be surprised if it's pneumonia myself. He's that sort, thick chested, you know.'

'Oh, I hope not,' Jess said. 'I don't know what we'd do without Mr Churchill. He keeps us all going. Pneumonia'd be serious, specially at his age. He's not a young man, you know, he'll be seventy next year.'

'Be a good thing if he handed over to a younger man, then,' Olive said. 'Someone who might get us out of the war instead of digging us further in. You needn't look like that, Mum,' she said to Annie. 'There's quite a lot of people would like to see the back of Mr Churchill. This war's been a godsend to him. He was nothing before it started – nothing. Now he's cock of the walk and he's enjoying it. Playing soldiers like a little boy, that's what he's doing – playing soldiers. The only difference is, he's got real live soldiers instead of tin ones.' She stood up suddenly. 'Sorry, Auntie Jess, I didn't mean to carry on like that, but Uncle Frank's not the only one who's fed up with it. It's people like me whose lives are being ruined. Our blokes sent away, God knows where, for years on end – getting wounded and killed – and no chance of us settling down and starting our own families. And all because high-ups like Mr Churchill say we've got to go to war. *We've* got to go to war, while they stay comfortable at home and move us around like – like counters on a Ludo board! Well, it's time they took their turn, that's what I say, time *they* went off and lived in tents in the desert, never knowing whether they might be shot or blown up. It's time they gave decent people a bit of rest from it all.' She turned back to her mother. 'I'll have to go now, Mum, I'm due back on duty. I'll come in again some time during the week. Take care of Gran for me.'

She went out and they heard her footsteps fade away up April Grove. Jess, Annie and Cherry looked at each other and sighed.

'Well, it's up to us, as usual,' Annie said after a moment. 'Keep the home fires burning, keep smiling through, keep our peckers up and all the rest of it. Thank goodness for nippers like your Tim who can still find something to laugh at, that's what I say. And little innocents like Maureen here, who don't know what it's all about.' She bent and kissed her niece, who was in her usual place on the floor, playing with her bag of marbles and box of bricks. 'You're a little love, you are, and you're going to have such a lovely time when peace comes back again.'

Maureen looked up at her. The familiar little frown of puzzlement creased her smooth forehead and she rubbed her chin.

'Where's peace *been*, Auntie Annie?' And then, as they all looked at her, 'Auntie Annie, what *is* peace?'

Clifford got a few days' leave just before Christmas, and came to spend it with his uncle and aunt in April Grove. The minute he had dumped his kitbag in their back bedroom, he was off down to number 13 to see Gladys.

'She's not here,' Bert Shaw said, peering at him suspiciously as he stood at the front door. 'She sent word to say she'd be here Christmas Eve, and she can only stop for dinner and tea then. You'd think they'd let a girl come home of a Christmas,' he went on indignantly. 'Specially when she knows her dad's here all on his own.'

'Aren't you going in next door for Christmas Day, then?' Cliff asked innocently. Gladys had told him that the Budds had invited him to dinner with them. Bert snorted and looked down his nose.

'Up Annie Chapman's, that's where I got to go. I'm not saying it's not good of them, mind, but a bloke wants to be in his own home of a Christmas, not with strangers. In his own home, with his family round him.' He glared at Cliff as though it was his fault. 'I never bin in Annie Chapman's house. I won't know where to sit.'

Cliff suppressed a grin. 'I expect they'll tell you. So when's Gladys expecting to get here, then? In the morning?'

'I told you, she'll be here for her dinner.' Bert gave him an unwelcoming stare. 'She won't be wanting no visitors, neither. It's her dad she's coming to see.'

'Well, I hope she'll have time to say hallo to me as well,' Cliff remarked. 'I think a lot of your Gladys, you know. Always have done, ever since we were kids.'

'I dunno about that. As I remember it, you was always pulling her hair and running off. Anyway, it won't be no use you coming in and expecting your tea at our house. We're on rations. There's a war on, in case you didn't know.'

'I had noticed,' Cliff said dryly. 'They do tell us the news in the Army, Mr Shaw. You needn't worry: I don't want to eat your rations. I just want to see Gladys and perhaps go for a bit of a walk, that's all.'

'I told you, she's only here for the day—'

'It's all right. I won't take her away from you.' Cliff looked at the older man and felt suddenly sorry for him. Until now, he'd been irritated with Bert and considered him selfish and possessive, but for a moment he saw him with different eyes – a bewildered man, too old for all this change, who had lost both his daughters and his wife within a few weeks, and who didn't even know when he would see his son again. He saw Bert, standing in his shirtsleeves, his braces dangling, his eyes tired and his face unshaven, and thought of how he'd been when Peggy Shaw was alive: always tidy, his clothes pressed, his body strong and healthy. Now, he sagged and his flesh looked muddy and sallow.

'I won't take her away from you,' he repeated gently. 'We'll just sit in the front room for half an hour and have a talk, that's all. I don't want to spoil your Christmas.'

Bert shrugged and turned to go back indoors.

Cliff went slowly back up April Grove, feeling oddly saddened. Bert hadn't said he couldn't go to see Gladys, and in any case Cliff was determined that he would, but he knew that whatever time they had together, it would be too short. Since the day he had first realised that he was in love with Gladys Shaw, his feelings had grown steadily stronger. He knew that he wanted her for his wife. He had told her he was prepared to wait until after the war was over, but now he wanted to know that she was his, that she was at least promised to him, before he was sent away.

He had intended to propose to her at Christmas, but he saw now that he would have to wait a little longer. It wasn't just Gladys who needed time – it was Bert Shaw himself.

He could not just take his daughter away from this pathetic man.

Christmas came and went without any sign of a truce. The RAF bombed Berlin on Christmas Eve and the people of Portsmouth felt a wry satisfaction in having been revenged for the Christmas Eve attacks on their own city in previous years. Even so, Jess couldn't help feeling sad for the little children over there who might have been just opening their own Christmas presents when the raid began. She thought of the broken dolls and shattered toys, and wept a little, but said nothing to Frank. He was low enough himself these days.

Cherry spent Christmas with them and the two families got together as usual in Annie's house, though their numbers were sadly depleted. Colin Chapman was still in Japanese hands and his short, infrequent letters told Annie and Ted very little. They knew that there were horrific stories circulating about what was going on in the prison camps and could only hope that they weren't true, or were confined to camps other than the one Colin was in.

Betty and Dennis stayed out on the farm at Bishop's Waltham. Old Jonas had died at last, succumbing to a bad attack of bronchitis which had turned to pneumonia, and they moved into his cottage a few days before Christmas. It needed a lot of cleaning and scrubbing, Betty had written to her mother, and it didn't seem right to take too much time off when Mr Spencer had already lost one farmhand, so they were going to spend most of the short holiday settling in.

'Pneumonia,' Cherry said. 'That's what Mr Churchill's had. I told you it was serious.'

'He's getting better, though,' Jess said. 'He's been treated with some new sort of medicine. Penicillin, they call it. It's a wonderful thing, they reckon it'll cure all sorts of diseases. They're using it on the troops too, Frank says.'

The lack of turkeys didn't bother the Chapmans and Budds. Jess and Frank had never been able to afford such luxuries, and although Annie had taken a pride in providing a good table at Christmas, she kept her grumbles to herself. Frank killed one of the cockerels which he'd been fattening up and they all had a bit – not a very big bit, it was true, but it went down well with a couple of sausages and plenty of vegetables from the allotment. The women had put together all their ration of sugar and butter and dried fruit to make a Christmas pudding every bit as good as in peacetime.

Bert Shaw came in for his Christmas dinner and tried to be cheerful, but his face kept settling into lugubrious lines, like a jowly, mournful dog. He missed Peggy badly, and resented the fact that both his daughters had left him to join the Services. Diane was on the RAF station, and Gladys had been posted to one of the numerous small Naval stations that had been set up in unlikely places all around Portsmouth – hotels, schools, even (on Hayling Island) collections of bathing huts. She came home when she could, but never said anything about her work, and this annoyed Bert even more.

'Given up my whole family for this bloody war,' he said. 'There's Bob out in Africa, my Peggy gunned down in the street and neither of those two girls got the common humanity to stop home and look after their dad. I mean, what can bits of girls like that be doing that's more important than family responsibilities? I dunno what the world's coming to.'

'Everyone has to do what they think's right,' Jess said. 'And you know they'd have been called up anyway. At least they got a bit of choice through volunteering.'

'They didn't have to go in the Forces, though, did they?' he said argumentatively. 'Coulda gone down one of the factories like that Ethel Glaister, or gone out Eastney doing tailoring like her Carol. I tell you what, it don't make sense to me, that young madam getting a plum job like that and stopping at home in comfort while decent girls like my Gladys and Diane has to go and sleep in tin huts. They talk about justice, but where's the justice in that, I ask you?'

'You don't know what Carol's been through,' Jess said. 'I know she did wrong, but to hear her mother carrying on at her sometimes I reckon she's getting her punishment all right. Anyway, you're changing your tune a bit, aren't you? A minute ago you were moaning about your girls, now you sound sorry for them.'

Bert looked startled at Jess's sharp tone. He bent his head over his plate but everyone could see the dark flush spreading up his neck. He muttered something nobody could hear, and Cherry said something about the Bevin boys who had been chosen by ballot to go down the mines.

'Six hundred of them, they're starting with,' she said. 'They want thirty thousand. Think of that – thirty thousand! There's a lot of lads going to get a shock when they find out what it's like to work down the pit.'

Everyone knew about the Bevin boys, but Cherry was the only one who knew what it was like to live in a mining area. There were a lot of mines where she came from, near Birmingham. She described the conditions to them and they tried to imagine what it must be like, living under a constant pall of smoke with coal dust being trodden everywhere.

'That's why they call it the Black Country,' she said. 'It gets everywhere. In your eyes, in your nose, sometimes you seem to be eating and drinking the stuff. And the washing! You can see the smuts landing as you hang it out.'

'Why hang it out, then?' Tim asked. 'I mean, if it's getting dirty again straight away . . . ' He wasn't really interested in washing, but it was a long time since he'd had anything to say, and it did seem a bit silly. 'Why don't they hang it round the fire, like Mum does when it rains?'

'Oh, you've got to have some fresh air blow through it,' Cherry said. 'It's not the same else.'

Annie thought it would be horrible to live in such a dirty place. 'It's bad enough in Pompey sometimes, and those smoke machines they use make it worse. But to live where it's like it all the time – how do they keep their steps white, and their windows clean and all that?'

'Just keep doing them, every day,' Cherry answered. 'Mind you, some of the really poor streets don't bother, right slums they are.'

Tim wondered what it would be like to go down a coal mine. His imagination showed him a picture of deep tunnels, with sparkling icy formations, like those he'd seen in pictures of Cheddar Caves. 'They have trains, don't they? With trucks to carry the coal. I wouldn't mind driving one of those.'

'Not like the trains that go by the bottom of the garden,' Frank told him. 'And you wouldn't like driving them, either. It's not a funfair down a coal mine. It's dark and dirty and it's hard work. You be thankful you've got a good apprenticeship on the ferry, and haven't been picked to be a Bevin boy.'

Tim looked mutinous. He didn't like being told what he would enjoy and what he wouldn't. He wanted to experience everything, to know for himself what it was like. 'I bet they get paid more than me,' he said. 'And I bet they don't have to give it all to their mum – they don't live at home.'

'They don't get much, all the same,' Cherry said. She seemed to know a lot about them – perhaps she was more interested because she knew about mines and miners. 'I read about it. Two pounds ten shillings and six a week – yes, I know it sounds a lot, Tim, but you mind what they have to pay out of that. They got to pay for their hostel, their meals, their washing, insurance, and their fares to the mines and anything else that comes along. The bit I read said they got three and sixpence pocket money. That's not much for spending twelve hours a day underground, hacking coal out of the rock, with never a sniff of fresh air.'

After dinner, Olive got up to go. She and the other ATS girls who had come out to have Christmas dinner with their families were due back at the camp by three, so that the rest who lived locally could get home for a few hours. She walked off up March Street, feeling fed up, trying to picture Derek away in Africa.

It couldn't seem a bit like Christmas, out there in the hot sun and with all that sand as far as the eye could see. She wondered what they'd had for dinner. Or if they'd even *had* their dinner yet. It must be quite a different time of day where he was, and she'd almost given up trying to remember what the difference was.

In fact, Olive was finding it more and more difficult to relate to her thoughts of Derek these days. It wasn't that she didn't love him just as much, but he'd been away so long that she could hardly remember what it was like to be with him. She couldn't even picture his face sometimes, without the aid of the photo she kept by her bed. It frightened her — the fact that when she tried to imagine him, all she could conjure up was a sort of blur. It made her feel guilty, as if she was betraying him.

'I wonder sometimes just how we'll get on when he eventually comes home,' she'd said to Claudia one day. 'I mean, what will we talk about? Suppose we don't have anything in common any more?'

'I should think you'll find plenty to talk about,' Claudia said, polishing her nails. Nothing kept Claudia from making sure she looked her best, though she wasn't vain and silly like one or two of the girls in their hut. 'You'll have years to catch up on.'

'Years! Oh, don't say that, Claud.' But it was already one year, and no sign of the unit returning, and the world seemed to be sinking deeper and deeper into a permanent state of war. 'What I'm worried about is that we'll have changed. Both of us. I mean, it's bound to change us, isn't it? Me being in the ATS and working on guns, and him out there in the desert. We were going to live an ordinary life, in our own house with our own children, and Derek would have had a good job as an accountant, or perhaps taken over his dad's building business.'

'And I daresay that's just what you will do.' Claudia spoke briskly, then paused and looked at Olive's woebegone face. 'I'm sorry, Livvy. I know what you mean. You *will* be different. We all will. Somehow we're all going to have to find out how to live normal lives again, and it might not be as easy as we think.'

Olive was beginning to think it wouldn't be easy at all. We'll be different people, she thought, Derek and me. Two different people. Living in a different world.

Back in camp, she didn't go straight to her hut. Instead, she wandered on along what used to be Southsea Common, now cordoned off from the town and barred to civilians. There was something going on out on the beach, something you were supposed to pretend you hadn't noticed. A lot of concrete was being mixed and slipways being built, but it wasn't just that. There were big sections, like floating walls, that nobody knew the use of.

'Happy Christmas, Livvy.'

The voice was quite quiet, but it made Olive jump. She looked round and saw Ray, leaning against a wall, watching her. His mouth was smiling but his eyes were serious.

'Ray—'

'Don't tell me to go away,' he said, before she could go on. 'Not on Christmas Day.'

She shook her head. 'I wasn't going to. Happy Christmas, Ray,' and then, 'That's a daft thing to say. It can't be very happy for you, not being with your little girl.'

He shrugged. 'I'm getting used to that. Anyway, seeing you makes up for it.' He shifted away from the wall and came towards her, one hand in the pocket of his greatcoat. 'I've got something for you, Livvy.'

'Oh.' She watched uncertainly as he drew out his hand and held it towards her. 'Ray, you mustn't – I can't . . . '

'Please.' He held a tiny parcel. 'It doesn't have to mean anything, Livvy. It's just – well, I wanted to give you something, that's all.' He added a little desperately, 'I've got to be able to give *someone* a Christmas present.'

'Oh, Ray.' Olive gazed at him, struck to the heart by the implication. 'D'you mean to say you couldn't – your wife wouldn't even let you . . . '

'I sent Dorothy a few bits and pieces,' he said flatly. 'Not much – there's not much you can get for kids these days, but you'd have thought Joan would've still . . . I'm her *dad*, for God's sake. Anyway, she sent 'em back. Came in yesterday's post.' His lips twisted. 'I thought for a minute it was a present for me – then I realised it was my own writing and I knew what she'd done. I took 'em round to the children's home last night and left 'em on the doorstep. Proper Father Christmas!' He laughed, but Olive heard the bitterness in it, and felt the tears in her eyes.

'That's the meanest thing I ever heard,' she said indignantly. 'Not letting your little girl have the presents you sent her. I think that's really horrible.'

'So do I, as a matter of fact,' he said. 'So will you let me give you this, just to make up for it a bit? Because we're friends?'

Olive held out her hand and he dropped the little parcel in it. It's jewellery, she thought, and knew she shouldn't take it, but she couldn't bear to see the misery that lurked behind his eyes. That mean bitch, Joan, she thought. And stupid as well as mean. Can't she see what a catch she's got? Why, if I weren't already married to Derek, I might—

Swiftly, she put an end to that thought. She began to unwrap the brown paper and found a small box. Her heart suddenly quickening, she opened it and stared with delight.

'Ray, it's lovely.'

'I thought you'd like it,' he said with a little self-conscious grin. 'I thought of you the minute I saw it.'

She looked at him. 'So it wasn't—'

'I wasn't going to give it to Joan,' he said, anticipating her question. 'I'd never have thought of *her*. It's for you, Livvy – only for you.'

'Oh, Ray.'

It was a brooch. A small, gold brooch – not real gold, she knew, and she would have been embarrassed if it had been, but it *looked* like real gold. It was in the shape of a rose, with daintily cut petals just opened, a little stalk and two tiny leaves.

'It's lovely,' she said again.

'It looks like your mouth when you're just going to give someone a kiss,' he said quietly. 'It's all right, Livvy. I said it didn't mean anything and it doesn't have to – not to you – but it means a lot to me to give it to you. I'd really like to see you wear it some time.'

'I will,' she said. 'I will wear it. And – it means a lot to me too, Ray.' Suddenly, on impulse, she reached up and gave him a quick kiss on the cheek. 'Thanks.'

'Come and do that again where no one else can see us,' he said with half a grin, touching his fingers to the spot where she had kissed him. His voice sounded odd, hoarse and a bit cracked. He looked at her again and Olive saw the misery of his loneliness flood his face. 'Oh, *Olive*.'

Olive stepped back quickly and glanced around, but the camp was deserted in the early winter dusk and there was no one within sight. She turned towards him and felt her own loneliness sweep across her. She yearned suddenly for a warm body close to hers, a pair of strong arms about her, lips that could kiss . . . They were here, here within her reach. Not Derek – but Derek was so far away, and his face was fading, had almost disappeared, his voice had gone from her memory. And it was so long since he had held her close . . .

'Ray . . . '

'Livvy,' he said, and the crack in his voice almost broke her heart. 'Livvy, I don't want—'

'You do,' she said, so quietly she barely heard her own words. 'And so do I. Oh, *Ray* . . .'

She was in his arms, warm and close, as she had been when they had first danced together, but now there was a difference. A tension in his body, a quivering in hers. An ache, a tingle, a sensation of fire that crept in little tongues of flames from a white heat in some deep, central core, along each vein till it reached to the very tips of her fingers, to the tiny pads of flesh on the end of each toe.

She lifted her face to his and their lips touched as delicately as the touch of the petals of a rose, and then with the spreading, burning heat of fire.

'*Ray . . .*'

# CHAPTER TWELVE

The bombing of Berlin continued into January, 1944. Diane, who was now a flight mechanic (E for Engines), said that the pilots were horrified when they heard they were to continue their bombardment. Some were appalled by the damage they were doing, and they were all only too well aware of the risks they took, night after night. The nonchalant bravado that they had adopted in the early days, as a defence mechanism against the toll war was taking of them, had begun to wear thin.

'The bastards will be waiting for us with their guns already sighted,' one pilot said bitterly. 'We'll be lucky to come back alive, any of us.'

As it turned out, he was one of the lucky ones, but over a hundred and fifty other airmen failed to return that night, and nobody needed much imagination to know what their fate must have been.

A few days later, nearly four hundred American Liberators were almost lost when they took a wrong bearing and lost radio contact. Luckily, the film actor James Stewart, leading a bomber squadron based in Norfolk, saw what had happened, followed them and gave fire cover until they were safely back, saving all but eight of the big aircraft and averting real disaster.

'I bet he'll never go back to film acting,' Bert Shaw said. 'He wouldn't be satisfied with a namby-pamby job like that, not after he's been a hero.'

'I reckon even heroes only really want their ordinary lives back,' Frank said. 'Not that it's an ordinary life being a film actor, not to you and me, but I suppose it must be to him.'

The two men were standing in their back gardens, chatting as they worked to prepare the ground for next season's vegetables. The humps of the Anderson shelters looked as if they'd been there for ever: Frank had a thick layer of earth over his, with vegetables growing all over it, while Bert's was more neglected, nothing but rough grass and weeds. He said Peggy had done most of the gardening, but just lately he'd perked up a bit, started a bit of digging and asked Frank's advice about what to plant. 'I don't need much when it's only for me,' he said, beginning to sound sorry for himself again, 'but I suppose I'd better do me bit.'

'Well, if I was you—' Frank began, when his words were drowned by a sudden scream of noise, slicing through the air like a giant whistling kettle coming to the boil. Both men jumped violently and stared up at the sky. Frank shielded his eyes with one hand.

'What in God's name is that?'

'It's a new sort of bomb,' Bert said, his voice edged with panic. 'Get in the shelter, quick!'

'Don't be daft, bombs don't fly by themselves.' Frank cringed as the noise grew louder. It was screeching almost overhead now, yet still he could see nothing. Out of the corner of his eye, he saw that Bert was already half inside his Anderson, and he made an involuntary movement towards his own. Perhaps Bert was right . . . but there was Jess, inside the house, and little Maureen, he couldn't go in without them. He began to run towards the back door.

Jess was already on her way outside, with Maureen in her arms, her face full of fear. 'What is it? Frank, what is it?'

'I don't know.' Suddenly, he saw it – an aircraft, flying ahead of the banshee screaming, vanishing over the houses towards Southsea. It was a glimpse, no more, and then it had gone, leaving only its shrill, fading whistle. The sky was empty. He let his shoulders sag. 'Whatever it was, it's gone now. It's all right, Jess. You're quite safe.'

Tears of relief stood in her eyes. 'Frank, I was so scared – it came so sudden. I've never heard anything like it.' She shivered. 'They say you hear a bomb whine just before it hits you – I thought that was what it was, a bomb, falling right on top of us.'

He put his arms round her. 'I know. Bert thought it was a bomb too, but it looked like a plane to me. I dunno what sort of plane goes that fast, though – or makes that kind of noise.'

'Well, I hope we don't get any more like it. It was awful, Frank.'

It was, he thought, but it had also been unbelievably fast. Although he'd caught no more than a glimpse of it before it vanished from sight, he'd been pretty sure it was British. If it was, it was surely something to crow about.

They found out what it was only a few days later.

'A "jet aircraft",' Frank said, reading the report in the *Evening News*. 'That's what me and Bert saw. It's the first one, but the inventor – a bloke called Whittle, it says here, thirty-six years old – says it's been well tested and ought to be going into full production soon.' He looked up. 'That's something to make the Germans think!'

'It's the fastest plane there is,' Tim said, sneaking the newspaper away. 'It doesn't have any propellers, it fires out jets of steam and they sort of push it along. Gosh, I wish I'd seen it.'

'Well, I still hope we don't get too many over here,' Jess said. 'It nearly frightened me to death. D'you know one of the worst things about this war, it's so noisy. I mean, it's nothing but rattles and whistles and screeches, and explosions and bangs and crashes, and goodness knows what else. My head's tired with just listening to it all.'

The new drug, penicillin, seemed to have cured Mr Churchill's pneumonia and he went to Marrakesh to convalesce. The Free French leader, General de Gaulle, went to see him there. His recovery was another thing that heartened people – apart from the fact that they'd soon hear his mellifluous tones on the wireless again, it meant that the soldiers and sailors who were also being treated with penicillin had a good chance of getting better.

'I just hope they're using it in those camps in Japan and Burma,' Annie said despondently, although it didn't seem likely, when everyone knew it wasn't even available to civilians in Britain yet.

General Montgomery came to Portsmouth at the end of the month. He'd been rather an unknown quantity when he'd been put in charge of the 8th Army, out in the desert, but now he was a hero and he drove through the city, his arm raised in a victory salute for the cheering crowds, to take over as Commander-in-Chief of the British Invasion Forces under General Eisenhower. People were surprised by how small he was in comparison with the big American.

'I always thought he was quite tall,' Jess said, but Frank shook his head.

'A lot of the best leaders are short. Look at Napoleon. And Nelson. I reckon they have to fight that much harder when they're nippers and it makes 'em tough.' Whatever the reason, 'Monty' was tough all right.

It was only a few days before everyone needed their own toughness as the Germans began a new attack, soon to be called the 'Little Blitz', raiding London and the south coast night after night. Groaning, fed up, and probably even more scared than they'd been first time round, they took to the shelters and once more the sky blazed with the red, angry flames of burning buildings, and the streets were a chaotic welter of firefighters and rushing ambulances.

'You just don't know how long they're going to last,' Jess said, getting Maureen's socks on while Rose crouched under the stairs, begging her to hurry. 'We might as well just go down there to sleep without waiting for the warning to go.'

Rose and Maureen were sleeping upstairs in the double bed, while Jess and Frank made the best of the settee and floor in the front room downstairs. It was easier to get everyone out that way. Rose seemed to know the siren was going even before it began its whining. She would grab Maureen and fly down the stairs, her feet scarcely seeming to touch the steps, and could hardly contain her anxiety while Jess got everyone dressed. Maureen would look at Rose curiously, unable to understand her sister's fear, but Rose could remember all too well the first big Blitz, the explosions that had rocked Portsmouth and the fires that had engulfed some of its biggest buildings.

'Come *on*, Mum,' she said, but Jess wrapped Maureen firmly in her winter coat and then picked up the tin box that contained all the family's 'papers'.

'There's no point in getting pneumonia, like Mr Churchill. It's bitter out there.'

Once they were in the Anderson, Rose felt safer, though she knew that if the shelter got a direct hit it would be completely destroyed. She sat on one of the two bunks, bending forwards, her head almost on her knees, listening to the snarl of the German planes passing overhead and the harsh rattle of the ack-ack. Her cousin Olive was out there, helping to work the guns, and sometimes you could hear an explosion when a plane was hit and the strange scream of its engine as it went out of control and spiralled down in a crash.

As a firewatcher, Frank spent most of his time outside the shelter. He had a stirrup pump ready to put out any fires that started on his patch and he kept his eyes skinned for incendiaries. Tim crept out to join him and they stared up at the sky, watching as the long spears of light from the searchlights split the darkness, catching their breath as a flock of black specks was caught in the brilliance and the rattle of ack-ack began.

'There goes one! Look at that – *wowee!* – Straight down into the drink!' Tim was mad about planes and had caught all the Air Force expressions from Diane Shaw when she'd been home on leave. 'Oh, wizard shot!'

'Let's hope it did go down in the sea and not over a street full of houses.' Frank peered down at his watch, flicking his torch on just briefly enough to see the time. 'How many more are there, for heaven's sake? There must have been hundreds over tonight.'

Tim watched anxiously. He hated Frank flicking his torch on like that. The blackout had been in force for so long now, he could hardly remember a time when you were allowed to show a light, and he was still half convinced that even that minute pinpoint of light might be enough to guide in a German bomber. However, they didn't seem quite so interested in Pompey these days: most of the bombs on the south coast seemed to be dropped at random ('Where's Random?' Tim had asked, predictably) by bombers who had been turned back from their real objective.

'Here,' he said suddenly, 'what's that? Look – coming down over there.'

Frank turned and stared in the direction in which Tim was pointing. A flickering light hung in the air just over the allotments. It was difficult to tell how big it was or how far away, but it seemed to be descending rapidly, and as it did so it got bigger and easier to see.

'It's an incendiary!' he said. 'Get the pump, Tim.'

'It's a parachute,' Tim said excitedly. 'Dad, it's a *parachute!*'

There was a commotion in the shelter at their feet.

'What's going on? What's happening?' Keith scrambled out, ignoring Jess's remonstrances, and stood beside his brother. 'What've you seen?'

'It's a parachute, look. I thought there was a German on the end of it but Dad says it's an incendiary. We're going to put it out.' Tim had passed his father the pump and was halfway to the gate with a bucket of water. 'Bring a sandbag. *Quick.*'

Keith dashed after him, dragging a heavy sandbag with him. They collided in the gateway, then sorted themselves out and Tim scrambled over the fence between the alley and the allotments. He reached back to take the bucket and Keith heaved the sandbag after him. Frank was already over, heading for the spot where the parachute seemed likely to land. It floated down, a pale ghost lit by the crimson glow of the flames beneath.

'It'll get burned,' Tim gasped in anguish. 'Don't let it get burned, Dad. It's the best souvenir we've ever had . . . Gosh, look at that!'

The device on the end of the parachute was hovering just over a patch of cabbages. It looked like a gas-ring, with flames spouting all around it. Above it, the parachute drifted sideways and the device dropped the last foot or so and came to rest on the frozen ground. The parachute collapsed with a sigh and lay in a crumpled heap of glistening silk.

'Oh, *smashing*,' Tim breathed, longing to gather it up in his arms. However, Frank was snapping at him and Keith to help with the pump, to fetch more sand and water, and it wasn't until the fire was well and truly out that they were able to turn their attention to the parachute again.

By then half a dozen other men had arrived and were watching with some envy. Bert Shaw even tried to assert that he'd got to the scene just as quickly as Frank, but Frank wasn't having that. As official firewatcher for April Grove, he was taking charge, and Tommy Vickers backed him up, saying that he'd seen Frank and the boys lit up by the flames before Bert got anywhere near.

Tim laid his hands on the fine, slippery silk and lifted it from the ground. He didn't want to tear it on the cabbages, but he knew that however thin and delicate the fabric was, it was really very strong. He sent his brother to the other end and together they carried it in a streaming flow of white, like water in a brook, into the garden of number 14.

'It stretches all the way from the gate to the back door,' Tim said in awe, and when the all-clear had sounded and the rest of the family came out to inspect it, they marvelled at its length and fineness. 'Everyone's going to be really jealous of us.'

'What are we going to do with it, Mum?' Rose asked. 'I know someone who had some silk from a parachute and they made a lot of clothes from it, nightdresses, and petticoats and things. Can I have a nightdress made of it?'

'No, you can't,' Tim said indignantly. 'That's our parachute, mine and Keith's, we went and got it. And Dad,' he added fairly. 'It's not going to be cut up for stupid nightdresses. I'm going to—'

'You're going to do nothing,' Frank said sharply, 'and it's not going to be cut up, either. That's a German parachute and it's got to be reported to the authorities. We'll probably have to hand it in.'

Jess and Rose stared at him in disappointment. 'D'you really mean that, Frank? It seems an awful shame. I mean, they can't use it again, can they?'

'Perhaps they'll give it back to the Germans,' Tim said, trying to hide his own disappointment. Not that he'd ever expected to be allowed to keep the 'chute for himself, not really. 'Perhaps they send them all back in a parcel.'

'I don't know what they do with them.' Frank was nearly as disappointed as the rest of the family, but he knew what his duty was and he had never overstepped the mark yet where Duty was concerned. 'It's not our business, and it's not our parachute. I'll have to go down the police station on my way to work and report it.'

'Well, I still think it's a terrible waste,' Jess said. 'I mean, with rationing so bad and hardly any material in the shops . . . I could've made some lovely things with that.'

They left the parachute where it was until all the neighbours had had a look at it – Ethel Glaister peered with sour envy over the fence when she thought no one was looking – and then rolled it up into a tight bundle and put it away in the cupboard in the front bedroom.

Frank went into the police station, but they were too busy to do more than take a statement. They were getting ready for a police ball to be held at South Parade Pier, with Jack Payne's Orchestra and Carole Carr singing. They tried to sell Frank two tickets for twenty-five shillings.

'Twelve and six a ticket!' he said disgustedly. 'And what are they doing, having a "ball" when there's a war on?'

'I suppose you'll just have to go again,' Jess said. 'When they're not so busy.'

'When they've got enough spare time to do a bit of work, you mean,' Frank said, and put on his boots to go over to the allotment.

To everyone's relief, the 'Little Blitz' was soon over, but it was unsettling. It meant that the Germans were still making a lot of planes, and you still couldn't feel safe. Olive and her companions on the ack-ack did their best, but they could only bring down a few of the hundreds that flew over every night. Even after the bombing had apparently stopped, the sky was still pierced by the spears of the searchlights every night, and the guns were still on the alert.

'I've forgotten what it's like to go to bed knowing we can sleep safe until morning,' Jess said sadly, as she tucked little Maureen into bed. 'And you've never known.' She smoothed back a strand of fair hair. 'Sometimes, I wonder if you ever will.'

On 1 February, it was announced that men's trousers could have turn-ups again, and suits be fitted with pockets. Popular opinion had killed the 'austerity suit'. The limit of four pleats to a skirt and the number of buttons on women's clothes was also removed.

'Well, at least they've seen sense over that,' Ethel Glaister said. 'Daft, that was. I mean, how much material did they actually save? It's all rationed, as it is. People have got to be able to dress up a bit, to look nice.'

'You'd dress up for the invasion,' Carol told her. 'I bet if a German came knocking on our door, you'd be upstairs in front of the mirror putting on fresh lipstick.'

'You mind your mouth, my girl,' Ethel snapped. 'Are you calling me a collaborator or something?'

'I'm not calling you nothing. It just don't seem much to get worked up about to me – an extra pleat or couple of buttons on a frock.'

'That's because you don't understand the importance of having things nice. Though I'm sure I've done my best to bring you up right.' Ethel examined her face in the mirror that hung over the fireplace. 'I must say, I've kept my complexion. There's not many women my age can say they've got a skin like mine. Porcelain, that's what it is.' She dabbed another layer of Pond's face powder over her nose and cheeks. '*And* my figure's just like when I was a girl, too. You look after yourself proper, Carol, and you'll always be able to look smart.'

'I can't see the point.' Carol watched her mother's titivating with faint disgust. Mutton dressed up as lamb, that was her opinion, though she didn't dare say so. 'Anyway, where are you off to, all tarted up?'

'I told you to mind your mouth,' Ethel retorted. She turned sideways, craning her neck to see her back view. Her skirt was tight across her bottom, and so short that it rode up above her knees when she sat down. 'I'm going out for the evening with my friend Violet, not that it's any of your business.'

'Violet? Who's Violet? First I've heard of anyone called Violet.'

'I don't have to tell you everything about my friends,' Ethel said haughtily. 'She's someone I know at work, that's all. She's like me, didn't ought to be grovelling about on the floor at all, but got pushed into it. We've decided it's time we had a bit of entertainment. We work hard enough, not like some I could mention.'

Carol turned away. She wasn't really interested in what her mother did. She wasn't interested in anything much these days. Dragging herself to work of a morning was just about all she could manage, and she sat at her machine all day silently oblivious of the chatter of the other girls. When she came home in the evening, she nearly drove Ethel mad by hunching herself in a chair doing nothing, or going upstairs to lie on her bed.

'I don't know what's got into her,' Ethel said angrily when she met Violet in the pub. 'Got everything a girl could want, she has – a good home, a mother that's ready to stand by her through all her trouble, a nice job where she can learn a proper trade – and she just moons about as if the world owes her something. Don't know she's born, that's her trouble.'

Violet Parsons nodded. She was the only person Ethel had confided in over Carol's 'trouble'. She had caught Ethel's eye because she wore her hair tidily tucked away in a turban made out of a real silk scarf, not the old cotton ones that most of the rivet-sorters wore, and she always had a bit of make-up on, as if she took a pride in her appearance. She looked the sort who would have a nice home too, and understand how things should be done – a definite cut above most of the rather rough women they had to work with.

At the same time, in Ethel's estimation, she wasn't *quite* so attractive as Ethel herself. Ethel Glaister had never really taken to women who outshone her, and it gave her quite a lot of pleasure to be able to advise her new friend on how to put a frill on her blouse, now that frills were allowed once more, or on a prettier way to hang her net curtains.

159

Even so, it was only when Violet had confided that her own sister had an illegitimate son that Ethel had told her about Carol.

'I can see you'd understand,' she'd said. 'I mean, it's not the sort of thing you wants everyone to know, is it? My neighbours are a nosy lot, and it's only because I had the wit to get her out of the way before she started to show that they didn't all know what was up.'

'That was clever of you,' Violet said. 'My mum didn't know what to do when she found out about our Beryl. Beryl never said a word till she was five months gone, and it was too late then – she was already showing, only we never realised what it was. They didn't have these mother and baby homes then, there wasn't nothing we could do but just let her stop home and have it. I mean, you couldn't throw her out on the streets, could you?'

Ethel thought you could, but she didn't say so. She wasn't really interested in Violet's sister. She went on talking about the people of April Grove.

'Of course, they'd have been tickled pink if they'd cottoned on – they're jealous, you see, jealous because we've always been a bit above them. Well, it's not the sort of street *I'd* have chosen to live in, it was just somewhere to start us off while we looked around for something a bit better, and if it hadn't been for this awful war we'd have moved out long ago. But my husband insisted – you know what men are – and then he went off to the war and left me to manage on my own. She was always his favourite, of course, always a daddy's girl. He let her have her own way over everything and that's what came of it. Of course, it's her mother what gets the blame.'

'It always is,' Violet said sagely. 'Doesn't matter what you do, it's wrong. But that's men all over.'

Violet's husband had gone to the war as well. He was a stoker in the Navy and so far he'd been on three different ships. The first two had been sunk and he'd survived both. His ship was in Portsmouth now, but he didn't get home much. He told Violet they were allowed hardly any leave at all.

'It's daft, if you ask me,' she said to Ethel. 'I mean, they're not doing anything, are they? Just sitting there, from what I can make of it. He'd be just as well off at home doing a few jobs about the place.'

'They use it as an excuse, I reckon,' Ethel said. 'Half the time they could get home if they wanted to and they just don't bother. Sooner sit in the mess, playing cards and smoking with their mates.'

The two women had taken to calling in at the Coach and Horses for a glass of port and lemon on the way home from work. They took off their turbans as soon as they were outside the factory gates, so that no one

160

would recognise that they were factory women, and combed their perms and put on fresh lipstick. Sometimes, as they sat showing their legs – stained brown with gravy mixture to look like stockings, with lines painted down the back for seams – they were approached by men, mostly the older soldiers and sailors, who wanted to sit and chat with them for a bit of company. They always haughtily repulsed these approaches, but it didn't stop them making up their faces or colouring their legs.

'I don't know why it is,' Ethel said huffily. 'You try to keep up appearances and people take you for a tart. For two pins, I'd give them all a good slap on the face, if it wasn't for the war.'

'You've got to make allowances,' Violet said, turning her back on a sailor who had been in the Coach the last three nights and spoken to her every time. 'They're a long way from home, and they'll be going off on this invasion any time, that's if it ever comes to anything. You can't blame 'em for wanting a bit of decent female company.'

'So long as that's all it is,' Ethel sniffed. 'Some of 'em want a bit more than that, if you ask me.' She stared icily at a Marine who was eyeing her legs. 'Look at that one – been giving me the once-over for the last five minutes, bold as brass, the monkey.'

Violet giggled. 'P'raps he's a brass monkey.'

'You've had too much port and lemon,' Ethel told her severely, and then giggled herself. 'Here, he's not bad looking, though, is he? A bit better set up than my George, I'll say that for him. I like the dark types, myself.'

The Marine got up and sauntered casually towards them. He was tall and smart in his uniform, with a thin moustache. He looked down at Ethel.

'You seem to be having a good time, you and your friend. Mind sharing the joke?'

Ethel tossed her head a little. 'I don't know about that. Depends what you're thinking of sharing in return.'

'Oh-ho,' he said, 'like that, is it? Well, I daresay we could come to some arrangement.'

'Now don't you go getting any wrong ideas,' Ethel said sharply. 'Me and my friend are respectable women having a quiet drink together after a day's work, that's all. You needn't think there's any more to it than that.'

'Why should I think there is?' he asked. 'I can see you're decent women. I wouldn't have spoken to you else. There's too many tarts around Pompey these days, out for everything a man's got in his trousers – his trouser *pockets*, I mean, of course,' he added with no more than a flicker of one eyelid. Violet squealed and Ethel gave her a reproving glance.

'Don't encourage him. They're all the same, these Marines.' She looked the man up and down. 'I suppose you'll be telling us next you've got a friend who'd like a bit of company too.'

'Well, it just so happens I have. We always go about in twos, you know, like the police.' He winked again. 'Not that I blame 'em in some streets down Pompey. Why, in Queen Street they'd be better off by the dozen. The tarts down there . . . !' He rolled his eyes and gave a little whistle. 'But this is a better area altogether. No tarts, just nice respectable women like yourselves, who aren't too hoity-toity to pass the time of day with a couple of blokes who're fighting for their country . . . Shall I call him over?'

'Call who over?' Ethel said, touching the corner of her mouth with one fingertip.

'My mate, of course. Percy, his name is, and I'm Reg. Who might you two lovely ladies be?' He sat down, beckoning to another Marine sitting in the corner with a half-empty pint glass in front of him.

'I don't remember saying you could join us,' Ethel said haughtily. 'As a matter of fact, me and my friend were just thinking of going, weren't we, Violet?'

'Violet, eh?' he said. 'That's a nice name. A name like a flower for a lady like a flower. I bet they call you Vi, don't they?'

Violet hesitated. She had told the other women at the factory right from the start that she never allowed herself to be called Vi. 'It sounds so common,' she'd said to Ethel, who had heartily agreed. The other women hadn't taken any notice, which infuriated her, but it was different with a man, you couldn't tell a man what to do like that.

'I don't—' she began, but the Marine had already turned to Ethel.

'And what's your name? Another flower? I bet it's a pretty one. Let me see if I can guess.' He screwed up his face and began to recite flower names, while the other Marine came across with his glass. 'Rose, is that it? Or Iris? Or maybe it's Daisy. Or Petunia. Or *Chrysanthemum*.' His dark eyes teased Ethel, who was growing pinker and pinker as he continued. 'Or—'

'Oh, for goodness' sake!' she exclaimed, tossing her head again. 'If you must know, it's not a flower at all. It's Ethel – a plain, honest, ordinary name with no silly nonsense about flowers or anything else.' She ignored Violet's indignant indrawing of breath. 'I think it's time we were going. I've got a meal to cook.'

'I thought you said your Carol was doing that,' Violet said, getting her own back.

'I also said she's walking about in a dream these days and can't hardly be trusted to make a slice of toast,' Ethel snapped. The two Marines were both sitting at the table now, grinning, and she flung them an angry glare. 'You can stay here if you like, Violet, but it seems to me the whole tone of the place has gone down in the past few minutes, and I'm off.'

She put both hands on the table and made to get up, but the first Marine put out his hand and laid it on hers. He gave her a grin that was half cheeky, half apologetic.

'Here, Ethel, don't go off in a huff. It's too nice an evening for bickering. Let's have another drink, shall we, all cosy together? I daresay it won't matter too much if you're a bit late home, will it? Or will the old man be waiting with a rolling-pin?'

Ethel pretended to hesitate for a moment or two more. Then she gave an exaggerated sigh and sat down. 'Well, I suppose a few more minutes won't hurt, and my Carol's in such a state, she won't notice if I don't come home till next Tuesday. Not that I've any intention of stopping more than five minutes,' she added sharply to the Marines, 'and that's only out of the kindness of my heart, seeing as you're likely to be going off again any time soon. Since you're offering, I'll have another port and lemon. A large one.'

Reg grinned and winked at his friend. 'You get 'em in, Perce. I'm not letting go of this one – she looks to me as if she'll fly away the minute I take my eyes off her.' He kept his large hand on Ethel's, and stared at her face. 'My, but you're a pretty little thing,' he said. 'Who's this Carol who's getting your supper ready? Your sister, is she? I can't believe you're old enough to have a daughter old enough to cook.'

'I married very young,' Ethel said with hauteur. 'And Carol's no more than a child herself.'

'What – about ten? Twelve? Old enough to be left on her own?'

'She's old enough to look after herself, and that's all I'm saying. How do I know you're not a spy? And take your hand away, if you don't mind. I'm very particular who I let touch me.'

'I bet you are.' He winked at Violet. 'That's what I like about respectable women.' The drinks arrived and Percy sat down close to Violet, who moved away slightly. Reg raised his glass. 'Here's to respectable women. What would we do without 'em?'

Percy sniggered. 'What would we do *with* 'em?' He attempted to slide an arm around Violet's waist and she brushed him away indignantly. He was fatter than Reg, with a red face and gingery whiskers. He slurped some beer into his mouth and sucked it through his whiskers with a loud noise.

Ethel gave him a cold glance. She picked up her glass, holding it almost as if it were a tea cup with her little finger held out at an angle, and sipped daintily, staring at the opposite corner of the room. Reg nudged his friend sharply.

'Give over, Perce, and behave yourself. You're embarrassing the ladies. I've told 'em, all we want is a quiet drink with some pleasant female company. We don't want none of your crude humour.'

'Sorry, Reg.'

'I should think so, but it's the ladies you ought to be apologising to. He's not really used to such genteel company,' he said to Ethel. 'He's a good bloke, but he never had the advantages I had. I've taken him in hand, though, and I'm teaching him his manners. You'll see, he'll be a credit to me in no time at all. I'll be able to take him to Buckingham Palace to meet the Queen by the time I've finished with him.'

'I'm sure she'll be delighted to meet you both,' Ethel said sarcastically. 'I daresay you'll be expecting to collect medals too.'

'Already have.' He showed her the ribbon on his chest. 'Military Medal. I'll show you the real thing one day – it's got the King's head on it.'

The two women stared at it. 'The Military Medal? What did you get that for?' Ethel asked.

'Oh, nothing much. Bit of a shindig at sea – we were under heavy fire, couple of blokes got blown overboard and I pulled 'em back in. Nothing to it, really. I was always the best swimmer, so it had to be me, didn't it? Matter of fact, I reckon they just had this medal lying about spare, see, and had to find someone to give it to. If my name hadn't started with an A, they'd have passed it on to the next bloke in the line. There was plenty on board that day deserved it just as much as I did.'

'The Military Medal,' Ethel said. She put out her hand and touched the ribbon. 'Well, I reckon you ought to be proud. They don't dish out things like this for nothing.'

'Go on,' he said, 'they're chucking them about these days. Nearly everyone you meet's got a ribbon pinned on him somewhere.'

'Sometimes it's somewhere you can't see, mind,' Perce put in with a leer. 'Services to the nation, and all that. Got to keep the flag flying, ain't we?'

'Oh, *you*,' Ethel said, but the tartness had gone from her voice and as she turned back to Reg, she noticed that Violet had moved back into her original position. 'Look, Reg, I'm sorry we were a bit sharp to begin with, but you know a girl can't be too careful these days. We've got our reputations to think of. We don't want people to start talking about us.'

'Go on,' he said, 'I bet they talk about you all the time. Smart, well set-up woman like you, they're bound to wish they could match up to you. We don't want to cause any gossip, though. Just a quiet drink with friends, that's all we're suggesting.'

'Well, in that case,' Ethel said, 'I'll have another port and lemon, but that's the last one, mind. After that, I'm off home.'

'Well, we'll have to see how long we can make it last,' he said, and winked at her. 'And now, why don't you tell me all about yourself? What's your hubby do, eh? Away in the Forces, is he?'

Ethel hesitated for no more than a moment. Then she looked again at the dark stripes of the ribbon on his jacket.

George Glaister had never won a medal, nor was ever likely to. All he'd ever done was play at soldiers in the Territorial Army and then gone off to build tin huts in Africa. And the last time he'd been home, he'd told her he was never coming back.

She arched her eyebrow at Reg and moved slightly closer.

Olive and Ray had stopped trying to stay apart. There didn't seem to be any point after Christmas Day. We didn't do anything wrong, she told herself, not really wrong. It was just a kiss – well, a few kisses, then. And it was Christmas, everyone has a few kisses at Christmas. It's all right if we don't do any more than that, and we'll never go all the way. We just wouldn't.

She would not let herself think of the heat that had spread through her body, the surge of desire that had left her shaking in Ray's arms. At the same time, she couldn't forget it. It was still there, a tingle ready to leap into life whenever she thought of him, whenever they met. She lay awake at night, letting her thoughts drift, letting the memory waft in like a gossamer mist, and the tingle grew to a fire. She burned to be in his arms. Just a kiss, she thought, just a kiss . . . and pretended that she didn't want more.

Afraid of what might happen if they were alone together, she refused to go for walks with him, but agreed to go dancing or to the pictures. They went to South Parade Pier, which was open again – though not to the expensive police ball – and to the cinema where they sat together in the back row watching Humphrey Bogart and Ingrid Bergman in *Casablanca*.

'That was gorgeous,' Olive sighed afterwards. 'Humphrey Bogart makes me go all shivery. And Ingrid Bergman is lovely. I like her sort of husky voice, and her accent. She's Swedish, you know.'

'I thought the bad guys were good too,' Ray said. 'That bloke Conrad Veidt was smashing as the Nazi – and Claud Rains and Peter Lorre, they were good too. But d'you know what I thought was the best thing in the whole picture?' He paused. They were walking along a deserted stretch of road, and he drew her into a dark corner. 'It was that song, the one the Negro sang.'

'"As Time Goes By,"' Olive said softly. She made no resistance as Ray slid his arms around her body. She laid her lips against his ear and sang softly, as if they were dancing.

> Moonlight and love songs, never out of date,
> Hearts full of passion, jealousy and hate,
> Woman needs man . . .

Her voice shook, and she stopped, catching her breath. Ray joined in, supplying the words she could not utter:

> . . . and man must have his mate,
> That, no one can deny . . .

'Olive,' he muttered hoarsely, 'Olive, oh my darling, my darling, my Livvy, Livvy . . . Let me love you, let me love you properly. I need you – I can't go on any longer, not being able to show you how much I love you, how much I need you. Please, Livvy, *please* . . .'

'Ray . . .'

'We can't help it,' he went on, his hands moving desperately on her coat buttons. 'We've got to do it. You know we've got to.'

'Ray – Derek . . .'

'I know. I still can't help it.' He had her coat unbuttoned. 'I love you just as much as he does, Livvy – more – and you love me too, I know you do. We're here, we're together . . . It's wartime, Livvy, everything's different in wartime, we've got to take our happiness while we can, we might not even be alive this time tomorrow . . . Livvy, please . . .'

'Oh Ray,' she gasped, knowing she couldn't withstand him any longer, could not withstand herself. The desire was burning in her again – she had felt it all evening: felt it in her shoulder and arm as they pressed against his in the cinema; felt it in her fingers as his hand touched and held them; felt it in her body as he slid his arm around her shoulders and drew her close. She had known it would end this way. She had known, and done nothing to stop it. She couldn't stop it. She didn't want to stop it.

'Ray, I love you.' Her blouse was unbuttoned too and his hands had slipped inside, dragging aside the heavy Army issue brassière she wore, cupping her breasts in his palms. He kissed her face, then ran his lips down the arch of her neck and buried his mouth in the softness of her breasts. She shook with anguish. 'Ray, I love you, I love you.'

He lifted his face. 'I want to do it properly, Livvy. I want to love you properly, not here in an alleyway. Oh, God –' his voice sounded strangled, tormented – 'I want you so much.' He wrapped his arms about her and kissed her again on the lips, hungrily, as if he were devouring her. 'Livvy, it's driving me mad – *you're* driving me mad . . .'

'Darling.' She had never called him that before, never used any endearment. She didn't even call Derek that, it wasn't a word the people she knew used much. 'Darling, let's go back to camp. I know a place – it's not much more than a cupboard. There's some mattresses stored there. Nobody goes there, I'm sure.'

'Now?' he said. 'Now?' He sounded like a child, promised a treat, who is afraid that it would be snatched away. 'You – you won't change your mind?'

She looked at his face, a pale glimmer in the moonlight, and felt a sudden desperate pity for him. He had never known what it was like to make love with a woman who really wanted him, who was prepared to give him joy. He had only ever known the harsh discomfort of the relief of lust with a woman who gave her body reluctantly – except, presumably, for that first time when little Dorothy had been conceived – and nothing more at all. It was as if he had been offered a rainbow and pelted with hail.

'I won't change my mind,' she said gently, and then as her voice began to shake again, 'Let's go, Ray. Let's go *now*.'

# CHAPTER THIRTEEN

Not all the aircraft which crashed came down in the sea. Some were caught inland, by gun emplacements on Portsdown Hill or the South Downs, and they fell into fields and woods. Often they exploded or caught fire on impact, and if the crew hadn't been able to bale out they were burned to death. Some crashed planes weren't enemy aircraft at all, but British or American, limping back to base badly damaged from their own raids. When this happened, it was almost as important to save the plane as its crew, and the WAAF flight mechanics were often the ones called out to the rescue.

'*Bomber crashed!*'

The call came before dawn, before the girls in Hut 19 were properly awake, but the effect of the words was better than any alarm clock or reveille. Her eyelids still struggling to part, Diane found herself out of bed and groping for the clothes she had left piled neatly on the wooden chair beside her locker. She was in her regulation knickers, her blouse and tunic almost before someone had snapped on a torch, and out of the door before she had finished doing up all the buttons.

It was a far cry from mornings at home, yawning and stretching in bed, reluctant to leave her dreams, while Mum called impatiently at the bottom of the stairs.

Thinking of Peggy still brought a lump to Diane's throat, but there was no time for grieving now. Somewhere, out in the darkness of the Hampshire countryside, a bomber had come down, and it was her job to help go and bring it in.

'I wonder if he baled out,' Miriam said. She clambered up into the lorry behind Diane and squashed against her. All the girls Diane had trained with were there: Shirley, the driver, tall and fair, who had been to a private school and still thought herself a cut above the rest of them; Joan, who was a bit plump with mousy brown hair and not much opinion of her own; Iris, who had been married and widowed before she was twenty; and the twins

168

Liz and Ellie Owen, who had been given names beginning with E just because they were twins, and shortened them because they were determined to be different.

'We got fed up with nobody being able to tell us apart,' Liz had told Diane, 'so we shortened our names and got these brooches – see, mine's an L and hers is an E. Now all you have to do is look.'

Unfortunately, WAAF regulations forbade them to wear their brooches and the uniform made them look more alike than ever. Most of the other girls didn't even bother to try to tell the difference and called them Lizanellie One and Two (according to which one they spoke to first), while the officers simply used their surname, as if only one Owen existed.

The girls sat silent in the lorry after Miriam's remark. They were seldom sure what they were going to find when they went out to salvage a crashed aircraft. The crew might have escaped before landing, drifting unhurt to the ground on their parachutes – or they might have been trapped in the wreckage, injured, perhaps burned to death.

That was what had happened to Iris's husband, and Diane could never understand how the girl could bear to go to such a scene. Didn't it bring back terrible memories every time she heard those words – 'bomber crashed' – and set forth in the lorry, behind the long trailer? She asked Iris about it once and the girl shrugged her shoulders.

'I have nightmares about it every night, so I might as well see what it's really like. And I might be able to save some poor bloke's life, like someone could've saved my Billy's if they'd got to him in time.'

All the same, Diane thought she'd rather have just had the nightmares and not gone through it all again during the day. It's best to put it behind you, she thought, looking at Iris's pale face in the dimness of the lorry. Forget. You can't do any good by keep remembering.

The trailer was too long to negotiate the country lanes at any speed, and the girls could feel Shirley's frustration at having to follow so slowly.

'I dunno why they don't let us go first,' Miriam grumbled. 'There could be blokes dying up there.' They knew that was unlikely, though: an ambulance would have been sent to pick up any survivors of the crew who might have baled out. Any still inside the plane would have little chance of survival.

The last stretch of lane was up a steep hill on to open downs. At this time of the year there wasn't any crop growing, though the winter wheat would soon be sown and that meant the ground had to be cleared as quickly as possible. There was always some reason why the plane had to be shifted fast – grazing animals, harvest to be gathered – apart from the need to get the aircraft back to the station and repair it, if possible, to make it operational again.

That was the job Diane and her comrades were there for: to dismantle the wreckage before it was transported back to base. Each one of them was now a flight mechanic, qualified either as 'A' (for airframes) or 'E' (for engines), and when the lorry finally came to a stop beside the crashed plane they jumped out and ran over to it, confident of being able to do their job.

'Hey,' Diane said, stopping a yard or two away from the huge body, 'that's not one of ours.'

'It bloody well isn't,' Lizanellie One said. 'It's a bleeding Flying Fortress.'

'Americans!' Miriam exclaimed. 'Think they've got a few pairs of nylon stockings aboard?'

'They'd better have. I'm not salvaging their plane if they haven't.' Diane had met one or two Americans already and disliked their lofty attitude. She had not forgiven them for delaying so long before entering the war. It could have been all over by now, she thought, if they'd come in to begin with. Now they were flooding over and treating the British as though they were children who had had to turn to big brother for help against the school bully. 'Anyway, they ought to have their own salvage teams.'

'Never mind that.' Shirley, as driver, was in charge of the operation, and the RAF men who had brought up the trailer were already examining the wreck. 'We've got a job to do. We've trained on Fortresses, we all know the form, so get moving.'

The girls switched into action. The short exchange had taken up only a few seconds and none of them was seriously interested in nylon stockings – at least, for the moment. Later, they might drop a few hints to the crew, if they met them – if they were lucky enough to have survived.

There was no sign of anyone around the plane, but it didn't look too badly damaged and there hadn't been any fire. They stood for a moment assessing the big aircraft and then began work.

There was more to this job than just picking up pieces. It wasn't like clearing away a few broken toys. You had to know what the pieces were – what part of the plane they came from – and you had to be able to dismantle the undamaged parts without causing further harm. Everything would be removed, packed away and taken back to the repair depot, and the better the WAAF flight mechanics did their work, the more chance there would be of at least some of that plane taking to the skies again.

The girls had been trained to salvage every kind of plane they would be likely to encounter. The American Boeing B-17 – known as the Flying Fortress – was a big bomber that had already been proved in the Pacific. It had come to Britain in 1942 and begun carrying out raids over railway marshalling yards and airfields in France during the Dieppe landings. It had then concentrated on the war in Africa before returning to Europe and beginning to raid Germany itself. By the summer of 1943, everyone had heard of the Flying Fortress, and had seen it on the Pathé Pictorial news at the cinema. The American habit of giving aircraft names, like ships, and even decorating their fuselages with pictures, had given it an added glamour which culminated in the fame of the *Memphis Belle* – the first Fortress to complete an entire quota of twenty-five missions – which was filmed in action and later taken on tour all over America, to boost morale and sell war bonds. The girls had all seen the film and felt almost a part of it as they began their work, but even that glamour couldn't compete with the reality of a bitter winter's morning and the twisted metal of a plane which hadn't made it back to base.

The airmen had already lifted the body of the machine and jacked it up so that there was no danger of it falling. As Shirley brought the lorry to a halt, they had seen the armourers coming away with the last of the guns and ammunition. Sometimes there were bombs left too, which were brought out.

The WAAFs didn't waste time. They swarmed all over the body, each going straight for her own particular task. Diane's was to dismantle the engines with Miriam and Lizanellie. Shirley and Iris used special bowsers to drain the oil and fuel, then turned their attention to the airframe. The girls worked swiftly and surely, their small fingers quicker and nimbler than men's at doing these often fiddly jobs. However, the cold gripped their bones, and the metal of the plane seemed to stick to their skin, making the job all the more difficult, even painful.

'They should only have bombing raids in summer,' Diane grumbled, blowing on her frozen fingers. 'It'd be quite nice, getting up early on a summer's day, with all the birds singing. I wouldn't mind that at all.'

'You're not paid to mind things,' Miriam said. 'You're paid to do as you're told, and no back answers.'

The girls laughed. This had been one of the favourite sayings of their sergeant during training. It seemed a long time ago now since they were rookies, attending lectures on everything from venereal disease to aircraft maintenance. By now, most of the RAF had accepted WAAFs as a fact of life – and a useful one – but there were still a few of the old school, who believed that women had no place in war and shouldn't be doing men's jobs.

'For every one of you that comes on the station,' one had told Diane in the early days, 'there's another one of us can go off and get killed. Think that's a bloody comfort, do you?'

Others had expressed their doubts that women could ever handle the jobs a man did. Cook and clean, yes, if you had to have them around; do a bit of nursing – cheered a fellow up to have a pretty face looking after him – keep a chap's laundry up to the mark – that sort of thing was women's work. But mend engines, maintain the kites, operate the RT? Never in all your life!

However, women were doing all these jobs, and more. Doing them efficiently and well. And the old school, the diehards who were mostly pre-war RAF and looked back to the old days with longing and nostalgia, had mostly grumbled themselves into silence.

Salvaging the Fortress took several days. Some of it was buried amongst the trees it had fallen on, and the broken branches had to be cleared before the team could get at it. The tail had broken off and buried itself in a crater, and had to be dug out again. A lot of the wreckage was buckled and twisted, but amongst the tangled metal there were instruments that could be extracted and used again. There was no waste allowed. 'It's no good asking people to give up their saucepans to build Spitfires,' the NCO told them, 'if we're going to let a whole bloody plane go to pot.'

Back at the station, the crew who had baled out of the Fortress were in the canteen. They didn't need to buy cigarettes or chocolate – the Americans had their own generous supply – but it was a good place to meet. The WAAFs soon singled them out from the rest of the airmen, and Diane made a beeline for the pilot. He was tall, with a craggy face, corn-coloured hair and crinkling blue eyes. He looked as if he'd be at home in a cowboy film, swinging a lasso.

'I can tell you're a Yankee,' she said, eyeing him cheekily.

He looked down at her. 'Oh yeah? Guess it's not too hard – the uniform kinda gives it away.'

'We've just finished salvaging your plane,' she said. 'It was a real wreck. You must've come down ever so hard.'

He shrugged. 'I wouldn't know. I wasn't in it by then.'

'Just as well,' Diane said. 'You'd have been a real wreck too.' She tilted her head in the way that men seemed to like. 'I suppose you didn't have any nylon stockings with you?'

'No,' he said, drawling a little, 'we took bombs, and I guess we dropped most of 'em over the Huns. Kinda careless, that, wasn't it?'

Diane smiled. 'We got most of your plane out. It's like a big jigsaw puzzle now, waiting to be put together again. I suppose they'll give you a new toy to play with while you're waiting for it.'

'I guess so. We're bits of machinery too – gotta be kept operational, look after you guys over here. I guess you need it pretty bad.'

Diane's eyes narrowed. 'What d'you mean by that?'

'Well, you'd have been in a pretty bad way if we hadn't come into the war, now wouldn't you? Just about on your knees to the Hun from all accounts. Reckon you'd have been invaded by now if it hadn't been for Uncle Sam.'

'You think a lot of yourself, don't you?' Diane said coldly. 'As I remember it, you only came into the war after Pearl Harbor.'

'So?'

'So it was only to save your own skins. The Japanese tore strips off you, and they'd have beaten you to a pulp if you hadn't come in. You just use us as a jumping-off point.'

He stared at her. 'If you were a man, I'd take you outside and beat *you* to a pulp for saying that.'

'If *you* were a man,' Diane said, 'I might take you on.'

They stood glaring at each other for a few moments. Diane could feel her heart thudding. She couldn't understand what had got into her, why she was saying these things. There was just something in his eyes, in the cool drawl of his voice, that had got under her skin. That and the attitude so many Americans seemed to have: that if they hadn't stepped in, the British would be crushed under the Nazi heel by now.

If you'd come a bit sooner, she thought, my mum might still have been alive.

The American laughed suddenly, and his face looked quite different. 'Hey, what're we doing? I ain't got no quarrel with you. So you brought my crate home again, did you, in a cardboard box? Well, I'm sure glad I wasn't inside that box as well. I guess I owe you a drink as a thankyou.'

'It doesn't matter,' Diane said, stiffly, unwilling to unbend. 'We don't need thanks. It's our job. We're paid to do it.'

'Sure, but a little oil never hurts on troubled waters.' He touched her arm. 'C'mon, what'll it be? Bourbon? Or – what is it you Britishers drink? Gin?'

'I don't drink gin. Or bourbon.' Diane didn't even know what bourbon was, though she'd heard it mentioned on films sometimes. 'I'll have a beer,' she added. 'A half.'

'A half of beer coming up.' She watched him shoulder his way to the bar. Lizanellie came up behind her and stood one on each side. They nudged her simultaneously.

'Getting off with the Yanks? You want to watch it, Di. You know what they're saying about them: overpaid, over-sexed—'

'—and over here,' Diane finished. 'Well, I don't mind a bit of overpaid, but as for the rest of it—'

'—you don't mind that either,' the other Lizanellie said. 'You ought to be careful, though. You don't know where they've been.'

'Or what they brought back with them,' her twin added. 'And I don't mean nylon stockings and chewing-gum.'

'Well, whatever he's got, he can keep it,' Diane said. 'He thinks a sight too much of himself, this one. Says we'd have been under the Hun by now if it hadn't been for America stepping in.'

'Catch *me* under a Hun,' Lizanellie Two said, and they all laughed.

The pilot came back with two glasses. He looked at Lizanellie and did a double take.

'Say, they mass-producing you now? How many more are there? I sure like the model, mind. Can we put in an order for half a dozen?'

'Ha very ha,' Lizanellie One said coldly. 'I suppose you don't have twins in America.'

'Sure we do,' he said comfortably, 'and triplets, and even quads sometimes. And if they all looked like you, nobody'd have any objection at all. So you're WAAFs as well, are you? Did you help bring my crate home in a brown paper bag too?'

'He's the pilot of that wreck we salvaged,' Diane put in. 'The one that had been landed so badly.'

'Oh, that one,' Lizanellie Two said. 'They reckoned it could have been brought home in one piece if the pilot hadn't panicked, didn't they?' She turned kind eyes on the pilot. 'It *is* a bit frightening, being in a real war, but we can't afford the time to come up and hold your hands for you. We're too busy picking up the pieces.'

He raised one eyebrow and whistled. 'Phew! You girls sure are straight out of charm school. What is it you've got against us guys, huh? I thought British girls fell for us Americans like ninepins.'

'That's probably what we've got against you,' Diane said, sipping her beer. 'You think you're God's gift to women. You think we're all sex-starved and man-crazy. Well, maybe we are – but we'd rather wait for our own men, thanks very much. The ones who went off to war in *nineteen-thirty nine*.'

The American's other eyebrow went up. 'You sure have got it in for us, haven't you? Maybe we oughta continue this discussion somewhere else, a bit more quiet.' He cocked his head at Diane. 'How about it? I'll dig up a coupla guys for the lookalikes here too.'

'No thanks.'

'C'mon. There's a good little pub in the village, so I've heard. I really like these little village pubs you Britishers go for. I'd sure like to go into one with a gal on my arm, just like the local squire. Let's make it a date, whaddya say?'

'I said no. Thanks. Or just plain no.' She finished her beer and set the glass down. 'Thanks for the drink, and I hope you get your new toy soon. Be more careful with it next time, or Father Christmas won't bring you any more.' She glanced at Lizanellie. 'Coming back to the hut? The air's fresher there.'

The twins looked at each other, then shrugged and followed her. Outside, they each took an arm and danced her across to their hut.

'What on earth was all that about, Di? He seemed all right. We could've had a good time down at the pub with him and his mates.'

'Yes, and pigs might fly,' Diane said tersely. 'I dunno. He just got my goat. Anyway, I'm off men. More trouble than they're worth.'

She tossed her head and went into the hut. A kettle was hissing on top of the stove and she mixed cocoa powder with sugar and a few spoonfuls of dried milk in a mug, then poured on boiling water. She took the mug over to her bed, still stirring.

The American pilot had been altogether too sure of himself and his welcome. Give him the slightest encouragement and he'd have had her behind the NAAFI canteen before you could say 'get 'em off'. And while Diane liked a bit of fun, she didn't like being taken for granted. There are plenty of British boys to have fun with, she thought. I'm not that hard up for a pair of stockings.

The offensive against Berlin continued, with huge formations of planes going out whenever the weather was suitable. The slaughter was so great that even those who hated the enemy began to feel uneasy and ask why Bomber Command was attacking civilians rather than major industrial areas.

Jess said little these days about her own worries for the old people and children who were the innocents in these attacks. Some people were all too ready to call you a collaborator. However, she read the report of the Bishop of Chichester's speech in the House of Lords, during which he voiced almost identical concerns, and felt comforted that she was not alone, that really important people thought the way she did.

' . . . A tornado of smoke and flames,' he had said, 'with seventy-four thousand persons killed and a policy of obliteration. That is not a justifiable act of war.' Referring to Air Chief Marshal Sir Arthur Harris's declared intention to bomb Berlin 'until the heart of Nazi Germany ceases to beat', he maintained that 'to justify methods inhumane in themselves by arguments of expediency smacks of the Nazi philosophy that might is right.'

'He means we're making ourselves no better than them,' Jess said to Tim. 'It's like when you used to fight with Micky Baxter and we told you always to fight fair, even if he didn't. That's why your dad taught you and Keith how to box, so you could always defend yourselves properly.'

'But you can't beat someone who doesn't fight fair,' Tim objected, 'and Micky Baxter never cared where he kicked you. It's no good knowing how to box when someone kicks you like he did.'

Jess sighed. It was difficult for her to know what was right in such cases – she'd never had to fight like the boys did – but, like Frank, she believed strongly in being fair and that doing what they'd been taught was right, even if other people didn't. You didn't have to sink to their level. But when it meant being kicked where it would hurt the most? Being trodden underfoot, like the rest of Europe?

'I don't know, Tim,' she said. 'I just don't know what to say, but it still seems to me we've got to do things right. One day this war will be over, and then people will look back and ask questions. You've always got to think of that.'

That day still seemed far away, however, and meanwhile, the attacks went on. In six days, towards the end of February, nearly four thousand heavy bomber sorties were carried out, with thirteen major attacks against the German aircraft industry. Of a thousand bombers and almost as many fighters, not many more than two hundred aircraft were lost – an acceptable number, apparently.

'It's still a lot of young men, though,' Jess commented to Annie as they walked down to Commercial Road to do some shopping. A few of the stores were open, even though the Landport Drapery Bazaar and several others were still little more than huge waste areas. 'Pilots and airmen – and they're so young, most of them. Diane Shaw was telling us when she was home on leave the other weekend – no more than nineteen or twenty years old, as often as not. There's a lot of mothers grieving over their boys.'

'It makes you wonder why we brought 'em into the world, just to suffer and die like that,' Annie agreed. 'And it's not just the RAF, it's all the Services. I can't get our Colin out of my mind at all. You hear such terrible things about what's going on out in Japan, and Malaya and Burma. Dying like flies, they say – and tortured to death, starved and beaten. God knows what else. I lie awake at night going over it all in my mind till I think I'm going to go mad. He was such a cheery little boy – always on the go, always up to mischief, and when he went into the Navy, he was so proud in his square rig and bell-bottoms. I just can't bear to think what he's going through now, Jess, I just can't – and yet I can't *stop* thinking about it.' She shook her head sadly. 'You know, sometimes I almost wish we hadn't never had him at all. It would have been better than what he's suffering out there.'

'Annie, you mustn't think like that. He'll be all right. I know he will. And you wouldn't have been without him, you know you wouldn't. All mothers have to suffer.'

'It's not me I'm thinking about,' Annie said, 'it's him.'

They walked on in silence. Jess was holding Maureen by the hand. They came to the square, still dominated by the Guildhall, no more now than a gutted shell yet still a proud, lovely building. They stood for a moment looking up at the clock tower which had so miraculously survived the blazing fires of the Blitz.

'There's a lot of people about,' Jess said suddenly. 'Look over there – a whole crowd. There must be something going on. Let's have a look.'

She set off across the square, towing Maureen. Annie followed, peering to see what was happening. It looked as if there was someone walking about, someone important enough to attract the crowds. She saw a Naval officer in his dark blue uniform and peaked cap with 'scrambled egg' adorning it to show he was a captain or commander or something, but that couldn't be what was attracting people – Naval officers, even high-ranking ones, were a common sight in Portsmouth's streets. Then she saw the man walking beside him – a stocky bulldog of a man, with head slightly lowered as if about to charge, a big cigar stuck in his mouth . . .

'Annie!' Jess turned excitedly. 'Annie, look who it is! It's Mr Churchill himself – Winston Churchill, come to have a look at Pompey. Look, Maureen, look at Mr Churchill.'

She lifted the little girl up so that she could see over the heads of the crowd. Annie stood beside her, Colin momentarily receding to the back of her mind – he never really left it entirely – and they stared and waved and cheered with the rest of the crowd. 'Hooray! Hooray! Three cheers for Mr Churchill – hip, hip, hooray, hooray, hooray!'

The bulldog's head turned. He nodded and smiled, and waved his hand. His fingers came up in the well-known Victory V sign and Jess turned and clasped Annie's arm.

'Did you see that? Did you see him, Annie? He looked straight at us when he did that, and he smiled specially at our Maureen – didn't he, my love? He smiled at *us*.'

'He did,' Annie said slowly. 'You're right, Jess – I saw him too. He did.'

Mr Churchill had moved on now and the crowd swirled around him, hiding him from view, but Annie and Jess didn't need to see any more. They drew themselves away from the thrusting people and walked back to a quieter part of the square. They stood for a moment and looked at each other.

'It gives you some heart, doesn't it?' Jess said at last. 'Seeing him like that – looking so cheerful and so determined. I mean, with someone like that in charge, we've just got to win, haven't we?' She touched her sister's arm. 'Colin'll come back,' she said. 'I know he will.'

Colin wasn't the only one of her children that Annie worried about. Betty, married now and out on the farm, seemed settled and happy, but the same couldn't be said about Olive. Annie watched her elder daughter with a feeling of helplessness, knowing that things were going wrong in some way, but unable to ask why, and not daring to give advice.

Olive had stopped coming home quite so often. She knew her mother missed her regular visits, and she was sorry about that, but now that she and Ray had finally given in to the desires that had been eating at them for so long, she couldn't really think about anything else. She even pushed the thoughts of Derek out of her mind – she felt too guilty, and at the same time exhilarated, about her affair with Ray.

I'm sorry, Derek, she thought, I really am, but I just can't help it. It wouldn't have happened if you hadn't gone away – I'd never have looked at another bloke . . . It was wrong to blame Derek for going away, she knew, but she couldn't help thinking it. Anyway, it was the war and the high-ups like Mr Churchill – and, most of all, Hitler himself – who really took the blame.

'I love you, Livvy,' Ray said as they sat close together in a deserted bus shelter one night. 'I've loved you ever since that night we first met, at the pier. Only I couldn't ever say so.'

'I'd have run a mile if you had.' She laid her head on his shoulder. 'Oh Ray, I don't know what I feel. I love you too, but I haven't stopped loving Derek. It's as if I loved you both. *Can* you love two people at once, Ray?'

'I don't know. I never loved Joan at all, so it's never happened to me.' He paused. 'You're the only girl I've ever felt anything for, Livvy, and you're the only one I ever will.'

'Oh, Ray . . . ' There was a long pause. She turned her face up to his and he bent his head and kissed her, slowly and tenderly, on the lips. 'I do love you,' she whispered at last. 'I couldn't kiss anyone like that unless I loved them . . . What are we going to do, Ray? What's going to happen?'

'I don't know. I don't think there's any point in us doing anything. Nobody knows what's going to happen – the Germans might invade yet, or there might be fighting somewhere else that me or Derek might have to go to . . . Everyone in Pompey knows there's something big going on, what with the sea front being barricaded off and all those Canadians arriving last week, and there's soldiers everywhere . . . but we can't do anything about any of it. All we can do is make the most of what we've got.' He touched her lips again. 'I don't want to make things bad for you, Livvy. I don't want to break up your marriage or anything like that. If I can just love you, while I can . . .'

'Oh yes,' she breathed, 'you can do that. We've got to do that, Ray.'

'Livvy.' It was cold and uncomfortable in the bus shelter, and they were both wrapped in khaki greatcoats, like stiff cardboard blankets. 'We've got to find somewhere better than this to go. That place where they store the mattresses – well, it's all right, but we've only got to get caught once and there'd be real trouble. We could be court-martialled for it. It's not me I'm worried about, I just don't want to get you on a charge. I want to love you properly – not in dark corners like this, that stink of pee.' He hesitated. 'Would – would you come somewhere with me? A bloke I know told me about this little place off Fawcett Road. It's a kind of boarding-house, people used to come to it for their summer holidays. It's really respectable,' he said hastily as she drew in her breath. 'I mean, there's nothing funny going on there. Maybe we could go there sometimes, like, as if we were married . . . That's if you wouldn't mind.' He sounded miserably uncertain. 'I'm sorry, I shouldn't ever have said anything about it.'

'It's all right, Ray. You're right, we've got to go somewhere.' She hesitated, then said in a low voice. 'I don't know if it's wrong or not – I suppose most people would say it was – I just can't help it, I've got to be with you. I'll come wherever you say.'

'Oh, Olive . . .' He caught her hard against him, even the muffling greatcoats unable to dim the passion flaring between them. 'Are you really sure, though? You've got to be sure. I mean, some people might say it was – well, a bit sordid. I don't want you doing anything that might seem like that to you.'

'It doesn't.' She considered the thought. Going with Ray to a small boarding-house in a quiet street in Southsea. Signing in as if they were man and wife. Going to bed together, properly to bed, with a nightdress and everything – not that she supposed she'd have that on for long, and her stomach tingled at the idea – and spending hours, a whole night, just making love . . . Yes, maybe some people would say it was sordid – her

179

own mother would say it – but they didn't have to know about it, and it wasn't their business anyway. It was just her and Ray, and to her it didn't seem sordid at all. It seemed . . . beautiful. Just beautiful . . .

It became a regular habit for Ethel and Violet to meet the two Marines in the Coach and Horses for a drink or two on a couple of evenings a week. There was nothing in it, they assured each other, nothing at all. They were both respectable married women, after all, and Reg and Perce were decent men, not like some of the roughnecks you saw around Pompey. Marines were a cut above the other Services anyway, with their smart uniforms and brilliantly white belts. You could look up to a Marine.

A drink or two led to three or four, and the evenings stretched until closing time. Sometimes the women found the night air affecting them when they came out, and needed a gentleman's arm to escort them home. What happened at Violet's front door, Ethel didn't know, but she always made Reg stop at the corner of April Grove.

'I've got my reputation to consider,' she said, hiccuping slightly. 'You don't know what the neighbours are like down here. Nosy as a pack of monkeys. I'll say goodnight now, if you don't mind.'

Reg didn't seem to mind too much. He gave her a pat on her bottom and rubbed his bristly face against her cheek.

'You're safe with me, Ethel, never fear. I won't get you into no trouble.' His patting fingers pinched and she gave a little squeal. 'You go on in to that lovely daughter of yours. I bet she's got the kettle on, waiting for you. A nice cup of tea, eh? That's what you want.'

He didn't add that he could have done with one himself, but one evening, as they sat in the Coach and Horses, Ethel gave him a coy look and leaned closer.

'I've been thinking, Reg. It don't seem right, you buying me drinks all the time and me never giving nothing back. And looking after me the way you do – seeing me back to my door, and all that. I know I've been careful – a woman in my position has to be careful of her reputation, what with George away fighting for his country and all – but I don't see as anyone could make anything out of an innocent friendship. And those that do aren't worth bothering about, that's what I reckon.' She stopped, trying to drag together the thread of her thoughts. 'What I want to say is this: well, if you wants a bit more comfort than you get in a pub – a bit of home cooking, you know, that sort of thing – you've only got to say. I can't promise nothing special, mind, but whatever I've got, I'm happy to share with you. There.'

'Well,' he said, pretending to consider, 'I must say that's very handsome of you, Ethel. Very handsome indeed. And I appreciate all you say about your reputation, and that. I wouldn't want to harm a lady's reputation, specially a lady as pretty and dainty as you. So if you'd rather I only came in the blackout, when all those nosy neighbours of yours have got their curtains drawn, well, that's all right with me. And as for your offer to share whatever you've got – I'd be more than happy to bring along some little contribution of my own. *More* than happy.' He paused to glare at Percy, who was snorting into his beer. 'So all in all, I'd say yes, thank you very kindly, I'd like to take you up on your offer. I'd like it very much indeed.'

'And the same goes for you,' Violet said to Percy. 'I agree with Ethel – I think you boys deserve a bit of home comfort when you're so far away from home. You can come along and sit by my fire any time you like.'

They lifted their glasses and drank deeply. Then Reg set his down and stared solemnly at Ethel.

'There's only one thing worrying me. What about this little girl of yours? Little Carol? I mean, I wouldn't want to frighten her in any way. I wouldn't want her to see anything she shouldn't – you know?'

'Don't worry about her,' Ethel said. Her face had gone rather red, and her eyes were pink. She set her glass on the edge of the table and fumbled to catch it as it tipped. 'Don't you worry about my Carol. She won't see nothing. I'll make sure of that.'

There wasn't much to cheer Bert Shaw up these days. He was learning, in a grudging manner, to look after himself – scrambling together his meals and doing his bit of washing on a Sunday evening because he'd be out at work first thing Monday, and Peggy had always said Monday was the day washing should appear on the line. He didn't bother too much with the ironing. It was far too much trouble to heat up the old flat iron and get it to just the right temperature, sprinkling water on clothes that had dried too much (he never did get the knack of fetching them in from the line while they were still damp) and then pressing his shirts and folding them in the way Peggy had done.

'It's an art in itself, that is,' he said to Jess as she gave him his Sunday dinner. 'I dunno how it is, but there's always one sleeve that gets sort of crooked up and then falls out, and then the whole lot's in a heap again, worse than it was to start with. Anyway, I don't see as it matters. I've got me jacket on over the top so who's to know whether me shirt's creased or not?'

Jess shook her head and smiled. Part of her wanted to tell Bert to pass his ironing over the fence to her, but Frank had told her quite firmly that she wasn't to take on all Bert's work.

'He's just sitting there listening to the wireless half the time,' he said. 'He keeps saying he'll do something about the garden, but it's going to rack and ruin again. I know it's hard on him, being left on his own, and I know Peggy was your friend, but you've got more than enough to do.'

'I know, but it seems so pathetic, somehow. The other day he came in and asked me how to fold an egg. He'd got this recipe he was trying out, and it said to fold in an egg. He said he couldn't do it with the shell on so he broke it and tipped it into a bowl and he *still* couldn't work out how to fold it. I couldn't help laughing, but it seemed sort of sad as well, a great big man like him standing there wondering how to fold eggs.'

'He's lucky to have an egg to fold,' said Frank, who wasn't altogether sure himself what it meant. 'I daresay it was one of our eggs anyway, wasn't it?'

The hens Frank had installed in a run at the end of the garden, between the Anderson shelter and his workshed, had been a success and there were enough eggs for the family as well as a few left over for friends. You weren't supposed to sell them, but who was to say how many had been laid? Jess collected them every day and marked the date on them with pencil before putting them in a bowl.

'Anyway, Gladys is coming home at the weekend on a forty-eight-hour-leave pass,' she said. 'That'll put a bit of a smile on his face. I just hope he isn't saving up too many jobs for the poor girl to do!'

Gladys was working at Fort Southwick, on the slopes of Portsdown Hill, the long ridge which rose behind Portsmouth Harbour and sheltered it from inland Hampshire. Fort Southwick was one of the range of nineteenth-century forts, part earthwork and part brick, which encircled Portsmouth and Gosport, and were known collectively as 'Palmerston Follies'. They had been constructed under the orders of Lord Palmerston, Queen Victoria's Prime Minister, who had envisaged a time when Britain might be attacked again by their old enemy, France.

The invasion had never come and Palmerston had been laughed to scorn by his own enemies for wasting money, but now the forts were all in use as Service headquarters and ammunition depots. Out in the Solent, there were three others, grim chequered bastions built of stone on the seabed itself, which were now part of the 'boom' – a long fence of thick, pointed staves which stretched across from Portsmouth to the Isle of Wight, with only one or two gaps for shipping to pass through.

Fort Southwick was the HQ now of Admiral Sir Charles Little, who was Commander-in-Chief of Portsmouth Command. Gladys was training as a 'plotter', bending over a huge map of the seaways which was spread on a vast tabletop in the operations 'room' – a maze of old brick tunnels a hundred feet below the ground, which radiated out from a central corridor lined with steel. Here was all the new, and still secret, radio telegraphy equipment needed for keeping in touch with ships in the Channel and forces on the French coast.

All the ships known to be in the area were represented by models, and these were pushed across the maps by Gladys and several other Wrens as the news of their position came through on the RT. In this way the progress of a sea battle far away could be monitored by the Admiral and his staff at home.

Gladys smiled and shook her head when Bert asked her what she did, and he scowled and almost spoiled the visit before it had properly begun.

'All dressed up in a posh uniform you might be, but you're still my daughter and under my jurisdiction, and don't you forget it. I don't see as there can be anything that secret that you can't tell your own father. If you ask me, you're just using it as an excuse not to come home and do your rightful duty.'

'I've told you, Dad. We're not allowed to talk about it.' She hadn't even told Cliff, and he knew better than to ask. Their letters talked of themselves and the small happenings of their daily lives, and to Gladys the arrival of the small envelopes, crumpled sometimes from being carried about in Clifford's pocket before they got posted, was becoming more and more important. It seemed that Cliff was the only one she could talk to properly these days, and it helped to think of him while she was trying to cope with her father.

Maybe he's right, she thought. Maybe we are suited to be together, but I can't think about that till after all this is over. There just isn't *time*.

She had told Cliff as much when he had asked her to marry him, the last time they'd met. They'd gone to the pictures together and he'd turned to her quite suddenly, in the interval between the big picture and the little one, and asked her straight out. She'd been so surprised she'd almost said yes – and then she'd bitten her tongue.

'Cliff, I've told you. I don't want to think about anything like that till the war's over. I can't.'

'If it's your dad . . . ' he began, but she shook her head.

'It's not just Dad. Look, I've seen friends of mine who've got married in a hurry, and some of them are regretting it already. Some of them haven't seen their husbands for a year, *two* years. What's it going to be like when they try to start again, after all they're going through now? They'll be like strangers.' She shook her head. 'I want to get back to normal before I think about settling down.'

'D'you mean you don't think it'll last?' he asked. 'You think it's just a flash in the pan?'

'I don't know. I don't *know*. But I think we ought to give ourselves a chance to find out – before we do something that can't be undone.'

The lights had dimmed then and the second picture started. After a few minutes, Cliff had put his arm around her shoulders and drawn her close. Gladys resisted a little at first, then relaxed against his shoulder. It felt comfortable and strong.

'I'd like to say yes,' she whispered, 'but I just can't – not yet. I'm sorry.'

'It's all right.' He squeezed her shoulders gently and turned to kiss her cheek. 'It's all right, Gladys. So long as we can go on being friends. I told you before – I'll wait.'

It seemed wrong to make him wait, but what else could she do? Meanwhile, she must be patient too. Patient with herself, and patient with her father. Above all, patient with the war that was holding up all their lives.

'Cooking and cleaning,' Bert grumbled. 'That's what the women's Services are for. You could be doing that just as well at home and still be doing your bit for your country.'

'We don't do cooking and cleaning. At least, some do, but so do some of the men. We do all the other jobs as well.'

'What sort of jobs, then?' he challenged her, but Gladys refused to rise to the bait.

'Secret jobs, Dad. Honestly, we're not allowed to say. I'd tell you if I could, I would really.'

It was quite clear to Gladys why her work should be secret, although she was also aware of something larger behind it all, something that wasn't yet known to anyone but a very few. It was to do with the gradual amassing of troops and ships along the south coast, the sudden flood of Canadians, and the mysterious building work that had begun in unlikely places.

You could see some of it from the top of the Hill. Langstone Harbour, on the eastern side of Portsea Island, was full of huge concrete caissons and massive floating blocks, like a giant child's playground. And when she went over to Gosport to see Elsie Philpotts, Gladys heard about the building that was going on in Stokes Bay.

'It's all along the beach,' Elsie said. 'I know we're not supposed to talk about things, but everyone knows, you can't help knowing. I mean, you can *see* it – huge scaffolds, big as three houses on top of each other, they are, must be getting on for a hundred feet high. God knows what it's meant to be. I mean, it's never going to float, whatever it is.'

There was a constant coming and going of vehicles too. Tanks and

DUKWs were gathering at the far end of the bay, where the Royal Engineers were quartered in Bay House. They ran down the beach on the hard concrete slipways that had been built all the way along, and were tested in the water. The gigantic caissons were floated as well – despite Elsie's misgivings – and towed away. Nobody knew where they went, but someone told Charlie Philpotts they were just taken out to sea and sunk. There didn't seem to be any rhyme or reason in it.

'They reckon one of 'em turned over, when they were hauling it down the beach,' he said. 'Squashed three blokes flat. They got to wash out all the sand and seaweed now before they tries to move 'em.'

There were other mysterious things going on too. Talk of plywood ships that would never be seaworthy, inflatable dummy aircraft that would never fly. It was almost as if the powerful men who had run the war so far – and run it badly, some said – had retreated into a second childhood and started to make monstrous toys. There had to be some reason for it all, though, and no one knew anyway which was truth or which was just talk. Perhaps it really was best, after all, to close one's ears to gossip and not talk at all.

Generally, people didn't discuss what was going on. They stood aside as the tanks rumbled through the streets, leaving the imprint of their tracks on the kerbstones, and did what they could for the throngs of Servicemen who crowded the town. Gladys, who probably knew more than any of them, from her work at Fort Southwick, kept her own mouth firmly shut.

'I'm sorry, Dad,' she said again. 'If it got out that I'd breathed a word to anyone at all, I'd be on jankers for the duration. Or worse. You wouldn't want that to happen to me, now would you? Who'd come home and bake you a cake now and then, and darn all those socks you keep wearing through?'

Bert opened his mouth to say that she ought to know he wouldn't go blabbing it about, but he closed it again with the words unspoken. Gladys was right, he knew. Everyone had to keep quiet about what they did. If you never said a word, there was no chance it would get out. He still couldn't help feeling fed up about it, though.

The trouble with Dad, Gladys thought, watching his grumpy face, was that he was missing Mum's constant flow of brisk chatter. He might have seemed as if he wasn't listening, half the time, but in fact he'd depended on her for his entertainment, and a lot of his information. He tried to fill the gap by having the wireless on whenever he was in the house, but although he liked hearing comedians like Arthur Askey and programmes like *Stand Easy* and *Much Binding in the Marsh* – and, of course, *ITMA*, which had been running since the war began – it wasn't the same as having a real live person about the place, and the quickfire humour sometimes left him flummoxed. He liked to take his time listening, and if you missed a joke it wasn't any good asking them to repeat it, they were on to the next three before you could blink.

'I just wish something good'd happen in this war,' he said lugubriously. 'Something to take our minds off it a bit.'

So perhaps it was people like him that Field Marshal Montgomery had in mind when he agreed to become the first president of Portsmouth Football Club. People remembered that he'd been a keen supporter when he'd been Garrison Commander in Portsmouth. He'd watched games at Fratton Park several times and said, proudly, that he'd never seen Pompey lose.

Bert saw him at Fratton at the end of March, when Pompey played Brentford. Both teams were lined up to be presented to the great man, and he was cheered as Churchill had been cheered in the Guildhall Square a month earlier. Jess Budd was right, Bert thought, it did give you a bit of heart, seeing these people who had to run the worst war the world had ever known, taking time to walk about and talk to ordinary folk, and do ordinary things like go to football matches. Somehow, it made you feel as if they still knew you were there after all – they hadn't forgotten about the ordinary man in the street.

Churchill was well over his illness now, and made another of his famous wireless broadcasts. He never pulled any punches, did Churchill, never pretended that things were better than they were – almost the other way about, indeed – and yet somehow the fact that he faced up to the worst with everyone else seemed to give strength. It was as if he was saying, 'We're all in this together, mates, and if we pull together we'll win . . . ' This time – and Jess could imagine that bulldog head thrust forward as he spoke – he was telling the nation that 'the hour of our greatest effort is approaching'. Our greatest effort! she thought. How could anyone make any greater effort than they'd been doing? But somehow, she knew, with this pugnacious and determined man leading them, people would find that extra bit of strength he demanded, and the effort would be made.

However, as April took over from March with its softer air and promise of springtime, it seemed as if the effort required might be just too much. The relentless attacks on Germany had been a failure, won without doubt by the Luftwaffe. In a single raid over Nuremberg, nearly 550 airmen died. During the past five months, well over a thousand bombers had been lost and, as Jess had said, most of the crews were young men under twenty years old. Many of them were shot down on their first operation; for the others, there was only a fifty per cent chance of completing their tours of thirty operations.

On 1 April, a ten-mile-deep belt of coastland from Land's End to the Wash was declared a Protected Area and closed to the public. Nobody who did not either live in this vast area, or have official business there, was permitted access, and everyone must carry their identity card at all times. There would be a hundred per cent check at railway and bus stations, and on any other public vehicles, as well as in hotels, guest houses and places of amusement, and anyone not carrying their card would be arrested at once.

The residents of April Grove, together with all those in Portsmouth and in all other towns and villages along the south and south-east coasts, heard the announcement with a mixture of bewilderment and apprehension.

'They're expecting an invasion,' Jess said fearfully. 'After all this time. That's what all this is about. All these troops and secrets and things we're not supposed to have noticed. Oh, Frank . . .'

Frank and Cherry, who had both been involved in the strange and secret activities in Portsmouth harbour and the dockyard and knew about the huge constructions, and unfamiliar equipment being built in some of the workshops, glanced at each other and shook their heads.

'No,' Frank said quietly, 'it's not going to be an invasion, Jess. At least – not in England.' He paused for a moment, as if deliberating whether he should say any more at all. Jess was reminded of his admonitions to Tim and Keith – 'Walls Have Ears. Be Like Dad – Keep Mum' – but they were at home now, and their walls didn't have any ears. After all, what could Frank know that everyone else didn't?

'So what do you think it *is* all about?' she persisted. 'What d'you reckon *is* going to happen?'

'Something big,' he said. 'Something very, very big.' He glanced at Cherry again and decided that it wasn't fair to Jess to keep them from her, the things he knew and the things he suspected.

'They're getting ready to invade Europe,' he said. 'We're sending our men into France again, Jess, and this time we're going to win.'

# CHAPTER FOURTEEN

Soon, it was apparent to everyone that the country was moving towards the full-scale invasion of Europe.

All military leave was stopped. Mail and telephone communications were allowed under only the strictest supervision. The British Isles were effectively sealed off from the outside world, and the south coast of England was the jumping-off point for thousands of Service personnel. The whole place seemed to be crawling with uniforms, and yet still they poured in, until it seemed that there couldn't be space for even the smallest cadet.

'They're going all out this time,' Frank said, adding, 'Let's hope it won't be another Dunkirk, or Dieppe.' But nobody could believe that the Allies could make another mistake like those. Surely this time, and with so much preparation, they would get it right.

Frank had just been down to the police station for the third time, about the parachute that had dropped on to the allotments.

'They didn't seem to be interested at all,' he told Jess, who was still hoping she'd be able to use the fine silk for sewing. 'I suppose they've got a lot more things to think about. I'm surprised anyone can think about anything else, really, with all this going on.'

'Someone still can, though, thank goodness. We're getting a better jam and sugar ration – two pounds of jam and two pounds of sugar for preserving, or three pounds of sugar and no jam, or six pounds of jam and no sugar.' She laughed at his face. 'Well, there's no need to look like that! It's quite simple. See, if you want to make jam, you get—'

'Never mind,' Frank broke in. 'I've got quite enough trouble doing my own work without trying to understand yours. Ration books are a mystery to me – it's no wonder poor old Bert gets a bit down in the mouth trying to master it all. I wouldn't like to have to manage without you, I know that.'

Jess thought of Peggy and felt a sudden lump in her throat. It *was* awful for Bert, losing first his wife and then his daughters who had joined up at almost the same time, left all on his own and having to manage by himself. It wasn't just a matter of a bit of washing and cooking – it was having to learn it all at once, after years of having it done for him, and doing it with no one to help, no one to have a bit of a laugh with, even no one to speak to him a bit sharp now and then.

She imagined Frank, left alone in number 14, fumbling about in the scullery with a frying-pan, trying to scrub his working clothes, going to bed by himself. Well, he hadn't made a bad job of it when she'd gone away with the first wave of evacuees at the beginning of the war, but she'd soon come back to look after him. A working man needed his wife at home – and Jess had needed Frank, too.

'Poor Bert,' she said. 'I know I still miss Peggy every day. It must be much worse for him. Poor, poor Bert.'

Diane Shaw came home for the occasional weekend to see her father, but she had changed from the effervescent, frivolous girl who had gone into the WAAF. Her eyes were dark with fatigue and her sparkle seemed dimmed. She sat in her mother's chair beside the fire, opposite Bert's, darning the big pile of socks that always accumulated while he was on his own, and listened to the wireless.

She spent quite a lot of her time thinking about the pilot of the Fortress they'd salvaged. He was stationed at the American air station a few miles down the road, and there was quite a lot of coming and going between the two camps. The WAAFs were invited to dances there, and after some persuasion Diane had gone along with Lizanellie, pretending indifference.

'Aren't our boys good enough?' she'd sniffed, but she couldn't help feeling envious when Lizanellie showed her nylon stockings and chocolates they'd been given. 'Well, if they've got stuff to give away, we might as well get the benefit, I suppose. So long as they don't go thinking it gives them any rights over us.'

The dance was held in an empty hangar. It was almost full when they walked in, with American airmen and local girls as well as the WAAFs who had been invited from all the neighbouring stations. At one end, a stage had been rigged up and the band was already playing – mostly tunes they all knew, like Glenn Miller's 'String of Pearls' and 'In The Mood'. The floor was packed with dancers, and Lizanellie immediately began to jig about in time to the music.

'Isn't it smashing! I think the jitterbug's the best dance there ever was.' A couple of airmen had swept them on to the floor almost before Lizanellie One had finished speaking, and Diane was left alone by the wall. She stood hesitating for a moment, unused to the feeling of being a wallflower, and not liking it much.

She glanced around the hangar. It had been decorated with streamers and balloons – *balloons*! Diane hadn't seen a balloon for years – but the lighting had been left dim. Nearly everyone was dancing. The quickstep and waltz were supplanted by the feverishly energetic jitterbug, which all the girls had practised in the hut before coming. Diane had thought she was pretty good at it, but some of the couples seemed to be almost frenzied. She watched, fascinated, as they swung each other to and fro.

'Well, hi there.' She turned, startled, at the sound of a familiar voice, and saw the pilot of the Fortress standing close beside her. 'So you've decided to give us a look-over. Having a good time?'

'Oh, hullo,' she said, collecting herself. 'You still around? I thought you'd have got fed up and gone back to the States by now.'

'Now, why would you have thought a thing like that?' he drawled. 'We're having far too much fun over here. Or hadn't you heard.'

'Oh, I've heard,' Diane said. 'Overpaid, over-sexed and over here. Haven't seen much sign of it myself yet. Except that you're over here, of course. We can't miss that.'

'You mean nobody's tried to prove the other two to you?' He shook his head. 'That's too bad.'

'They probably know better than to try,' Diane retorted. She glanced around in a bored fashion. 'I don't know that I'll stop much longer. I've got things to do – you know, letters home, that sort of thing.'

'Better things than being here? Now that's a real shame – I was hoping you'd give me a dance.'

'Really?' Diane said coolly. 'Won't any of the other girls dance with you, then?'

The American raised his eyebrows. 'Why, sure they would. I was hoping to dance with *you*.'

'Well, sorry to disappoint you and all that, but I don't think so, thanks. I'm not really interested in dancing.' That must be the biggest lie I've ever told, she thought. 'I only came along because my friends wanted me to.'

'The double act?' He grinned as one of the Lizanellies went past, squealing with excitement as her partner twisted her this way and that. 'Well, they seem to be having a whale of a time. C'mon – give it a try, why don't you?' Diane shook her head. Part of her badly wanted to accept and show just how good a dancer she was, but another part recoiled from the thought of being in this man's arms, or even held at arm's length. I just don't want him to touch me at all, she thought.

'Try one of the others. The queue starts over there.'

They faced each other for a few moments. His blue eyes narrowed and Diane felt her chin lift a little in defiance, then he shrugged and turned away.

'Suit yourself. Like you say, there are plenty of other pebbles on the beach.' He walked off and a moment later Diane saw him lead a petite brunette in civilian clothes on to the floor.

She watched, feeling an odd tightness in her chest. He was even better looking than she remembered. And probably twice as conceited too, she thought grimly, turning her back.

Dancing with the Americans was quite different from dancing with British boys and Diane could see that her friends were soon breathless from being whirled and twisted on the floor to the jazzy music of the band. She caught sight of Lizanellie, dancing with equal vigour, laughing all over their faces as they swung this way and that, and she saw the pilot too, lifting the brunette right over his shoulder. She squealed and kicked her legs. Showing everything she's got, Diane thought scornfully.

It was surprising how often she caught sight of the pilot after that. He always seemed to be dancing with a different girl and didn't seem to notice Diane at all, but he came up to her again during the interval and gave her a quizzical look.

'Still here? Reckon you must be getting pretty fed up, just standing around watching.'

Diane shrugged. 'I only came to please my mates. I'm going soon.'

'Well,' he went on as the band struck up again, 'you might as well have one dance before you go. You never know, you might like it. Or are you scared you might smile and crack your face?'

Diane drew in a deep breath, but before she could answer he put out his hand to take her wrist. Her yelp of surprise was lost in a sudden blast of music, and before she could resist he had swung her into a fast jitterbug. For a moment or two, she tried to pull away, but his fingers had hers fast and he only jerked her harder into the dance. Her feet slipped almost of their own volition into the rhythm she had practised so often in the hut, and when he swung her over his shoulder she squealed and kicked her legs in just the same way as the little brunette had done. He set her back on her feet and grinned, and to Diane's own amazement she found herself smiling back at him. Her barriers crumbled and by the time the dance ended and he pulled her towards him and threw her across his shoulder again, she was laughing.

They sat down and the pilot looked at her and grinned again. His eyes were just as crinkly as she remembered.

'Who's a little liar, then? Not interested in dancing, huh? I reckon you owe me something for that.'

'I don't have to tell you everything I can do,' Diane said.

'You mean there's more?' He raised his brows and she flushed. 'You can't fool me this time – you're a pretty good dancer. Want a drink?'

Diane shrugged. 'I don't mind.' Now that the dance was over, she was re-erecting the barriers, though she didn't know why. Somehow, she felt safer behind them.

'If I go and get us one,' he said, 'you won't disappear while I'm away, will you?'

'Why shouldn't I? It's a free country.'

'For the time being,' he said. 'That's what we're fighting for, as I understand it.' He looked at her again. 'I'd rather you didn't, all the same.'

He went off and Diane watched him uncertainly. There was something about this man that disturbed her. It was as if he was in charge, and where men were concerned Diane was used to being in charge. She had grown accustomed to the power that her sex gave her, and the sense that although this man was quite well aware of her attraction he was not intimidated by it, scared her a little. It was as if she had lost control.

She toyed briefly with the idea of slipping away. Who was he, after all, to order her to stay where she was? However, before she had made up her mind, he was back with a glass of beer in each hand.

'It's cold!' she exclaimed in surprise, and he laughed.

'That's the way we like it. Coffee hot, beer cold.' His eyes crinkled again. 'My name's Charles M. Caraway. Chuck, for short. What's yours?'

'Chuck? That's not short for Charles. *Charlie*'s short for Charles.'

'It's Chuck where I come from.' He was still looking at her interrogatively. 'You haven't told me your name yet.'

'It's Diane.'

'Diane, huh? That's pretty. Do they call you Di?'

'Sometimes.' Nobody had ever told Diane her name was pretty. She'd always thought it very ordinary. It was probably just one of the lines Americans liked to shoot. She sipped her beer, looking at the floor.

'I've seen your pals here,' he said after a minute or two. 'The lookalikes. I guess it gets pretty confusing for them, with the guys, I mean.'

'I don't think so. They've been twins all their lives, they know who they are.'

It took a few seconds for him to get her meaning. Then he laughed. 'Oh, I guess they know themselves all right. It's the guys must get confused. You kiss a girl one night and the next day she acts like she's never seen you in her life. Happens to all of us, but with those two it could be true. How's a guy to know what to do the third time?'

'I think Lizanellie would let him know all right,' Diane said, laughing despite herself.

'Yeah, but suppose it wasn't her – whaddya call her, Lizanellie? What's the other one's name?'

'That's what they're both called. At least, it's what we call them. One's called Liz and the other's Ellie. We just call them Lizanellie – Lizanellie One and Two.'

He stared at her. 'You mean you can't tell the difference either?'

Diane shook her head, her lips twitching. Chuck stared a moment longer, then threw back his head and laughed, and this time she laughed with him. It suddenly seemed very funny.

'Well, if that don't beat popcorn,' he said at last. 'Lizanellie One and Two. I wonder if their own mother can tell 'em apart!' The band was striking up again, a Glenn Miller tune that Diane loved. He grabbed her wrist. 'Come on, baby – we're missing all the best dances. Let's jitterbug!'

There was no more talk of Diane leaving early. Instead, they danced every dance together, pausing only for drinks of beer to replace the sweat that poured down their faces as they jived. At the end of the evening, they stood in a corner of the hangar and looked at each other.

'That was great,' he said. 'I'd like to do it again. How about you?'

Diane lifted her shoulders. 'If there are any more dances . . .'

'Oh, there'll be more. As long as we're here.'

Diane remembered suddenly why he was here. She tilted her head.

'Crashed any more kites lately?'

He narrowed his eyes. 'If I did, would you come out and pick up the pieces?'

'Depends what pieces you want me to pick up,' she said, looking him in the eye.

There was a tiny pause. Diane wished she hadn't said it. It was the kind of flippant remark she would make to any man, but it wasn't the sort of thing she wanted to say to Chuck. Despite their abandoned dancing, she still didn't want him to get past those barriers.

It didn't seem, however, as if he shared her inhibitions. He cocked one eye at her and said, 'Why don't we discuss it over a drink at that pub I was talking about? But just you and me, hm? Don't bring the double act.'

She had hesitated only for a second. Then, in the manner that was fast becoming a habit, she shrugged and said, 'I don't mind.'

He grinned. 'One of these days,' he said, 'someone's going to say "Neither do I", and leave you flat, but not just yet, pretty Diane. Not just yet.'

Towards the end of April, Gladys was moved from Fort Southwick down into the village of Southwick itself. It seemed an unlikely place for a war headquarters, but this was the centre that had been chosen, and Southwick House was the heart of it. Surrounded by several hundred acres of walled parkland, it was quiet, secure and yet within easy reach of Portsmouth. And it could be protected from enemy attack by the gun emplacements along the hill, and those scorned 'Palmerston Follies'.

There had been Wrens at Southwick House ever since the navigation school had come here, when the estate was first requisitioned in 1941. It had all been quite primitive then, one of them told Gladys when she arrived: only an old oil-fired generator for electricity, and no proper mains water, just a well. The Navy had soon taken that in hand, in its normal efficient manner, and now everything worked. They had also built a few Nissen huts and set up over seventy Bofors guns at strategic points on the slopes.

'There was an old man living here before,' Judy said, sitting on her bed to cut her toenails. 'His family'd been here for generations. They chucked him out – *really* chucked him out, I mean. He just wouldn't go. They put him in a house in the village but he went on being a pain in the you-know-what and they shifted him down to Broomfield House. That's on the edge of the estate. He's dead now – died last November – but we used to see him sometimes, being pushed about in a wheelchair and swearing about Admiral James – he was the one who got the Navvies moved here.'

'Poor old man,' Gladys said. 'It's horrible to have to move out of your home.'

'Well, that's war, isn't it?' Judy observed. 'And it's not as if he was in a hovel. *I* wouldn't mind living at Broomfield, I can tell you.'

Gladys thought she wouldn't have minded living in Southwick House itself. It was a huge mansion, three storeys high and with a row of tall stone columns running along the whole front. She stood on the lawn one day and counted twenty-seven windows on the front of the main part alone, and that was without counting the two-storey building at one side. She wondered what people did with all those rooms. Some of them were big enough in themselves to put her dad's house in and still have room for the coalshed, and the whole house would have taken April Grove and half of March or October Street without any trouble.

Judy said that the Wrens had lived in South Lodge, on the edge of the grounds, when they'd first come to Southwick. 'But that was too comfortable. We weren't used to it, so they got in some Nissen huts to make us feel more at home.'

There were over forty Nissen huts in the South Lodge gardens and in the old paddock beside the spinney, which was a spinney in name only now, covered with concrete and buildings. On one side of the clock tower was a Nissen hut which acted as a meteorological office, and the stable block had been taken over by the Action Information Training Centre (AITC for short) and converted into plotting rooms which were filled with models, and huge table charts and maps of the south coast and seaways. The main house was used by the Naval C.-in-C., Admiral Sir Bertram Ramsay and his staff, and it was rumoured that more high-ups – no one knew, or would say, just who – were coming as well.

The grounds of the park were filled with tents and caravans, looking like a huge camping site. Judy told Gladys that she'd once been to a camping site on the Devon coast that looked just like this. It was run by the Co-op, where her dad worked, and employees could go there for a week every summer.

'It wasn't all that different from here, actually,' she remarked. 'We used to get up early every morning and do drill and go for route marches – only they called them hikes – just the same!'

Everyone knew now that the massive operation was the preparation for the invasion of Europe. With the lessons of Dunkirk and Dieppe firmly in mind, and knowing that this had to be the last chance, nobody was going to make any mistakes. The whole campaign must be planned in meticulous detail and in total secrecy. Anyone who asked too many questions was firmly told, 'Yours is not to reason why . . .' The rest of that quotation was '. . .yours is but to do or die', but no one needed to complete it.

Gladys worked hard at her plotting. Most of the training consisted of 'mock' battles played over the RT, while the girls moved model ships about on the sea-charts to denote their progress. With information from both ships and spotter planes, the controller could see an overall picture that an individual captain couldn't, and give guidance and even orders, while a ship that had been hit or might even be sinking could be sent aid.

The real thing was going on all the time, of course, but once the invasion had begun the scale would be far greater. That was when Gladys and the other Wrens would be expected to be able to work swiftly and accurately, and all their training was geared to that end.

In the evenings, she and Judy and some of the others would walk into the village. After a day in the plotting room, they were glad to be able to get out in the fresh air, and Southwick was a pretty and friendly village, its flint-walled church and timbered houses dreaming around a tiny green with a pump where many people still drew their water. It had a minute village shop that seemed to find room for almost everything anyone could ever need, from tobacco for the Admiral's pipe to writing paper and pens for letters home. You could get these things in the NAAFI too, of course, but it was more fun to go to the shop, and it gave life that touch of ordinariness which they all craved.

'I dunno what is ordinary any more, mind,' Gladys said as they came out of the shop and lounged against the church wall. 'I mean, I used to come over here on my bike before the war started. It was really quiet then – you wouldn't see a soul, just a cat washing itself on a wall, or a dog laying in the sun, or maybe someone doing a bit of gardening – but now there's people all over the place, and you don't know who you're going to walk into when you turn a corner.'

'You're right,' Judy agreed. 'I never saw so much scrambled egg in my life! Never thought I'd get within spitting distance of a real live Admiral, let alone stand rubbing shoulders with him in the village shop. The people who live here don't seem to take a bit of notice. It's as if they don't even *see* our uniforms.'

'They all know there's something big happening, that's why. What you don't know, you can't pass on.'

There was a pub as well, the Golden Lion, which was more or less taken over by the Navy. Its two lounge bars were named Blue and Gold, after the colours of the Lloyd Loom furniture they sported, and the Blue Room was immediately adopted by the Naval officers as their unofficial mess. The public bar was a cheerful mixture of Service men and women, and locals, all lifting their stone mugs of beer high, cheering and singing.

The village school was just along the street. Gladys had been in there yesterday, taking a message to the fat American general who presided in the schoolroom. There'd been a meeting in progress, with brigadiers and colonels as well as one or two other generals, all looking awkwardly large and cramped as they tried to sit at small desks normally used by children under ten. The American general had been talking about the big map that was pinned on the wall – a map of the world, such as could be found in any classroom in the land, with the deep pink of countries belonging to the British Empire showing up bravely against the others. We're still king of them all, Gladys thought with a sudden lump in her throat, we've still got most of the world behind us . . . But as she stood at the back of the schoolroom, waiting to be noticed, the general unrolled another map and pinned it over the first, and she saw that this was a map of France, and that there were strange names written on it, names that weren't French at all, that weren't the names of any places that she had ever heard of.

Mulberry, she saw before the nearest officer turned sharply and held out his hand for the message she carried. Neptune. Omaha. Sword.

Overlord . . .

The roads and lanes that led through Hampshire to the seaports of Portsmouth, Southampton and Lymington, were choked with vehicles. They flooded through the villages – British, Canadian, American, in lorries, tanks, armoured cars and DUKWs, the strange amphibious carriers that could be used as both wheeled vehicles and seagoing vessels. There were other vehicles too, peculiar-looking things which nobody could recognise and which were quickly dubbed 'the Funnies'.

'They'll be able to do all sorts with them,' Ray said. 'They'll be able to lay tracks over boggy ground or soft sand for the others that can't manage it, and they'll be able to sweep up mines and rescue tanks and stuff that get caught . . . They can think of anything these days.'

He and Olive spent every possible spare moment together. The little boarding-house off Fawcett Road was their second home now. They went there whenever they could and the woman who ran it always kept the same room for them. She had few enough visitors now, and was glad of even the little Olive and Ray could pay her. There'd been a nasty moment when the ban on movement was first laid down and all her guests checked, but she'd tipped Ray the wink when he'd come in to book up and he'd pretended he was just asking directions. The redcap who was looking through her visitors' book gave him a narrow stare and demanded to see his ID, but had seemed satisfied enough, and after that it had been all right.

The room was small and rather dark, with brown wallpaper and cold linoleum on the floor, but there was a double bed, and that was all Olive and Ray cared about. They lay there for hours, close in each other's arms, neither wanting to waste the time by sleeping, and tried to pretend they were really married.

'I think we'll decorate this room,' Olive said one morning, gazing up at the cracked ceiling. 'Strip off that horrible wallpaper and give the walls a coat of distemper. A nice duck-egg blue, what d'you think? D'you like blue in a bedroom, Ray? I do.'

'I'll like anything you like,' he said sleepily. 'My mum always says it's a woman's job to make a home, and I reckon you'd be a lovely little homemaker, Livvy. What shall we do downstairs?'

'In the back room?' She considered. 'I'd like wallpaper there. With flowers on. My gran had some lovely wallpaper in her room with big blue roses all over it. Grandad grumbled because it was hard to put up – the roses had to match exactly – but it looked really nice when it was done. I'd like something like that.'

'Blue roses,' he said. 'You like blue, don't you? What would you have in the kitchen? Blue again?'

'I don't know. Everyone says green and cream look nice in a kitchen, but I think blue could look lovely. Fresh, you know.'

'Mm.' He kissed her neck. 'Let's forget about the kitchen. I'd rather talk about bedrooms. You know, I never liked wallpapering and that sort of thing before, but I reckon with you it'd be fun. Doing up our own home – that'd be smashing.' He was silent for a moment, then added with a touch of bitterness, 'That's if we're not past it by the time this bloody war's over.'

'Past it?' Olive said, pinching his thigh. 'Don't be daft – you'll never be past it.' She squealed and giggled as he grasped her hand and squeezed it hard against him. 'You see?'

'Past decorating, I meant. Anyway, it's too soon – give me another twenty minutes and I'll show you who's past it.' He looked thoughtful. 'I wonder when people really do get past it. You hear some of the older blokes in the mess talking sometimes as if they were just lads, but I don't reckon they really get up to half what they say they do. To look at some of them, you wonder if they ever did. I mean, what girl would fancy old Toady?'

Olive laughed. Toady was a sergeant with a wide, flat face and a big, loose-lipped mouth. He wasn't simple, or he'd never have been a sergeant, but he was slow-thinking and easy to tease.

'Well, someone must have. He's married, isn't he?'

'I know, it's amazing. Makes you wonder what his wife's like.'

'Probably a princess who got caught out,' Olive said wickedly. 'He told her he'd turn into a prince if she kissed him, and she's still waiting.'

'Still trying to pluck up the courage, I'd say.' They lay in silence for a few moments and then he said, 'All the same, Olive, I think we've got to take what happiness we can while we've got the chance. We're all in danger – you, me, Derek – and if we get bombed or shot that's it, finish, goodbye. I don't see how anyone can expect us to live like monks just because there's a war on.'

'I know, but all the same . . . ' Olive stared up at the ceiling. The questions tormented her mind, night and day. There had never been any quarrel between her and Derek. They were as much in love now as the day they married, and yet . . . if that were true, how could she lie here in another man's arms, giving him the heart and body she had given to her husband? How could she look into Ray's eyes as he held himself above her, and tell him she loved him – and mean it? Because she *did* mean it. She believed in her love for Ray, as wholly as she believed that she loved Derek.

You can't love two people at once, she thought, and even if you do, you can't marry them both. Or live with them both.

For a few minutes, she was quiet and then she turned into his arms and clutched him tightly against her. 'Oh Ray, Ray . . . what are we doing? We know it can't ever happen, not for us. It's just a dream, a lovely, impossible dream, and one day we're going to have to wake up . . .'

'Moonlight and love songs,' he said quietly. 'That's what dreams are made of, Livvy. If that's really all we can have, let's just enjoy them while we can. Forget everything else and just love each other now.'

He held her close against him and laid his lips against her ear. She could hear him singing softly, feel the quiver of his body against hers, and she closed her eyes and cast aside all thoughts of the outside world, of the war, of her parents and, most of all, of Derek, and became just Olive, lying in the arms of the man she loved.

> Moonlight and love songs, never out of date,
> Hearts full of passion, jealousy and hate,
> Woman needs man, and man must have his mate,
> That, no one can deny . . .

'I don't know about that bit "jealousy and hate",' she murmured. 'I don't feel a bit of jealousy about you, Ray, and I couldn't ever hate you.'

He held her a little more closely and didn't answer for a moment. Then he said, 'Don't let's think about that, Livvy. Let's just think about the good bits. Moonlight and love songs. That's all we have to think about now.'

'Moonlight and love songs,' she repeated, and turned her face to his for a kiss.

Dispensing home comforts became Ethel's 'little bit of war work'. She brought Reg home of an evening two or three times a week, and gave him a bit of supper and a cup of cocoa. Carol, startled when she encountered him for the first time, eyed him with hostility.

'I don't know what you want to give him our rations for,' she muttered to Ethel out in the scullery. 'They get fed like fighting cocks in the Marines. I've seen 'em up Eastney Barracks.'

'You mind your own business. Men like that need a bit of home life. We've all got to do our bit to make things easier for them.'

Carol sat at the table, aware of Reg's hot eyes on her, and spent the rest of her evenings upstairs in her bedroom. She could hear her mother and the Marine downstairs, talking, and then the voices would fade and she realised they had gone into the front room. Ethel had bullied George into buying a three-piece suite just before the war, and it had been sat on less than a dozen times. It looked as new as when it had first arrived from the shop, with starched white antimacassars laid over the backs of the chairs and settee, and a little table in the window with a green glass vase on it that Carol had won at a fair.

Carol sat on her bed, stroking her doll, its battered face mended roughly with thick, coarse sticking plaster. She pretended that it was Roderick, holding it as she had held him on that last morning, bathing him tenderly, washing in all the creases of his plump body, brushing and fluffing his hair, drying him with soft pats of the towel. She imagined dressing him in the new clothes she had made for him herself, and she looked down at his face and saw the smile break out again, the real smile that was for her alone, the smile that told her he knew her for his mother. She played 'Round and round the garden, like a teddy-bear', on his fat little hands, and 'This little piggy went to market' on his toes. She tickled him until he almost choked with giggles and she clutched him to her and buried her face in the sweet, milky creases of his neck, her love for him swelling and growing within her until she thought she would burst with it.

And then, just at the moment when her pretence was most real, she felt the cold, hard china of the doll's face against her cheek and knew that it was nothing but a dream.

They'd told her at the home that she would get over it, but it wasn't true. It was getting worse. When she woke from such dreams and felt her joy dissolve into agony, the pain was like a huge lump of jagged, broken glass that she carried inside her wherever she went. It actually hurt her to move, to bend her body, to walk. It hurt to speak and it hurt most of all to laugh, because in the middle of a laugh she would remember the smiling baby Roderick and his father Roddy, and her whole world would fall away and the lump of glass pierce her all over her inside.

She got up and went over to the chest of drawers to get out the letter Roddy had given her. It was addressed to his mother, and he'd told her that if ever she needed help she was to go to that address and give his mother the letter. Carol turned it over in her hands, wondering if Mrs Mackenzie would really welcome her. Or would she slam the door in Carol's face, for bringing such dreadful trouble on her son?

It hardly mattered. There was no chance that she could ever go to Scotland. Even if she had been able to afford the fare, the present restrictions would have stopped her from leaving the Portsmouth area, and in any case she knew that she couldn't even have mustered either the energy or the courage to go.

She wondered what her father would have thought of Ethel bringing home a Marine several times a week. Perhaps he wouldn't have minded, but it didn't seem right that they should go and sit on the best chairs, that Dad was only allowed to use at Christmas and sometimes on a Sunday. She listened to their voices, Ethel's high and rather giggly, and the rumble of Reg's deeper tones.

After a while, the voices stopped. Carol decided that he must have gone. Good riddance, she thought. I'll go down and get a drink of water and go to the lav.

She put down the doll and went down the stairs, opening the door into the tiny scullery. The lavatory was outside, its door opening from the 'conservatory' that George had built by glassing a roof across the walls of the small, square yard. Carol opened the back door, and jumped back, startled as a huge figure appeared.

'Oh! I thought you'd gone.'

Reg stared at her. There was a funny look in his small eyes, the sort of look small boys sometimes had when they'd been caught doing something they enjoyed but shouldn't do. His face was flushed and, most disconcerting of all, his shirt was off and his braces dangled round his legs.

Just as if he lived here! she thought indignantly, and stepped back quickly as he brushed against her in the doorway.

'Just having a bit of a wash,' he said easily. 'Your mum's been very kind to me, having me over for supper and all that, and she said I could make free with the kitchen sink for a few minutes. We don't get much chance of any privacy at the barracks, you know.'

Carol looked at him. It sounded a bit funny to her, but there was no accounting for the way people behaved sometimes. She went into the back room and found her mother just coming through from the short passage which led to the front room and the door to the street. Her face was pink and she was fastening the top button of her blouse. She gave Carol an unwelcoming stare.

'What're you doing down here? I thought you'd gone to bed.'

'I just came down for a drink and to go to the lav.' Carol glanced over her shoulder. The scullery door had been closed and she could hear the sound of water running. 'What's *he* doing, Mum? He didn't look to me as if he needed a wash. And it's not true about the barracks, they've got proper bathrooms and showers there and everything. What's he want to wash in our sink for?'

'I told you before,' Ethel said sharply, 'you mind your own business. It's nothing to do with you what me and my friends do. If I say he can have a wash if he feels like it, that's what he'll do. And I'd take it kindly if you'd keep out of the way in future, see? Stop upstairs, and you won't have nothing to worry about.'

'Suits me. I don't want to have to sit and be stared at by every Tom, Dick and Harry you bring home.' Carol began to fiddle with the knobs on the wireless. The usual crackling and series of burbles and squeaks began as the set warmed up, and then they heard the voices of Tommy Handley and Mrs Mopp. She sat down in her father's armchair.

'You needn't think you're going to settle in there, either. Sergeant Allen's going to have a cup of tea before he goes.'

'Well, I can't go out to the lav till he's finished in the scullery, can I?' Carol got up again and snapped off the wireless. She felt uneasy, almost frightened. There was something odd in her mother's manner, something that tied in with Reg Allen's flushed face, and she didn't like it. 'I wish you wouldn't bring him back here, Mum. I don't like him. I don't like the way he looks at me.'

'Don't be daft. Reg is a decent man and he needs a bit of company when he's so far away from home.'

'Far away my foot!' Carol snorted. 'He lives up Cosham. Joy Brunner told me her auntie knows him. Got a wife and three kids and all – *ouch*!' She put a hand up to her cheek, stinging from the slap her mother had just swung at her.

'Don't you dare say such things!' Ethel panted. Her face was white, stained with angry patches of scarlet. 'Don't you *dare*. That's not him. It's not him at all. He comes from Leeds. She's just spreading spiteful rumours, trying to get her own back on me for what I said about her dirty German father.'

'I don't blame her, neither,' Carol retorted. 'Her dad's a smashing chap, or was till they took him away, and her mum's always been nice to me. It's just you what puts everyone's backs up with your nasty remarks and thinking you're so much better than they are—'

'I'll put *your* back up for you if you go on like that, my girl, see if I don't!' Ethel glared at her. 'Don't you forget you're here on sufferance. I didn't have to take you back after you got yourself into trouble – I could've shut my door against you and told you never to come home again, told you to get down in the gutter with all the other tarts. There's plenty would have done that, I can tell you. It's not every mother's got the kindness of heart to take back a girl that's brought shame on the family the way you did.'

'Kindness of heart!' Carol exclaimed. 'So it's kindness of heart, is it, that makes you yell and shout at me from morning till night? It's kindness of heart that makes me slave away like a skivvy, after I've done a day's hard work at the barracks. It's kindness of heart that made me give up my baby, *my own baby*, and give him away to strangers who won't even call him by his proper name.' Her voice thickened with tears. 'Kindness of heart! You're a grandmother and you never even had the common decency to come and see him. You never held him in your arms or touched him, or anything. You treated him and me as if we were dirt.'

'And so you are,' Ethel said in a low, bitter tone. 'Dirt. Common, mucky dirt.'

Carol stared at her. Her face whitened. Her lips lifted at the corners, her nostrils widened, her eyes narrowed. For a moment, she looked almost frighteningly like her mother.

'Dirt?' she said in a voice that trembled. '*Common, mucky dirt?* And just what d'you think *you* are, our Mum, bringing home Marines and giving them their home comforts along with a bottle of port in Dad's front room? Don't you think *you're* dirt as well? Don't you think *you* belong right down there in the gutter with all the other tarts?' Her mouth curled with scorn. 'You think you're so much better than anybody else, don't you? But you're not. You're just a slut. I gave my baby away, all because of you!'

She turned away from Ethel's fury, and jerked open the door to the front passage. In a moment, she was out on the street and running, running up the road, running blindly with tears in her eyes and grief rising in her breast. At the top of April Grove, she almost cannoned into Annie Chapman, hurrying out of her front gate with her mac slung hastily around her shoulders, but Carol barely noticed. In the few moments since she had run from the house, she had almost forgotten her mother and the bitter quarrel they had just had. Her mind had room for one thought only.

Roderick.

She ran until she was breathless. She ran until it was almost dark, and then, exhausted, she turned with slow, dragging footsteps for home, and the dim fog to which she had become accustomed settled down again over her mind.

Despite all the official warnings about rumours, they spread all along the south coast. Three hundred German soldiers were reported killed trying to invade along Stokes Bay, and almost a thousand Americans were said to have been slaughtered by German E-boats while doing manoeuvres on a beach in South Devon. Nobody knew whether to believe the rumours or not.

The RAF was bombing coastal towns in France day and night. It couldn't be helped that they were Allies – they were occupied and in the front line, and it could only be hoped that the French citizens were able to take cover.

The whole of the south of England was now a vast armed camp. Wherever you looked, there were tanks and trucks, masses of artillery, and soldiers camped in parks and fields, even along the roadside. Those around Portsmouth and Gosport alone numbered over a million, and this was repeated all along the coast.

Nobody was in any doubt now that it was the invasion. The biggest push of all. The last massive onslaught against the enemy forces waiting across the Channel.

What they didn't know, was when it would take place. And so, silently, they waited, living life each day as it must be lived. Knowing that one morning soon they would wake to the news that the attack had begun.

The nation held its breath.

# CHAPTER FIFTEEN

Since the night of the dance, Diane had been out with Chuck half a dozen times. Irritated though she was by his cocksure manner, she hadn't been able to get him out of her mind. Probably that was *because* he irritated her, and because, although he'd invited her and Lizanellie to the pub, he hadn't seemed at all bothered when they'd refused. Imagined he was God's gift to women, Diane thought. Expected them to fall at his feet in droves. Well, here was one who wasn't going to.

She'd gone out with him, all the same. To the pub, to other dances, to the cinema the Americans had rigged up in one of the hangars, where they showed all the latest Hollywood films. She tried to be prickly at first, but he refused to be baited and after a while she relaxed and simply enjoyed herself. However, she still couldn't quite forgive him for being an American.

'How long have you been flying?' she asked him one day, as they lay on their backs in a field, chewing blades of grass. Chuck had acquired a car and they had gone out into the countryside for a jaunt. She didn't ask where he had got the petrol – it seemed to be like chocolate and nylons, supplied with unending generosity to the Americans. When she thought about it, she was very conscious of the resentment she had felt towards them ever since they'd first arrived.

'Flying? Oh, for ever.' He turned his head and grinned at her. 'About five years. I'm an old man.'

In RAF terms, she thought, that was true. Not many British pilots lived to say they'd flown that long. 'You started before the war, then?'

'Oh, sure. Pa had a light plane and he taught me. We rounded up the cattle in it.' He had already told her that his father owned a ranch, and her disbelief when he'd told her the size of it had caused him some amusement. Now, she looked at him with some caution.

'I don't believe you.'

He grinned. 'You don't believe anything I say.'

'Well, how can I?' she exclaimed in exasperation. 'You tell me you've got a farm the size of Hampshire and about fifty thousand cattle, and now an *aeroplane* – how can I know what to believe? I never even knew anyone who *worked* on a farm until Betty Chapman from our street joined the Land Army, and the place she's at is just tiny.'

Chuck laughed. 'Well, OK, we didn't actually round up the cattle that way,' he admitted. 'We do it the good old-fashioned way, with horses, just like in the movies. But it's true we had a plane. Still do. When I left school and decided to branch out a little and leave the ranching to my brother Larry, I went into flying commercially. There's a big future in it – or will be, once this war's over. It's the quickest way to travel, y'know.'

Diane nodded. 'I've always wanted to fly. I'm still hoping to get into transport – delivering the planes to the airfields – but it looks as though I'm stuck with being a flight mechanic for the time being.' She glanced at him. He was staring up at the sky, still chewing his blade of grass. He had a nice profile, she thought, just comfortably craggy enough to prevent him from being too good looking. There was a bump in the middle of his nose; perhaps it had been broken at some time. 'Is your brother still on the ranch?'

Chuck shook his head, not removing his gaze from the sky. 'Uh-*uh*. He joined the USAAF just before me. Went down in an attack over Bremen in April last year. A hundred and fifteen Fortresses raided the Focke-Wulf plant there and sixteen of 'em never came back.'

Diane stared at him. 'He was in Fortresses too?'

'Uh-huh.'

'But – what happened?'

'Whaddya think? They got shot down by the Luftwaffe. See – ' he raised himself on one elbow, tracing his meaning on the grass with one finger – 'the B-17's got blindspots that neither the top-turret gunner nor the nose guns can cover. One of the Luftwaffe flyers cottoned on to this and the Germans started coming at us from twelve o'clock high.' He glanced at her. 'Know what that means?'

'Yes, it's when they get directly ahead. It's even better if they've got the sun behind them. You just can't see them.'

'Nobody can see them when they're coming out of the sun,' he said, 'but with the Fortress, they didn't even have to bother about that. Just being ahead was enough. That's what they were doing, and that's why we lost sixteen planes that day, and one of the poor bastards who went down was my big brother Larry.'

Diane said nothing for a few moments. She thought of her mother, gunned down in the street by the German sneak raider. 'I never really thought of Americans losing their relatives in the war,' she said at last. 'I mean – you're so far away.'

'Not when we're over here,' he said quietly.

Diane rolled on to her side and put her hand over his. 'I'm sorry. I thought – well, you seem to make such a game of it all. And you've *got* so much – all those chocolates and nylon stockings, and ranches and aeroplanes and everything. It seemed as if—'

'None of those things really matter,' he said. 'It's people who matter. My folks would give it all up, just to have Larry back again. So would Jeanie – the girl he was supposed to marry. She lived on the next farm to us.'

'But what about you? How can you do the same as he did – fly out on raids, day after day? Suppose they lose you too? Isn't there anything else you could do?'

'Look,' he said, 'this war's got to be won. It's here. We can't just walk away from it. We found that out when the Japs hit Pearl Harbor. And I can fly better'n I can do anything else. Anyway, I was in before Larry copped his share, and I don't reckon Uncle Sam'd let me off on that account.'

Diane shook her head. 'But to let you go on flying, in a plane that isn't even safe . . .'

'The Fortress is as safe as the next plane. There isn't one that's perfect. You ought to know that. And they've done something about it, anyway.' He grinned a little cynically. 'At least, they say they have. They've given us extra guns in the nose, but the real problem was bad positioning, not lack of guns.' He shrugged. 'When it comes down to it, we just have to take our chance. The poor old plane's still got a rather nasty tendency to burst into flames when it catches a load of flak, so what the hell?'

Diane lay back on the grass. She knew that every pilot flew with the knowledge that he had a high chance of being killed. It happened with almost every raid – some of the young men who had been in the mess the night before, or at a dance or drinking in the local pub, just never appeared again. You didn't talk about it much, except when someone remarked casually that Nick or Mike or Sandy had 'bought it', but she had seen the fear lurking in their eyes, and she had heard about the way they died. The sudden enveloping flames. The splintering fragments as a plane exploded in mid-air. The screams that sounded over the RT as an aircraft spiralled into the ground.

She had seen for herself the result of some of those crashes, when she and the other girls had been called out to salvage a wrecked Spitfire, or Hurricane. Sometimes they had to watch as the bodies of men they had joked with the day before were lifted out and carried away.

Sometimes the plane they had to salvage was an American plane. A Liberator, or a Flying Fortress.

Chuck's Fortress.

It was time to go back to the station. Chuck raised himself again on one elbow and leaned over her. His blue eyes looked down into hers.

'It's OK,' he said easily, reading her mind. 'I'm like a cat. Got nine lives. There's still quite a few to be used up before I'm finished.'

Diane couldn't speak. She looked up into his face. There were little papery crinkles around his eyes, as if he'd spent a lot of time out in the open, looking into the sun. His mouth was wide, splitting into a wicked, three-cornered grin to show very white teeth. One of them was slightly crooked, overlapping the one next to it.

'Don't look so worried,' he said gently. 'This cat's going to live to catch quite a few mice. One of these days, this war's going to be over, and then I'll be high-tailing it back to the ranch. I reckon I'll have done enough flying by that time, and I can take over Larry's job and look after the old folks.'

There was a long pause. Diane felt the rapid beating of her heart. His face was very close to hers. She wanted to look away, but the blueness of his eyes held her, and she felt her lips part slightly and ran the tip of her tongue across them to ease their dryness.

'And marry the girl next door?' she said, without thinking, and then felt the colour run up her neck. 'Chuck, I'm sorry—'

'That's OK,' he said. 'Jeanie wouldn't want me anyway. Which is just as well, because there's another girl I'm interested in.'

There was another silence. He was looking grave. He's going to tell me he's got a sweetheart back home, she thought, and felt suddenly angry. Why didn't he tell me before? He *ought* to have told me before.

'Di—'

A sudden roar sliced the air, and the brightness of the sky was darkened by the shadow of a huge plane. Diane cringed involuntarily as it thundered over their heads, and Chuck lifted himself to look after it.

'Hey, look at that! It's the old *Casablanca Rose*. The bastards – they saw us here and buzzed us, just to give us a scare. *I'll* scare 'em, when I get back to the station!'

'The *Casablanca Rose*?' That was the plane that Lizanellie's boyfriends flew. 'But what's she doing up? I thought she was in your squadron.'

'So did I.' Chuck was on his feet now, frowning as he shielded his eyes against the sun to peer after the plane, now vanished from sight. 'Maybe there's something on. I'd better get back, Di.'

'Yes.' She scrambled up beside him, brushing bits of grass from her uniform. They had both taken off their jackets and she handed him his and shrugged into her own. 'So had I.'

Chuck turned suddenly and looked at her. He laid his hands on her arms. His eyes were very dark, their blueness no more than a rim around the wide black pupil.

'It's been a great afternoon.' He hesitated, and Diane thought: here it comes. He's going to tell me we've got to stop seeing each other.

'I guess we've got some talking to do some time, you and me,' he said quietly, 'but we'll have to take a raincheck on it. That OK by you?'

Diane had only a vague idea of what a raincheck might be. It was something they said in American films, and generally it meant that someone was trying to get out of something they didn't want to do. It was a way of pretending you'd do it some other time, when really you had no such intention.

Her heart was beating quickly, but she looked straight at him and forced her voice to remain light and flippant. 'Sure,' she said in mock imitation. 'That's OK by me. A raincheck it is.'

She flicked his arms away from her and turned and walked across the grass. Inside her, she was conscious of a strange, bitter heaviness. They got into the car in silence and she stared straight ahead, refusing to meet Chuck's glance.

Back at the station, he stopped the car and looked at her.

'Well, I guess that's it. I thought for a minute—'

'Yes?' she said, turning to meet his eyes at last. 'What did you think, Chuck?'

He stared at her for a long minute. She kept her eyes steady, her eyebrows slightly raised, challenging him to say what was in his mind, daring him to tell her the truth.

Then he dropped his glance and shrugged. 'Oh, it doesn't matter. I guess I was mistaken, that's all. Thanks for everything, Di. See you around, huh?'

He slammed the car into gear again and Diane got out. She stood irresolute for a moment, willing him to look at her again, but he was already turning the car to return the way he had come.

'Yes,' she said quietly, as dust spurted up from under the wheels. 'I'll see you around, Chuck.'

And, unhappily conscious of the eyes of the sentries on her, she walked slowly through the gates.

The next time there was a dance at the American air station, Diane refused to go. Lizanellie went and had a marvellous time. Chuck had been there, they said, dancing with a small brunette. He'd seen them and asked if Diane was OK and just shrugged when they told him she hadn't wanted to come. He'd sent no message.

He didn't get in touch to ask her to the pictures either, or to go out for a drive or a walk. He didn't write her a note, and he wasn't hanging around the station gates when she went out.

Shrugging and trying to pretend that it didn't matter, Diane carried on with her work. At least here she felt that she was beginning to be appreciated. Her keenness had brought approval from the airmen in charge of the WAAF. Working on the planes gave her a deep satisfaction, and being on an operational station gave her and the rest of the girls the feeling that they were almost in the front line themselves. Men they knew went out, night after night, to meet the enemy in aircraft they themselves had serviced. They heard them go, watched them in the sky, counted them out and back. There were never as many to count back, and they went about their work each day with the knowledge that some would never return. Often, when they went to salvage a crashed plane, they knew the crew who had crashed with it.

As spring drew on, the work intensified. Everyone on the station knew that there was something big on the cards. All leave had been cancelled from the beginning of April. Planes were going out day after day, night after night, in black waves, returning to be serviced round the clock and then going out again. The flight mechanics were exhausted. The special duties girls, who never mentioned their work to a living soul, looked even more impassive than usual. And a new kind of aircraft arrived.

It was a glider – a huge, wooden glider. It was called the Horsa, and Diane had seen it before, at the Airspeed factory where it had been developed and built. It had also been used in the invasion of Sicily, but most of the WAAFs on the station had never seen one. They looked at it with some doubt.

'A *glider*?' Lizanellie One said. 'You mean it's got no engine? It's towed by a plane?' She looked up at the blunt nose, where a propeller ought to be. It looked too big to fly without an engine.

'Well, they didn't think carthorses would be much good,' Diane said. 'Of course it's towed by a plane, you twerp. It can carry nearly thirty men. It can take a howitzer too. And there's a bigger one – the Hamilcar – that can take a *tank*.'

'Go on, I don't believe you,' Lizanellie Two said. 'You couldn't lift a tank off the ground in one of those things.'

'Ask the corporal. He'll tell you.' Diane gazed lovingly at the big wooden aircraft, its wings bare of any sign of an engine. 'They'll be taking all sorts over to France in these.'

Work began on the gliders as soon as they arrived. There were modifications to be made and, as far as the WAAFs and RAF mechanics working on them could tell, they all needed to be done yesterday. There was no leave, almost no time off duty. The men barely had time to shave, the girls forgot about hairdos and make-up. They fell into bed when their watch was over and rolled out again a few hours later to don the same boiler-suits and boots and start again.

'They're calling it D-Day,' Lizanellie told Diane. 'That's when they start the invasion. D-Day.'

D-Day. Nobody knew when it would be. They just had to work like slaves to get everything ready, in case it turned out to be tomorrow. Or the next day. Or the day after that . . .

D-Day.

The highest men in the land were arriving now at Southwick Park: General Eisenhower, the American Supreme Commander; General Montgomery – Monty to everyone in the nation, 'the great man' to those who knew and worked with him; Winston Churchill, in his greatcoat and trilby, the famous cigar forever held between his fingers as he gave the victory salute with the other hand; and – at least once – King George VI.

Gladys saw them all. She saw the caravan that Monty lived in, parked close to his HQ, Broomfield House. She saw Eisenhower's enormous trailer at the bottom of New Barns drive. She saw Mr Churchill stumping through the grounds with Monty, and she saw the King arrive in his Army uniform. She stood with especial pride to be inspected, wearing the medal awarded for her courage during the Blitz. There were tears in her eyes as she bobbed her curtsey and saw his glance rest on the ribbon.

'You're doing a f-fine job,' he said, with only the faintest trace of a stammer. 'Young women like you are helping us win this war with your p-pluck.'

Gladys didn't know what to reply. She felt her cheeks flush scarlet and muttered something incoherent, but he seemed to understand her nervousness and just smiled again and moved on. She longed to follow him with her eyes, but dared not. Instead, she kept her gaze rigidly ahead and stored up his words to be treasured in her mind.

Messages were flying back and forth every day. The high-ups and staff met every morning in the old library and conferred together. In the plotting room, where the information from Fort Southwick was relayed on to the huge table-map, Gladys marvelled at the changes that were taking place every day. There seemed to be no end to the massive accumulation of shipping that was arriving off the south coast. From Falmouth to Beachy Head, the fleets were gathering, and she thought that the sea must be so thick with ships that soon none would be able to move.

'They're a sitting target,' someone muttered to her as they came off watch one day. 'The Germans could blitz 'em all out of the water as easy as winking.'

'They've got to get past our boys first.' Everyone had seen the waves of aircraft flying overhead on their way to France, and could identify them – the Hurricanes and Spitfires, heroes of the war, the Liberators and Flying Fortresses, the Dakotas, the Mosquitoes and Typhoons. They watched as the squadrons passed overhead in tight formation; watched again as they straggled back.

There were never quite so many, coming back.

There were other objects on the big table map, objects that weren't ships, weren't even shaped like ships, more like huge walls, yet seemed to be afloat. Nobody seemed to know just what they were or, if they did know, weren't saying. They were simply called 'Mulberries'.

Mulberries. Gladys and the others pushed them around the table, getting them into their places. She remembered those enormous constructions that had towered above the skyline on Stokes Bay beach, mystifying the inhabitants of Gosport, the massive concrete caissons that had been towed away out to sea only – as some had said – to be sunk. All part of a massive plan, now being slowly worked out. Yet Gladys pushed the thoughts away. 'Ours is not to reason why . . .'

Towards the end of May, even more troops arrived, cramming themselves and their lorries and trucks and tanks into spaces no one would have believed possible. They parked beside hedgerows and along roadsides all the way into Portsmouth and Southampton. Another long trail wound its way through the sheltered clearings of the New Forest to Lymington. Where they could, the men pitched tents and slept under canvas. Where they couldn't, they just stayed in their vehicles.

Clifford was somewhere amongst them. Gladys hadn't heard from him for a while now, and didn't expect to as long as mail was so restricted, but it stood to reason that he must have left his camp in the north of the county. She still wrote to him every evening before going to bed, wondering when he would read the words she wrote, and where he would be. Perhaps in France, she thought, and a cold hand touched her heart. She hated to think of him cold, wet and in danger. She hated to think of him injured again.

Or killed.

There were Americans and Canadians as well as British filling the narrow lanes and camping in the fields. They threw sweets and chocolate to small boys who ran alongside their huge wheels, calling out for 'gum, chum'. They whistled at the girls who walked past and shouted invitations for dates none of them would be able to keep. In some of the more established camps, they held dances and parties and invited all the locals. Late at night, they danced arm-in-arm in a long line across the meadows, or did the conga around the tents.

There were no dances or parties at Southwick. Security was at its tightest. You couldn't move without showing your identity card, Judy said wryly, and there wasn't time for fun and frivolity anyway. Whatever was going to happen, this was the place where it would all be set in motion.

Monty and Eisenhower came regularly into the ops room to watch the progress of the plotters. They would move around the table, studying the positions intently and discussing them in low voices. Gladys and the others grew used to working with the American Supreme Commander at their elbows, and concentrated on listening to their headphones and moving the blocks across the map.

The density of vessels around the coast was almost as great as that of vehicles choking the lanes and byways.

D-Day . . . Somehow, the girls and men in the ops room grew to understand that the date had been set. They didn't know how or when they had realised this, nor what the date was, but they knew that there was now a specific day in the minds of the commanders.

It didn't take much intelligence to guess that it would have to be close to the full moon. The next nights when that would happen were 5–7 June. There was discussion about tides and sunrise as well, and several mysterious remarks about a 'window'. Whatever sort of window could they mean? Gladys wondered, and then realised it was a period of time during which the big push would be possible.

Full moons and tides could be predicted, but weather couldn't. At almost any time of day, you could walk outside and see Monty or Eisenhower – whose men referred to him as 'Ike' – staring up at the flags that fluttered from the top of the flagstaff and talking about the weather.

As well as her plotting work, Gladys was used more and more as a messenger between the various HQs. The CPO said it was because she was quick, reliable and quiet. Gladys herself thought it more likely that it was because she was the only Wren who could ride a motorbike. She'd learned years ago on her brother's bike, and the moments when she was speeding through the narrow lanes, oblivious to the wolf-whistles of the soldiers waiting at their wheels for the next order, were among the best she knew. She could almost believe she was back in peacetime, sitting astride Bob's old BSA, taking an illicit ride along the rough, narrow back lanes around Purbrook and Denmead. It gave her a small shock one day to realise that she was riding along those same lanes, now widened and resurfaced in order to take the heavy, rugged Army vehicles using them.

Not only the road was used to deploy troops. The little Meon Valley railway line, running from the main line near Alton down through Droxford and Wickham to Fareham, was used to transport mines and machinery as well as men. There was even a suggestion that a spur should be built as far as Southwick, but by then there was no time for such an enterprise and, as D-Day drew nearer, the members of the British War Cabinet came down from London in a special coach and held their conferences in a siding at Droxford.

All this, Gladys and her friends knew without speaking of it, as if they absorbed it through the atmopshere. As they went into the bar of the Golden Lion of an evening, to snatch a rare few minutes' relaxation, they would look at the locals and wonder if they, too, knew just what was going on, but the wise country eyes looked back at them, bland and blank, asking nothing, giving nothing away.

'Ours is not to reason why . . . '

The sunshine of May was cooling to a damp, chilly June. A stinging wind whipped through the streets of Portsmouth, and heavy clouds massed overhead. At Southwick Park, eyes were turned first to the meteorological maps and then to the sky. Out on Southsea Common, the gun-crews stayed at their positions, watching the RAF and USAAF planes fly out in waves, scanning the skies for intruders. In the Solent and all along the Channel, the ships swayed at anchor, while on the beaches and all along the roads leading to them, stretching the whole distance of the ten-mile exclusion zone and far beyond, the long lines of tanks and trucks, lorries and 'Funnies', waited for the order to start.

It seemed as if it would never come.

In the streets of Portsmouth, people went on living their everyday lives. As if there were no lines of vehicles, no throngs of soldiers and Marines, they walked to work and to the shops, queued for bread and vegetables and sugar to make jam, argued with the butcher over their meat ration, unravelled jumpers to knit socks for soldiers in Africa, dug their gardens and swept their houses clean.

Some of them had babies. Some of them died, of illness and old age.

'It doesn't matter what *they* do,' Jess said to Annie. 'They get us into wars and out of them – if we're lucky – and they put taxes on things and tell

214

us what we can buy and what we can't, and how much we should eat and all the rest of it, but they can't stop ordinary life going on. Nothing can stop that.'

She had walked up the street to see their mother. Mary spent all her time in bed now, lying in a small crumpled heap that scarcely seemed to make a mound in the bedclothes.

'Hello, Mum. How're you feeling today?'

The withered lips moved in a faint smile. 'Jess? Is that our Jess?' Her voice, once so strong, was little more than a papery rustle.

'It's me, Mum.' Jess sat down on the chair Annie had put beside the bed. Her throat ached with tears. 'And what're you doing still in bed at ten in the morning, eh? Don't you know there's a pile of ironing to be done?'

'Ironing's afternoons.' Mary had little interest in the world now. She was back in the past, her own past. She lay with her eyes half closed, recalling the days when Jess and Annie had been children. 'I used to take you and Annie all along Southsea on Sunday afternoons.' The papery voice rustled on, dredging up memories of long ago. 'You looked so nice in your little white frock with your hair tied up in a ribbon. Yellow hair, you had.' Her eyes drifted to look at Jess's head. Her hair was brown now – the colour of beechnuts Frank had said once, when he'd taken her for a walk in the country when they were courting – but strands of grey had begun to appear. It was the war, Jess thought, it was enough to turn anyone grey, and after all, she was forty-five. Plenty of women were grey before that.

'I felt so proud of you,' Mary whispered. 'Were you proud of yours when they were little?'

'Yes, I was.' Jess thought of the three older children: Rose, at five years old, shepherding her two brothers along the same stretch of beach, her dark hair tied up in a ribbon just as Jess's had been all those years ago; Tim, at three, sturdy and handsome in his blue romper suit, with his golden curls brushed and shining in the sun; Keith, only just able to walk, staggering between them, already his brother's faithful shadow.

Maureen hadn't been born then. She didn't come along until Rose was twelve, arriving the day they'd delivered the Anderson shelters. Jess had lain in bed in the front room at number 14, listening to the clatter and the shouts, and wishing they'd go away. The fear of war had been lying heavy on everyone's mind then. At the beginning of July, 1939, they'd still hoped it could be averted, but the preparations had already been under way, just in case. Just as well, she thought, remembering the Blitz – and it's not over now, not by a long chalk.

Involuntarily, she glanced at the window. You couldn't see the long lines of vehicles from here, but they weren't far away. One day – or one night – soon, they would begin to move towards the sea, towards the ships that were waiting to take them across the Channel. Towards France and the battle-torn fields and cities of Europe.

'So proud of them,' Mary was whispering. 'So proud . . .'

Her voice was fading. Soon it was no more than a thread of sound, and then it drifted into nothing. Her eyes closed and the bedclothes rose and fell with the minutest of movements.

Very gently, Jess disentangled her hand and slipped quietly out of the room. She went into the kitchen and found Annie making a mock apricot tart. She had lined an enamel plate with pastry and baked it, and now she was grating a few carrots into a bowl.

'What d'you think of her?'

Jess sat down at the kitchen table. That was one of the nice things about having a bigger house, she thought: you could have a kitchen big enough to have a proper table in it. At number 14, she had to manage with a wide shelf Frank had built over a couple of cupboards or else work on the dining-table in the back room.

'She's going, isn't she? Poor Mum.'

They tried to take their minds off it by talking of other things. They talked about the huge masses of lorries and trucks that had streamed through the streets. The tanks had crushed the kerbs all along September Street, Jess said, and left big grooves in the paving stones. Annie told Jess about the family. Olive hadn't been home for a fortnight. Everyone knew there was no leave, but Annie was worried about her anyway. She'd seemed different the last few times she'd been down: bright eyed and excited almost like she'd been when she'd first started going out with Derek, but trying to hide it. That wasn't right in a young woman whose husband was out in Africa, and had been for the past year or more.

'I just hope she's not losing her head. There was that young chap who walked down here with her one night in the blackout and waited up in the pub. Ted went up and gave him a look-over, said he seemed a decent enough chap, but you don't know what they're getting up to on these stations, with no one to keep an eye on them.'

'Your Olive wouldn't do anything wrong,' Jess said. 'She's been brought up right, and she thinks a lot of her Derek.'

'I don't know that either of those things is enough, not these days. You hear such things – young women going with other men, soldiers and sailors and that. Bringing them home and letting them stop the night.' Annie shook her head. 'You know what that leads to. There's going to be a lot of decent chaps come home from the war to find they've got a bigger family than they expected. I don't want to see that happen to Derek.'

'Annie! How can you talk like that about your own daughter? Of course it won't happen. Olive would never do anything like that, never.'

'She'd better not,' Annie said grimly. 'You know what me and Ted have always told both the girls: "Don't ever bring trouble to this doorstep." They know what'll happen if they do.'

Jess knew what she meant. It was what a lot of parents told their children. The sight of a policeman at the door, or a girl with a baby born out of wedlock – anything that would bring shame on the family – was their biggest dread. Ethel Glaister wasn't the only one who would try to hide such shame – and if it couldn't be hidden, the son or daughter who had caused such trouble was likely to find themselves turned out.

Jess didn't know if she could ever bring herself to turn either Rose or Maureen out if they brought shame on the family, but she knew it would create endless unhappiness for all the family. She knew it would affect the whole street. She hoped with all her heart that Annie was wrong about Olive.

'What about Betty and Dennis?' she asked, changing the subject. 'How are they getting on?'

Annie's face brightened as she gave Jess the latest news of her younger daughter. They weren't allowed to visit at present, of course, because Bishop's Waltham was outside the ten-mile zone, but Annie had had a postcard from her. It said they were happily settled in Jonas's cottage, Dennis was finding his way about and could work as well as when he'd had his eyesight, and they weren't sure just yet, but they might have some good news for Annie in a month or two's time . . . 'A baby,' she said, her face softening. 'That's what she means by that. Oh, it would be nice to have a grandchild at last. Do the whole family good, that would.'

News about Colin was not so good. Only a few letters ever got through from the Japanese prisoners of war, and what little they did say, you couldn't believe. Nobody at home believed that they were being well fed and looked after. It was well known by now that the Japanese were treating their captives with ruthless cruelty. All you could do, Annie said, was hope and pray that your boys would come through alive, and that you'd be able to look after them when they finally did come home.

The carrots were cooked. Annie stirred the thick, orange pulp one last time and then tipped it into the pastry case. She smoothed it out.

'If anyone mistakes that for apricots, I'll cook my best hat next time and eat that,' she said caustically. 'Not that anyone can really remember what an apricot tastes like anyway, so I don't suppose it'll make any odds.'

Jess smiled and got up to go home. She walked back down April Grove, thinking sadly of Colin, out in Japan, and her mother, fading away in bed. The war had taken the one from the family, and ceased to have any meaning for the other. If a bomb fell on Annie's house tonight and killed Mary, it would be a merciful release.

It was very hard to understand.

# CHAPTER SIXTEEN

'It can't be long now,' Ray said.

He and Olive had found a sheltered spot on the grassy bank above the moat round Southsea Castle. Like all the other old earthen forts in the area, it had come into use now as a military installation, and was heavily cordoned off with barbed wire. Palmerston would have been proud, thought Olive.

'I feel sorry for the soldiers,' she said. 'Just sitting there in their lorries and tanks, waiting. And the ones already on the ships, they must be fed up to the back teeth with it all. Though I suppose I'll feel sorrier for them in a week or two's time, when they're in France.'

'It won't be much fun.' Ray plucked a piece of grass and chewed it, his face grave. It wasn't really much of a day to sit outside, with the wind whipping sand from the beach across the embankment, and an occasional splatter of rain scuttering down from the lowering clouds, but there were so few places he and Olive could go to be private. Here, in this corner almost entirely fenced off with barbed wire, wasn't very romantic but at least it was quiet.

It had been hard enough to find time to be together anyway, just lately. Like everyone else, the anti-aircraft gun-crews had been on top alert, although the aircraft squadrons had been flying incessantly to prevent the enemy from even reaching as far as the coast. As well as bombing strategic positions across the Channel, they had kept up a constant patrol to see that no bombers or reconnaissance planes could get through. It was essential that information about the forces still massing off the British coasts should not get back to German headquarters.

Even now, they were still passing overhead, their constant roar so accustomed a background that Olive and Ray scarcely noticed them. It had become just another part of life, like the barbed wire and the constant checks for IDs, and the neverending, round-the-clock watch that must be kept.

'I reckon it'll be in the next few days,' Ray said. 'As soon as the weather improves.' It was raining harder now, the cold drops blowing under the greatcoat he was holding over his and Olive's heads. 'Talk about flaming June!' His voice altered slightly. 'Olive . . .'

'I suppose it depends on the tides as well,' she observed, not noticing his change of tone. 'And the moon, if they go at night. I suppose they *will* go at night. It'd be daft to set out in broad daylight. What d'you think—'

'Olive,' he interrupted. His right arm was around her shoulders, holding one corner of the greatcoat. Now he let go of the other end and put his hand on her shoulder, turning her to face him. 'Olive, there's something I want to talk to you about.'

She looked at him in surprise, her eyes reading his. 'What? What is it?' There was a sudden glint of panic. 'You're not going away? They're not posting you?'

'No, nothing like that. It's all right, Livvy, they're not parting us.' He paused, then added in a low tone, 'Yet.'

'What do you mean, *yet*? Stop making these hints, Ray, and tell me what's going on. You *are* going away, aren't you? Is it Dorothy, has something happened to Dorothy?'

'No, it's not that. Not that they'd tell me if anything did,' he added bitterly. 'I haven't heard from Joan in five weeks and then it was just to ask for money. She didn't say a word about how the baby was.'

'So what – ?'

'It's about us,' he said, his voice rushing as if he'd kept the words pent up inside for a long time. 'One day, Livvy, this war's going to be over. I reckon we're going to win it, too. What's happening now – they've been planning that for a long time, they must have been, to be able to get it all ready. All those trucks and tanks and things, all the food they've got to take, all the guns and ammo and all that . . . Anyway, the point is it's going to come to an end and then all the men'll be coming back. *All* the men,' he added, looking into her eyes. 'Including your Derek.'

'Yes,' she said. 'I know. But—'

'But we've been putting off thinking about it. We've tried to pretend it's never going to happen.' His face looked tight, the skin drawn taut over his bones and stretched around his eyes and mouth 'It *is* going to happen, Livvy. Perhaps by the end of this year. Perhaps it really will be "over by Christmas", like they said in the beginning. Perhaps it won't be till next year, but it's going to happen and we're going to have to think about it.'

Olive looked away. She picked at the grass. The rain had stopped again, but the wind felt cold and damp. She said miserably, 'I don't want to think about it now, Ray. Can't we just leave it till—'

'No,' he said, 'we can't. There was a short pause, then he added, 'Try to look at it from my point of view, Livvy. I love you. I really do. I want to spend the rest of my life with you. I want to marry you—'

'But we can't! We're already married, both of us, and Derek—'

'I know,' he said bitterly. 'You love Derek. He's your husband and he's got the rights over you. When he comes home you'll go back to him, and forget all about me. *Won't* you?'

Olive twisted the grass between her fingers. 'I'll never forget you, Ray.'

'But you'll leave me,' he said. 'You'll go back to him.'

'He's my husband . . .'

'And Joan's my wife, and we've got a daughter, but that doesn't mean I'm going back to her when this is all over.'

'That's different!' she cried. 'You and Joan don't get on, you never did, you only got married because—'

'Because Dorothy was on the way. That's right. But we *are* married, and most people would say we ought to stay together. And she's RC too, she'll never divorce me. All the same, I shan't go back to her. Whatever else happens, I'm never going to live with Joan again, and she doesn't even want me to.'

'But you see,' Olive said quietly, 'Derek *does* want me. And I – I want him.'

'I know.' Ray reached over and took the mangled piece of grass away from her. 'Here. Have a new bit.' He looked at her downcast face and spoke more quietly. 'And you love him. In spite of everything that's happened between us, it's still him you really love.'

'Yes. No. Ray, it's not like that.' The new piece was already crushed between her fingers. 'It's – I don't know, it's as if I love you both. I *do* love you both.' She raised her eyes. 'I don't know what's going to happen when Derek comes home,' she said honestly. 'I'll have to go back to him – I can't let him down like that – and I think I'll want to. But, oh, it's been so long and we might both have changed – this war *is* changing people, especially people like me. I'd never have done the sort of job I'm doing if it hadn't happened. I'd have stayed in Derek's dad's building yard, doing the invoices and typing, until I had a baby, and then I'd have stayed at home. I'd never have known any different, so I wouldn't have missed it, but now, I do know different. I've been independent. I can do what I like with my spare time. I don't have anyone to say I've got to be at home doing the ironing or waiting for them to come back from work and take me to the pictures or something, and I don't know what I'll feel like when I do.'

'D'you think Derek will expect you to do those things?'

'I don't know. I suppose so. I'm his wife.'

'So you'll just be the little woman again. Staying at home cleaning and washing and looking after the children.'

'Well, yes.' She looked at him again. 'Isn't that what you'd want me to do if we were married?'

'If we were married,' Ray said in a low voice. 'I'd want you to do whatever you wanted to do. I'd be happy enough just to have you with me.'

Olive put out her hand and he took it in his and held it against his breast.

'Ray . . .'

'I love you, Olive,' he said simply. 'I love you through and through, more than I've ever loved anyone else in my whole life. I don't think I'm going to be able to live without you, but I've got to, haven't I? That's what you're saying. When this war finishes and your Derek comes home, I've got to live without you.'

'Ray, no—'

'Ray, *yes*. That's what it comes to. You'll go back to Derek and never give me another thought.'

'I told you,' she said in a low, shaking voice, 'I'll never forget you.'

'All right, you'll never forget me, but you won't see me again. You won't walk on the Common with me, or go swimming or dancing, or any of those other things people do when they're in love. You won't ever make love with me again.' He caught her to him, looking down into her eyes. 'That'll all be over, Olive. It'll be finished. For ever. Full stop.'

Olive wriggled in his arms. 'Ray, you're hurting me.'

'And don't you think,' he said, not loosening his grip, 'that it's going to hurt me too? Don't you think it's going to rip me apart?' He paused. 'Do you think it might even hurt you, just a little bit?'

There was a silence. Ray slackened his hold a little, but Olive didn't move away. She stayed close, her face buried against his chest, her shoulders quivering, and he knew that she was crying.

'Livvy, I'm sorry,' he said at last. 'I shouldn't have said all those things. You're right, we shouldn't even think about them. I'm sorry. Forget them and let's enjoy what we've got, like we always said we would.'

Olive shook her head. She tried to speak but her voice was thick with tears and her nose was running. She felt in her pocket for a handkerchief and blew her nose hard.

'No. We can't forget it. *You're* right. The war'll be over some time – perhaps some time soon – and we're going to have to decide what to do.'

She looked up at him again. 'Ray, I don't know what to do. I do love you, and – and I think I'd want to marry you and live with you and be your wife, yes, *and* stay at home and do the cooking and cleaning and all that for you – if only – if only . . .'

'If only you weren't already married to Derek,' he said, and she nodded. 'Livvy, suppose you weren't married to him? Suppose you were just engaged?'

'I don't know. I'd still feel I ought—'

'Suppose you weren't engaged? Just going out, steady? Suppose there wasn't a war and you knew us both and knew we both loved you, what would you—'

'Ray, stop it!' she cried. 'I don't *know* – how *can* I know? It's not fair, asking me all those questions. I can't tell you what I'd feel, and it wouldn't make any difference if I could. I *am* married, and so are you, and we *can't* marry each other, and that's all there is to it.'

'People don't always get married to live together,' he said very quietly, and Olive stared at him.

'You – you mean, live in sin?'

'That's what they call it.' He tried to smile. 'Joan would say I was damned for eternity, but I should think she'd say that anyway. And it depends if you believe it.'

'I don't know if I believe it or not,' she said slowly, 'and like you say, if it's true, we've done that anyway. But living in sin . . . I don't know. Hardly anyone does that, Ray.'

'A few do. It's not against the law.'

'I know, but – nobody'd want anything to do with us. My mum would be really upset and I don't think Dad'd ever let me in the house again. It was bad enough when our Betty wanted to marry Dennis, and told us he was a CO. But living in *sin* – we'd have to move right away. We couldn't go on living in Portsmouth.'

'Well, that wouldn't bother me. I don't come from Portsmouth anyway. We could go as far as you like. We could go to London. Or Devon. Or somewhere up the other end of the country, if that's what you'd want. Nobody'd know the difference. You could call yourself Mrs Whitaker – who's to know?' He lifted her left hand and stroked the third finger, with Derek's plain gold ring gleaming on it. 'I could buy you another ring. *Our* ring.'

Olive stared at him. Then she snatched her hand away. Hot colour ran up into her face and the tears sprang to her eyes.

'Ray! *Ray!* Don't say things like that. Of course I can't do that. I'm *married*.' She rubbed her finger furiously, as if to wipe away his touch. 'I'm married to a man who loves me – a man *I* love. I can't take his ring off and put someone else's on, and just pretend. I can't.'

'So I'm just "someone else", am I?' Ray demanded, the shock and hurt of her reaction injecting his voice with anger. 'A minute ago you were saying you loved me and wanted to marry me – now you're calling me "someone else" as if I were a stranger.'

'I'm not. You know I'm not. I do love you. But what you're suggesting – people like us don't do that sort of thing, Ray. You know they don't.'

'And sometimes they do. When they really love each other and can't live without each other, they have to.'

'I can't.'

There was another silence, a longer one this time.

'So now I know,' Ray said at last. 'You love me, but not enough. You want to go to bed with me, but only as long as the war lasts. And when it's over you'll say goodbye and thanks, and go back to your Derek and your cosy life washing his shirts and cooking his dinner. Where does that leave me?'

Olive shook her head miserably. 'I don't know.'

'I'll tell you where it leaves me,' Ray said savagely. 'I'll tell you *just* where it leaves me. In hell, that's where. In bloody, shitting *hell*.'

He got up abruptly and walked away. Olive sat under the folds of his greatcoat, staring after him. She wanted to call him back, wanted to tell him that she would do whatever he wanted, that she would live with him and wear his ring and call herself Mrs Whitaker, that she would go anywhere he wanted to take her.

But Derek's ring was still gleaming on her finger, and the words would not be uttered.

Wind and rain seemed to have settled in for the summer. Weather forecasts had not been given out since the beginning of the war, but you didn't need to be a prophet to see that this was going to be a typical English summer – no glorious hot sunshine, day after day, as the country had had for the first two or three years of the war, just dull, chilly days and wet, stormy nights.

The invasion couldn't possibly be made in this weather. Everyone knew that.

In Gosport, the whole town turned into a garrison. Many of the streets were prohibited areas, with barriers across the roads and the people who lived there given passes to enable them to go in and out of their own homes. Military police were everywhere, checking and rechecking. The village of Alverstoke, close to the beach, was virtually taken over, its large houses requisitioned for military and Naval offices and accommodation, the children's home evacuated and turned into an emergency hospital, and a signalling station set up on the beach near the end of Jellicoe Avenue.

A vast marquee – intended as an annexe to the emergency hospital – made the putting green look like a scout camp, but there was no holiday atmosphere amongst the thousands of soldiers and Marines who were massing along the beaches. They marched up the ramps, or drove their tanks and DUKWs and Funnies into the huge maws of the landing craft, with a mixture of grim determination, relief that at last they were to be given the chance to 'get Hitler' – and, although they tried to hide it, fear.

Each one of them knew, as everyone in the country must know, that some of them were never going to return. Some would not even make it off the landing craft, on to the beaches of whatever part of the French coast they were heading for. Secret as the entire massive operation had been, concealed from German eyes and ears, an invasion on this scale could not remain hidden for long. All too soon, the German defences would swing into action, the battle begin, and men would die under enemy fire as they waded ashore through the chilly waters, or struggled up the beach, weighed down by heavy packs and waterlogged clothing.

It might be you, their eyes said to one another as they huddled on the decks of the ships that were massing in the Solent, or it might be me. It might be all of us.

The memories of Dunkirk and Dieppe were vivid in their minds. Some of them had been there, shared in the terrible experiences of those disasters, knew what lay ahead. Some could only guess.

This time, they must not fail. This time, the powers that had sent them to this place must have got it right.

The waiting went on.

On the RAF station, the airmen and women worked round the clock. Planes were flying out all the time, never mind the weather, bombarding the coast of France and keeping intruders away from the British beaches. As soon as they returned, the pilots and crew climbed wearily out of the cockpits and staggered away for a few hours' rest before taking off again, while the flight mechanics descended on the aircraft like vultures, going over every inch. While some worked on the engines, others replenished the ammunition, refilled the fuel tanks, washed the Perspex of the cockpit clear and repaired any rips and tears made in the fuselage by bullets. It was their aim, the NCOs told them, to send every plane out as if it were new.

The troop transport planes were ready and every corner of the airfield was crammed with the men and vehicles they were to transport. In the Dakotas and Albemarles would go paratroopers, wearing the sixty-pound packs which carried all they would need, including weapons strapped into special containers. As Diane had said, the huge wooden gliders could take both men and vehicles, and jeeps and even small tanks were loaded into the big, hollow bodies. The tails of the gliders could be unbolted to allow for easy unloading, but there was always the danger that the craft would be damaged on landing. 'At least it'll smash easy,' the NCO observed. 'We'll just have to hope they can get out through the holes. And there's no fuel aboard to catch fire or explode.'

It seemed like cold comfort. Diane and the other girls watched the paratroopers practise their jumping, and shivered, thinking of the real thing happening in the dark over strange country, not knowing who or what might be waiting below.

'This must be why they wanted all those holiday snaps and postcards a while ago,' Lizanellie One said. 'Remember, they put out appeals for any pictures of France that people had? They must have been looking for good places to land them then.'

Diane saw nothing of Chuck. Lizanellie were still meeting their own American boyfriends in every spare moment, and Ellie said she would be engaged soon, and was hoping to get married and go to America with him after the war. Liz didn't like the thought of her twin going so far away, but when someone suggested she might do the same, so that they could still be close, she pointed out that the two men lived at opposite ends of America – one in Florida, the other in Seattle. 'I might as well stay in England. At least she'll have to come back sometimes to see Mum and Dad and the rest of the family.'

The others laughed, and Lizanellie laughed too. There was a lot of water to flow under the bridge before anyone could think of peacetime living. It was all a dream, a fantasy, that might never come true.

Perhaps that's all Chuck was, Diane thought sadly. A fantasy. And that last afternoon, when we lay in the grass and he almost kissed me, nothing but a dream.

At Southwick, the atmosphere grew more and more tense. Weather reports were coming through all the time from the meteorological office. The sky was black and lowering, the rain drumming on the wooden shutters of the windows, the wind tearing at the flags. Wrens, sailors, officers, ran between the buildings, swathed in mackintoshes. The lawns were sodden, the tents streaming, the pathways running with water. The village seemed half drowned, the flowers and shrubs in the little gardens tossed and torn, with petals lying like soaked confetti on the roads.

If they didn't go now, it would be another two or three weeks before the tide was right again, and by then the weather might be even worse. Yet if they did send the men out, on ships that were heavily laden with armoured vehicles, ammunition, provisions, troops . . . it could be a bigger disaster than Dieppe, than Dunkirk itself. It could mean the end of the war for the Allies.

The decision rested in a few men's hands. Gladys watched them pacing to and fro – Eisenhower, Montgomery, the admirals and brigadiers, the prime ministers of all the Dominions – and her heart ached for them. In those hands, she thought, lie the lives of millions of people, and nobody can know what will happen. It would be like starting up a huge machine that couldn't be stopped.

The fourth of June.

All day at Southwick, they had been watching the weather. Watching the trees toss their branches in the wind, watching the rain splatter on the sodden lawns. Watching for a glimpse of the full moon which should be in the sky, above the heavy clouds.

There had been another strange delivery at the house. Workmen had arrived in a large wagon, all the way from a toy factory somewhere in the Midlands. Gladys had seen them unload a series of big, flat cartons and carry them into the house. There, in the library she had seen some of them unpacked.

'A map,' she said to Judy, who had also been in the library. 'That's what it is. An enormous wooden map of the south coast.'

'It's more than that,' Judy said. 'It's a map of the Channel, and France. They've got the Normandy beaches on it, and they're drawing huge lines and arrows, and writing names.'

Gladys saw the names for herself, the next time she went into the library. As she stared at them, she recognised them from the time when she had walked into the village schoolroom and seen a similar map up on the wall. Omaha, she read. Juno. Gold. Sword. Utah.

Overlord.

The men were still installing the map. It had come in sections and there were far more than were needed. One of them, working with a mouthful of nails, told her that they'd made a gigantic wooden jigsaw puzzle of the entire coast of Britain and brought it all here.

'We won't be putting the rest up, though,' he said in his flat Midlands accent. 'That was just so that no one would know which was the important bit. And you know what the buggers have done on us?' He waited, while

227

Gladys shook her head. 'Only told us we can't go back home, that's all. Got to stay here till the whole bloody job's over and done with, whenever that is.' They looked at the map. 'Stuck here for the duration,' he went on indignantly, 'and what d'you reckon the missus is going to say about that, eh? I was supposed to be doing a few jobs round the house at the weekend, once we'd got this lot out of the way.'

Gladys grinned. 'She probably won't believe you.'

'She won't get the chance,' he said morosely, filling his mouth with nails again. 'We're not even allowed to tell 'em where we are.'

The map had been in position for some time now, and was filling daily with new details. Every time Gladys went into the library, a few more ships had been added, or some more of the Mulberries. It was clear now what they were for – they were artificial harbours, constructed in portions so that they could be towed across the Channel and set up off the Normandy beaches to make havens for the troop-carrying ships. Sixty feet deep, the huge blocks would form long pontoons, bridges and piers in the sheltered bays which were to be the landing grounds for the invasion.

Still only a handful of people knew for certain just where those landing grounds would be. And nobody knew when the invasion would take place.

'They've given all the soldiers little books about France,' Judy said. 'Useful phrases, and that sort of thing. They reckon they're hilarious. Mind you, some people will get a double meaning out of anything.'

'Well, they've got to get some fun out of it,' Gladys said.

There certainly wasn't much else. Leave had been stopped for everyone now. The landing craft had begun to fill up with troops and, as each one became fully laden, it departed from the beach to make way for another. They swayed at anchor, tossing in the rough winds as they waited in the Solent for the word that would send them away.

Nobody knew what, or when, the word would be.

The great men who had charge of the war – Montgomery, Eisenhower and the others – conferred hourly. They came into the ops room and stared at the table-map, at the wooden blocks that represented ships and Mulberries, at the constant moving about that went on as more and more signals were sent through from the fort up on the Hill. They went into the library and studied the wooden wall-map. They could not conceal their tension, and it spread throughout the entire personnel.

'It was supposed to have been tomorrow.' Nobody knew how the information got out, but suddenly it was common knowledge. 'June the fifth was supposed to be D-Day, but the weather's put a stop to it.'

The weather. It seemed ludicrous, offensive, that a war waged all over the world, should be held up by the weather in the English Channel. A madman had been let loose, countries had been over-run, millions of people had died in a war lasting almost five years – and now, at its most crucial point, the weather could spoil a plan that had been two years in the making, as surely as it might have spoilt a picnic.

'What do you expect, if you *will* have a war in England?'

The joke was muttered all over the estate, but nobody laughed. All eyes were turned towards the sky and the tossing, scudding clouds. All ears were tuned to the gales that swept amongst the trees.

The direction of the war – the destiny of them all – depended entirely on the weather.

Out in the Solent, soldiers so young that they had barely completed their basic training, tossed in a misery of seasickness and fear. On the air stations, pilots and paratroopers, loaded with packs and weapons, waited with their aircraft. And at Southwick House, as the new day crawled slowly towards dawn, the Supreme Allied Commander, General Dwight D. Eisenhower, left his caravan and walked through a wind that tore at the trees like a hurricane, lashing him with rain that swept almost horizontally through the park, and came again into the library, dominated by the huge wall-map, where the rest of the commanders were gathered.

Admiral Ramsay. Air Chief Marshal Tedder. Air Marshal Trafford Leigh-Mallory. And, dominating them all with the stature of his personality if not his size, the 'great man' himself – General Montgomery.

They looked at each other. They looked at the wall-map. They studied the latest report from the meteorological office, handed to them with quiet self-effacement by Gladys Shaw.

'They think there'll be a slight improvement in the weather.'

'For a short spell. No more than that.'

'It may be our only chance.'

Nobody said any more. Monty moved to the table and stared at the plots. The others followed him. Eisenhower drummed his fingers lightly on the back of a chair. His face was half in shadows, drawn with concentration. Watching him, Gladys thought that he looked as if he were reviewing the entire progress of the operation as it must be, once set in motion. And it must be set in motion. At some point, the decision must be made. Once the order was given, thousands of men would move into action. Thousands of soldiers, sailors, airmen, Marines would cross the Channel to begin the assault on Normandy. On Europe. And, ultimately, on Germany itself.

Thousands of men, many of them already doomed to die on the beaches, or in the water before they ever reached a beach. Doomed to die in the skies as they parachuted from the gliders and aircraft that ferried them across, to be shot down or mined as they moved through the streets of foreign towns and villages. Doomed to die in horrors that could scarcely be imagined, unless you had already seen such things. Unless you had been through the Blitz, or served in a fighting ship, or flown in a bombing mission, or fought for your life and your country in a foreign land. Then, you knew that there was no way too horrible to die, and you knew that nobody was immune.

Eisenhower looked once again at the great map. The decision was his alone.

At just a quarter past four, as the first blackbird began to sing in the storm still raging outside, he lifted his head and looked his commanders in the eye.

'OK,' he said. 'OK. Let's go.'

# CHAPTER SEVENTEEN

The fifth of June.

Rain and wind. The sort of day to stay indoors, even think about lighting a fire – if only there hadn't been a war on.

During the whole of that day, the loading of the ships had intensified as more and more men poured through the streets and on to the barricaded beaches. The air was filled with a steady rumble of engines as tanks and jeeps and lorries inched slowly forward, heading over Portsdown Hill and down through the streets of Portsmouth and Gosport, in the biggest traffic jam ever known. The Solent was a mass of floating steel and concrete as the landing craft and Mulberries were taken out past the Isle of Wight, to assemble near its southernmost point.

The rumble was accompanied by the roar of planes overhead, as they flew out across the Channel to bomb France. It came in great waves, a swelling groan that grew to a thunder, vibrating through the streets and houses, shaking the floors and ceilings, making furniture tremble. In some places, they said they could hear even more – the barking rattle of German ack-ack guns, and the explosions of the bombs as they landed.

Everyone knew what was going on. Yet for the rest of the country, for the rest of the world, it was a normal day. For months, while the preparations had been taking place, no hint had been given to outsiders. There had been no mention on the wireless of the long lines of trucks and lorries and tanks crowding the roads to the south coast, no pictures in the Pathé Pictorial at the cinema. The closure of the ten-mile-deep strip of town and country around the coast had effectively sealed it off from the outside, and even the most innocent of communications had been severely restricted. Everyone was in on the secret, yet until now nobody had known just how or when it would happen.

Now there was no hiding it. The armies were on the move. The greatest invasion of all time was about to begin.

\*

The sixth of June.

D-Day.

The D stood simply for Day – the day on which the invasion would begin – and H was the hour at which the first landings were to take place.

That morning, between seven-twenty-five and seven-forty-five and while many people at home were still having breakfast, the first of the landing craft swept up to the Normandy beaches and, as their giant maws opened, thousands of men, tanks and trucks flooded into France. At the same time, the sky was darkened by the first wave of aircraft, many bearing paratroops, others to defend the advance against the enemy. The sea was a floating island of steel; the air a shimmering ceiling of wings. Along the south coast of England, barrage balloons filled the skies to keep away any vengeful invader. There was none. The enemy had, at last, been taken by surprise, and Overlord looked set for success.

At Southwick, where it had all begun, there was a curious mixture of excitement and anti-climax.

Once the decision had been made, there was a flurry of messages to be sent. Fort Southwick must be notified, every commander and captain made aware. Montgomery himself was on his way to France almost immediately, to take charge on the spot. Eisenhower too was away – the decision taken, there was nothing left at Southwick for him to do. Winston Churchill – who had longed to go into battle himself and been prevented only by the King's announcement that if the Premier went, he must go as well – was already back in London, addressing Parliament. His speech was reported in the *Evening News* that same day:

An immense armada of upwards of 4,000 ships, together with several thousand smaller craft, have crossed the Channel. Mass airborne landings have been successfully effected behind the enemy's lines. Landings on the beaches are proceeding at various points and the fire of shore batteries has been largely quelled.

There was a photograph of General Montgomery as well, with his affirmation of 'complete confidence in a terrific Allied team', and a description of the area of Normandy where the landings were being made.

Gladys and the others tried to imagine what it must be like over there during that first day and the ones that followed. They had all known men who had returned from Dunkirk. Some survivors of that first great catastrophe had refused to speak of what they had seen, but others had told graphic stories. Gladys had heard of it from Derek Harker's lips, and needed only to close her eyes for a moment to visualise the landing craft advancing up the beaches from grey, heaving seas under a rain-whipped sky.

The beaches at Dunkirk had been thick with men waiting to be rescued and brought home, men who stood for up to three days waist-deep in the water, shelled and bombed by the enemy planes which ranged without mercy over their heads. The only ships able to get near the beaches were the ferry-boats, tugs, trawlers built to float in shallow water. The bigger ships had been forced to stand off and wait for the burden of exhausted and injured men to be brought out to them. An entire army might have been lost, had it not been for those little ships and the men – many of them civilians – who had answered the call of their country.

This time it was different. As at Dieppe, there would be no chance of rescue, but this time, the operation had been planned to the last, tiny detail. It had been two years or more in the planning, a vast scenario of action drawn up months, years, ahead of time. It had meant equipment, vehicles and weaponry designed and built specifically for the task – and, if there was time, tested. Some of the newest equipment went untried to the battlefield.

Many of the men – boys of eighteen, men of forty – were without experience of battle, their basic training the most that they could be given. They had as good a chance as the toughest of diehards. When you went over the top, someone had once said to Gladys, it didn't matter whether it was your first day in the Army or your thousandth, the bullets hit just as hard.

The lessons of Dunkirk and Dieppe had been well learned for Overlord, and while nobody could pretend that men would not die, as much cover was given to protect them as was possible. All day, the sky had been black with aircraft, heading across the Channel to guard the great armada. From the Normandy beaches themselves, the approach must have been fearsome – a multitude of ships, prow to prow as they advanced, with scarcely room between them to set a pin, under a lowering cloud of aircraft flying in wingtip to wingtip, as close as the ships beneath. It must have looked as if the entire sea had turned to steel, Gladys thought, and wondered if the Germans would even dare to stand against it.

The lanes of Hampshire had fallen silent again. The long convoys had gone, the trucks and lorries disappeared, and the Tommies and gum-chewing Yanks gone with them. At Southwick House, the big jigsaw wall-map was abandoned, and the men who had made it were allowed at last to go home. Nobody used the library now. The admirals and brigadiers had vanished overnight; the camps were quiet.

Gladys returned to Fort Southwick and the operations room deep inside the Hill. The model ships that had been massing on the south coast on the vast table-map had all been moved across the Channel, and she could see just what a mighty operation it had been. She stared, fascinated, thinking again of that silent moment in the library, as the wet and windy dawn of an English June morning had driven night from the sky and General Eisenhower had lifted his head at last and spoken those few, quiet words. The words that had sent those thousands of craft across the Channel. Those thousands of men.

She knew that Clifford must be amongst them. She thought of the last time they had met, when they had walked together through the crowded streets of Portsmouth, and had stopped in a quiet corner for a last goodbye kiss. Even now, he was on a landing craft heading across the Channel in the wind and the rain, somewhere on that sea that was so thick with ships, the sky above him thick with aircraft as they flew above to defend the invading army.

And on the distant shore . . . what?

The Germans weren't fools. They must have known an invasion was on the way. The Allies had done their best to mislead them, sending the mock-up ships, the plywood and dummies, to make them think the invasion would happen somewhere else. They'd kept their reconnaissance aircraft at bay with incessant waves of planes that bombarded their own defences. Even the weather, which had seemed to be against their plans, had been a help in that the Germans had been lulled into a sense of security, thinking the invasion couldn't possibly take place under such conditions. You still couldn't forget those previous two attempts, though, and Gladys looked at the great map and wondered if it was all going to happen again.

D-Day. It had come and gone. Now all they could do was wait, while the greatest battle of them all began at last.

Jess heard the news just after half-past nine. She had run up the street to Annie's house, anxious about her mother, but Mary was lying in bed, peacefully asleep, and the two sisters closed the door softly and left her there while they made a cup of tea.

They scarcely heard the wireless programme of *Music While You Work* that Annie had switched on, but when it stopped abruptly, they lifted their heads to listen. At the first measured words, they looked at each other with sudden awareness.

'This is London.' The BBC always began like that when it was about to make a particularly serious announcement, and it always employed one of its most senior announcers to do the job. Today, they recognised the voice of John Snagge, one of the best known and most respected broadcasters of all. 'Under the command of General Eisenhower, Allied Naval forces supported by strong air forces began landing Allied armies this morning on the northern coast of France.'

'That's it,' Jess whispered. She remembered all the other announcements she had heard during the past five years beginning 'This is London', bringing news of battles, of losses, of hope and despair. Dunkirk, Dieppe, the Battle of Britain – they passed through her mind in a steady stream. 'They've got to get it right this time,' she said. 'We can't send all our boys over there to get killed, like the last lot. We've got to win this time.'

'We will,' Annie said. 'You can tell, by all the work they've done getting it ready. All those tanks and things they've been getting together, and all those things they've been building out on the beaches, whatever they are. There's some big plan in it all. They're bound to get it right.'

'I hope so,' Jess said quietly. 'I really hope so.'

The sisters sat quietly together for a few minutes, thinking over all that had happened. The war had been going on for so long, it was difficult sometimes to remember just what life had been like before it started – and even more difficult to think what it would be like when it ended.

After a while, Jess got to her feet. 'Well, I suppose I'd better get back. I've got a lot to do at home. Frank says there's gooseberries over the allotment, ready to be picked, and I want to make some jam. I'll just look in and see if Mum's awake.' She opened the door to the front room and peeped inside, and when she spoke again her voice had changed. 'Annie . . .'

'What?' Annie was on her feet at once, but she didn't need to ask what had brought that note into her sister's voice. She crossed the room swiftly. 'Jess, she's not—'

'I thought she was asleep when we looked in just now,' Jess whispered. She was beside her mother's bed, her palm laid on the still forehead. 'I could've sworn she was just asleep. She looked so peaceful.'

'She still does.' Annie stood at her shoulder and laid her own hand over Jess's. 'She looks as if she's just slipped away. Oh, Jess.'

The two women stood gazing down. Their mother looked small beneath the bedclothes, small and at rest, her skin like pale silk over the fragile bones. Her limbs were relaxed, the painful joints and stiffness gone for ever. Her eyes were closed and her lips just parted, as if in a tiny smile.

'Oh, Mum,' Jess murmured. Tears came to her eyes and slid down her cheeks, but she knew that she wasn't weeping for the old woman who lay in the bed, whose hold on life had become so frail, who had been more than ready to depart.

She wept for the mother of her childhood, the mother who had borne her and cared for her. The mother who knew when she had had her first tooth and taken her first step. The mother who had always been there, and now would never be there again.

At number 15 April Grove, Ethel Glaister was missing Reg.

He hadn't been near her for days, nor had Violet seen Perce. They'd vanished, the pair of them, as if they'd never been there, and Ethel Glaister was furious. She didn't believe that he was married with a wife and three kids and a home in Cosham, but Carol's words had sown a seed of doubt.

She was just being nasty, the spiteful little bitch, Ethel told herself. All the same, it was true that Reg hadn't been back, and Ethel missed him. More than that, she missed the presents he had brought her – the chocolates and the scent, things she hadn't had for years, it seemed. Black market, of course, she knew that, but she didn't care. It had been a little bit of heaven just to be given them, and worth what he wanted in exchange.

She heard the announcement on the wireless that morning. She was at the factory, sorting bits and pieces in her usual resentful way, half listening to the chatter of the other women, when it came over the loudspeakers. Later, she bought a paper and read the big headlines. The landings had been reported in Germany, where they said the Allies had landed in the Channel Islands. Again, there were descriptions and maps of France, and another report said that the King would broadcast to the nation at nine o'clock that evening.

The long lines of trucks and tanks had disappeared from the streets. Over the Hill, and in Gosport and Southampton, they were still moving as more and more men embarked on the ships that were constantly taking their place close to the beaches. Soon, they would be all in France, and then the traffic would begin to come the other way – dead and wounded, brought back to the emergency centres.

Ethel wondered if Reg would be amongst them, or if he would ever return. She knew that he must be on his way to France. It hardly seemed to matter now whether he had a wife and children in Cosham.

At the RAF station, Diane and the other girls worked in the hangars all day, servicing the planes and the gliders which were still going out. They listened to the news bulletins on the wireless whenever they went back to the mess for a hasty meal. Those whose boyfriends were flying were tense and pale. Lizanellie squeezed each other's hands tightly whenever they met, and asked Diane if she had heard from Chuck.

'Why should I?' she said tartly. 'I've finished with him. I'm off men altogether, as a matter of fact.' But she watched the sky as intently as the rest, and her eyes strayed in the direction of the American air base. The Fortresses were over the Channel too, bombing German defences and oil production centres. She thought of Chuck's brother Larry, going down in flames, and of the American rancher and his wife, waiting for news of their remaining son.

Life's too short for quarrelling, her mother used to say, and Diane found her eyes filling with sudden tears at the unexpected memory. But we didn't quarrel, she wanted to say, it was just that he wasn't interested in me. 'So why was he out with you that afternoon?' her mother seemed to ask from somewhere inside her head. 'Why did he ask you to dance in the first place? And when did you ever let him see that you were interested in him?'

Perhaps it was all a misunderstanding, she thought miserably. Perhaps if that plane hadn't flown over at just that moment, he might have said something else. I was sure he was going to say something else, but then it all changed and I didn't know what to think.

'And you were too silly and stuck up to let him see you cared.' Peggy's voice came again, as clearly as if she were there by Diane's side. The blunt common sense that had always been so much a part of her mother, and which both Diane and Gladys had inherited from her, seemed to pierce the defensive barrier she had built up against her own feelings. As she stared at the sky, she felt it crumble inside her and knew with a rush of anguish that Chuck had been on the brink of finding his way into her heart. I love him, she thought, and I believe he could have loved me. We never told each other, and now it's too late. He's gone, like all the rest. Flown over in his Fortress, and I never even knew it was him.

The hiatus did not last long. Within a few days, the traffic was beginning again, this time a long line of wounded returning to the beaches on their way to the hospitals and emergency medical centres that had been set up in readiness. As the armies gained slow but steady footholds in France, other Service personnel crossed to join them – administrators, nursing staff, other auxiliaries. Then, even as Britain began to let out a sigh of relief and dare to believe that perhaps the tide might at last be turning in their favour, Hitler's secret weapon was unleashed and a new terror began.

The flying bomb.

# CHAPTER EIGHTEEN

It was as if the war had begun all over again, with all the ferocity that had only been imagined back in 1939.

While the Army continued their landings in France, supported by the thick ceiling of aircraft above, and the steel ocean of ships in the Channel behind, the Germans began to attack with their long-threatened 'secret weapon' – a bomb that flew under its own power, that could be launched from France and set to travel all the way to London before its engine cut out and it fell from the sky to destroy whatever lay beneath.

The flying bomb. The doodlebug. The V1.

To begin with, nothing was said about this new and terrifying turn of events. The first explosions that occurred were said to be caused by gas, but as the days wore on and the bombs kept coming, the truth could not be concealed. The steadily mounting statistics told their own story.

Exactly a week after D-Day, four bombs fell on London, killing six people in Bethnal Green. After that, they came in increasing numbers, until on 17 June over seventy rained from the sky in just a few hours, and two dozen people, drinking in a pub, lost their lives in a single explosion. The next day a hundred and twenty more were killed attending a service in the chapel at Wellington Barracks, only a short distance from Buckingham Palace, and nearly two hundred office-workers died in Bush House, in the Aldwych. In less than a fortnight, nearly two thousand were dead and six thousand seriously injured.

It was news that could no longer be suppressed.

The new bomb created its own special terror. There was something creepy about a bomb as big as a small aeroplane, flying without a pilot, which could sneak in under the range of the anti-aircraft guns and set what seemed to be an inexorable course on its target. With the ordinary aircraft, you felt you had some chance of fighting back – there was a pilot in there who could be shot at; you were fighting human beings. The V1 was described as a 'robot', and the thought of fighting a war against robots was peculiarly horrible and unnerving.

At the sound of the droning engine, people would watch fearfully as one flew overhead, giving a collective sigh of relief as it passed – or throwing themselves to the ground as the engine sputtered and died.

They seemed quite inescapable, as if their destination had been pinpointed before they left France, and there was no way of preventing their devastation.

The airmen did their best. They flew daringly close to the missiles and shot them down or, even more courageously, close enough to tip the stubby wings with their own and send them off course. Even these tactics could not prevent the explosions and the risk of more deaths on the ground, so the fighter patrols were moved away from London to the south and east coasts over which the bombs were approaching, and a curtain of barrage balloons brought nearer to the city.

On 6 July Mr Churchill announced that, in less than a month, 2,754 flying bombs had been sent to England and 2,752 people had been killed. There were now eight thousand people in hospital suffering from their injuries. He added that the new drug penicillin – to which he owed his own recovery from pneumonia and which had previously been restricted to the Forces' use – would be available for those who needed it.

In 'Bomb Alley' – the flight path of the bombs across Kent, Sussex and the south-east suburbs of London – two hundred thousand houses were destroyed or badly damaged, and on 18 July, half a million women and children were evacuated from London. For those who stayed behind, shelters a hundred feet deep with bunks for eight thousand people, built after the Blitz of 1940, were opened for the first time.

'I don't know,' Jess said as Frank switched off the wireless after the nine o'clock news. 'It doesn't seem to be getting any better. I thought once D-Day was over, we'd be looking forward to the end of it all, and then when we heard that they'd actually tried to assassinate Hitler . . . Now it's worse than ever, with these awful bombs. I mean, what will they be doing next?'

'It's going to take more than a few weeks to beat Hitler,' Frank said grimly. 'He's had things his way for too long. He's got his foot in the door all over Europe, and he doesn't seem to have any trouble making more and more planes and munitions.'

'Well, he wouldn't, would he?' Cherry remarked. She was winding wool unravelled from an old jumper and washed to get the crinkles out. It was a peculiarly muddy shade of green, rather like half-dried seaweed. Jess wondered where she'd got it. She'd never seen anyone but Cherry wearing these strange colours that looked as if they'd been dredged up from a riverbed. She hoped the wool wasn't intended for a cardigan for Rose or Maureen. Kind as the thought would have been, she doubted if either of her daughters would have been very grateful.

'What do you mean?' she asked.

'Well, he's got all those countries working for him, having to do as he tells them. He's got all their factories and stuff, and they say he's using the people as slave labour.' Cherry finished one ball and started another. 'I'm surprised we can make any new planes at all. They must have used up all those old saucepans and iron railings they took off us.'

Frank went across to his big wall-map. The pins showed Allied advances through Normandy. There had been some criticism of Montgomery, who had had trouble breaking out into the open country-side and failed to take Caen. Cherry was right, he thought, the Germans had it all their own way with the manpower of so much of Europe under their domination. On the news tonight, they'd talked about our losing five and a half thousand men and several hundred tanks. There must be a limit to how long we can go on.

He sat down again in the armchair he'd made when he and Jess had first got married. He'd built quite a lot of their furniture – the dining-table with its extending leaves, the cabinet that housed the gramophone, their bed and a couple of boxes to store things in. He'd made their first wireless too, with headphones, and the one that they were using now that everyone could listen to at once.

Frank would have liked to work with wood, making furniture perhaps, or with wrought-iron as he'd been trained to do when he'd been apprenticed as a blacksmith. He liked making things as much as he liked growing his own vegetables. Fate had forced him into the dockyard, though, where he could only work as a skilled labourer in a hot, steamy boiler shop. He did his job well, as he would always do anything that he undertook, but sometimes he would rest from his heavy work and think longingly of the open air, or the sweet smell of wood in a carpenter's shed.

He'd thought of it more than ever just lately. Five years of war was wearing Frank down, just as it was wearing down everyone else. He was sick of the bombing, the blackout, the fear. He was sick of the unending grind, the long hours of work, the sheer tedium of it all. He was sick of getting up at five-thirty every morning, of walking to work for seven and back home again late in the evening, of spending his nights firewatching. He was too tired to do the things he enjoyed doing – tending his garden, improving his house, spending time with his family. He felt that his children were becoming strangers to him. They were growing up while his back was turned, growing away from him and out of his reach.

He thought of the plan he and Jess had made to get a tandem and go out into the countryside of a Sunday afternoon. The dream seemed even further from coming true than it had when he'd first suggested it. He looked at the map again and pictured another map hanging in the same place, a map of Hampshire and Sussex, with pins stuck in to show where they'd been on their tandem.

I'm fed up, he thought. I'm fed up with the whole bloody lot of it.

As soon as the restrictions on movements around the coast were lifted, Olive went out to Bishop's Waltham to see Betty. Annie had been right to suspect that there was a baby on the way, and although Olive still felt a bitter pang of sadness at the thought of her own miscarriage three years ago, she was excited by the news and wanted to congratulate her sister in person.

'You're not showing at all,' she exclaimed, admiring Betty's slim figure. 'Sure it's not a mistake?'

'There's no mistake about morning sickness, I can tell you,' Betty retorted. She looked the picture of health, her bright curls gleaming and her skin radiant. 'Anyway, I'm only three months gone. I shan't be showing for weeks yet.'

'You are lucky.' Olive sat down and accepted a cup of tea. 'Wish it was me having a baby.' She looked around wistfully. 'And you've got a home together as well. This is really nice.'

Betty sat down beside her on the little settee. She and Dennis had furnished the small cottage with a few bits and pieces the Spencers had given them from the farmhouse, together with whatever they'd been able to buy secondhand from the villagers. It was simple but looked cosy and cheerful, with Dennis's books on the shelves and a jug filled with hedgerow flowers and greenery on the table.

'I don't suppose we'd have a home if Dennis wasn't blind,' she said quietly. 'I thank God every day he wasn't killed, and that he's not still working on bomb disposal. Not many survive that, you know.'

'I know. I'm being selfish – thinking of myself.' Olive's lips quivered suddenly and she reached for her sister's hand. 'Oh, Betty, I'm so miserable. Everything's going wrong, and I don't know what to do.' Her face crumpled and she burst into tears.

Betty gazed at her. She took the cup away and set it on the floor, then put both her arms around Olive's shoulders. She held the shuddering body for a few moments, then said, 'What is it, Livvy? What's the matter?'

'Oh, what do you *think's* the matter?' Olive fumbled for a handkerchief. 'It's this horrible war, isn't it? Taking our men away from us. Ruining all our lives. Stopping us *living* our lives. I'm fed up with it all, sick and fed up with it, and I'm fed up waiting around for my marriage to get a chance to begin.'

'I know. We're all fed up with it, but it looks as if it won't be for too much longer. Things are getting better. I mean, I know the flying bombs are awful, but apart from that we seem to be winning. People are saying it could all be over by Christmas.'

Olive snorted. 'We've heard that before! *Which* Christmas? And anyway' – her voice shook again – 'I don't know that that's going to make it any better for me.' She lifted her head and stared at Betty. 'Sometimes I think it'd be easier if it didn't end,' she whispered, and buried her face in her hands again.

Betty looked at the bent head. She moved one of her hands, a little uncertainly, and stroked the shining chestnut hair. She bit her lip, started to speak, hesitated, and started again.

'Livvy – whatever is it? What's happened? Is it Derek? Have you had some bad news?'

Olive shook her head and said something in a muffled voice. Betty leaned closer.

'I can't hear you. Look at me, Livvy. Tell me what it is. It's not just the war, is it? *Tell* me.'

At last Olive raised her head. She looked at her sister with reddened, hopeless eyes and said, 'I've fallen for someone else.'

'Someone *else*?' Betty stared at her. 'What are you talking about? How can you have – Livvy, what do you mean?'

'It's plain enough, isn't it?' There was a trace of bitterness, tinged with defiance, in Olive's voice. 'It's what happens to a lot of women whose men have been away for years. I've got friendly with another chap and – well, it's led on from that. That's all.'

'That's *all*?' Betty drew her hand away. 'You're letting your Derek down and you say that's *all*?'

'Yes, and that's how everyone else will see it, isn't it?' Olive retorted. 'Letting Derek down. They'll look at the outside of it, and they'll call it sordid and bad, and want no more to do with me. They'll turn against me, just like you, not wanting to touch me. Nobody'll want to know what it feels like inside, how it hurts – oh *God*, how it hurts—' Her voice broke again and the tears streamed down her cheeks.

Betty reached out again, quickly, and pulled her sister close. 'I'm sorry, Livvy, I never meant to do that. It wasn't the way you thought. Of course I'm not turning against you. I'm your sister. Sisters stick together, whatever happens.' She held Olive by the shoulders and looked into her face. 'Tell me all about it, Livvy, and I promise you I'll do whatever I can to help.' She hesitated, then asked in a quiet voice, 'Are you – are you . . .'

'In the family way?' Olive laughed shortly. 'No such luck! No – I don't really mean that. That would make everything worse, but – oh, I just wish everything could be normal. I wish I could just love one chap and be at home with him and have lots of kids with him and just be *ordinary*. Like Mum and Dad, or Auntie Jess and Uncle Frank. Like you and Dennis.'

'Tell me,' Betty said quietly, and handed Olive her cup of tea.

Olive sipped it and sat staring out of the window at the garden. Dennis had dug it over and Betty had planted salad vegetables in it – lettuce and radishes and spring onions. She hadn't planted them in rows, as her father or uncle would have done – instead, she'd made a picture of them, planting them in rings so that it looked more like a flower garden than a vegetable garden. They were green and healthy looking, ready to be eaten. Olive had seen some in the kitchen, prepared for tea.

'It's Ray,' she said at last. 'We're both on the gun. We didn't meet there, we met at South Parade Pier when I went with Claudia. I only went to hear the music, but Ray asked me to dance and it seemed daft not to. And then he got put on the same gun as me and – well, we just liked each other. That's all it was to begin with,' she added, turning her head to look at Betty. 'We were just friends. We never meant it to get any further, never. I don't really know how it did,' she finished miserably.

'So – how far has it gone? I mean, are you . . .'

'Sleeping together? Of course we are.' A spark of anger lit Olive's eyes. 'We're human, aren't we? What does anyone expect? He's a nice bloke, I liked him. After a bit, I realised I loved him. I'd never have done it if I hadn't.'

'No, but – Livvy, what about Derek? Don't you still love him? What are you going to do?'

'Yes, I still love Derek, of course I do, he's done nothing to hurt me, but I – I . . .' Once again, the tears came and Olive covered her face with her hands, then she lifted her head and looked wildly at her sister. 'Betty, I just don't *know* what I'm going to do. Whatever happens, I'm going to hurt someone. Derek – Mum and Dad – you. Or else Ray. He needs me, he loves me, and I can't give him up, I *can't*.'

'But you're married to Derek—'

'I *know* that!' Olive twisted the ring on her finger. 'D'you think I don't remember that every day, every time I'm with Ray and we – we—' She shook her head violently. 'Look, I know all those things as well as you do, but I know what it's doing to me and Ray as well. It's tearing us apart. He's got no one else, only me. Well, he's got a little girl, but she hardly knows him, his wife won't have anything to do with him and—'

'His *wife?* Livvy, you're mad, you can't go on with this.'

'I can't stop. I've tried. We've both tried. We *love* each other, Betty.'

'But if he's married too . . . You know what people say about divorce. Mum would never—'

'His wife's Catholic. She'll never give him a divorce.'

'That's even worse!' Betty shook her head. 'You're not seriously thinking about just . . . living with him? Living *in sin?*'

'I told you, I don't know. I don't know what I'm thinking about. My mind just goes round in circles. All I know is, I love Derek and I love Ray, and I don't want to hurt either of them. I don't want to hurt Mum and Dad either, or anyone else. Sometimes I just think it'd be better if I wasn't here at all,' she added quietly, staring into her cup.

'*No!*' Betty snatched the cup away and almost dropped it on the floor. She grabbed her sister's shoulders and shook her violently. 'You're not to talk like that! Don't you ever, *ever*, say such a thing again. It's wicked. *Wicked*. You know what you've got to do. You've got to give him up. The war'll be over soon and Derek'll be coming home, and he'll want to set up a proper home with you and start a family, and he's *entitled* to that. It's what he's fighting for, and you've got no right to take it away from him.'

'Derek isn't fighting, he's building—'

'He's in the Army,' Betty said inexorably, 'and he's away from home. It's the same thing. You know it is.'

Olive was silent. She looked at her hands and then up into her sister's face. 'I thought I might get a bit of sympathy from you.'

'And so you have.' Betty's face softened and she drew Olive into her arms again. 'Livvy, don't think I've turned against you. You're my sister and I love you, and I always will. I feel really sorry about all this. I can see it's hurting you. I can see you really believe you love this Ray. But you know it's not possible. You've got to give him up. You've got to.'

'I can't,' Olive whispered.

'Livvy, you must.'

Olive shook her head. 'You don't understand. You don't know what it's like. I can't live without him. I need him. I need to see him and talk to him and – and feel him. I need to love him.'

'If he wasn't there, you'd manage.'

'I wouldn't.' Olive spoke without drama, the words as clear and quiet as tiny stones dropping into a pool. 'If he wasn't there, I think I'd die.'

'Oh, Livvy,' Betty said. 'Oh, my poor, poor Livvy.'

They sat in silence for a while, then Betty said, 'Something will have to happen. The war *is* going to end, and Derek will come home. You've got to face it. You can't have them both, and—'

'I know. Derek's my husband and I've got to stand by him. I've told myself that a hundred times. I've told Ray. And I want to stand by him, I really do. I love him – nothing's changed about that. I just can't bear to think—' Olive raised her tear-streaked face. 'How am I going to do it, Betty? How can I do it?'

'I don't know,' Betty said honestly. 'I'm trying to think what I'd feel like if it was Dennis, but I can't imagine . . . ' She shook her head. 'I just know you're going to have to be really strong, and I'll do anything I can to help. You know that. If you just want to come here and talk to me, you always can. And Dennis, too. He's so wise, and he won't turn against you either. Quakers don't. If you need any help at all in giving Ray up—'

'And if I still can't?'

'Then we'll stand by you,' Betty said. 'Whatever you decide, Livvy, we'll stand by you.'

There was another long silence. They sat close together, looking out at the quiet garden. Betty moved slightly and laid her hand lightly on her stomach. In there was the baby she and Dennis had made, from their love. She thought of Olive, loving Derek, of the baby they had lost. She thought of Olive loving this other man, and not knowing what to do.

Dennis is right, she thought, we don't have any business going to war. And not just because of the killing, but because of all the other harm it causes – harm that goes on and on.

Whatever Olive did about this unlooked-for love, nothing would ever be the same again, and the consequences would follow her throughout her life.

August Bank Holiday was another stay-at-home holiday. There were no long-distance trains or buses. All transport was required for troops returning from France – the wounded, coming back in a steady trail to be put together again and sent over for another go. The weather was fine, though, and thousands of people flocked to the beaches that were open to them, swimming in the sea or lounging on towels or in deckchairs they had dragged along with them. Jess and Frank took the family to Southsea, and for a few hours pretended that the war was over as they played in the sea with an old car tyre. Rose sat self-consciously in an old swimming costume of Jess's and Maureen paddled cautiously at the edge of the water in a pair of knickers that Cherry had made for her.

'Come on,' Tim said, lifting her up. 'Let's teach you to swim.' He held

245

her across his arms while Keith pulled her legs this way and that. Maureen squealed and half choked as a wave slopped across her face, and struggled to be set free. The boys laughed and let her go, and Tim found a patch of sand amongst the shingle and started to build a sand-castle.

Keith wandered away. There were still parts of the beach closed off with barbed wire. He found a small knot of boys about his own age, peering over the rolls. The shingle looked bare and innocent, and far more alluring than the crowded stretch behind them.

'It's just mean, not letting us go down there,' one boy said. 'I bet they keep it for the soldiers. The high-ups – I've seen 'em.'

'What, here? Swimming?'

'Well, not here,' the first boy said. 'Farther up, by Eastney Barracks. You got to have a permit to go up there but I got past the guard once and I saw 'em, all along the edge of the water. They had canoes and stuff. And little tiny submarines.'

The other boys stared at him unbelievingly, but who knew what the soldiers might have had? They had all seen the Funnies that had been lined up along the roads before D-Day. There might just as well have been miniature submarines.

'I bet there weren't. I bet you're making it up.'

'I'm not, then.' The boy stared at them aggressively. 'Show you if you like.'

'Go on, then. Show us.'

There was a challenging silence, then the first boy shrugged and turned away. They followed him along the line of barbed wire.

Keith hesitated. He knew that he was likely to be missed quite soon, and that there would be trouble if he didn't go back to the family, but he was torn between his awe of his father and a desire to see the midget submarines. And like most of the boys he knew, he was fascinated by what had been going on on the beaches, and longed for some souvenirs.

'There's a place where we can get in,' the leader said. 'It's just up here.' He glanced round at them. 'Bet you're scared.'

The boys moved forwards at once. No one was willing to be called a coward. Keith was third through the hole, with two others following him.

Once through the wire, they felt a surge of excitement. Not only did they have a vast stretch of beach to themselves, they were on forbidden territory, on military land. This was what it must feel like to be soldiers across the Channel, fighting for your life. They crouched and ran, darting glances to right and left, crooking their arms to hold imaginary machine-guns. At the edge of the water, they paused and then ran in, letting the waves lap over their plimsolls. Soldiers had to do that. They had to jump

246

off landing craft and wade ashore, up to their waists, never mind getting wet and cold. Soldiers didn't feel the cold, anyway.

'Bang-bang! You're dead.' The leader had forgotten his claims about midget submarines and was pointing his imaginary gun at Keith. 'You're a German and I've shot you, you're dead.'

'You can't shoot me. I'm English.' Keith stood upright at the edge of the water. 'I never said I'd be a German.'

'*I* said so. This is my place. You wouldn't never have come here if I hadn't shown you the hole.' The boy was advancing threateningly. He was bigger than Keith, and Keith was aware suddenly of his position. The other boys had all been together, they were friends, and he was the outsider who had tagged along. He looked a little nervously along the beach, but no one was in sight.

'That's right,' the rest chorused. 'It's our place. Who're you, anyway? Whose gang are you in?'

'I'm not—' Keith began, but his words were drowned by a sudden call from above the wire. The boys all stopped at once and looked around. At the sight of the large, burly man who was watching them, they fell silent and scuffled their feet in the sand.

The man eyed them for a moment. They couldn't see much of him above the rolls of barbed wire, but he seemed to be dressed in a dark blue uniform, like a policeman. Keith thought uneasily of the trouble his brother Tim had got into with the police. Keith hadn't been in Portsmouth at the time, he'd been away at Mr Beckett's, but he'd heard all about it and how upset Mum had been and how angry Dad had got. He didn't want to cause the same sort of trouble.

The man had no helmet on, however, and they breathed a quiet sigh of relief. Perhaps he was ARP. They were a bossy lot, but you could get away from them a bit easier. They waited to see what he would do.

When he spoke, his voice was surprisingly normal and friendly. 'Hullo, boys. Having a good time?'

They glanced at each other uneasily, then nodded. He nodded back, smiling affably. Perhaps he was a bit soft in the head, Keith thought. Like Desmond, who'd got hurt by Micky Baxter's gun and had to go to hospital.

'Just stay there,' the man went on, still in the same friendly tone. 'Don't move. I'll just go and get some help.'

'We don't need help—' the boy who had led them here began, starting up the beach, but the man lifted his hand and spoke much more sharply.

'*Stop!* I said *don't move*.' He stared at them, and the boy who had moved froze. 'I mean it, lads. Just stay right where you are – don't move an *inch*, d'you understand? I'll be back in less than five minutes.' He paused again, and added quietly, 'I'll know if you move. I'll know right away.'

The boys looked at each other. There had been a note in his voice that told them he wasn't joking. Nor was he soft in the head. They believed him when he said that he would know if they'd moved, and Keith had a nasty feeling that he knew why.

'It's mined,' he said, and his voice sounded hollow in his own ears. 'The beach is mined. That's why it's wired off.'

The others looked at him uneasily.

'It's not. It can't be. You'd be able to see if it was mined.'

'I bet it is. They bury them in the shingle. They go off if you step on them.' He glanced fearfully up the beach. 'I bet there's mines all over the place. It's in case the Germans invade.'

'Well, I don't believe it,' the leader said, 'and I'm not going to wait here while he goes to fetch a copper. I'm off.'

'*No!*' Keith cried as he made to walk up the sloping shingle. 'No, don't. My brother nearly got blown up. A boy in the next street to us did, and he got his leg blown off. And another one got killed, they never found the bits. And they put Micky Baxter in *prison* for it.'

The bigger boy paused and stared at him. 'It's not true. You're making it up.'

'I'm not,' Keith said desperately, wishing he'd never come. 'I'm not, honest. You can ask anyone. Ask my dad. Ask the police. Ask Jimmy Cross—'

'Jimmy Cross?' one of the others butted in. 'Here, I know him. My auntie lives next door to him. It's true, he did get his leg blown off. He's got a wooden one now.' He looked at Keith with something approaching awe. 'Were you there when it happened?'

'Well, no, I wasn't actually there then,' Keith admitted, 'but our Tim was, when they got shot. They had all these guns, see, and ammo as well, and—'

He was interrupted again, this time by another shout from the man on the other side of the wire. His fascinated audience looked up and Keith felt slightly annoyed. He'd just started to enjoy himself – it wasn't often he had all the attention. Tim did most of the talking at home, and Keith generally found himself referred to as 'the quiet one.'

However, his irritation disappeared in a surge of relief as he saw that the man had brought several soldiers back with him. They were already getting through the wire, and they had strange devices on long handles, which they held in front of them as they moved slowly down the beach. He also noticed that the man was a policeman after all. He must have taken his helmet off when he called to them before, and now it was back on his head.

'Just keep still, boys, and don't be scared,' the policeman called in a calm voice. 'Nothing to worry about. Nothing's going to happen to you. Just wait where you are . . . ' His voice went on, quiet and soothing, but somehow that frightened Keith more than if he'd yelled at them. It must be really bad, he thought, for a copper to talk to boys like an ordinary human being, especially when those boys were so clearly trespassing. Keith had been brought up to regard the police with respect – there to be called on for help if you needed it, but more likely to give you a clip round the ear for scrumping apples or breaking a window with your football. Mostly, he'd kept out of their way.

However, just now, he was less afraid of the policeman than of the mines that were buried under the shingle. I don't care if he does wallop me, he thought, I don't even care if he tells Dad. I just don't want to be blown to bits like Cyril Nash. I don't want to have a wooden leg like Jimmy Cross.

The soldiers had reached the edge of the water. There were three of them, and each lifted a boy in his arms and draped him over one shoulder in a fireman's lift. Keith and the leader of the gang were left behind, watching the men tread delicately back up the slope. Don't let them tread on a mine, he prayed. Don't let them get blown up . . .

The three boys were safe. They were dumped on the other side of the wire. Two of the soldiers turned and started to come carefully back down the beach.

'Come on, sonny. It's all right now.'

Keith found he was shivering. The water that lapped around his ankles was suddenly icy and the warmth had gone out of the August sun. He looked up at the soldier, and felt his lips tremble.

'It's all right,' the man repeated. He had a young face, like Bob Shaw next door, who used to take Keith and Tim to football matches. He'd taken them to see the Pompey team come back to Portsmouth after they'd won the FA Cup, just before the war started, and Dad had been really cross because they'd been late home. He'd wanted to cane them both, but Mum had stopped him.

'Come on.' The young soldier lifted Keith in his arms. The bigger boy was already being carried up the beach. Keith felt the roughness of serge against his cheek, and the hard buttons pressing into his body. He saw the shingle beneath and shut his eyes tightly as the man's body began to move.

The journey up the beach seemed endless. He could not believe that they had come so far.

At last he felt himself swung off the man's shoulder and opened his eyes to find himself standing safely on the right side of the wire. He blinked and looked around. The other boys were standing in a silent huddle, and the policeman, looking bigger than ever, was surveying them all grimly.

'Well, you're a fine lot and no mistake,' he began. 'Ain't there enough beaches open to you that you've got to come poking around here and risking your lives? And not just *your* lives – it's these soldiers here, soldiers who're needed to fight for their country, not tramp about rescuing silly young twerps like you from getting themselves blowed up. And what about your mums and dads, eh? What do you think they're going to feel like when you're brought home to them in a paper bag? Don't you think there's enough trouble in the world, without you adding to it? Don't you think people have got enough to worry about? Don't you have no consideration at all?'

Keith was near to tears. He stared down at his feet, blinking hard. He could see the others shuffling, as if they felt much the same. The policeman's voice went on above their heads, telling them in every way he could think of how stupid they were, how they deserved to be blown up and might have been if he hadn't come along. 'And I only stopped then because I thought of your mums and dads and how they'd feel,' he told them. 'Not because I thought a lot of silly little boys was worth saving. But I suppose they want you back, though Gawd knows why.' He paused for breath and seemed to run out of steam. 'Well, you'd better get off back to 'em, seeing as you're safe. And don't let me catch you round here again. *Hang* on a minute' – as they prepared to flee – 'ain't you got summat to say to these brave soldiers, what risked their lives to get you back? Ain't you even going to say ta?'

The boys stopped and looked nervously at the three soldiers, who stared solemnly back. Keith looked at the one who had reminded him of Bob Shaw. He didn't even look as old as Bob Shaw, he thought, and suddenly realised that the soldier was trying not to laugh. There was a twinkle in his eyes, and as Keith met his glance he dropped one eyelid in a suspicion of a wink.

Feeling suddenly better, Keith grinned back. 'Thanks,' he said. 'Thanks a lot.' He looked at the policeman. 'Sorry we caused so much trouble.'

The policeman wasn't looking nearly as stern as he'd sounded either. His face was broad and kindly, and there were wrinkles round his eyes as if he smiled a lot. He pursed his lips and nodded. 'Well, just you remember next time and don't be such a silly little fool. I ought to be taking you in charge, really, but – well, seeing as it's August Bank Holiday, you get off back to your parents before I change me mind.'

Keith turned and ran. He didn't look to see which way the other boys went. He was anxious only to get back to the family before his father realised how long he'd been away. If he could just pretend he'd only been for a wander along the beach, or for a swim . . .

There was no hope of that, of course. As he drew nearer to the little patch where they'd settled themselves, he could see Frank on his feet, peering out to sea, while Jess stood beside him, gazing anxiously this way and that and Tim held Maureen's hand. Only Rose was unconcerned, sitting on her towel in her borrowed swimsuit, trying to pretend she wasn't interested in the boys who went past.

'There he is! Oh, thank goodness.' Jess swooped upon him and Keith shrugged her away, terrified that she was going to kiss him or burst into tears. 'Wherever have you been?'

'Yes, where have you been?' Frank was on him too, and there was no chance that he would burst into tears. He looked furious. Keith had been going to pass off his absence lightly by implying that he'd just been talking with a few mates, but when his father looked at him like that he dared not lie.

'I went along the beach. There were some other boys . . . ' He wanted to stop the words, but they tumbled from his lips. 'We went through some barbed wire and a policeman saw us and got some soldiers to fetch us out. There were *mines*.' He stared up at his father. 'They came down with detectors to see where they were buried, and they carried us up the beach. Dad, there's all mines under the stones.' The terror of it hit him and he gazed around at the people sitting near by, the swimmers in the water, the children floating on the old tyre. 'Let's go home,' he said in a small voice. 'I want to go home.'

Jess looked at her husband. Frank's temper was liable to explode at times, especially when he'd been worried, and there was no doubt he'd been almost frantic with worry over Keith, who wasn't yet a really strong swimmer. She put out a hand to stop him from laying into Keith there and then. Wait till we get home, she begged him silently. Wait till you've had a chance to cool down.

Frank made no move towards his son, though. Instead, he sat down rather suddenly on the old blanket and drew in a deep, unsteady breath.

Jess sat down beside him, and Keith stood rather uncertainly in front of them both, expecting punishment but unsure as to what it would be.

'This bloody war,' Frank said at last in a low, tight voice, and Jess stared at him in alarm. Frank seldom swore, and never in front of the children.

'This bloody, *bloody* war.' He turned his head and looked into her eyes, and she read the fear and the misery in his face and knew that he was close to breaking point.

'Frank . . .'

'We can't even have a day on the beach without being reminded of it,' he went on as if she had not spoken. 'A nipper like Keith can't even walk along the shore without risking his life. *Mines*, Jess – on our beaches. Barbed wire. Places we can't go, where we used to play when we were kids. What sort of a world is it, eh? What's gone wrong with it all?'

Jess could not answer him. She could only reach out her hand and lay it upon his. They sat together, the six of them, silent as they gazed out to sea, at the Island that floated on the horizon, at the Channel beyond that stretched across to France where men were fighting at this very moment, where the war was being waged as it had been for five long years.

I don't know how long we can go on like this, she thought. We've managed to be strong so far, but there must be a limit. What happens when we reach it? Will we *ever* be able to get back to normal?'

# CHAPTER NINETEEN

For some people, normality was beyond dreaming of.

Carol Glaister wasn't even sure what it was. Surely not the dreary life she'd lived with her mother, before Roddy had come along and swept her away on the tide of his love. The frightened months in Bournemouth, after they had run away together and lived in that horrible little room, afraid every moment of discovery. The terror of thinking she had something awful wrong with her, barely assuaged by the realisation that she was pregnant. The misery of Roddy's arrest and her return home, only to be sent to the mother-and-baby home where little Roderick had been born and then taken away from her.

Surely none of these were 'normal'?

Nor her life now, working at the barracks, sewing uniforms that would soon be covered with blood, living that same cat-and-dog life with her mother just as if nothing at all had happened. When, really, everything had happened.

Ever since the night she'd spent wandering in her nightdress, Carol had passed her days sunk into a grey fog. She went to work, sat silent amongst the other girls, came home and got tea ready for her mother and herself, spent the evening half listening to the wireless and went to bed early. That suited Ethel, who was still finding plenty of 'gentlemen friends' – invariably soldiers or Marines – to bring home for a drink and a bite of supper. It suited Carol to be out of their way. She disliked them all, and hated the way they looked at her. Like Reg Allen, some of them seemed more interested in her than in her mother.

She was disconcerted and a little scared when she came home one evening to find Reg Allen himself waiting on the doorstep.

She stopped dead and stared at him with suspicion. As he grinned, his mouth a little slack, she smelt the beer on his breath and drew back.

'What are you doing here? We thought you were in France.'

'Well, I'm not, am I? Bin sent back to recover from me wounds.' He grinned and lifted one arm. She could see a plaster, but otherwise he didn't seem much hurt. His voice was slurred and he swayed slightly. 'Come to see your ma. Any objection?' He sniggered. 'Objection overruled!'

'She's not home yet,' Carol said shortly. 'She said she'd be late tonight. They're on overtime.'

'Doesn't matter.' He leaned against the door-jamb. 'I'll come in and wait for her. You can make me a cuppa.'

'I don't think you should.'

'Oh, and why not?' He lunged towards her. 'I'm your ma's friend, ain't I? She'd want me to come in and wait. Specially when she knows I'm a hero, bin wounded in battle, and what's more—' He stopped.

'What?' Carol said. 'You don't look wounded too bad to me. A bit of plaster on your arm's not enough to get you sent back.'

Reg lowered his eyes and looked shifty. 'I'm on secret work, see. I ain't supposed to be here, but I got a permit to come out, said my old woman was poorly. Only I come to see your ma instead. So let me in and I'll wait indoors.'

'Secret work?' Carol said disbelievingly. 'Go on, pull the other one. They wouldn't put you on secret work. Seems a bit funny, if you ask me.'

A scowl crept over his reddened face. 'You mind your tongue,' he growled. 'Nobody's asking you, and nobody's going to, see? And if they do—' He stopped again and gave her a quick look. 'Let me in. All I want is to sit in a proper armchair for a few minutes, and drink a cuppa tea like an ordinary bloke. That ain't too much to ask, is it, to give a bloke what's likely to be killed fighting for his country in a coupla days?'

Carol looked at him uncertainly. She didn't fancy the idea of being alone in the house with Reg, but she knew that a man in his condition could turn very awkward if thwarted. And her mother would be home soon. It was true she was working overtime tonight, but it had only been expected to be for an hour.

'All right,' she said, and took out her key. 'Let me past, then.'

Reg stood aside as she unlocked the door and for a moment she toyed with the idea of slamming it in his face, but he was too quick for her. As soon as she had it open, he was pushing past her into the narrow passage. Carol followed him reluctantly. For two pins, she would have stayed outside, but she didn't want to leave him alone in the house, and she didn't fancy standing out on the pavement until her mother returned.

'What about that cup of tea?' he demanded, standing in the middle of the back room.

Carol went past him to the scullery and filled the kettle. 'It'll be ready in a minute.' She came back and looked at him. 'Why is this the last time?'

He looked sly again. 'Wouldn't you like to know! That's why we're not allowed out. So's we can't tell no one, see? And so's we're ready when they gives the order.'

'What order?'

'For the next big push, of course.' He sneered at her puzzled face. 'Don't tell me you don't know there's an invasion on? They've bin sending us all across the Channel, the whole bleeding lot of us, and never mind how many gets killed so long as we can all take a few Jerries with us. That's what it's all about, young Carol. Happened before, ain't it? Dunkirk. Dieppe. Bloody catastrophes, like the rest of this whole bleeding shambles of a war, and who's the one that suffers? Joe Gubbins, that's who.'

He pushed his face against hers. Carol backed away, suddenly frightened. There was something mad in his hot little eyes tonight, something that reminded her of dreams she sometimes had about being chased by a bull. The smell of beer almost stifled her and she turned her face aside. He shot out his big hands and gripped her arms.

'Let go. You're hurting me.'

'Hurting you! And what about *me* getting hurt, eh? You think this hurts?' His fingers dug into her flesh 'Well, little girl, you don't know nothing. I *seen* men hurt. I seen 'em at Dunkirk. Laying on the beaches with half their body blown away and their guts spilling on the sand like pounds and pounds of sausages. That hurts. And a bloke with his leg hanging on by a thread – and a feller with the muscle out of his arm just like it was an orange picked off a tree. *That's* what hurt is. And another one with his face smashed in and nothing but a hole to scream out of . . . And it's going to happen again. I'm going to see it again. All – over – a-bloody-*gain*. Only this time it's supposed to be *me*.'

He was shouting at her now, shaking her as if she were a rag doll. Carol's body jerked backwards and forwards between his hands. She put up her hands, trying to ward him off, but they flailed uselessly with the force of his shaking. She sobbed and shook her head, trying to scream for help, but her voice refused to work.

'Only they ain't going ter get me,' Reg said, dragging her close against him. 'I seen enough of it, and I ain't going to be the next bit of cannon-fodder. I got meself wounded – just a bit – and sent to the field hospital. Then I managed to kid 'em that I was serious. They sent me back here, see, and the idea is that as soon as I'm fit again I'm off back to the front line. Only I'm not. I've had enough. They've had all they're going to get of Reg Allen, I tell you straight. I'm on the run and your ma's going to help me.'

'Help you?' Carol stared at him. 'You've deserted,' she whispered. 'You've done a bunk.' She thought fleetingly of Roddy, poor gentle Roddy, who had never wanted to join the Navy, never wanted to go to war. But Reg Allen was a Regular, he'd always known what it would mean . . . 'How can my mum help you? She won't keep you here.'

'She's got clothes,' he said. 'Your dad's clothes. She can kit me out. She's got money, too, keeps it under her bed. I don't need to ask where she gets it from – I ain't the only bloke she's brought back for a few home comforts. And talking of home comforts . . .' He pushed his face against hers. 'A little bit of that won't come amiss, and since she ain't here, I reckon you'll do instead.'

'What d'you mean?' He had stopped shaking her but the look in his eyes, so close to hers, frightened her even more. 'Let *go* of me.'

'Oh no,' he said, and held her hard against him with one hand while he ran the other down her back. 'Oh no. I'm not letting you go. Not yet. I've fancied you for a long while, little Carol. I reckon you'll be just as tasty as your ma. Tastier, in fact. Younger and tastier.'

He jerked her face up to his and laid his open mouth against her lips. She felt his tongue, harder than she would have believed a tongue could be, force its way past them and thrust itself against the roof of her mouth. She struggled in his arms, but he was holding her too tightly to allow her to kick or punch him. All she could do was pull his hair, but it was cut too short to give her any grip.

'Very tasty,' he muttered, removing his mouth for a moment. Carol drew in a deep breath to scream, but before she could utter a sound he had plunged upon her again, and she felt herself gag on the thickness of his slobbering tongue. While one hand still kept her firmly clamped against his body, the other was busy pulling at her clothes.

The room swam about her. She thought briefly of Roddy and the tenderness of their lovemaking. And she thought of Nancy Baxter and the man who had raped her.

It's not going to happen to me, she thought. I'm not going to let it happen to me.

She bit as hard as she could on the invading tongue.

Reg let go of her. He jerked backwards, both hands at his mouth, his eyes bulging. 'You little bitch! You spiteful little bitch!'

There was blood on his mouth, blood that Carol could taste in hers. She saw the pain and fury in his eyes and scuttled into the corner of the room, still facing him, her hands groping for the doorknob. For a few seconds, pain had rendered him helpless, but in a moment or two his rage would overpower them both. She got the door open, and ran down the passage and out into the street. Terrified that Reg would follow her, she shot like a rabbit up the narrow alleyway that ran along the back of October Street.

It was still light, but rainclouds hung like huge yellow bruises in the sky. A thin, spiteful wind scuttled along the alley, creating little swirls of dust that blew into Carol's eyes and mouth. She hardly noticed them. Casting frightened glances over her shoulder, she came to the top of the alley and turned right, towards the level crossing and railway bridge. Perhaps once over that, she would be safe. Perhaps Reg would have gone the other way. Perhaps . . . perhaps . . .

The bridge offered no comfort, for by the time she reached it, she had already forgotten the man who had attacked her. Her mind had reverted to the one thing that occupied it most. As the first spots of rain began to fall, she slowed to a walk, her head turning this way and that, her eyes wide and distracted as she sought the part of her that had been so roughly torn away. He must be there somewhere. And wherever he was, he would be wanting her, waiting for her, weeping for her.

Roderick, her baby. She must find him.

Reg Allen came out soon afterwards and slammed the door. He hadn't waited for Ethel to return. A quick search through the house had revealed that none of George Glaister's clothes remained, so he'd done no more than snatch the money that Ethel had hidden under her mattress and washed his mouth out in Ethel's kitchen sink. He could still taste the blood and his tongue was sore and swelling. He wished he could go to a doctor, one who wouldn't ask questions, and get it seen to. God knew what the little hussy might pass on to him. But he knew that he must put as many miles as possible between him and the city before he dared do that.

He'd go to London – that was the best place to get lost in – and then he'd find a sawbones and tell him it was a whore who'd bitten him. And so it bloody well was. A whore like her mother.

Carol ran blindly, not knowing where she went, not caring what was going to happen. During the scuffle with Reg, the fog that had swirled about her mind had cleared just sufficiently to allow her to save herself. As soon as she was out of the house, it descended again, more thickly than ever, like a heavy, muffling blanket that dulled her thoughts and blotted out memory. Only a few recollections stood out, like vivid pictures against its darkness.

Roddy. She had lost Roddy. She had to find Roddy again, or she would be lost for ever in the fog.

And Roderick, their baby. She had lost him too. She could never go home unless she found the baby Roderick.

The streets were quiet. Most people were at work. Only a few old people, or women with small children, came out in the wind and rain to stand in sodden queues outside the shops. They watched Carol with varying degrees of boredom as she fled past. If they saw the fear in her eyes, they were too accustomed to it to interfere. So many people were afraid these days. Soldiers, bored and tense, whistled and called after her as they did with every woman under forty who passed, but she ignored them. She had come out without coat or hat and was quickly soaked to the skin, but she took no notice. She simply walked, without aim or purpose. She walked as far as she could – from Copnor to Southsea, through the darkening and windswept streets – and when she was tired of walking, she stopped and huddled in a shop doorway.

Her mind was blank, except for the constant repetition, like hammer-blows to her brain, of her baby's name.

Roderick. Roderick. Roderick . . .

Dawn stirred her into life. She opened her eyes, unsurprised to find herself in a shop doorway, and struggled stiffly to her feet. She was wet through, cold and hungry, but these discomforts went unnoticed beside the anguish of her emotions. She was conscious only of a huge sense of loss, a sense that punched her in the stomach and smashed against her head. It hurt all over, and mere cold and wet and hunger could offer no competition against such pain.

She wanted desperately to escape it. Yet at the same time, she was afraid to let it go. For once that was gone, there would be nothing in her life, nothing in herself, only a great, yawning void that nothing would ever be able to fill. An emptiness that she feared more than death itself.

For a few moments, she leaned against the shop window. Then she began once more to walk.

She was looking for her baby.

She had lost track of the months since he had been born, forgotten that he would now be eighteen months old, a toddler, walking and even talking. To her, he was still the six-week-old baby she had held in her arms on that last morning, who had given her his first real smile. To her, there had been no months in between – no time in Devon, while Ethel told lies about her at home; no return on the day Betty Chapman had married that conchie from the farm; no tailoring job at Eastney Barracks; no enduring the carping of her mother; no Reg coming to sit at their supper table and stare at her with hot eyes; no doll with its face battered.

It had all been forgotten, wiped from her memory. She knew nothing now but the fact that she was in Portsmouth, wandering the rain-soaked streets, her hair in rats' tails, and with no baby in her arms. She had lost him. He had gone. She must have left him somewhere. At home, perhaps, if she could remember where home was. Or in the park. Or outside a shop.

Lost. Gone.

Panic swept over her, the terrifying panic of every mother who has ever had a child and believed, even for a second, that it is lost. Mothers in shops, blindly searching, mothers in the street convinced that their child has been run over, mothers in country lanes afraid that their child has been stolen.

Carol was gripped fast by this terrible fear. She ran through the streets, her heart torn by dread, her eyes darting this way and that. *There* was a baby! But no, it was dressed in pink. It was a little girl, it wasn't Roderick. *There* was another! But no, this one wore a sailor suit, and Roderick has never had a sailor suit, for all that his father was in the Navy . . . Another, *there*! This one was too old: its mother was just setting it down on the pavement and it was staggering beside its pram, its face laughing.

The shops were open now and the streets were filling with people. Men, women, girls and boys, going about their business. Carol stared at them wondering why they were so calm when her baby was lost. Didn't they know how serious it was?

There. She saw the pram, standing outside a baker's shop, and lurched forward, her heart in her throat. She had used that pram at the home. It was dark blue with high wheels. She must have brought it with her and gone into the shop for some bread . . . She could remember none of it, but it must have happened, and she'd come out and walked away, forgetting she had a baby, forgetting him and leaving him behind. But it was all right now, because she'd remembered and come back for him and soon she would be looking down into his little face and seeing that lovely smile break out again, just for her . . . Roderick . . .

A young woman came out of the baker's shop. She dropped a loaf into the pram and took the handle in both hands, leaning forwards to smile at its occupant. As Carol stopped, her mouth open with disbelief, the woman released the brake and began to walk away.

Carol shouted after her. She shouted that the girl was taking her baby away, her own baby, her Roderick who had smiled at her . . . but no sounds came from her mouth. Her throat was dry, her voice had gone.

Once again, she was back in her nightmare world, a world of fear and panic, a world in which neither her legs nor her voice would work, a world in which she had lost her baby and would never, never find him again.

She began to follow the girl with the dark blue pram. In her heart, she knew that the baby could not be Roderick, but she could not remember why she knew that. And perhaps, after all, it was; perhaps her heart was wrong. Her baby had to be somewhere. He was as likely to be in that dark blue pram with the high wheels, as anywhere else. She had given Roderick away, dimly she remembered that. Perhaps she had given him to this young woman.

Carol quickened her steps. If she had, it was a mistake. All she had to do was go after the other girl and tell her it was a mistake. Then she would give Roderick back, and everything would be all right again.

The girl with the pram stopped outside a greengrocer's shop. For once, there was no queue – perhaps because everyone was too busy discussing the invasion. She went inside.

Carol walked towards the pram. As she drew nearer, she slowed her pace, glancing to left and right to see if anyone was watching her. They'd taken her baby away before: they might as easily try to do so again. But this time she wouldn't let them. This time, she would hold on to him, and this time nobody would take her baby away.

The hood was up, to keep the rain out. Quickly, she unfastened the waterproof apron. The baby inside was bigger than she'd expected – more like six months old than six weeks, and already sitting up. That surprised her, but her surprise was immediately replaced by pride. Clever Roderick.

The baby was fastened in by two straps, buckled to a harness around his chest. Her fingers trembling, Carol snapped the fastenings open. She gripped the baby's waist and hauled him out.

He was much, much heavier than she had anticipated, and his legs got caught in the pram apron. He kicked and struggled, and Carol pulled harder, suddenly panic-stricken again. The baby opened its mouth and began to roar.

'No!' she panted in sudden desperation. 'No, don't cry, it's all right, it's Mummy here, I'm taking you home. Don't cry, Roddy, please don't cry or they'll never let me have you. They'll take you away again like they did last time, and I'll never find you again, never, never, never . . .'

She had him in her arms, clutched against her breast, his face pressed into her wet blouse. His cries were muffled as she ran down the street. Behind her, she could already hear the screams, the voice of the other girl, edged with the same jagged panic that Carol had felt as soon as she had realised that her baby was lost.

'*Johnnie! Johnnie! She's taken my Johnnie! Catch her, someone, for God's sake. She's running away with my baby . . .*'

Carol dodged into an alleyway. She stopped for a moment, listening. Others were shouting now, yelling out orders, screaming at each other that they'd seen her, she'd gone this way, that way, she was tall and dark, short and fat, she'd been wearing a red mac, she'd been thin and wispy with straggling wet hair—

Johnnie. Johnnie . . . *Johnnie?*

Panting, terrified, bewildered, Carol looked down at the bundle in her arms. The baby was still screaming, its face red with fury and its own panic. It had bright red hair, true carrot colour, and angry blue eyes. It bunched its hands into fists and waved them furiously, almost blacking her eye.

It was nothing like Roderick. In all his days, Roderick could never have looked like this.

Slowly, Carol came out of her hiding-place. The hue and cry had disappeared; everyone had gone running in the opposite direction. There was nobody about, but outside the greengrocer's shop she saw a pram. She scurried across to it and dumped her burden inside. It was only as she did so that she realised that the pram was dark green, not blue, and that it was already occupied.

She didn't bother to run away this time. She just walked, quite slowly, as if there were nothing else to be done. Behind her, she heard a fresh set of screams and a different kind of yell, and when the people caught her this time, she made no resistance. She said nothing, seemed to see nothing, and simply let them lead her away.

# CHAPTER TWENTY

By the beginning of September, it seemed as if normality could not, after all, be far away.

'We won't be getting any more doodlebugs,' Frank reported with satisfaction as Jess came in from the scullery with their cocoa. 'It's just been on the news; Duncan Sandys has made an announcement that our troops are overrunning the launching pads at the Pas de Calais. Only four out of nearly a hundred got through the other day anyway, thanks to the fighter patrols and the barrage.'

'Oh, that's something to be grateful for.' Jess set down the cocoa and went back for the chips she'd made to go with a couple of sausages for their supper. 'What with Paris being liberated and the Army getting on so well in Italy, it's looking ever so much better, Frank, isn't it? D'you think the war really will be over by Christmas? They say Monty thinks it will.'

'I'm not so sure about that. We've heard it too often before.' Frank picked up the newspaper. It was full of photographs and reports of the liberation of Paris. A huge crowd of American troops were pictured marching down the Champs-Elysées, watched by cheering Parisians. However, victory hadn't been won easily. Over three thousand French people had been killed in the uprising against the Germans, before the Allies had arrived. Now there were reports of collaborators being beaten and even killed, while women who had fraternised with the enemy had their heads shaved and were put on show with insulting placards round their necks.

'Well, it seems to me things must be starting to look up.' Jess ladled out the chips. 'There's been another bit of news, too. We're going to be allowed to stop putting up the blackout curtains in a couple of weeks' time. We're having "dim-out" instead. It's going to seem quite funny – the first time for five years we haven't had to worry about showing a light. That *must* mean things are improving.'

Somehow, though, Frank couldn't quite believe it. The cares of the past five years seemed to have grown into a heavy stone that he carried about with him wherever he went. While he was on dry land, he could manage, but just lately he'd felt as if he were sinking into a deep, sticky sludge that dragged at his feet and made his steps slow and difficult. He felt as if he were approaching deep water where, strong swimmer though he was, he would not be able to keep both the stone and his head above the surface.

'There's a long way to go before we can start cheering in the streets,' he said, looking again at the pictures of the French celebrating in Paris. 'A long way.'

Nevertheless, Jess was filled with sudden hope. As well as the blackout, other restrictions were lifted. People could travel again, and those with relatives in the Isle of Wight were at last able to meet once more. ('The Island's been liberated!' Tommy Vickers said with a grin.) Shoppers came from London for a day out by the seaside and spent their money in Southsea. The shopping centre was in ruins, but there were still quite a few shops open and people bought all kinds of household goods, from furniture and utility china to wire pot scourers and wooden spoons.

'They wouldn't be letting all that happen if they didn't think we were getting the upper hand,' she said to Annie. They had got the bus out to Southsea themselves, and walked out to the beach with a few sandwiches for their lunch. They sat looking at the blue water, with the green, wooded Island clear on the horizon. 'Honestly, I've felt so much better these past few days, since the doodlebugs stopped coming. And not having to put those awful curtains up last night – well, it was a real treat.'

'I know. I felt quite funny, sitting there with the lights on and only the ordinary curtains drawn. I half expected to hear Tommy Vickers banging on the front door, shouting, "Put that light out!" When I looked out and I could see all the windows down April Grove and up March Street, glowing . . . it was just like the old days, it put real heart into me.'

The two women sat quietly for a few minutes, thinking over the events of the past five years. So much had happened since that Sunday morning when Mr Chamberlain had made his announcement: 'I have to tell you that no such undertaking has been received . . . This country is now at war with Germany.' Already, Jess and the children had been evacuated along with thousands of others from the cities, and she had heard the broadcast in a farmhouse kitchen at Bridge End. Rose and Maureen, then just a tiny baby, had been with her, and the boys had been with that nice Corner couple, somewhere else in the village.

Now Reg Corner was posted missing, believed killed, and poor Edna had a baby he'd never seen. So many others had been taken from their homes, some still serving, some never to return. Some, like Annie's boy Colin, were prisoners enduring heaven knew what hardships. Others, like Betty's husband Dennis, had been maimed for life.

'Tell me a bit more about your Betty,' Jess said. Annie had been out to Bishop's Waltham on the bus a few days earlier and reported that Betty was indeed expecting a baby, some time in January. She and Dennis were nicely settled now in the farm cottage, and Dennis was proving a dab hand at the milking.

'Oh, she's blooming. Pretty as a picture, with lovely roses in her cheeks and a real gloss on her skin – you know how some young women look when they're in the family way. She's just beginning to show now, of course, and Dennis is that proud – he keeps putting his hand on her belly, just to prove there's something there.' Annie blushed slightly. 'Well, I don't say as that's something I'd like to see in the ordinary way, but with him being blind – I mean, he can't *see* what's happening, like another chap could. He uses his hands a lot now. He touched my face with his fingers when I arrived. It felt a bit funny but he told me that's how he's learned to recognise people. He said I had a lovely smile!'

Jess closed her eyes and felt her own face. She smiled and traced the upturned lips with her fingers. 'Yes, I can see what he means. I mean, I can *understand* what he means! So you think they're settled, then?'

'Oh, yes. He's a good husband, for all he can't see. And he works his turn. Mr Spencer says he won't know how to manage without Dennis after the war. Says he's the best cowman he's ever had.'

'Well, why can't he go on doing it?' Jess asked.

Annie shrugged. 'They've got two boys of their own, haven't they? Young Gerald, that Erica's married to, and Dick, what's never been home since the war started. I suppose they'll want to come back to the farm when it's all over.'

'I suppose so.' And that means more lives being disrupted, Jess thought. People who have got used to living in different places, doing different jobs, having to start all over again. Men coming out of the Forces. Women who've been doing the sort of work they never thought they would, having to give it up and be housewives again.

Their conversation was interrupted by a low, steady hum that grew to a roar. Startled, they looked up and behind them, into the sky over Portsdown Hill.

'My goodness, Annie,' Jess said in an awed whisper, 'just look at that . . .'

From the back of the Hill, in a wide black band like a thick cloud of gigantic insects, came a huge formation of aeroplanes. Heavy and thick bodied, they approached with a slow, almost majestic deliberation. As they passed overhead, the thunder of their engines almost deafening, it could be seen that not all of them were aeroplanes. Many were gliders, towed by long wires – the same kind that Diane and her friends had worked with in the weeks before D-Day, that had been developed and built at Airspeed, just up the road and that had taken men into France.

'Where are they going this time?' Annie breathed. 'Where are they invading now?'

The answer came on the nine o'clock news that night. The latest invasion was called Operation Market Garden, and it was aimed at Arnhem.

Operation Market Garden, which was supposed to bring the war to an early end, was not a success.

Of the paratroopers whom Jess and Annie had seen on their way to the fields of the Netherlands, many were shot as they descended from the planes. Others were trapped in the town as the Germans lay siege, and forced to surrender after holding the bridgehead for nine days. Of the ten thousand men who were landed, twelve hundred were killed and nearly seven thousand taken prisoner.

There was no more talk of the war ending before Christmas.

'It's terrible,' Jess said bitterly. Her disappointment was even more acute than Frank's. He had held out little hope, but she had set her heart on an early end to the misery they had suffered for so long. She had been looking forward to a Christmas without fear, for the children more than for herself, and little Maureen especially, who had never known a war-free Christmas at all.

Maureen had started school now. Jess had told her about it one afternoon, while she was doing the ironing. She was warming flat-irons on the stove and using them in turns, sprinkling the clothes with water to stop them scorching. Maureen was playing on the hearthrug as usual, and looking at one of Keith's comics – *Film Fun*, with Laurel and Hardy on the front page.

'It's a story,' she said, following the pictures with her finger. 'Can you read the words to me, Mummy?'

'Not now. I'm busy.'

'You're always busy,' Maureen said, with some truth. 'Why can't I read the words? Tim can, and Keith can, and Rose can. It's not fair.'

'You'll be able to soon,' Jess said, changing irons. 'When you go to school.'

Maureen looked at her in surprise. '*I* go to school? When?'

'Soon. When the summer holiday's over.' Jess laid a damp teacloth on her best blouse and smoothed the iron carefully over it. 'You'll learn all about reading and writing then.'

After that, Maureen had lived for the day she started school. Every morning, she had asked Jess if it was time to go yet, and she had talked incessantly about being able to read and write, until the whole family were sick of hearing about it. Tim finally took matters into his own hands and set himself to teach her, and by the time she actually started she could pick out quite a lot of the shorter words in *Film Fun* and *Beano* and *Dandy*.

School was quite bewildering to start with. The infants' department was at one end of the primary school, and all the children who were starting that day were herded into the biggest classroom and told to sit on long forms. They sat together, shuffling their feet and whispering. A few were still crying from having left their mothers at the school gates.

Miss Brown, the headmistress, was a large lady in a black dress and cardigan, with a long glittery necklace and glasses. She was sitting behind a large desk on a platform and talking to some of the other teachers. Maureen studied them, wondering which one would be hers. By now, she had been told quite a lot about school by her brothers and sister, and knew that she would learn a lot, but she also knew that it was easy to get into trouble and she was rather nervous.

Maureen wondered how soon they would be taught how to read and write. Once you could read, you could read stories that other people had made up, and when you could write, you could write down the ones you told yourself.

Maureen spent a lot of her time telling herself stories. Her marbles were, as Jess had once suggested, real people to her, and the houses and castles she built with her bricks were their setting. Some of the marbles had pleasant colours, clear with tiny bubbles inside and little swirling patterns. These were happy people, people it was good to be with. Others were opaque, usually white, with crude slashes of colour across them, and these were nasty people, people who would be spiteful and cross. She had once tried to explain this to Rose, remarking that she 'didn't like' these particular marbles, but when Rose had removed them from the bag she had been frantically upset and demanded them back. Nobody had been able to understand this, but for Maureen the 'nasty' marbles were as essential to her games as the 'nice' ones.

It was good to be able to tell stories in your own head, but it wasn't easy to remember them all. Maureen wanted to be able to write them down so that she could keep them.

Miss Brown now rang a little bell that stood on her desk, and addressed them. 'You'll all go into your classrooms now, with your teachers. When you come to school in the mornings, you'll stay out in the playground until the bell rings, and then you must line up in your classes until you're told you can come in, and your teacher will call the register in your own classroom. After that, you'll come here for prayers and then go back into the classroom for lessons.' She surveyed the rows of small faces, many of them still stained with tears. 'This is a happy school, and we all work very hard,' she said. 'I shall expect you all to behave yourselves and work just as hard. If you don't, your teachers will have to punish you, and if you are *very bad* they will bring you to me. Do you understand?'

Some of the children broke into fresh tears. Others simply looked bewildered. Half of what Miss Brown had said simply made no sense at all. What did 'lining up in classes' mean? What was a 'register', and how was it called? Most of them understood what prayers were, but the concept of work was something they understood only in relation to their own families. Fathers and sometimes mothers went to work. Did that mean they were going to have to do the same? Maureen saw her dreams of being able to read and write slipping away, and began to feel let down.

All of them were terrified of the idea of being brought to Miss Brown for being *very bad*.

Miss Brown then began to call their names from a long list, and the children whose names had been called, including Maureen, were told to follow one of the teachers. Her name was Miss Jenkins, and they were to be in her class. They trooped after her and found themselves in a large room with a lot of low tables and small wooden chairs. There was a blackboard on a big easel and several maps on the wall, like the one Maureen's father had at home. There were also a few pictures of Jesus.

The rest of the morning was spent in listening while Miss Jenkins told them all the things they had to do. Each day after prayers, they would be given a small blackboard each and a piece of chalk. This would have to be looked after carefully all day until the end of the afternoon, when it must be given back. Monitors were appointed for this task, and Miss Jenkins chose these at random from her list of names. There was also one duster for each table, to rub their blackboards clean.

'I don't want to see any of you drawing picures on your blackboards,' Miss Jenkins told them, fixing Maureen with a stern eye. 'Chalk is expensive. They're for writing and doing sums on, and nothing else.'

Maureen looked at hers with some disappointment. There wasn't much room on a small blackboard for writing the endless stories that went on in her head, especially if she had to do sums as well.

Next, they were given boxes of tiny wooden beads and bits of string on which to thread them. Some of the children enjoyed this, but Maureen couldn't get the string into the small holes and it reminded her too much of her mother's sewing, which so often took up all the floor space in the back room. By the time she'd managed to string a few together, Miss Jenkins was ringing her bell and telling them to unthread the beads again and put them back into the boxes. Maureen felt irritated and wondered again when they were going to learn to read and write.

They all went home to dinner. Jess was waiting at the school gate and Maureen skipped home, thankful to be out in the fresh air. She spent a little while after dinner on the rug with her marbles and bricks, and felt better when she went back in the afternoon. It was nice to come outside again almost immediately for 'drill', and then after another short playtime Miss Jenkins read them a story. She didn't read particularly well and some of the children fell asleep with their heads resting on their arms, but it was a story and Maureen listened with rapt attention.

She went to school each morning with Vera Baxter, from number 10, and they became friends. Jess wasn't too keen on this, but there was nothing to be done about it. The girls were the same age and in the same class, and they would be playing together in the playground, so there was little point in stopping them from playing together when they were at home, and allowed out into the street.

'You're not to go out of sight of the front door,' Jess told Maureen. 'Not even up October Street. I don't want to have to come looking for you, and I don't want you playing on the allotments or the bomb site.'

Maureen nodded and went out, to sit on the kerb with Vera and chant nursery rhymes. Sometimes Vera played with a tin of old buttons, threading them into necklaces as they did with the beads at school, but Maureen was more interested in stories. She regaled Vera with the ones she made up in an interminable serial.

'Look at them,' Jess said to Annie. 'Sitting there nattering away like two old women on a bench. I don't know what they find to talk about, two little scraps like that.' Still, she was too pleased to have Maureen occupied to think much more about it. Especially when Annie recounted her latest worries about Olive.

'She's not the same girl as she was. Doesn't come home any more than she's got to, and when she is here she's off in a dream most of the time. I just wonder what she does with the rest of her spare time.'

'Well, I suppose she's made friends with the others, it's only natural,' Jess said. 'They go about together, to the pictures and dances and that. They're still only young, Annie, and they've missed an awful lot.'

'She's a married woman,' Annie said. 'She didn't ought to be going to dances and out with men. She's got a husband to think about, and a home to make for him when he comes home.'

'But they haven't got a home. Olive's still living with you, when she's not in camp.'

'Yes, but that's what I'm saying – she doesn't seem to think she is, any more. She never even bothers to go up to that bedroom when she comes over. It's just like she was only a visitor.' Annie sighed. 'It's hard to explain, Jess, but she's changed. A little while ago she was all bright and laughing, *too* bright if you ask me, and now she's got a face so long it's nearly down to her knees. She don't seem interested in anything. I mean, with the war going the way it is, Derek could be home in a few months. She ought to be looking forward to it – thinking about where they're going to live. The papers are full of all the rebuilding that's going to be done, you know. They reckon there's going to be thousands of houses built for young couples and people that have been bombed out. She ought to be doing something about getting her name down for one of those. Or finding somewhere to rent.'

'I don't know, I think it's a bit early for that. What with all those paratroopers being lost at Arnhem, it doesn't seem to me as if the war's going to be over yet, not by a long way. Anyway, it takes a year at least to build a house – I don't see them getting all that under way the minute it finishes.'

'Well, she should be looking forward to it, at least,' Annie said stubbornly. 'She ought to be getting stuff together. I mean, there was all that stuff for sale out at Southsea and she never even bothered to go and have a look. It don't seem right to me.'

Jess looked at her sister. 'You surely don't think she's got someone else, do you? Another feller?'

'I wouldn't like to say.' Annie's mouth was a tight line of disapproval. 'But there's something not right, I'm sure of that. I know our Olive, Jess, and I know when she's keeping something back. I don't like it.'

Olive was well aware of her mother's suspicions. Indeed, she was surprised that everyone didn't know exactly what was going on. She felt as if her guilt must be written all over her face, for all to see.

Once again, it had been useless to try to keep away from Ray. They were together every day and could not ignore each other. Once again, they tried to push away the thoughts of what was going to happen after the war, and enjoy the time they had, but their happiness was tinged now with the bitter knowledge of the pain that lay in wait.

'It's like that song,' Olive said as they walked along the beach, their way lit by the full October moon. '"Hearts full of passion, jealousy and hate . . ." I don't hate anyone, Ray, but it's going to be there in the end, isn't it? And the jealousy. When Derek comes home—'

'Either he'll hate me or I'll hate him,' Ray said moodily, 'and we're both going to be as jealous as hell. I'm jealous already, because you're married to him and not me.'

'"Woman needs man, and man must have his mate,"' Olive went on. 'It's true, isn't it? It's as if our bodies take over and we can't do anything about it.' She stopped and turned into his arms, burying her face against his chest. 'But it isn't just that, Ray. I really do *love* you. I can't bear to think of hurting you – leaving you to go back to Derek. And I can't bear to think of hurting him, either. I don't know what we're going to do.'

Ray held her close against him. Together, they stared out over the darkened sea. The water was like hammered pewter, lit by a silver pathway that seemed to lead directly to the creamy white globe of the moon. It was like a promise that could never be fulfilled.

'When I was a little girl,' Olive said softly, 'I used to think that pathway really led somewhere. I used to wonder what it would be like to walk along it – across the sea, into a different place, a sort of fairyland.' She turned her head to look up into his face. 'I wish we could walk along it now. Leave all this behind and just be together, in our own little heaven where nobody could hurt us and we wouldn't be hurting anybody else.'

'Maybe we could,' he said. 'Maybe we could just walk on it now, hand in hand, and find our heaven.'

There was a brief silence. Olive felt her heart kick and tremble a little. She looked at him again. He was staring out across the sea, along the silver pathway, his expression remote and unreadable, as if in his mind he had already set out on the journey. She felt suddenly afraid.

'Ray.' Her hand tightened on his arm. 'Ray, what are you thinking about? What do you mean?'

He looked down at her and the tautness in his face relaxed as he hugged her close once more. 'I don't mean anything, Livvy. I was just thinking about that song. "Moonlight and love songs." They're not really there at all, are they? They're pretty and you think they're real, but you can't get hold of them. It's all a – what do they call it? An illusion.'

'No,' she said desperately. 'It's not. I do love you, Ray. I really do. It's real. It's *true*. We love each other.' She paused and added miserably, 'If we didn't, it would be easy. It wouldn't *matter*.'

'I know,' he said quietly. 'I know. I didn't mean that either.' He gave a small, mirthless laugh. 'I don't know what I meant. It's just the moon getting into my head, I reckon. Let's go back.'

They turned and walked slowly back along the beach to South Parade Pier, where they had first met. There were a few street lights on now, although they were hardly needed when the moon was so bright. A bomber's moon, it would have been called a year or two ago, Olive thought. Now no one expected bombers to come over any more, and the blackout had been replaced by the dim-out. It surely meant the war would be over soon.

'Tell you what I heard today,' Ray said suddenly, breaking the silence. 'They reckon there's a new sort of bomb coming. A rocket. There's been explosions in London. They've given out that they're gas mains exploding, but the bloke who told me about it reckoned that wasn't true. It's what they said when the doodlebugs started.'

Olive stopped and stared at him. 'They must be doodlebugs. They've found somewhere else to send them from.'

Ray shook his head. 'No, this one's different. You don't hear 'em coming. You hear a sort of double thunderclap – a kind of *crack-crack*, really loud – and then a noise like an express train. They've been coming over for the past month.'

'Why haven't we heard anything about them on the news?'

'Because we don't want the Jerries to know they're working, I suppose. We shouldn't be talking about them at all, really. They say they've started launching the doodlebugs again as well, from planes. They can't get the range otherwise, now that the Pas de Calais has been taken over by our people.'

Olive sighed. 'It doesn't matter what we do, they think of something else. I don't see how all this is ever going to end, Ray. I'm fed up with it. I want to get on with my own life.'

'I know,' he said. 'So do I.'

They were back to their own troubles again. Whatever they talked about to take their minds off them, the conversation always led back to the same thing. What was going to happen after the war. What they were going to do about this love that had come upon them, and would not be denied.

Moonlight and love songs, Olive thought. Ray's right. They're as hard to get hold of as morning mist, but you can't just wait for them to go away. They won't. They never will.

It's going to go on hurting for the rest of our lives, she thought, and there's no escape.

*

The plot to assassinate Hitler had failed, but there did seem to be dissension amongst his henchmen. The news that Rommel was dead – some said he had died of wounds caused by an Allied plane strafing his car, some that he had taken poison – was definitely cause for celebration. There was good news at home, too, when the House of Commons announced that more meat would be available for Christmas, as well as dried fruit such as sultanas and raisins. Christmas looked like being Christmas again, even if the war wasn't ended by then.

Although the fighting was continuing all over the world, it really did begin to seem that the Allies were gaining ground. In Greece, Athens was liberated, and in Germany itself the town of Aachen fell after a siege that lasted ten days. At the same time, thousands of miles away in the Philippines, the greatest sea battle ever was being fought between America and Japan, and America was winning.

There was still a constant flow of traffic across the Channel, as wounded soldiers returned and fresh units were sent out to replace them. Clifford Weeks was one of those who came back, and Gladys went to see him in the Army hospital. His head and one arm were bandaged and he looked tired, but he grinned when he saw her and stuck his good thumb in the air.

'You can't keep a good bloke down. I'll be back to give as good as I got before they can blink.'

'They'll have blinked their eyelids away by the time you're back.' Gladys sat down beside his bed. 'How can you be so keen, Cliff? This is the second time you've been wounded. Aren't you getting fed up with it?'

He shrugged and winced. 'It helps to pass the time. Besides, I want to get this war over and done with so that we can get married.'

Gladys sighed. 'I've told you, Cliff—'

'You don't want to talk about it till it's all over, I know, but you can't stop me thinking about it. You can't stop me hoping.' He looked at her seriously. 'I've got to have something to keep me going, Glad.'

'You could be just building yourself up for a disappointment.'

'I could be, but somehow I don't think I am.' He waggled his ginger eyebrows comically. 'I've got secret powers, you see, Glad. I can see into the future.'

'Oh, go on with you.' She couldn't help laughing. 'What can you see, then?'

'I can see us.' He screwed up his eyes as if peering into the distance. 'We're in church, and you're wearing a long white dress. A proper smasher you look in it, too. What d'you suppose that is, Glad?'

'I can't imagine,' she said tartly. 'Perhaps we've been to a dance. Is that all you can see?'

'No, I can see something else as well. It's us again. We're in a house. An ordinary house, but it's ours. We're sitting on a settee holding hands and – coo-er! I don't know how you're going to like this bit, Glad. Maybe I'd better not tell you.'

'Tell me what?' Her curiosity overcame her disbelief. 'What are you talking about?'

'Kids,' he said. 'Three kids. There's a boy about five and a little girl about three in a pink frock, and a baby. You're holding him in your arms and feeding him. Properly, I mean, not with a bottle. My, you look even more beautiful than you did in your wedding dress—'

'*Cliff!*' Gladys was scarlet. 'Don't you dare talk like that! You're making it all up, I know you are. Wedding dresses! Babies! And thinking about me – you know – like that. You've got a dirty mind. I don't know why I bother with you.'

'Give over, Gladys,' he said in an injured voice. 'There's nothing dirty about thinking about weddings. Or babies. I thought it was what girls thought about all the time.'

'Well, it's not. Not when there's a war on. And we know what *men* think about all the time.' She stared at him. 'I thought we'd agreed we'd just be friends, without all that kind of nonsense.'

'It's not nonsense. It's what makes the world go round.' He reached out with his unbandaged hand and laid it on her fingers. 'Don't be cross with me, Glad. I only think that way because I love you.'

Gladys looked down, suddenly surprised by the feeling of tears in her eyes. She knew that she wasn't cross with him at all, not really.

'I'm sorry, Cliff. It's just that all this talk of weddings and babies make me feel – well, sort of frightened. As though it's unlucky, somehow.' She gave him a shaky smile. 'Silly, isn't it? But I know a lot of people think that way. Diane's told me the aircrews have a superstition about girls who are jinxed – got a sort of curse on them, as if anyone they get involved with gets shot down.'

'Well, it's not going to happen to me,' he declared. 'I've told you, I've got secret powers and I know we're going to get married and have kids, and—'

'Cliff, *stop* it!' There was an edge of real panic in Gladys's voice. 'You *can't* know that. Anyway, if you've got these secret powers, why couldn't you see that you were going to get wounded? Why couldn't you do something about it?'

'I can't actually change things,' he explained, so seriously that she almost believed him. 'I just see them. Anyway, I wouldn't have wanted to change it. It gives me a chance to see you, doesn't it? And when they let me out of here I'll get a bit of leave and I'll come and spend it with Uncle Tommy and Auntie Freda, and I'll be able to see even more of you.' He grinned at her. 'When I've got an engagement ring on your finger, I'll go back and finish off the Huns and we can—'

'Cliff, *no*. I've told you and told you, I'm not even going to think about getting married, *or* engaged, until after the war's over, and I'm not going to promise it'll be you even then. You'll just have to take your chance.'

'Join the queue, eh?' He shrugged again and gave a little yelp of pain. 'I don't know how you can be so cruel to a man what's been injured in the service of his country, but if that's your last word—'

'It is,' she said, though she was hard put to it not to either laugh or cry, and either way to throw her arms around him and promise to marry him there and then, if only they could find a priest. 'I really mean it, Cliff, and if you want me to go on coming to see you—'

'Oh, I do, Gladys. I really do.'

'—well, you'd better just stop going on about getting married. Or engaged. We're friends, Cliff, that's all. Friends. All right?'

'All right,' he said humbly, but there was a look in his eye that told her she hadn't heard the last of it, and as she left the hospital and made her way back to Fort Southwick, she was conscious of a warmth deep inside that told her she didn't really want to.

Don't be daft, Gladys Shaw, she counselled herself. Don't let yourself get in too deep. Remember what you told him. Friends. That's all. That's *all*.

Gladys wasn't the only one visiting the wounded that weekend. Fifty miles away, her sister Diane was walking nervously into a burns ward in an American Army hospital.

She had not seen Chuck since the day when they had lain in the grass together and he'd told her about his brother Larry. They had been close then – closer than she'd ever expected to feel to this brash, cocky American – but something had gone wrong. She couldn't even remember what it was. Something to do with rainchecks, she thought vaguely, but she was conscious of a gnawing hurt inside her, as if she'd held out her hands and had them rudely slapped away.

Since then, she'd tried to push him out of her mind. She had gone out with one or two other airmen, but her heart hadn't been in it. Perhaps I've had enough of sex and all that stuff, she thought. It's not all it's cracked up to be after all. Slowly she'd stopped going out at all, and spent her evenings in the hut instead, reading or just lying on her bed.

Lizanellie had reported back to her regularly. The American air base still held dances and invited the WAAFs along, and the twins were still going steady with their own boyfriends. They said that Chuck had appeared a few times, and had danced a lot with the little brunette. They seemed pretty thick. Diane shrugged when they told her this, and turned away, but once when they didn't mention Chuck she found herself waiting for the sound of his name, and even asked – as casually as she could – whether he'd been there or not.

'I think he was,' Lizanellie One said thoughtfully. 'Did you notice?'

Her sister shook her head. 'Didn't see him myself. Perhaps he just looked in for a few minutes.'

Diane had a feeling they weren't telling her the truth, but there was nothing she could do about it. She went to bed and lay for some time staring into the darkness, trying to ignore the ache inside her.

And then she heard that he'd been shot down.

One of the twins brought the news. Liz had been out for the afternoon with her boyfriend – now her fiancé, she said proudly – and came back pale faced to find Diane doing her washing. She leaned against the door-jamb and blurted it out.

'Chuck's crashed again.'

Diane stopped what she was doing. She stared at the pair of RAF issue knickers she was holding, and waited a moment until the blood had stopped pounding in her ears. Her voice sounded quite calm as she spoke.

'Is he all right?'

'I don't know. He's been taken to hospital. The – the plane caught fire.' Liz's voice wobbled. Everyone knew that fire was what the pilots dreaded most. 'He was shot down. The rest of the crew—' She took a deep breath. 'Only two of them got out.'

Caught fire. *They have a nasty habit of catching fire from flak.* Diane could hear Chuck's voice in her ears as they lay on the grass. Casual, offhand, as if it couldn't happen to him. He'd known, of course, that it could, that the longer he went on flying the more likely it was to happen. And she had known it too.

She was suddenly aware of a feeling that time had been wasted, a vital opportunity missed.

'Do you know where he's been taken?'

'No,' Liz said, 'but I can find out if you like.'

She looked at Diane enquiringly, and Diane lifted her head and met Liz's eyes. She nodded.

'Yes. Find out. I want to go and see him.'

Liz had come back the next day with details of Chuck's whereabouts, and Diane had immediately set about getting a leave pass to go and see him. Now she was here, at the door of the ward, looking nervously about her and wondering what on earth she was doing.

He more or less told you it was over, she thought. Over before it even started. He won't want to see you now. He won't want anything to do with you.

But she had to go on. She had to see for herself.

She walked slowly down the ward. The nurse had pointed out to her which bed he was in, but she couldn't help looking at the occupants of the other beds as she passed. Some were heavily bandaged, and she wondered rather sickly what lay under those swathes of white – like everyone else, she had heard horrific tales of the disfigurements suffered by some burns victims. Others had had their bandages removed and as they turned their heads at her approach she saw the shocking rawness of flesh that had been eaten away by flames. A young man with hair over only one side of his head, the other a mass of puckered, blue-white skin. Another with his nose and upper lip almost obliterated. Another, whose face was untouched but whose hands were scarred and twisted like charred roots. Another whose eyes peered blindly from torn eyelids and whose mouth had been twisted into a travesty of a grin.

Diane's footsteps faltered. I don't know if I can go through with this, she thought. Then she thought of other girls who had gone through with it – and those who hadn't, who had run screaming and crying from such wards as this, leaving the men inside – men who had laughed and joked and made love with them only days before – to suffer the torment of rejection.

I won't do that to him. Nor to these others.

She was approaching his bed. He was lying down, his head turned away from her, not expecting visitors. As she came closer, she saw that he was smothered in bandages. His head was almost completely covered, and his arms were huge white sausages lying outside the sheets.

Diane stopped beside him. He can't hear me through all those bandages, she thought sadly, gazing down. He doesn't know there's anyone here at all.

She leaned a little closer. He smelled of ointment and soap and hospital. She remembered the crinkling of his eyes when he'd smiled, and wondered if he could smile now, if he would ever be able to smile again, and if his eyes would crinkle when he did.

'Chuck.'

Her voice was quiet, little more than a whisper. He made no response, and she tried again. 'Chuck.'

Slowly, he turned his head. There were holes left in the bandaging for his eyes, his nose and his mouth and she saw, thankfully, that his lips appeared untouched and his eyes were clear. She saw the pupils widen as he recognised her, and grinned awkwardly.

'Hello, Chuck.'

'Diane?' His voice was hoarse and roughened, as if it had been gone over with sandpaper. 'Di? It ain't really you?'

'Well, it was when I left camp,' she joked, but her own voice was cracked and she could feel the heat of tears in her eyes. 'Oh Chuck, whatever have you been doing to yourself?'

He lifted his bandaged arms an inch or two and she saw that the tips of the fingers of his right hand were just showing. 'Got a bit too near the fire. It was kinda chilly up there. Tell you what, the old Fortress'll be great for those bonfires they'll be lighting the day the Yanks win the war. Burn like tinder . . .' His voice faded as if it hurt to speak.

Diane gazed down at him, her throat aching, but she couldn't let him see her give in to her feelings. 'What do you mean, when the *Yanks* win the war? This is *our* war – we're only letting you in so that you can practise shooting straight.'

'Same old Di,' he said faintly. 'Gotta have the last word.'

There was a short silence. She wanted to kneel down beside his bed and lay her head on the hump of his body. She wanted to hold his bandaged head in her hands and kiss his pale, dry lips. She wanted his eyes to look at her with something other than guarded caution.

'Chuck,' she said quietly, 'don't let's fight.'

'I never wanted to.'

She closed her eyes. It was still there, the caution, the barrier that wouldn't let her pass. She said, 'Chuck, that last day, when we'd been out in the field. You said we had some talking to do, but we'd have to take a raincheck on it. What did you mean?'

'Why, just what I said, of course.' His voice was terribly cracked. 'We'd have to wait till another time. That's what a raincheck *is*.' She saw a faintly puzzled look creep into his blue eyes. 'What in hell did you think I meant?'

'I thought it meant you didn't want to talk to me,' she said. 'I thought it meant . . . never.'

There was another pause. Then Chuck said, 'Oh, my God.' He turned his bandaged head stiffly. 'This damnfool English language of yours. Why can't you talk *American*, for chrissake?'

'What?' Diane said, conscious of a huge relief blossoming inside her. 'And all end up speaking *Yankee*?'

For a moment, she thought she had gone too far, and held her breath. Let him not take offence, she thought, please let him see what I'm really saying to him, underneath all this joking and silliness. Oh, please . . . And then she heard a queer gasping, choking sound and saw the bed begin to shake. Alarmed, she looked around for a nurse, but Chuck lifted one of his sausage arms to stop her.

'It's all right, Di. It's all right. It's just so goddamned funny. I mean – all these weeks, we've both been trying to pretend the other one doesn't exist, and all over some stupid thing that I said that any American girl would understand right away. I mean, how are we ever going to be able to talk to each other when we're hitched? How're we ever going to know what we're saying?'

Diane stared at him. '*Hitched?*'

'Sure. That's American for—'

'I know what that one means,' she interrupted. 'It means married. But whoever said we were getting married?'

'Isn't that what we were going to talk about?' he enquired simply.

Diane went silent. Perhaps it was, she thought. Perhaps we did understand each other after all. As long as we didn't try to talk, perhaps we understood each other all along.

'But how do you know we still want it?' she asked cautiously, and saw the blue eyes narrow a little as they fixed themselves on her face.

'Why else would you come to see me, pretty Di?' he asked. 'Why else are you here?' He paused a moment and then said, 'You'd better be very sure, because I don't have time to waste, and I ain't going to be the pretty guy you used to know, once I get out of this lot.'

Diane stood quite still. She looked down at the bandaged face and wondered vaguely if he would be very disfigured. She thought of the man with the torn eyelids and shattered mouth, the one with no nose, the one with hands like burned tree-roots. She did not know what lay beneath those swathes of bandages, nor how horrible it might look, and she could not know what it would be like to look at such disfigurement every morning across the breakfast table.

But there was more to Chuck than a face, and the Chuck she had known was still there, and she wanted him just the same.

*Wanted* him? I always wanted him, she thought with amazement. I wanted him from the very start. I still do.

He was still watching her. She recalled his words and lifted her eyebrows.

'Pretty?' she repeated with just the right amount of scorn in her voice. 'Whoever said you were pretty in the first place?'

And then she did as she had been longing to do ever since she had arrived, and dropped to her knees by the bed. Carefully, so as not to hurt the burned and injured body, she laid her hand on the bandages that hid his right hand from view and kissed the exposed fingertips. 'Oh Chuck. Oh Chuck, I love you . . .'

# CHAPTER TWENTY-ONE

Ever since she had snatched little Johnnie and left him in another pram, Carol Glaister had been kept in St James's Hospital.

She had been taken to court and there had been talk of sending her to prison, but the doctor had gone to see her and said she wasn't responsible for her actions. That meant she must be mad, and it was a well known saying in Portsmouth that if you were mad they took you to St James's. It was also well known that not many people who went there came out again, and if they did they were never quite the same.

For Ethel Glaister, the shame was almost worse than that of Carol's having had an illegitimate baby.

'I don't know where she gets it from,' she said to anyone who would listen. 'Not my side of the family, that I do know. It must be George's. There was that uncle of his who kept a musket under his bed, he was as cracked as an old tin roof. And his gran was only ten pence in the shilling, now I come to think of it.'

'But she was an old woman,' Jess said. 'A lot of old people get a bit funny.' She thought sadly of her own father, who had sunk into despair and forgetfulness over the war, and her mother who had wavered in her last months between lucidity and hallucination. There's no fun in old age, she thought, and we've all got to come to it. All we can hope for is understanding. But poor little Carol, she's not twenty yet. It's a shame.

'Well, it comes from somewhere,' Ethel said doggedly, 'and there's never been anything like that in the Davies family, I can tell you.'

Jess looked at her and wondered. Ethel wasn't the woman she had been, there was no doubt about it. She still wore her powder-blue costume and frilly blouses, but the blue looked grubby these days, and her frilly blouses weren't kept as white. Her make-up looked different too: her lipstick was too bright and seemed to smudge easily, and her powder was thick and clogged over the rouged patches on her cheeks.

'Going to seed,' Annie said tersely when Jess mentioned it, 'and no wonder, the way she's carrying on.'

'What do you mean, carrying on?'

Annie gave her sister a look of mild exasperation. 'Oh, Jess. You must know about the men she brings home, what with her living right next door.'

Jess did know but preferred not to see. Living mostly in the back room, you didn't really see who went in and out of the other houses, and if she heard a man's voice through the wall she told herself it was the wireless. But if Annie knew as well . . . 'I daresay she's just being pleasant,' she said uncomfortably. 'Offering a bit of home comfort – a fire to sit by, that sort of thing.'

Annie hooted with laughter. 'Home comfort! I'm sure that's just what it is. Come on, our Jess, even you can't be that simple. The woman's a tart – no better than Nancy Baxter.'

Jess stared at her sister, shocked. 'You don't mean she – she—'

'She goes with men. Of course I mean that. And takes money for it, what's more. I reckon she always did, if the truth be known. Where else was she going all those afternoons, in that fancy costume of hers?'

'She said she was going to see her friend—'

'Yes, and so she might have been, but who was the friend? And where d'you think she got that money her Carol pinched when she ran off that time? George Glaister never earned enough for her to save up, not and buy all her clothes and make-up and silk stockings.' Annie shook her head. 'I don't blame you for not realising it, Jess, we've always been brought up decent and wouldn't think of it, but I'd bet my last silver threepenny bit that's what she was up to.'

'Well, I don't know.' Jess was reluctant to think such a thing of her neighbour, even when the neighbour was Ethel Glaister. 'I mean, I've got to admit we have noticed a bit of coming and going. And now I come to think about it, Frank's always a bit funny about her – doesn't like going out in the garden when she's about, that sort of thing – but I never thought—'

'She set her cap at him when you was evacuated at the beginning of the war,' Annie said. 'That's what that is. Ethel Glaister's always had an eye for anything in trousers, but she kept it off her own doorstep before. Now there's no one at home, she doesn't have to bother.' She leaned a little closer and lowered her voice. 'She's drinking, too. Ted's seen her in the pub a few times, and there was drink on her breath when I was standing in the butcher's queue just in front of her yesterday. In the *morning*.' She drew back and nodded her head up and down, her lips pursed.

Jess still didn't like to believe it, but once Annie had opened her eyes, she couldn't help hearing the murmur of voices from number 15, and the sound of the front door shutting late at night, and heavy footsteps tramping away up the street. She was upset and embarrassed, avoiding Ethel's eye when she met her.

'Stuck-up cow,' Ethel said to Jess's back one day, when Jess had hurried past with her eyes down. 'Thinks she's too good to talk to the likes of me just because I've had the bad luck to have a daughter that's gone to the bad. Wait till that namby-pamby little Rose of hers starts going out with boys – she'll find out what it's like then.'

Ethel went indoors and unpacked her shopping. There wasn't much, but she'd managed to get a bottle of gin and some sausages and a slab of rather dry madeira cake. She had a new gentleman friend coming round this evening – a sergeant who was stationed at the camp out on Southsea Common. Ethel had met him in a pub in Fawcett Road and struck up a conversation by asking him if he knew her friend Reg, who'd gone off to France on D-Day. He didn't, but it was enough to start them off and after a couple of drinks she'd suggested he might like a bite of supper by her fire one evening.

It was her usual pattern and she knew how it would turn out. He'd present himself at her door, punctually at eight (regular Servicemen were always punctual, she never had any truck with volunteers or conscripts, like George) and he'd probably bring a present – a half bottle of whisky or a bar of chocolate, or a couple of pairs of nylon stockings. They would sit down with a drink or two and then Ethel would produce supper, generally something out of the oven, like toad-in-the-hole or a savoury pie. After that, they'd go into the front room and sit on the settee. They'd have another few drinks and then the sergeant would grow maudlin and slip his arm round her waist. Ethel would squeal and try to push him away, but he'd kiss her with slobbering lips and say how nice it was to come and sit in a proper home for an evening, how much he missed being in his own home, how good it was to hold a woman in his arms again.

'I've never let my missus down,' he'd say sadly. 'Never wanted to. But what with this war – and never knowing when I'm going to get home again – and feeling so lonely . . . Well, it's not like you're a common tart, Ethel, you're a decent, respectable woman, you understand what it's like. You know it's just a matter of giving a bloke a bit of comfort, what he needs. I reckon it's women like you what win the war, when it comes down to it.'

They all talked like that, and Ethel, thinking of the drinks they'd paid for and the presents they'd brought, and the loneliness of the nights when none of them came, would let him paw over her with his big, beefy hands, and let him slobber her with kisses. And, finally, let him take her body with his own for the gasping, groaning release they all seemed to want so badly.

It wasn't a release for Ethel, and none of her gentlemen friends visited her more than a few times, but she found her own savage pleasure in those final moments, as she thought of George, walking away from her up April Grove as she screeched after him, walking out of her life as if she didn't matter. *I'll* show you I matter, she thought viciously, thrusting herself against the man who panted above her. *I'll* show you . . .

It was well into November before the government admitted at last that Britain had been under attack by the new rocket since September. It was called the V2 and it was even worse than the doodlebug. The V2 flew so fast that you couldn't even hear it until it had passed overhead, and because it was so fast, no warning could be given of its approach. The first anyone knew was the flash of blue light which immediately preceded it, and then either the roar, like a passing express train, which followed it, or the explosion itself. People took to sleeping in their shelters again, but during the day you just had to take your chance.

London was suffering the most through this new weapon, and hundreds of people had been killed before Mr Churchill made his announcement. A hundred rockets had landed since early September, the explosions being explained away as gas mains. Some Londoners had even begun to call them 'flying gas mains', but although those who lived with the new devastation knew perfectly well that the rockets were a new and even more dreadful weapon, the news could not leak far as long as newspapers and the BBC were forbidden to mention it. It was only, Mr Churchill said, to dispel the increasing rumours that he spoke now. 'There is no need to exaggerate the danger,' he insisted. 'The scale and effect has not been significant.'

However, the people who had been in London when a V2 had suddenly thundered overhead, and had seen and heard its huge explosion, didn't think it was insignificant at all.

'There's a letter from my cousin Lily, in Putney,' Jess said to Frank one evening when he came home from work. 'She says there was a direct hit on Woolworth's in New Cross last Saturday dinnertime. She reckons there was nearly two hundred people killed and as many hurt. Her next door neighbour was there and she said it was terrible – all the stuff in the shop blown up into the sky and coming down in bits and pieces, and bits of people as well, and there was a bus all full of dead bodies, squashed under a wall that fell on it, and a horse's head in the gutter, and a little baby's hand, still in its woolly mitten . . . and people under all the rubble, screaming and screaming . . . Frank, it's awful, *awful*. I don't know how people can bear seeing things like that. And little children too, how are they ever going to get over it? What's going to happen to the world, even when it does stop?'

'I don't know.' He took the letter from her hand. 'I don't think anyone knows, Jess. And there's nothing we can do about it, people like you and me. We've just got to carry on.'

'I'm fed up with living like this, I'm fed up with it all,' Jess said miserably. 'I just want to be able to walk up to the shops without being afraid I'll never come home again, and see you and our Tim off to work knowing you'll come back safe for your dinner.'

'I know.' He held her close for a few minutes. 'I know, Jess. I feel just the same, but we don't have any choice, do we? We've got responsibilities, and we can't just say we'll not have any more to do with it.'

The King had been to Portsmouth yet again but nobody from April Grove had seen him this time. Gladys Shaw knew that he had gone to Southwick House and seen the plotting rooms, but she was back on duty at the fort by then. She was more concerned with Clifford than the King anyway. He'd gone back to France to rejoin his unit, and the last she'd heard they'd started a new drive into Germany. Not that he was allowed to tell her that, but like a lot of people they'd devised a code so that she could know at least which country he was in. 'Remember that night at the Odeon?' meant France, South Parade Pier was Italy, and the Roxy was Germany.

Germany. Right into the heart of enemy territory. She listened to the news and read the papers with anxiety, and watched the progress of the war in her own plotting. She wrote to him every day, and at the same time she was still writing to Colin Chapman, out in Japan. It was said that Japan was on the defensive and America preparing to reopen the Burma Road. What that would mean for prisoners, already being cruelly and appallingly treated, nobody could guess.

By Christmas, street lights were switched on all over Portsmouth. The lights were on in London too, in Piccadilly and the Strand. Even though the V2s were still coming, there wasn't much point in having the blackout when there were no pilots to see the lights. The Home Guard, which had started in such a raggle-taggle fashion as the Local Defence Volunteers ('Look, Duck and Vanish', people had jeered then) and paraded with broomsticks instead of rifles, was disbanded in a final ceremony in the Guildhall Square. Firewatchers were allowed to stand down from their duties too, and Frank could be sure of getting a good night's sleep for the first time in five years.

The saddest news of the month was the loss of the great bandleader Glenn Miller, whose plane disappeared between England and Paris. His band weren't with him and didn't know at first that he was mising. When it was reported at last, people hoped he would be found, but the hope faded and was gone by the time Christmas was over. They heard his music played on the wireless and felt tears in their eyes. 'In the Mood', 'String of Pearls', 'Pennsylvania 65000' and 'Little Brown Jug' were played over and over again.

It was time for a new year. For the fifth year in a row, the country embarked on it in the hope that this would be the last of the war. The signs were good, although the past year had brought two new and terrible weapons – the V1 and V2. There was still talk of another, even worse, which would bring the war to a sudden and catastrophic end.

'God is on our side,' one of the archbishops said in his New Year message, and although the cynics might mutter that if he was, he was coming in even later than the Americans, most people looked to 1945 with hope.

'Did you hear all that racket last night?' Jess said to Annie on the first day of January. 'We haven't heard a din like that since before the war.'

It was bitterly cold. They said it had been the coldest night of the century and Tim and Keith had been up to Hilsea yesterday, skating on the lido. At midnight, the frosty air had crackled with the noise of Portsmouth welcoming in the New Year; clocks striking, trains blowing their whistles, factory sirens and ships' horns going off and even the church bells ringing.

April Grove had been alive with people coming to their doors to call out greetings to each other. The families in number 5 and number 6, who were cousins, had had a party going on into the small hours. Frank and Jess had spent the evening quietly, playing Ludo with the children and then having a glass of sherry together in front of the embers of the fire. Their big family party had been, as usual, over Christmas.

The papers were full of optimism. They had all published the lists of people named in the King's New Year Honours and everyone was delighted to see the name of Dr Una Mulvaney, the young woman doctor who had worked so hard and so bravely as MO in the first aid post in St George's Square, Portsea. She'd been awarded the MBE.

'She was so good to Ted when he had that bad patch in the Blitz,' Annie said. 'Wouldn't have it that there was anything really wrong – you know, in his mind. She said he just needed time to get over Dunkirk, and she was right.'

'Peggy knew her well, too, when she was in the first aid,' Jess agreed. 'And Gladys said she was always right on the spot after a raid, didn't care where she went or how dangerous it was. All she thought about was her patients.'

Doctors were much in Annie's mind at present. Out on the Spencers' farm at Bishop's Waltham, Betty was getting near her time. She and Dennis had got the small bedroom in the little cottage spick and span, with a cot someone in the village had given them and the walls brightened up with distemper. Now all they had to do was wait. The baby was due in the middle of the month, but in fact it was only three days after the New Year when Betty met Dennis from morning milking and told him her waters had broken.

'You'd better fetch Mrs Spencer, quick, and send for the midwife. I'll be all right here till you get back.'

Dennis touched her swollen belly. 'I can feel the difference. He's gone right down.'

'He!' she teased him. 'It's a girl, I keep telling you, and if you don't hurry up, she'll be here before the midwife. Put the kettle on before you go.'

He held her for a moment. 'Are you sure you'll be all right? I don't like leaving you like this.'

'I'll be all right.' She laid her palm against his cheek. 'Nothing's going to happen in a hurry. The first baby's always slow. But don't be too long, Dennis. I want you with me.'

She watched anxiously as he set off down the path to the garden gate. He knew every inch of the way now, but since the snow had fallen the lane was icy and treacherous and Betty had insisted he use his stick. He tapped his way quickly up the lane and out of sight.

Betty went back indoors. She had padded herself with thick sanitary towels, but already they were soaked. She renewed them and went to lie on the bed. Her back was beginning to ache, and the ache spread round her middle, tightening around her belly. That's a labour pain, she thought with a twinge of fear and excitement. A real labour pain.

The contraction tightened again, more strongly. It was more than an ache this time. It was like being squeezed in an iron band. She clenched her hands around the railings of the bed and gritted her teeth. She had never dreamed it would hurt so much. And this is only the beginning, she thought with another twinge of fear. Oh Dennis, come back quickly, *please*. She felt very alone in the small cottage, although the ache had died away.

It began again, even more fiercely, and in the middle of it, she had a sudden powerful desire to go to the lavatory. She didn't think she could get down the narrow stairs and outside to the earth privy quickly enough, so when the pain diminished she scrambled awkwardly off the bed and bent to drag the china chamber-pot out from underneath.

The desire passed and she hesitated for a moment, then it came again with a savage tautness, and she knew that if she didn't sit down quickly on the pot she would make a mess on the floor. She pulled away the padding towels and, holding the bed, lowered her cumbersome body and balanced on the cold china. The iron band tightened again and she had the sensation of something large pushing its way out of her body. It was like the worst constipation she had ever known. But I went this morning, she thought hazily, and then she realised that what was happening was nothing to do with the lavatory or constipation at all. The baby was being born.

A final thrust sent her tipping off the pot to the floor. She lay gasping as the wave of pain engulfed her and then receded. She could feel something large and slippery between her legs and after a moment, wonderingly, she reached down to investigate.

The baby had a hard, round head. She could feel its face and its tiny shoulders. A soft, slithering body no bigger than a doll, and legs that kicked her questing hands away.

Betty struggled to sit up. She looked down at the squirming body, covered in greyish slime, and drew it up towards her. For a moment their eyes met and she felt a rush of overpowering love.

'You're here,' she whispered in wonderment. 'You're really here.'

However, there was no time to be lost. The baby ought to be crying, and Betty didn't know how to make it cry. She patted it gently, hating the thought of slapping its little bottom. There was the dark, twisted cord too, that was supposed to be tied and cut. She didn't know what to do about it. With animals, the mother always knew just what to do and did it. Humans didn't seem to have the same instincts.

Betty began to feel afraid. Suppose the baby died. She stopped patting it and gave it a sharp slap. 'Cry. *Cry*. You're not to die, d'you hear me, you're *not* to die.'

To her immense relief, the baby let out a startled and furious yell. I hope you'll forgive me, she thought, looking at the wrathful face, but I had to do it, and now—

Somewhere below, a door slammed. She heard footsteps hurrying into the house and up the stairs. With a sigh of thankfulness, she leaned back and held the baby to her breast. A moment later, the door burst open and Dennis stumbled in, with Mrs Spencer close behind.

'Betty! Are you all right? I thought I heard—' He stopped, his head up like a hunting dog scenting its prey. 'Betty, what's happened?'

'It's all right,' she said, smiling, and reached up one hand to find his and draw it down towards her. 'The baby's here. It's here and everything's all right. Didn't you hear it cry?'

'The baby's *here*?' He dropped to his knees beside her. 'You mean – it's all over? He's been born?'

Betty nodded. Mrs Spencer, clucking like a hen, was busy with the cord and some cotton and a pair of scissors, but Betty didn't watch. Instead, she took her husband's hand and laid it gently on the tiny head, covered already with dark, wet curls.

'He couldn't wait. Dennis, he looks just like you.' Then a thought struck her and she looked more closely. Until that moment, she had been more concerned with whether the baby would cry or not than what sex it was. Now she smiled, and her smile turned into a laugh. 'Well, not quite like you, Dennis. Didn't I tell you all along? It's a girl – a *girl*! We've got a daughter, Dennis.'

'A daughter,' he said wonderingly. 'Just what I wanted.'

The news began to get better again. By the end of January, all Portsmouth's schools had been reopened, with children pouring back into the city from evacuation centres at Bournemouth, Salisbury, Winchester and the Isle of Wight. To give them some entertainment, the Regent Cinema at North End, and the Plaza at Fratton had both been opened on Saturday mornings. Because it was still so cold, there was a lot of fun to be had in the snow – skating at Hilsea and on Baffins Pond, sledging on Portsdown Hill, and snowball fights.

It was strange to hear children's voices again, laughing and shouting through the streets just as they'd done five years ago. There had always been a few about, of course, but never had the school playgrounds been filled like this or the parks so crowded. It made the city seem to come to life again.

'It's getting near the end,' Ray said to Olive. They were back in their little boarding house, spending the night there whenever they could manage it. The joy of the summer seemed to have disappeared, along with the sunshine. Now, the bitter cold brought them a dread of the future.

Christmas had been desperately lonely. They'd both had time off and had longed to spend it together, but it was impossible. Olive was expected at home, and could think of no excuse to give her mother for her absence. Ray had heard from his own parents that little Dorothy was going to be allowed to spend Christmas Day with them. He could not miss the chance of a Christmas with his own child.

'She probably won't even know me,' he said when he accepted the invitation, 'but I can't help that. It might be the last time I see her.'

'What do you mean?' Olive turned her head on the pillow to stare at him. He was lying on his back, one arm under her neck and the other crooked back behind his head as he gazed at the ceiling. 'Aren't you going to go back to your wife at all?'

'Never,' he said shortly, and she felt almost rebuffed. Then he turned and took her fiercely in his arms. 'How can I go back to her, Livvy? How *can* I? When it's you I love – you I want to be with. Living with her would drive me crazy. *Crazy.*'

'But you know we can't – I can't—' She couldn't bring herself to say the words, but he said them for her, in the grim, hard voice she hated to hear.

'We can't live together, you and me. All right. But that doesn't mean I have to go entirely to hell, does it?' She winced at the cruelty of his words. 'Just most of the way will be enough, believe you me.'

'Ray, don't talk like that.'

'I *love* you,' he said. 'I love *you*. There isn't anyone else for me and there never will be. I'm not going to spend my life putting up with second best. Not that Joan's second best,' he added bitterly, 'or third, or fourth, or even a thousandth best. It was the worst day of my life when I set eyes on her.'

'Ray, I'm so sorry. I really am. I love you too, you know that, but—'

'But you love Derek as well,' he said wearily. 'Don't let's go through it all again, Livvy, there's a good girl.' He turned on his back again.

Olive bit her lip. The tears crept slowly out of her eyes and began to soak the pillow. After a while she said in a small, lost voice, 'What are we going to do?'

She felt his arm tighten around her shoulders. He was still staring at the ceiling. Then he turned his head slowly and looked into her eyes. Their faces were very close. She could see the tiny specks of colour in the irises. In the pupils she could see minute reflections of herself.

'We know what you're going to do, don't we?' he said at last. 'You're going to go back to your Derek and have his kids and forget all about me. There's a life for you. But for me – there's nothing.'

'D'you think it'll be easy? Living with Derek as if nothing had happened, pretending nothing's changed and – and all the time, wondering where you are and what's happening to you. I don't think I can do it, Ray. It'll be like telling lies every minute of the day.' She was silent for a few moments, then she said, 'There's no way out, is there? What we've done – we can't go back. We can't stop people being hurt now, whatever we do.'

'There's only one way out for me,' he said. 'If I can't have you, I don't reckon I'll want to go on living at all.'

'Ray!'

'It's all right,' he said, still in the same flat voice, 'you don't have to worry about it. You won't even know. I'll get demobbed and go away, and you'll never hear from me again. You won't have a thing to worry about.' There was a brief, appalled silence and then he turned again and snatched her hard against him. His eyes were almost black now, hard and narrow with anger and misery. 'Well, isn't that what you want? Isn't it what you've always really wanted?'

Olive couldn't answer. She had held him tightly against her, her tears flowing freely now and mingling with his. She began to kiss his face, his lips, his wet eyes, his ears and neck, and he kissed her in return. They wrapped their arms tightly about each other. Olive felt his lips on her breast. She held his head close and moved her hips, feeling him harden against her thighs. With a swift movement she rolled on to her back, bringing him over with her, and drew him inside her body.

'Ray, I love you. I love you. You're not to do it. You're not. You're not. You're not . . .'

That had been before Christmas and they hadn't mentioned it again. Olive had almost persuaded herself that she had imagined it. Or that it had been only a momentary threat, which he would never dream of carrying out. But every time she saw Ray she felt a surge of relief, and knew that the love which had come upon them – unbidden, unwanted – had grown very deep.

I can't let him go, she thought. I can't let him go.

It was towards the middle of February when she realised that she was pregnant.

At first, she refused to believe it. It was the strain of the war: she had missed before, it was nothing to worry about – she'd had the same scare after she'd first made love with Derek, and it had turned out to be a false alarm. They'd always been so *careful*.

But it wasn't just a missed period, or even two. Her breasts had begun to grow larger and felt tender, and she felt slightly queasy in the mornings. Nothing very much – nothing like as bad as her sister Betty had told her she'd felt for a couple of months – but it was still there, passing off by about ten o'clock and then back again the minute she put her foot out of bed next morning.

It all added up.

And they *hadn't* always been careful, she thought with a feeling of doom. That time before Christmas, when Ray had been so down and she'd wanted so much to love him – there hadn't been a clean French letter handy, and they'd taken a chance with the withdrawal method. Only he hadn't withdrawn as quickly as he should: Olive had held him close and let him go reluctantly. They'd both thought it was all right, but obviously it hadn't been.

Once! she thought, railing at the unfairness of it. Just once, and this had to happen.

She went for a walk along the beach on her own, to think about it. Parts were still wired off, but you could look out at the Solent and see quite a bit of what was going on. Ships that entered Portsmouth harbour had to come this way, between Clarence Pier and the sea-wall at Haslar, on the Gosport side. The harbour entrance itself was narrow and guarded by the old bastions of Sallyport and Blockhouse, making it easy to defend from the sea. It was the air that had made the big natural harbour so vulnerable in this war.

We've done our best to look after you, she thought, gazing out across the broad expanse of water. People like Ray and me on ack-ack, and the RAF – we've kept a lot of planes out. We might not have shot all that many down, but we forced them to fly higher. And some of us have been killed doing it.

She sat down on a bench, looking at the grey sea. Pregnant. A baby growing inside her, a baby that would soon begin to be noticed by other people – by her mother, especially – and would then be born. It couldn't be stopped. There was nothing to be done about it.

Well, there *was*. People did stop babies being born, she knew that. There were things you could take that could start a miscarriage. Or you could have an operation. Some of the girls Olive had trained with had known all about it, and one or two had even had it done, but it was against the law, and it was dangerous. You didn't go to a proper hospital for it, or have a proper doctor or nurse. You went to someone who just had a couple of rooms in a back street and wasn't too fussy about hygiene. You just hoped they'd do it properly. If they didn't, there wasn't anything you could do about it, because you'd be in trouble as well as them.

Sometimes, girls died from it. There had been one Olive had heard about a year or two back. Claudia had known her and, being a doctor's daughter, had understood what had happened. A haemorrhage, she said. The girl had gone back home, gone to bed and quietly bled to death. Others caught infections, and sometimes, even if you got better, you would never be able to have another baby.

Oh God, Olive thought, is any of that going to happen to me?

She wondered what it would be like to have the operation. It was called an abortion, a word that was seldom uttered in more than a whisper. There were places in Portsmouth where you could get it done, places in Queen Street and some of the other areas that were generally most frequented by tarts. Would she have the nerve to go to such a place and have the baby killed? Because that was what it amounted to: having the baby killed, her and Ray's baby. And perhaps die of it herself, or end up never able to have a baby at all?

I can't, she thought. I've lost one baby already. I can't lose another.

But if she didn't . . . Everyone would know. Her mother and father would know, the whole family would know, the whole street. Her companions on the gun, the girls in her hut. Everyone. And she knew how they would react. She had seen other girls who had got into this predicament, seen the scorn and disgust in people's eyes. She had seen people turn aside, cross the street to avoid meeting them. She had seen Carol Glaister, coming home from the mother-and-baby home, seen the misery in her face. A slut, that was what people had called her. No better than she should be. A hussy.

Not all parents took their daughters back. Ethel Glaister had only taken Carol back because she wanted to pretend it had never happened. Olive remembered her mother's words – 'Don't you ever bring trouble to this doorstep' – and shivered at the thought of being turned away from her own home.

And then there was Derek.

How could she face Derek when he came home, with another man's baby in her arms? How could she even write and tell him?

She told Ray a few days later. They had gone to Fawcett Road and gone to bed, but she was anxious and tense in his arms and after a few minutes he stopped caressing her and raised himself on one elbow, looking down into her face.

'What's the matter?'

Olive stared up at him and felt the tears sting her eyes. Her face crumpled as she tried to speak, and she rolled her head from side to side on the pillow. A huge sob rose up from somewhere deep inside her and forced its way out, like a great lump of matter, in a choke. She tried to speak again, but her voice wouldn't work, she could only cry. Through her tears she saw the consternation on his face and wanted to reassure him, but there was no reassurance to give. She could not speak the platitude. 'It's all right, everything's all right,' because everything was not all right. Nothing was right.

'*Livvy!* What is it? What's happened? Is it Derek? Have you had bad news about Derek?'

She almost wanted to laugh at his words – 'bad' news about Derek could only be good news to him – but the agony of the situation washed over her again. She shook her head and pulled him down against her and sobbed all the more.

'Livvy, stop, please stop. Tell me what it is. You've got to tell me. Whatever it is, we can deal with it together. It can't be that bad. *Livvy.*' He held her close and rocked her in his arms, almost crying himself. 'I can't bear to see you like this.'

'It *is* that bad,' she gasped at last, struggling to overcome the sobs. 'It's the worst possible thing . . . Ray, I'm going to have a baby.'

During the silence that followed, she could hear the thundering of her own heart in her ears, and feel the sudden leap of Ray's against her breast.

'A – a *baby?*' he whispered. 'You mean – *our* baby?'

'Well, it couldn't be anyone else's,' she answered, and knew that he understood.

'Oh, God.'

'I don't know what to do,' she said desperately. 'I've thought and thought about it, and I don't know what to do.'

'How long have you known?'

'I don't really know,' she said miserably. 'I think I've known for a long time. I just hoped it couldn't be true, but now I'm sure it is. Ray, what can I do? How can I face Mum and Dad and tell them I'm pregnant? How can I face Auntie Jess and Uncle Frank and all the neighbours? There's a girl down our street, she had a baby and she went funny afterwards and now she's in St James's. Suppose something like that happens to me.'

'It won't. Nothing like that's going to happen to you, Livvy. I won't let it.'

'How do you know? How can you stop it?' She looked at him wildly. 'Ray, you don't know what it's like for a girl to have an illegitimate baby.' He met her eyes and she remembered that he had been in this position before, but that time it had been Joan, and he could marry her. 'Ray, how am I ever going to be able to face Derek?'

Ray drew away slightly and rested his head on one arm, and she stared at him, terrified. Suddenly, she was afraid that he was angry with her. She saw him abandoning her – getting out of bed, pulling on his clothes, walking out of the room. He could refuse to have anything more to do with her. He could deny that the baby was his, and leave her entirely alone.

'*Ray.*'

'It's all right.' He pulled her close again, and the tears that spilled from her eyes this time were of relief. 'I'm here. I'm not going to go away. You've always got me.'

They lay close in silence again. Olive felt the easing of some of her tension. Until now, the problem had been all hers. Now it was shared. She could wait for him to tell her what to do next. As soon as she had formed the thought, she knew it was wrong. Ray couldn't tell her what to do next –he was probably just as scared as she was – but she couldn't stop herself asking him, all the same.

'What are we going to do?'

He held her a little longer before replying. His head was pressed against hers and she couldn't see his face. She could only feel the beating of his heart.

'What do you want to do?'

'I don't *know*!' Her words were almost lost in fresh sobs. 'I've thought and thought about it and I just don't know what to do. I don't know which way to turn. I can't tell Mum or Dad, they'd go mad. They'd never want to see me again, and there's no one else. And Derek – I can't hurt him like this, Ray. He's been away so long – how can I have someone else's baby? How can I do that to him?'

'I don't understand how it happened,' he said. 'We've always been so careful.'

'We weren't. That time before Christmas, remember? It must have been then.'

'So when d'you reckon it's due?'

'September, I suppose,' she said dully. 'September. The war might be over by then, and us all back in civvy street. Derek home from Italy. He's going to come home and know right away. I won't be able to hide it from him. How's he going to feel, Ray?'

'How am *I* going to feel?' he said quietly, and she looked at him, startled. 'You're talking as if it's just your baby, Livvy, as if it's a problem between you and Derek, but I'm in this too, you know.'

'I know. I'm sorry, but I can't help thinking about what he—'

'What he's going to feel, coming home and finding you with another man's baby. But who says that's going to happen, Olive?'

294

She stared at him. 'I don't know what you mean. Of course it'll happen. Either he'll come home before it's born and he'll be able to see I'm pregnant, or he'll come afterwards. Either way, I can't hide it and—'

'What you haven't thought about,' Ray said, 'is how I'm going to feel, letting another man have my baby.'

There was a long pause. He met Olive's gaze and held it steadily. At last, she dropped her eyes.

'Ray, I'm sorry. I'm *sorry*.'

'You never even thought about it that way, did you?' Ray said. 'You thought I was just going to go away and leave you with it. Is that what you want me to do?'

'No,' she whispered. 'No, it's not.'

'You want me to help you, don't you?' he said.

'Yes, I do. I can't face it by myself. I just can't.'

'I can't help you and then just go off and forget all about it. It's my baby too, Olive. *Our* baby.' His voice shook. 'I've already lost one, you know.'

'I've lost one, too,' she said in a small voice. 'In one of the air-raids. I had a miscarriage.'

'Oh, God,' he said, 'it gets worse all the time.'

They lay again in silence, holding each other. After a while, Olive spoke again.

'I thought you'd want me to – to get rid of it.'

'No!' His arms tightened around her. 'Don't even think about it. We're a family now, Livvy, and families stick together. If one of us goes, we all go.'

She pulled away, frightened. 'What do you mean?'

'You, me and our baby. We're a family—'

'No. Not that. About if one of us goes—' She stared at him. 'You're not thinking . . .'

'I don't know.' His voice was suddenly sombre. 'I don't really know what I meant, Livvy. Only that if we can't be together, especially now – life really won't be worth living at all.' He drew his head back so that he could look deeply into her eyes. 'I love you, Livvy. I love you more than I've ever believed it was possible to love someone, and I'm not going to give you up. I'm not going to give you and our baby up.'

Olive looked at him and knew that he meant it. She felt a shudder of fear run through her.

'Whatever we do, it's going to be awful,' she whispered. 'Whatever we do, it's going to be wrong.'

Ray did not reply. He held her close against him, and she buried her face in his neck. They clung together in the bed that had been their haven, and wept in each other's arms.

# CHAPTER TWENTY-TWO

Europe was now under attack as it had never been attacked before.

The Allies were steadily encroaching everywhere. British and Canadian troops swept across the Siegfried Line. After a siege that lasted for fifty days, Budapest fell to the Red Army. Towns, villages and cities were wrecked as the armies advanced, driving the enemy before them. In Greece, the civil war ended, and in Germany one of the most vital V2 launching sites was abandoned, although this didn't stop them coming over.

The greatest battle was still being fought from the air. Day after day, night after night, the bombers crossed the Channel and hurled destruction on the German cities. Berlin was smashed and set ablaze by a thousand bombers in one day, and Dresden, a city so seldom attacked that its people never bothered about warnings, was annihilated in a firestorm that swept like a hurricane through its quiet streets. Wave after wave of bombers came over that night, raining firebombs on homes and factories alike, until the inferno gathered its own power and sucked up all that lay in its path. People were swept like drifting leaves into the flames, and those who had taken cover in cellars and shelters died of suffocation.

There was no mercy.

Over the rest of the world too, it seemed that the end was in sight. The Burma Road was reopened. America was bombing Japan. The Japanese were fighting back, and still held Manila despite huge forces landed in the Philippines, but other countries could see the turn of the tide and the South Americas, led by Paraguay and Ecuador, began to declare war on Germany and the Axis.

'They want to be in the United Nations when it gets started,' Frank commented cynically. 'A bit late now. Where were they when we needed them?'

'At least they were neutral,' Jess said, but she didn't argue the point. She didn't argue the point much with Frank at all these days. The war's getting him down, she thought. It's getting us all down, and no wonder.

To cheer herself up a bit she made a lot of underclothes for herself and Rose and Annie, with the silk from the parachute that had landed in the garden. The police had never done anything about it and in the end Frank had stopped going down to the station. Jess had waited a while, then taken it out of the cupboard and cut it up before he could tell her not to. It was lovely material to work with, and she really enjoyed making pretty things again.

'I don't know why I want cheering up, though,' she said to Annie. 'With good news coming every day, I shouldn't need any more, but somehow, these days, I feel as if I'm wading through treacle. It's been such a long time, and we still don't know that it's really going to be over. We've still got those awful V2s, and people say he's working on something even worse.'

'We'll never feel safe while Hitler's alive,' Annie agreed. 'Here, have you heard about those new houses we're going to get in Pompey? Phoenix prefabricated houses, they're called. They're made of sort of thick boards instead of brick, and they can be built really quickly. They say there's going to be thousands of them all over the country.'

'Well, we'll need thousands of houses to make up for the ones that have been lost,' Jess said doubtfully, 'but cardboard isn't going to last long.'

'I don't think it's cardboard. It's a lot stronger than that. They're going to have fitted cupboards in the kitchens, and fridges, *and* an inside bathroom! They sound really nice. I'm going to tell our Olive to put her name down for one.'

'I can't see Derek wanting to live in a cardboard house, not with his dad being a builder,' Jess said. She bit off an end of Sylko and held up the garment she had been making. 'There. That's a petticoat for our Rose. Doesn't it look lovely?'

'It does. You're really clever with a needle, Jess. That parachute silk's gorgeous to wear. I feel like a film star in the one you made me!' Annie gathered up her bags. 'Well, I'd better get back. Ted will be home soon and wanting his tea, and I was hoping our Olive would be looking in.'

Something in her voice made Jess stop what she was doing and look up. 'What's the matter? Are you still worried about Olive?'

Annie bit her lip. 'I can't stop worrying about her. There's definitely something not right there. She's getting thinner, and she looks drawn. And it isn't just because she's missing Derek.' She shook her head and Jess saw the fear in her eyes. 'I know Olive, and I know when she's trying to hide something from me. She won't look me in the eye, Jess, and I don't like it when my children won't look me in the eye.'

Jess felt uneasy. Annie was clearly upset, yet it was difficult to see why.

She and Ted had never liked Olive joining the ATS, and Jess suspected that there was no more to it than that. They simply didn't like Olive living like a single girl, and away from home and their supervision. There were plenty of parents who felt like that these days.

'Well, I suppose she thinks she's old enough to run her own life now. She's nearly twenty-six, after all, and a married woman.'

'I know,' Annie said. 'I just hope she remembers it too.'

She let herself out of the house. Maureen was playing outside with Vera Baxter and a couple of other little girls from October Street. They were making a snowman in the road. The snow was getting dirty now, with smoke from the fires, and the snowman looked as grimy as a coal-heaver.

'Our Micky's coming home,' Vera said to Annie as she paused. 'He's not going to that school any more.'

'Coming home, is he?' That wasn't the best news April Grove could hear, Annie thought grimly. Micky's two years in an approved school had been a respite for them all. She wondered if Jess knew.

She walked carefully along the icy pavement. Some bigger children were playing on the bomb site in October Street, where poor Kathy Simmons's house had been. She saw one of them clamber up the side of the static water tank and called out to them.

'Get down from there! You know you're not allowed to play in there.'

The boy turned. It was Alan Atkinson, from the greengrocer's shop in September Street. 'We're skating. It's smashing.'

'Skating! You get down at once. You'll get yourself drowned.'

Alan stuck out his tongue and turned away. Annie frowned. He used to be such a nice, quiet little boy. She toyed with the idea of going and dragging him out forcibly, but she knew she couldn't manage it. She ought to go and tell his mother, Molly, but Molly had enough troubles since her husband Dave had been killed in action. After a minute or two's hesitation, she shrugged and walked on up the street. The ice was probably several inches thick, and anyway boys seemed determined to kill themselves these days. If you stop them one way, they'll think of another, she thought, remembering little Cyril Nash and Jimmy Cross. Only a couple of days ago there'd been a nipper in the dockyard, one of the young apprentices, who'd found a German shell somewhere or other and was sitting on a bench filing it when it blew up in his face. Where he'd got it, nobody knew, and by the time someone realised what he was doing, it was too late.

She reached home to find Florrie Harker having a cup of tea with Ted, who had got home early. Florrie was looking excited.

'I was hoping Olive might be here. Have you heard the news?'

299

'What news?' Annie poured herself a cup of tea and sat down. 'From the look of you, it's something good. Is Derek coming home?' It must be about Derek, she thought, for his mother to make the effort to come down here.

Before Derek's mother could answer, the front door opened again and Olive herself came in. Annie gave her a quick glance. The girl was looking tired and there was a shadow in her eyes. There's definitely something wrong there, Annie thought, and made up her mind to have it out with Olive the minute she could get her alone.

Olive looked quickly round the room and went pale. 'What is it? What's happened?'

'Nothing's happened—' Annie began, but Florrie Harker cut across her words. She was waving a bit of paper. She looked excited and triumphant all at once, as if she was pleased with herself to be first with the news, whatever it was.

'Look at this. Apparently they're going to give building workers priority release when the war's ended. They're going to need thousands and thousands of new houses then. My Derek'll be bound to be one of the ones they send home first!'

*My* Derek, indeed! Annie thought indignantly. He's Olive's Derek now, if you don't mind, but she bit back the words. A son was always a son, when all was said and done, and you couldn't blame Florrie for being a bit possessive with her only child.

Olive went paler still. She put out her hand and laid it on the back of a chair. She was trembling slightly.

'But he's not a builder. He's an accountant.' Her voice was panicky. 'And the war's not over yet, it could be months—'

'It's not that far off,' Florrie said confidently. 'Mark my words, it'll be all finished with by the summer. Look at the papers. They're full of what's going to be done after the war. New town plans, new houses – *proper* houses, not these daft cardboard cut-outs, a waste of space and money, that's all they'll turn out to be. The building trade's the one to be in, you'll see. You'll see then how lucky you were to catch a chap like my Derek.'

Olive sat down and Annie looked at her with concern. She looked almost frightened. Annie fetched another cup and saucer and poured her some tea. She tipped in two saccharins and stirred it thoroughly.

'Here you are, love. Drink that. It's bound to be a bit of a shock.'

'Shock?' Florrie said suspiciously. 'Why should it be a shock?' She darted a glance at Olive. 'Here – there's not been anything going on as there shouldn't have been, I hope.'

'Of course there hasn't,' Annie said sharply. 'All I'm saying is, it's bound to need a bit of taking in, after all the time they've spent apart.' And I hope to goodness I'm right, she thought. 'There's plenty of young couples going to find it a bit hard, adjusting to ordinary life again.'

Olive gave a sudden hiccup of laughter. 'Ordinary life? What's that?' Her voice was high. 'People like me and Derek never had any ordinary life to start with.'

'Well, you'll get some now,' Florrie said with satisfaction. 'And before you're very much older too, the way they're talking. Those Germans won't be able to stand the bombing we're giving them for much longer, and the Americans are doing just the same to the Japs. I heard on the wireless this morning, they reckon they've killed at least a hundred thousand in Tokyo with firebombs. That's what they deserve.'

Olive turned away. She had heard the news too, and felt sickened by it. All those ordinary people, killed in the most horrifying ways, just because of the greed of the men who led them. It was senseless. At the same time, she'd heard the stories of what was happening to prisoners of war in the German and Japanese camps, and felt equally disgusted, and terrified by the thought of what might be happening to her own brother, Colin. It's a madness that's spread over the whole world, she thought, and I've had enough of it.

She didn't stay long after Florrie Harker left, and she didn't give her mother a chance to talk to her alone. She'd seen the look in Annie's eye and knew she couldn't face it. Instead, she went back to camp early and found Ray.

'It could be over by the summer, that's what everyone's saying. Ray, I just don't know what to do. I'm at my wits' end. Sometimes I think I'll just write to Derek and tell him everything, and then I think what would it be like for him to get a letter like that, all those miles away in Italy, and I just can't do it. Then I think I'll run away with you – but how can we, while we're still in the Army? And then I think I'll just wait till he does come home – but everyone would know by then anyway, and his mother would write and tell him, I know. She's never really liked me.' She buried her face in her hands, clenching her fingers in her hair. 'I don't think I can go on, Ray. I can't see any way out of it.'

'There isn't one,' he said. 'We're *in* it, Livvy, just about as deep as we can get, and this is how it seems to me.' He looked at her gravely and held up his hand, bending back his outstretched fingers as he spoke. 'One: you've got to make up your mind which of us you really want – me or Derek – because you can't have both. You're the only one that can decide it, and you can't put off deciding much longer. Two: if it's Derek you want, we've got to decide what to do about the baby. And that's not just your decision, Livvy. It's my baby too. I don't know that I want it brought up by another man, even if your Derek agrees you can keep it.' He sighed. 'I suppose in the end I'd probably say yes, because I'd want it to stop with you, but I'd still want to see it and know about it. And suppose he doesn't agree you can keep it, what then? I'm not having it go to strangers—'

'Ray, stop!' she cried. 'You're making it all so complicated. I can't *think*.'

'It is complicated. It's about as complicated as you can get.'

There was a short silence. At last, Olive said, 'I don't think I can go through with this, Ray. Not any of it. I can't face Derek knowing what's happened. I can't face my mum and dad knowing, and my sister – she's just had her own baby and everyone's so pleased about it. I want them to be pleased when I have one, and they won't. They'll be disgusted.' She took her hands away from her face and looked at him. 'If we run away together, it'll be worse. I shall never see any of my family again. I don't think I can face that either.'

'So what do we do?' he said quietly. 'We haven't got long, Livvy. In a few weeks, you'll start to show, and then—'

'They'll throw me out of the ATS,' she said with sudden panic. 'They won't keep me in, not once they know I'm expecting. Ray – there's no way out, no way at all!' She was as taut and terrified as a cat caught in a cage. Her hands curled almost as if she were physically trying to claw her way out of the walls that surrounded her. '*Ray!*'

'Olive – no.' He caught her against him and held her tightly. 'Don't be so frightened. We'll think of something, I promise you. It'll be all right.'

'It won't. It'll never be all right.' She buried her face against his chest. 'Nothing's ever going to be right again, nothing, nothing, *nothing*.'

'I'll look after you—'

'How can you? How *can* you? You've got a wife already, and you know she'll never divorce you, you've said so. You're tied to her for the rest of your life. And your little girl. She needs you too.' She looked up at him. 'How many children do you think you *can* be a father to, all with different mothers?'

She heard her words with horrified amazement. I never said that, she thought, I couldn't say that, but the expression on Ray's face told her all too clearly that she had, and she clutched him tightly, the tears streaming down her cheeks.

'Ray, I'm sorry, I'm sorry. I didn't mean that. I don't know what made me say it. I just – I don't know what I *am* saying, half the time.' She beat her forehead against him. 'Tell me you still love me, Ray. Tell me. I can't bear to hurt you. I can't bear to lose you.'

'It's all right, Livvy.' His arms were around her again, folding her into his body. 'It's all right. I still love you. I'll never stop loving you.'

For a few minutes they were quiet, resting against each other, both shaken by the things that had been said and thought, the things that were yet to be said. At last, Olive raised her head and looked at him. The tears had paused in their flow and she felt a huge, grey sadness, and a cold certainty as to what would have to be done.

'I honestly can't go through with it,' she said. 'I can't. I think I'd rather be dead.'

For a few moments, Ray did not answer. Then he said, 'So would I.'

Olive stared at him. She tried to speak, shook her head a little, tried again, her voice no more than a whisper. 'Ray?'

'Don't let's do anything in a hurry,' he said, and took both her hands in his. 'Don't let's decide anything until we've got to, but – I've got something to suggest.'

'What?' she whispered, staring at him fearfully.

'I've got a mate who lives in London,' he said. 'Hampstead. He lives in a flat. It's empty – his wife's been evacuated because of the V2s. He told me we could use it any time we like.' He paused. 'I was going to suggest we had a weekend up there – some time, when we could both get a forty-eight hour pass. We've never been like that – you know, sort of at home together. I was thinking about us doing a bit of shopping, cooking our meals together, that sort of thing. You know. As if – as if we were married. *Really* married.'

'In our own home,' Olive breathed. 'Not like just going to Fawcett Road. Better.'

'Much, much better,' Ray agreed.

They sat silently for a while. Olive's thoughts roamed back over the eternal problem, worrying and worrying at it as restlessly as a terrier. She had thought of every aspect, of every course of action it was possible to think of. She had asked herself over and over again what she could do, but however many times she asked herself the question, she came back with the same answer. Shame. Shame and disgrace. And the pain that she would cause Derek, her husband, the man she had loved. The only man she had thought she could ever love.

She didn't even know how it happened. She really didn't know how it happened.

She looked at Ray again, at his funny, paper-bag face and the eyes that had once twinkled with such humour and were now as sad as a puppy's. He's being hurt too, she thought, and the hurt's going to go on, for all of us, for the rest of our lives . . .

Unless they stopped it. Now.

'What are we going to do?' she asked in a small, lost voice.

He looked at her, and then lifted her hands to his face. He kissed her fingers, one by one, and then held the palms against his cheeks. His face was wet with tears and she felt them, warm against her skin.

'We're both due a forty-eight hour pass,' he said. 'Let's go to London. Let's have our two days, being married together. And then—'

'Then . . . ?'

'It's the only way to stop people being hurt,' he said half pleadingly. 'They don't need to know for sure. Accidents happen all the time. Specially in London. But at least we'll be together, Livvy. We'll *always* be together.'

Ethel Glaister put the gin bottle down on the occasional table. It balanced precariously on the edge and she made a grab at it but her groping fingers knocked it to the carpet. Before she could grab it again, it rolled on to its side and spilled some of its contents.

'Oh, damn and blast it!' She picked up the dripping bottle and stood it upright again. This time, it stayed where it was. She looked at it, picked it up again and tipped it over her half-empty glass. There was just enough to fill it up.

Ethel looked again at the scrap of paper on her lap. A yellow envelope lay beside it, crumpled from when she had bent to retrieve the bottle. With shaking fingers, she smoothed it out and read the address again. There was no doubt that it was addressed to herself.

It was the second such envelope Ethel had received. The first had been from the matron of the home for unmarried mothers, to tell her that Carol had given birth to her baby. That was how the nosy parkers of April Grove had found out, she thought, because she'd thrown the telegram down in the gutter and Jess Budd had picked it up and read it. If it hadn't been for that, she would still have been able to hold her head up in front of them all.

If it hadn't been for George, she wouldn't have lived in April Grove at all. They'd have been in one of Portsmouth's nicer streets, in a house with three bedrooms and a bay window and a bit of garden between them and the pavement. She'd been just getting him to the point of agreeing to a move when the war had started. If it hadn't been for the war . . .

Her eyes returned to the yellow envelope and its scrap of paper. If it hadn't been for the war, Joe would still be alive.

Every wife and mother, every sister and sweetheart, dreaded the arrival of the telegraph boy on his red bike, with his canvas satchel full of yellow envelopes. Sometimes the news wasn't all bad. The son, or husband, or sweetheart would be reported as taken prisoner. That was bad enough, but it usually brought a sigh of relief: at least he was alive, at least he'd be coming home again some day.

All too often, though, the news was worse. 'Missing' . . . no more than that, and leaving you with another telegram to wait for, a telegram that might never come. Or 'missing, believed killed' . . . and, worst of all, baldly hopeless: 'died of his wounds' or 'killed in action' . . .

It was one of the last kind which Ethel had received this morning, the brief announcement of her son's death. She sat now, looking at it with blurred eyes, reading it over and over again as if she thought it might contain a different message, but it remained the same; starkly cruel.

Joe was dead.

Joe, her boy who had not long become a man and gone off to war. Joe, who'd looked so grand in his bell-bottoms and lanyards. Joe, who was to have been her comfort now that George had left her.

Joe, dead.

'It's not true,' she muttered, and screwed it up suddenly in both hands, ripping it across, shredding it between her fingers. 'It's not true. *It's not true.*' Her voice rose to a screech and she jumped up, knocking the little table flying. Once more, the bottle fell to the floor, and the glass went with it, its contents splattering on the carpet. 'He's not dead, he's not, he's not, he's *not*. I won't *let* him be. I won't let him be dead, not Joe, not my boy.' She stood in the middle of the small room, her body quivering with rage, and lifted both fists above her head. 'He's not dead. I won't *let* him be dead – I won't, I won't, I *won't*.' At the last word, her voice rose to a thin, keening wail and she tore her hair with both hands and stamped her feet in an agony of denial and despair.

How long she went on screaming, she had no idea, but a hammering on the front door brought her slowly back to awareness. She stopped and slowly lowered her hands. She felt as if she had passed through eternity, but the room looked just as it had a few moments ago, except for the small table which lay on its side, and the bottle and glass scattered beside it. For a moment, she stared at them uncomprehendingly, then she kicked them out of her way and went to open the door to the short passage.

'Go away. I don't want visitors.'

'Are you all right, Ethel?' It was Jess Budd's voice, she realised with a sinking heart. She must have heard Ethel crying and come nosing in to find out what was the matter. 'I thought I heard a noise—'

'Go away.' Her voice trembled. 'I don't want anyone. Just go away.'

There was a short pause. Then Jess said again, uncertainly. 'Are you sure? I don't want to pry, Ethel, but you did sound ever so upset. Have – have you got anyone in there with you?'

Ethel gasped. The cheek of it! What did Jess Budd think she was? In her indignation, she flung open the door and confronted her neighbour. 'No, I haven't got anyone in here with me. What are you insinuating, Jess Budd, eh?'

Jess jumped back, startled. She hadn't meant to insinuate anything, but since Annie had opened her eyes to Ethel's goings-on, she had been in perpetual dread of one of Ethel's 'visitors' turning nasty. You heard such things . . . There'd been a woman only a week or two ago, out at Southsea, found with her throat cut, and when she'd heard Ethel shrieking like that . . .

'I'm not insinuating anything, Ethel,' she protested. 'I just wanted to make sure you were all right.' Her eyes took in Ethel's dishevelled appearance and reddened eyes. 'You're not, are you? What is it? What's happened?'

Ethel seemed about to make another angry retort, but suddenly her shoulders sagged and she jerked her head for Jess to follow her indoors. Dazed and fearful, Jess did so. She found herself in Ethel's back room, where she had rarely been before, looking at the wreckage of the occasional table, the bottle and the glass.

'What's happened? Who did this? Ethel, has someone been attacking you?'

'Don't be daft!' Ethel's scorn was withering. She searched amongst the debris for the telegram, but could find only a few shreds of paper. The envelope lay on the arm of the chair and she grabbed it and thrust it under Jess's nose. 'Look at that.'

Jess stared at it. 'It's a telegram envelope. But where's the—'

'I tore it up.' Ethel was quivering again, with rage and grief. 'I tore it up. D'you know what it said, Jess Budd? *D'you know what it said?*'

Jess shook her head, staring at the half-demented face before her. She felt uneasy and began to wish she hadn't come in here alone. 'No, how could I? Tell me, Ethel. What did it say?'

'It said . . . it said . . .' Ethel seemed unable to get out the words. She took a deep breath and spat them out suddenly, like pebbles. 'It said that my Joe's been killed in action. *My Joe*.' She spoke as if it were an insult. 'He wasn't no more than a bit of a boy. He had all his life before him and now he's dead. Dead. Killed by that bugger Hitler, and that Churchill, he's no better, a lot of warmongers the bloody lot of them. Taking decent young chaps like my Joe and putting them with a lot of louts, and teaching them to kill people and then sending 'em off to get killed themselves. They got no right to do it. They got no *right*.'

She stared at Jess with manic, reddened eyes. 'They're spoiling everything. All what we've worked for and built up, they're ruining it all. Smashing it all to pieces. What did we ever do to get mixed up in it all, eh? Tell me that. When did ordinary people like us ever say we wanted to be in a war? Having to run and hide in holes in the ground when we ought to be able to sleep safe in our own beds, seeing our houses blown to bits with all the bits of furniture and stuff we've scrimped and saved for. Never a decent meal to fill our bellies, standing for hours and hours in queues for a bit of sausage and then finding out they're sold out when we get there. What's the point of it all? And they're still not satisfied. Oh no, we've got to give 'em our menfolk too, and our children, send off the boys and girls we carried for nine months and gave birth to and looked after and brought up decent, send 'em off to die like rats in holes or drowned at sea like my Joe.'

She stared at the yellow envelope again. 'D'you know what it must have bin like for him, Jess? Can you *imagine* what it was like? Out there in all that ocean, in the bitter cold, torpedoed just like my Shirley was torpedoed at the beginning of the war, only she was saved and he – he just had to *die* there. Die in that awful cold water, hundreds of miles from anywhere, *choking* to death—'

The tears came again and she collapsed on to the floor, her arms thrown across the seat of her armchair. The sobs burst from her throat and strangled her words as she went on railing, half choking herself. 'My Joe. *My Joe*. Oh, it's not fair, it's not fair, it's not *fair*.'

Jess stood beside her, feeling totally helpless. She had never liked Ethel much, but liking and not liking didn't come into it now. She laid her hand on the woman's heaving shoulders. There were tears in her own eyes, tears for Joe and for Ethel and for all the sons and mothers and wives and husbands who had been caught up in this terrible, seemingly endless war. Ethel's right, she thought, everything she says is right. We're told to keep smiling through and we're told our country needs us and we've all got to do our bit, and all those things, but when you come down to it, she's right. *We* carried them for nine months, *we* gave birth to them and it isn't right that they can take them away, just when their lives are really starting, and just feed them to the Germans as if they didn't matter. They do matter. Everyone matters.

'I'll make you a cup of tea,' she said, and went through to the scullery to put the kettle on.

A cup of tea. The answer to all ills, but a poor answer indeed for a mother who had just lost her only son.

# Chapter Twenty-Three

Ethel was taken ill the day after the telegram about Joe had arrived, and the doctor said it was a stroke. She might get better and she might not, but there was nothing that could be done about it. She would just have to stay in bed and someone would have to take care of her.

They brought Carol home from St James's. There was nobody else to look after Ethel, and it was clear that if she were left to herself there would be another tragedy.

Frank refused to allow Jess to take on the task. 'Popping in to make a cup of tea's one thing,' he said. 'Turning yourself into a fulltime nurse is another. You've got enough to do, Jess, with all of us at home. And you're still doing Bert Shaw's washing on the sly, I know.'

Jess blushed. 'Only his bits and pieces. Not his overalls and heavy stuff.'

'Well, I'm not that keen on you doing his bits and pieces, neither,' Frank said, trying not to think of Jess standing at the sink scrubbing Bert Shaw's underpants. 'Anyway, that's not the point. I know you feel sorry for Ethel, and so do I, but she's never been that good a neighbour to you. She's got her own family to look after her.'

All Ethel had was Carol, and Carol had been in St James's ever since last summer. She came home looking dazed and wary, like a cat that had been shut in a barn.

'You'll need to take care of your mother,' the doctor told her. 'She's had a bad shock. More than one bad shock.' He looked at her hard. He knew about the baby, of course, and about Carol's breakdown. She'd almost gone to prison over that, but in the end they'd relented and sent her to St James's instead. That had been just as bad, she thought. At least the people in prison would have known what time of day it was.

The doctor went away and left her alone with her mother. She stood in the middle of the back room and looked around her. Ethel was upstairs in bed, lying perfectly flat and still, her face turned to the wall.

Carol went out to the scullery and put on the kettle. The doctor had told her to make her mother a cup of tea. She found the pot in its usual place and spooned some tea out of the caddy that Ethel and George had brought back from their honeymoon over twenty years ago.

Once upon a time, she would not have dared take her mother a cup of tea without first spreading a lace-edged cloth on the tray and setting it out daintily with the flowered sugar-bowl and tiny silver-plated tongs. Now, she slopped the tea into one of the plain white utility cups Ethel had bought for everyday use after George had broken her best china, and carried it upstairs on its own.

She looked down at the still, silent figure with loathing. You took my son away from me, she thought, and now I've got to look after you because you've lost yours.

Micky Baxter was home too. His sojourn at the approved school at Drayton had filled him out. He had always been a big boy, but the hard physical work had put muscle on him and broadened his shoulders. He was almost as big as a man now when he strutted along April Grove.

'We bin growing vegetables,' he told his mother and grandmother as they sat at the table eating cottage pie. 'Taters as big as yer head. And cabbages, and carrots, and all sorts. They send 'em down the shops to be sold.'

'Well, you can get the back garden dug over, then,' his mother said. She was smoking a Woodbine in between mouthfuls of pie. 'Save us a bit of cash, that would.'

Micky scowled. He didn't mind showing off, but he didn't want to be taken up on his boasting, and it didn't suit his image of himself to spend his days gardening. 'I dunno about that. I might not have time.'

'Why, what are you going to do? You're not thinking of joining up. You're too young, for all you're so big.'

'Nah.' Micky curled his lip derisively. 'That's a mug's game, that is.' There had been a time when he'd longed to join the Army, had dreamed of winning the war single-handed, but two years in approved school had changed his ideas. 'There's better ways of bringin' in a bit of dough than that.'

'That's right,' his grandmother nodded. She beamed toothlessly and reached across to pat his hand. 'Get yerself a job, Mick. That's the style. You could be an apprentice, like Tim Budd. Doin' ever so well on the ferry, he is, and he'll have papers at the end of it. Papers, that's what you wants.'

'Papers!' Micky scoffed. 'Apprentice! Don't be daft, Gran. People like Tim Budd might think that's all right, but I ain't tying myself up to some potty little ferry-boat for years and years just to get a bit of paper. What good does that do yer? Tim Budd won't never amount to nothing.'

'He might get to be a skipper, like his uncle.'

'Skipper! If I was going to be skipper,' Micky said grandly, 'I'd want to be skipper of something a bit bigger than the *Ferry King*. Ocean liner, that's what I'd want. But I don't want to do that anyway,' he added hastily before his grandmother could point out that he'd still need papers to start him off. 'There's better pickin's than that to be had.' He laid his finger alongside his nose and winked.

The two women stared at him. Micky had always had big ideas, but now there was a new assurance about him. 'What you got in mind?' his mother asked dubiously. 'You don't want to get into no more trouble.'

'I won't be gettin' in no trouble. I bin talkin' to people while I bin up Drayton. People who knows things. This war ain't goin' to last much longer, Ma, and when it's over there's goin' to be all sorts of things happening. There'll be a lot of chances for anyone what's got his eyes open.'

'I don't see—' Granny Kinch began, but her daughter interrupted her impatiently.

'Black market, Ma. That's what he's on about.' She looked at her son. 'That's right, ain't it, Mick?'

'Call it what you like,' he shrugged. 'All I'm saying is, there'll be a bit of stuff about and a lot of people wantin' it. If they can pick it up cheaper from blokes like me, they're goin' to take the chance, ain't they? That's all there is to it. Simple.'

'You can still get into trouble,' Nancy said. 'I don't want you ending up in jail.'

Micky shook his head and helped himself to the last of the cottage pie.

'I won't end up in jail. I got me head screwed on too tight for that. You don't need to worry, Ma. I learned a lot more than growin' cabbages when I was up Drayton.'

Ray and Olive managed to get their forty-eight hour pass together in the middle of March.

'Fancy us going to London together,' Olive said with a nervous giggle as they boarded the train at Portsmouth Town station. 'It makes me feel really funny.'

Ray put his arm round her waist. It wasn't something he did often, in broad daylight in the middle of Portsmouth, but it didn't seem to matter now. The station was full of Service men and women anyway, going on leave or coming back, and there were plenty of relatives hugging and kissing them. The station loudspeakers were playing Vera Lynn singing 'We'll Meet Again' and nobody was taking any notice of Ray and Olive.

Olive looked around her and remembered the times she'd come here with Derek, to kiss and wave him goodbye. The last time, especially. She'd been broken hearted, wondering if she would ever see him again, and how long it would be before they could start their married life properly.

Now, it looked as if they never would.

Oh Derek, she thought, I'm sorry. I'm really, really sorry.

They climbed into a carriage and Ray led the way along the corridor, looking for two seats together in a compartment, but there were no seats at all, and in the end he gave up and dumped their kitbags at the end. They sat down on them and looked at each other.

'Well,' Olive said, still feeling nervous, 'this is it.'

Ray reached for her hand. 'We don't have to do anything you don't want—'

'Don't let's talk about it,' she said quickly. 'Let's just enjoy ourselves. For a couple of days. Let's – just pretend everything's all right. Please.'

'All right,' he said, and he drew her closer so that she could rest her head on his shoulder. She felt his arm around her shoulder, warm and strong, felt the beat of his heart beneath her cheek. If only we could stay like this for ever, she thought, and nothing change, nobody get hurt.

The train rattled towards London. The corridor filled with smoke from cigarettes and from the open window. Whenever they went through a tunnel, smoke from the engine blew back and covered everyone with black smuts. At Guildford, someone got on with a large, smelly dog. It flopped down beside Olive's kitbag and lay heavily against her knee, snoring.

Olive alternately dozed and stared out of the window. The countryside was just beginning to show signs of spring. A few trees had started to open their leaves, dusting the woods with a haze of green, and there were primroses growing along the embankment. Olive thought of Sunday afternoons before the war, going with Betty and their mother to pick primroses and coming back with a basketful which they distributed all over the house and still had some over for Auntie Jess.

Spring did not appear to have made much impact on London. The streets were grey and dusty, with few flowers to be seen. Olive could remember women who sat around the entrance to Waterloo station with great baskets of violets and primroses for sale, and stalls with buckets of daffodils and stacks of fresh fruit. There were none of these now, and people would probably not have lingered to buy them if there had been.

Instead, they hurried past with their heads down and their brows furrowed. They looked as grey and depressed as the streets.

Ray and Olive caught the Underground to Hampstead. The flat was in a side street of large houses, with three floors and a basement and big bay windows. The flat was on the second floor, overlooking a small garden which was almost filled with a big weeping willow.

'What huge rooms,' Olive said. 'You could fit almost all our house in this.' She gave the gas fire a quick glance, then walked across to the tall windows and looked down at the tree. 'They don't seem to grow any vegetables or anything around here.'

'I don't know who looks after the garden,' Ray said, coming to join her. He stood behind her with his arms wrapped around her body. 'It's all separate flats, you see, not like one house.'

'Perhaps the one at the bottom does it. It's called the garden flat.' Olive leaned back against him and closed her eyes. 'Did you bring any civvy clothes?'

She felt his face smile against hers. 'And where would I get things like that? All we've got in camp is uniform. I haven't had any civvy clothes for years. The ones I've got at – at home wouldn't even fit me now.'

'Of course. Daft of me.' She turned and grinned. 'I brought a frock.'

'A real one? A proper, pretty civvy frock? I've never seen you in one.'

'I know. I thought I'd dress up a bit for you. It would be a shame if you never saw me—' Her voice faltered and the grin faded. 'Ray . . .'

'Don't,' he said, holding her more tightly. 'Don't talk about it. Don't even think about it. We're here to enjoy ourselves. We're going to be married – just for a little while, before it's all over. That's what matters. Being together. That's all that really matters.'

Olive turned in his arms and put hers around his body. She held him close and laid her face against his chest.

'I love you, Ray.'

'I know. I love you, too.' He stroked her back and they stood close together, by the window, for a long time, not speaking, just holding each other, just feeling the closeness of their love.

It's funny, Olive thought. I'd imagined we'd want to go to bed the minute we arrived, but there doesn't seem to be any hurry after all. It's as if we had all the time in the world . . .

The first thing was to do some shopping. There wasn't much you could do, with rationing the way it was, but they stood in a queue or two and bought what little they could. Sausages, a few potatoes to boil and mash, an onion to fry. They both had their Service ration books, which everyone needed for weekend passes and leaves, but there were no eggs to be had, nor the bacon they were accustomed to in camp. Service people were fed better than civilians.

Taking their shopping back to the flat and cooking dinner together was fun and made them feel closer, but it was strangely awkward as well. Neither of them had ever experienced ordinary married life, just two people together in their own home, and they didn't know quite how they should behave. They each turned to their parents' way for reference, but Ray's family had lived differently from Olive's.

'You sit down there and read the paper while I get the potatoes on,' Olive said, pointing to the armchair in the living-room.

'No, I'll do those. You do the onion and sausages.'

Olive looked at him. 'I can do them. I want to.'

'I want to help. I won't feel right, sitting about while you do it all.'

'But I want to cook a meal for you.' She felt unexpectedly near to tears. 'It's the first one we've ever had. I've never had a chance to cook for you before . . .'

'And I've never had a chance to help you.'

They stood looking at each other, nonplussed. Olive didn't know what to say. The idea of a man actually helping in the kitchen was almost too outlandish to believe. Her father had never lifted a finger to help her mother. He wouldn't have dared: Annie had been trained as a cook and worked in some of the big houses in Portsmouth before they were married. She'd taken a lot of trouble to pass on her skills to her daughters, and never allowed either her husband or her son anywhere near the stove, except to make a cup of tea or cocoa.

Olive could see that Ray really did want to help, and she didn't want to spoil their weekend at the outset with a silly tiff, so she smiled at him and reached up to kiss his lips.

'All right. You can do the potatoes. Don't peel them too thick, that's all.'

'Look,' Ray said with mock sternness, 'I was a squaddie once. I've peeled more spuds than you've had hot dinners.' They both laughed, and after that it was all right.

When the meal was ready, they sat down to it with as much enjoyment as if it had been a pre-war Christmas dinner with all the trimmings. If only it could be like this all the time, Olive thought, setting the two laden plates on the table. Just the two of us, living in our own home, with nobody to interfere or look down their noses.

But that was what she'd wanted to share with Derek too, and now it would never be.

After dinner, they went out to have a look around London. It was a depressing experience. There were even more bomb sites than there had been in Portsmouth, and because the buildings were bigger, so were the gaping holes where they had been. A lot of them were overgrown with grass and weeds, and even quite big bushes, and some had static water tanks on them, with the usual warnings to keep off being ignored by local children. It wasn't warm enough yet for swimming, but Olive had no doubt that once summer arrived they'd be using them for bathing just the same.

There were signs of hope too. As the afternoon drew on, lights began to be switched on in the shops and no blackout curtains were put up. There were even a few street lights on – not as many as pre-war, because it was now officially 'dim-out', but enough to see your way. Cars and buses were allowed to have lights on too – not the big, bright headlights, but sidelights that at least told you they were coming.

At the same time, people were still using the air-raid shelters. There were signs to point out the big street shelters and to tell you which Underground stations were being used. It seemed funny to think of raids still going on, when there was no effort being made to hide the city from the sky.

'It's because it's the V2s,' Ray said. 'They don't need lights to tell 'em where to fall – the Germans just aim them from their launch sites and over they come. All you know of it is the bang.'

Olive nodded. She had heard a V2 over Portsmouth. It wasn't like the doodlebug, with a droning engine that could be heard stuttering before it finally cut out. The V2s went faster than the speed of sound and created a huge thunderclap as they went over, and when they fell it was with a noise like an express train going through a tunnel.

Air-raid warnings were useless against such a weapon, and the blackout didn't mean a thing, but people still wanted to know they'd wake up in the mornings. They still needed the shelters.

'We're not going to one of those, are we?' Olive said. 'I don't fancy being in a shelter with a lot of strangers. Or down the Underground.'

'Not likely. We didn't come all this way to spend our nights like rabbits in a hole.' Ray squeezed her hand. 'We're married, remember? There's a lot to do when you're married.'

Olive giggled. 'I can see it's going to be a fulltime job, being married to you.'

'Well,' Ray said, pretending to consider, 'we could put you on to just night duty, if you find it gets a bit too much.'

They walked a bit further and came to a cinema. Olive stopped dead.

'Ray. Look at that. They're showing *Casablanca*.'

'So they are.' They looked up at the poster with the picture of Ingrid Bergman and Humphrey Bogart, cheek to cheek. 'You know, that was a smashing picture. I wouldn't mind seeing it again.' He turned to Olive. 'Shall we?'

'Oh, yes – let's.' She hugged his arm. An evening in the cinema, and then back home – *home* – to bed together. Then waking up tomorrow to another whole day – and night.

She pushed out of her mind what was to happen after that.

The second film was halfway through when they went in. An usherette showed them to a seat with her torch. Ray had asked for the back row and there were just two spaces left, between two other couples. Nobody was paying much attention to the picture.

Olive and Ray sat down and he slipped his arm around her shoulders. She sighed and nestled against him, lifting her face for his kiss. This was what the small films were for, she thought, drifting away into pleasure. 'The pictures' were somewhere to go for warmth, darkness and privacy, where you could kiss and cuddle and be sure no one was watching you – except sometimes when the usherette's torch shone its beam suddenly along the rows of seats and lit up one blushing couple. That stopped anyone going too far.

After the small film there was a Pathé news, showing the most recent events of the war. They watched sombrely as the images flickered before them. There was heavy bombing everywhere. The Dambuster squadron had dropped their largest bomb yet on the viaduct at a place called Bielfeld, the Americans were still hammering Japan, and nearly seventy German prisoners of war had escaped from a camp near Bridgend, in South Wales. They had tunnelled forty-five feet under barbed wire and broken out at four in the morning. By evening, over forty had been recaptured, but Olive shivered as she thought of all those desperate men roaming loose around the countryside.

'I'm glad they're a bit more careful in the camps around Pompey.'

At last the news was over and they settled down to watch the big film. The usual picture of a roaring lion came on screen first, followed by the certificate that said that the film had been passed for adult viewing, and then the music began and they lost themselves in the story.

Olive and Ray had already seen it twice. There were no surprises left, but they followed it with anticipation of their favourite parts. They watched as tough bar-owner Rick first set eyes on Ilsa Lund, the girl he had loved years ago in Paris, as she walked into his cafe. 'Of all the gin-joints in all the world . . .' How must it have felt, Olive thought, to see the woman you loved and had lost, and know that she was married to someone else? She felt a sudden wave of tears and turned her head against Ray's shoulder.

Sam, the Negro pianist, was played by a man called Dooley Wilson. He had dark velvet eyes and a voice to match, and his touch on the piano keys was almost unbearably tender and poignant – like Ray's fingertips when he touched her in their lovemaking, Olive thought with another wrench of sadness – and although he was as gentle as his songs, he was totally devoted to the tough Rick. He knew, you could see, that the song Rick wanted him to sing was going to hurt him, and he pretended he'd forgotten it, but Rick insisted, and the soft, velvet voice hummed the words to begin with, before it became a duet with Ingrid Bergman herself joining in.

> Moonlight and love songs, never out of date,
> Hearts full of passion, jealousy and hate.
> Woman needs man, and man must have his mate,
> That, no one can deny . . .

'Oh, Ray . . .'

The tears were flowing freely now and there was nothing Olive could do to stop them. She leaned her head on his breast and sobbed. Ray kept his arm tightly around her shoulders and she felt his head close against hers. There was a dampness on her hair.

'Let's go,' he muttered into her ear. 'We've seen enough. Let's go back to the flat.'

They got up and squeezed past the other couples, barely conscious of the grumbles at the disturbance they were causing. The usherette glared at them suspiciously as they stumbled up the aisle and through the door, but there wasn't any law against people leaving a cinema halfway through a film, and they hurried out to the street and stood for a moment in the darkness. The dim-out didn't exactly make the streets as bright as day – there were just isolated pools of gaslight around lamp-posts at street corners – but it was enough to help them find their way back to the flat.

People were queuing to go into the shelters or down into the Underground now. Olive shuddered again. There had been a horrible accident at one of the London Underground stations, when a whole crowd of people had fallen down the stairs and got crushed to death. She'd remembered it when they'd been on their way to Hampstead by Underground, and she hadn't felt happy until they'd been back in the fresh air.

They turned the last corner. The house was halfway along the street, and they went up the steps to the front door. Ray had a key for it, and another for the door of the flat upstairs. They groped their way up the steps and along the passage, and let themselves in.

'There.' Ray switched on the light. 'Home again.' He took Olive into his arms.

Home. She stood close to him, trying to recapture the feeling of being married that she'd had earlier, but the film, the film that had meant so much to them, had taken it away. The song was still sounding in her ears, the dark velvet tones of Dooley Wilson merging with the soft voice of Ingrid Bergman. 'Moonlight and love songs, never out of date, Hearts full of passion, jealousy and hate . . .'

'"Woman needs man, and man must have his mate."' Ray sang softly in her ear. '"that, no one can deny . . ." Oh, Livvy, I love you so much . . .' He caught her hard against him and began to kiss her frenziedly, little passionate kisses all over her face and neck, down into the collar of her dress – the dress she had worn for him, to look pretty for him. She twisted her head this way and that, trying to capture his lips with her own, and at last their mouths touched and held, and they sank into each other, lost to time, lost to the world, lost to everything but each other.

The tingle of desire, beginning low in Olive's body, spread over her, from thigh to breast, from finger to toe, and was then joined by another sensation, so brief that she barely registered it, so delicate that she almost missed it.

For a moment, she was very still. Then it came again.

'*Ray.*'

'What?' He responded with alarm. 'Livvy, what is it? What's the matter?'

'Nothing. I don't know . . .' She waited, unsure, unbelieving. 'It felt like – *oh*!' It had come again, a tiny flutter of movement, so minute that if she had never experienced it before she would not have known. 'Ray, it's the baby.'

'The *baby*?' His alarm grew. 'What do you mean? You – you don't think it's started? But you're only—'

'No. No, it's not that.' She held herself a little away from him and laid one hand over her stomach. 'It's all right, Ray. Nothing's wrong. It – it's just the baby moving. I've quickened.'

'Moving? *Quickened*? You – you mean you can *feel* it?' He stared at her.

Olive laughed a little, breathlessly. 'Yes. Oh, it's nothing very much – just a tiny flutter, almost like a butterfly – but that's what it is. I know it is.'

Ray gazed into her face. Then his glance dropped to her stomach, still with her hand laid across it. There was, as yet, only the smallest sign of a bulge though her waist had begun to thicken. 'It doesn't seem possible. Our baby, starting to move.' He laid his hand on hers. 'Can I feel it too?'

Olive laughed again and shook her head. 'I told you, it's only tiny. Anyway, it's stopped now. It'll be a long time before anyone else can feel it, but I'll tell you the minute—' She stopped abruptly and her eyes met his, all laughter gone. 'Ray . . .'

'Don't think about it,' he said roughly, pulling her to him again. 'Don't think about it. We've got all tonight and all day tomorrow and then another night before we have to think about anything else. Let's just go on being married. Let's just be at *home* together.'

He took his arms away and they walked into the living-room together. It looked empty despite its furniture – empty of us, Olive thought. There was nothing of theirs in the room; no shoes lying about, no newspapers or books or knitting. No family photographs on the mantelpiece, no toys pushed half under the sofa. She had a sudden desire to untidy it, to make it look as if someone lived there. As if she and Ray lived there.

Ray pushed her gently on to the sofa. 'You sit there and I'll make you a cup of cocoa.' He lifted her feet on to a small stool.

Olive laughed. 'I'm not an invalid. I can still stand up.'

'You're my wife,' he said quietly. 'You're the mother of my baby, and I'm going to look after you.' He knelt suddenly and took her hands in his. 'I want to look after you always, Olive. For the rest of our lives. I want to love and cherish you, like it says in the wedding service. "For better for worse, from this day forward, in sickness and in health, as long as we both shall live." I don't know if I've got it all right, but that's what I want to do.'

They looked into each other's eyes. Then Olive smiled tremulously and said, 'You forgot "for richer, for poorer."'

'Oh, money,' he said dismissively. 'That's not important. That doesn't count.'

'No,' she said, 'it doesn't. Not if you really love each other.'

They stayed like that for a few moments and then Ray got up and went to make the cocoa. Olive lay back on the sofa, her eyes closed, listening to the faint sounds from the kitchen.

*To love and to cherish . . . from this day forward . . . as long as we both shall live . . .*

Oh Ray, she thought, as another tear squeezed itself from her eye. How long will that be . . .'

'Woman needs man, and man must have his mate, that, no one can deny . . .'

The morning light filtered through the curtains and Olive stirred and opened her eyes. She was still wrapped in Ray's arms, her body curved against his, the warmth of his skin flowing against hers. She lay savouring it, delighting in the sensation of skin against skin, counting and treasuring the tenderness of every particle of flesh that touched. Sex is good, she thought dreamily, but this is even better. This is what binds us close, this sensation of being close even while we're asleep, of knowing that someone loves you and trusts you enough to let you be with them while they're asleep, enough to let you have such closeness. Enough to let you touch them if you want, to look at them – just to be with them.

That's why married couples share the same bed, she thought. Because they have that trust and love and they want to show and share it. Because they know that closeness is the most important part of their marriage.

She lifted her head slightly and looked at Ray's old alarm clock. He hadn't set the alarm, but it was ticking gently. It was almost nine o'clock.

Nine o'clock! She hadn't slept as late as that for years. She let her head rest on the pillow again, smiling. It had been late last night when she and Ray had finally stopped making love and fallen asleep. The tall windows had been dark and the house silent. There was no one to hear their whispers, their whimpers, their cries, no one to witness their ecstasy. The skies too had been silent: no aircraft, no bombs, no V2s. It had been almost possible to pretend it was peacetime.

Olive moved a little. She needed to go to the bathroom, but she didn't want to disturb Ray. She felt him shift against her, then he sighed and loosened his arms a little. Holding her breath, she slid gently away from him and then eased herself out of the bed.

Ray turned in the bed, as if feeling for her, and then settled down again. Olive knelt beside him for a moment, looking at his face, studying it as intently as if she needed to memorise each tiny detail.

Asleep, he looked less like a crumpled paper bag. The cragginess was smoothed out, the lines disappeared, and his skin looked fresh and young. It was the muscles that made him look crumpled, she thought, the creases of laughter and smiles. When he was older, they would be wrinkles, but they weren't yet, and when they were he would look just as attractive, just as funny and nice.

*When he was older . . .*

A shiver ran over her body. She put her hand on her stomach in a sudden gesture of protectiveness. What are we doing, Ray? she asked silently. What have we done? But he lay quietly, not replying to her, and she could find no answer in his smooth and sleeping face.

Abruptly, Olive got to her feet. She went into the bathroom, revelling in the idea of a real bathroom with a lavatory, indoors, and then padded into the kitchen. She would make some tea and take it back to bed. By then, Ray would be awake and they could stay there, drinking tea and cuddling, perhaps even making love again, very gently. If they wanted to, they could stay there all day.

She filled the kettle and looked for the matches.

The box was empty.

Olive bit her lip in annoyance. They'd known yesterday that they were short of matches, and had meant to get some more, but the film had upset them both, and they'd come straight back to the flat and forgotten all about them. Ray must have used the last one to light the gas last night. He'd probably intended to go out first thing this morning to get some more.

Well, she could do that herself. It meant leaving the flat, and Ray might wake to find her gone, but he'd see the kettle and cups put out and guess where she'd gone. There was a little newsagent's shop at the corner of the street – she need be gone no more than a few minutes. She needn't even bother to get dressed – Ray's Army greatcoat was on the back of the door, and she could just slip that over her pyjamas. It came right down to her feet, so no one would know.

The March morning air was chilly as she hurried to the shop. There were quite a lot of people about, some still on their way to work, though most people must have started by now, and some on their way home, perhaps from night shifts, or from being down in the Underground shelters. You see, Olive thought a little smugly, there wasn't any need to have gone down there after all . . . But she hadn't lived through the last year's bombardment of flying bombs, so she didn't really know what it was like. All the same, she'd done her best, with all the other ack-ack teams round the coast, to shoot down as many as possible and stop them getting to London at all.

V2s were different. Nothing could warn of the approach of a V2 in time to do anything about it.

She went into the shop and bought the matches, aware of curious eyes on her. It must look a bit queer, a girl out in a soldier's greatcoat. She had a sudden idea of what they were thinking, and blushed scarlet. The man handed her the matches and she gave him the right money and hurried out, thankful that she didn't have to wait for change.

It doesn't matter, she thought. We don't really live here and they'll never see us again. It doesn't matter what they think . . .

She was just crossing the road to the house when the sky was suddenly split by a huge double bang, like a giant clap of thunder.

She stopped dead, and looked up, but there was nothing to see. There was only a roar like that of an express train going into a tunnel, and then a crash that filled her ears and took away her senses and left her spinning, alone, into darkness.

# CHAPTER TWENTY-FOUR

They brought Olive back to the Army hospital. She lay in the ward, pale and silent, refusing to answer her mother's questions. She had had to tell the Army doctors the truth, of course, and she'd had to tell the officer who came to see her that Ray had been in the house that was hit, but she would tell her mother nothing.

'It's my own business. I can't talk about it.'

The implication was that it was to do with the war and therefore secret, like Gladys Shaw's work, but Annie wasn't satisfied. There had been a look in Olive's eye before she went anywhere near London, a look that didn't come from being proud to serve your country. More from doing something you didn't want to be caught at. And it didn't need much imagination to think what it might be.

'I never liked her going around with that gang of men and girls from the camp,' she said to Ted. 'Young people like that, all split up from their families, some of them married and some not – it's bound to cause trouble.'

'What I want to know is what she was doing in London at all,' Ted said heavily. 'She never told us she was going. If she'd got a leave pass, she ought to have been here, with her own family.'

'Oh, use your head, for goodness' sake,' Annie said impatiently. 'What do you *think* she was doing? Look, it said in the paper about them being there, didn't it? "Soldier killed and ATS girl wounded in London V2 bomb blast." I know it didn't give no names, but that was our Olive, I'd go to the King's court and swear on it. And the soldier—'

'Well, who was he?' Ted demanded pugnaciously. 'I'd have tanned the hide off him if I'd known about it. Leading a decent young woman like our Olive astray.'

'Our Olive's old enough not to be led anywhere she don't want to go, and you know who he was as well as I do. That bloke she brought here once – the one that walked her here one night, back before Christmas, and waited for her in the pub. I knew at the time it wasn't all above board. I knew it.'

Ted shook his head, trying to come to terms with it all. He'd always set his face firmly against any 'funny business' and told both the girls that they needn't ever think they could bring trouble to the house, meaning a baby born out of wedlock, or carrying on with someone else once you were married, that sort of thing. He'd seen a lot of changes since the days when you could tell girls that, though: they'd all gone off and got jobs or joined the Land Army or the ATS, or whatever else took their fancy, and you couldn't tell 'em a thing. Sometimes he wondered whether it really mattered. So many people of his age were losing their children in the war – blokes he worked with, like Sam the engineer whose son had been blown up in France, and young Ben who'd been apprentice before Tim and joined up, all full of pride, in '41 and been killed the first time he saw action . . . He'd been a good nipper, had Ben. They'd gone to Dunkirk together and he'd been scared but he'd gritted his teeth and carried on, and now he was dead like so many others . . .

Ted caught up his rambling thoughts. The upshot of it all was that Olive could easily have been dead too, but she wasn't. And really, all he could feel was thankful for that. Despite his pugnacious words, he didn't really want to tan the hide off the young chap she seemed to have been with. He was dead, wasn't he? That was enough punishment.

Olive had been punished too. She'd been hurt quite bad, enough to keep her in hospital for several weeks, and she'd told Annie on her last visit that she was being invalided out of the Army. Annie was still aware that she wasn't being told everything.

'There's more to it all than meets the eye, but once a girl's married, the mother doesn't count any more with these officials. It's only the husband they'll talk to, and Derek's not here.'

Olive was thankful that Derek wasn't here. She lay in her narrow hospital bed, thinking of him and trying to disentangle her feelings. All the time she'd been in love with Ray, she'd told herself she still loved Derek just as much. There was room to love two men. But now that Ray had gone, he seemed to have left nothing but a huge gap of emptiness, and it was as if he'd taken all her capacity to love anyone at all. When she thought of Derek now, there was nothing, only a huge grey sadness that seemed to spread all through her body.

The blast of the bomb had taken her clear along the street. It had ripped Ray's greatcoat and her pyjama trousers from her body and left her with only her pyjama jacket on. Flying debris had broken her arm and bruised her legs and body, and her face had been lacerated with glass. One of her eyes had been badly scratched and they still weren't sure she'd ever see properly with it again.

It was a fortnight before they let her look into a mirror. The grazes and cuts had mostly healed by then, but there were still angry red weals crisscrossed over her cheeks and forehead. She stared at them, wondering dully if they would ever fade. Some of them still felt quite deep, like the wrinkles on the face of an old woman.

She laid the mirror aside. It didn't seem to matter. Nothing really seemed to matter.

She had lost the baby, of course. She seemed doomed to lose babies in air raids, she thought bitterly. When they'd found her, the miscarriage had already started and she was lying in a pool of blood. The people who had rushed to pick her up hadn't realised what it was at first, thinking it was some terrible injury, and Olive hadn't been able to tell them because some of the flying debris had knocked her unconscious. Later, she discovered that she'd reached the hospital only just in time. 'You nearly bled to death,' the doctor had said, and she wished she had.

Well, there would be no more babies to lose, either in air raids or by any other means. It was very unlikely, the doctor had continued, looking at her with some sympathy, that she would ever conceive again. The blast and the miscarriage had damaged her internally, and there was nothing they could do about it.

It would be no use the Queen coming this time to say there would be other babies for her and Derek to raise.

Derek . . .

I love him, she thought experimentally. He's my husband. I love him.

But there was nothing. No quickening of the heartbeat. No flutter of the pulse. No warmth, spreading through her body. Nothing.

Perhaps if she thought of Ray . . . but that was something she couldn't bear to do, yet couldn't stop. Her mind kept conjuring up pictures of what had happened: of him waking to find her gone, getting out of bed, coming to the window and watching her cross the street before that terrible thunderclap; of him hearing the bang, perhaps even seeing the rocket as it hurtled towards him; of him knowing for a brief, eternal second what was going to happen, before the world disintegrated around him.

Or perhaps he hadn't woken at all. Perhaps he had died believing she was still close in his arms. Together, the way they'd planned to be.

The thoughts kept coming into her mind, relentlessly, and she kept pushing them out. I won't think about it. I won't.

She tried instead to think of the times they'd shared, the happiness they had known. That first dance on South Parade Pier. The walks along the beach, before it was wired off. The nights they had spent in Fawcett Road. Going to the pictures together and cuddling in the back row. Going to see *Casablanca* . . .

No. It hurt too much. The grey sadness turned a virulent green and a vile yellow. It stabbed at her deep inside; it clawed at her mind. She turned away from it, thrust it from her. It was too much, too much.

I wished I was dead before, she thought. I thought I couldn't live with what was happening, I thought the pain was too bad, but it was nothing like this. I didn't know about this.

She laid her hand on her stomach. Only two weeks ago, there had been a baby in there. A living baby who had begun to kick, whose first tentative movements she had detected, like a butterfly within. A baby who might have looked like her or like Ray – if it had ever been born.

She turned her face aside again, swept by a terrible remorse. My baby, my baby. You were never going to live anyway. She felt like a murderess.

Florrie Harker came in to see her. Annie had done her best to dissuade her, but Florrie had been insistent. 'She's my daughter-in-law. I owe it to Derek to visit her.' She brought a bunch of daffodils bought from Atkinson's shop, and stuck them in a thick glass vase on the windowsill. Then she stook beside the bed and looked down at Olive, her arms folded.

'Well. You've been in the wars.'

Olive tried to smile. 'You could say so.'

'Don't reckon those scars'll ever go, not properly,' Florrie pronounced. 'What a shame. You always had quite a nice skin, too.'

Derek had said she had skin like porcelain. Well, even porcelain could crack. Olive shrugged.

'It's not so bad as some.'

'I'm glad to see you can take it in the right way.' Florrie settled herself on a chair. 'Beauty's only skin deep, after all, and my Derek's not one to let a little thing like a few scars change him. *He* knows what loyalty's all about.'

Olive closed her eyes. She didn't have the strength to fend off Florrie's hints. She knew that both families were suspicious about what she'd been doing in London – it was inevitable that they should be – but she was determined to tell them nothing. It was between her and Derek, and if Derek had to know, he should know it from her. She didn't want Florrie Harker writing a spiteful letter, telling him his wife had been running around with another man. I owe him better than that, she thought. Even if I had stopped loving him, I'd owe him better than that.

'So how long d'you think you'll be in here, then?' Her mother-in-law's voice came from above her head.

'I don't know. Another couple of weeks.'

'Well, they won't be wanting you back on ack-ack anyway. They reckon the bombing's over now. They shot down the last doodlebug over in Suffolk at the end of March and there's been nothing since. Our boys are marching all over Germany. They've liberated Vienna, and they reckon Berlin's next, and we've got Arnhem at last, too. Hope they gave the buggers all they deserved for what they did to our lads. They say they're about to set nearly twenty thousand prisoners free from one of the big POW camps – Colditz. Yes, we've got Hitler on the run now all right.'

Olive had heard most of the news already. Everyone in the ward followed it with intense interest. They were all ATS, and most of them were burning with frustration at not being out there, sharing in these last days of the war, for everyone knew it must soon be over now. The only question was: when?

'It was a shame President Roosevelt died,' Olive said. 'He's been all through it with us, and it would have been nice for him to see it end.'

Florrie snorted. 'Better if he'd come in at the start instead of dithering about till the Japs pushed him into it. And *they're* still causing a lot of trouble, out East, slimy little yellow bastards. I don't reckon they're going to give in just because Hitler does.'

She got up to go, and Olive lay back thankfully. At least talk of the war had kept Florrie's mind off Olive's trip to London, and it had even kept Olive's mind off her problems for a short time, but now that she had gone, there was nothing once more to stop the thoughts and fears and memories flooding back.

One day soon the war was going to be over. One day soon, Derek would come home. And somehow or other, Olive was going to have to face the final consequences of what she had done.

The news of the progress of the war cheered everyone, but hard on its heels came other news, of a more disturbing kind. On a Sunday evening in the middle of April, the nation listened in shock and horror to a broadcast by American war correspondent Ed Morrow who had been present at the liberation of Buchenwald.

Buchenwald.

The name had never figured before in war reports, but now it was branded into everyone's hearts.

Jess and Frank listened to the report in silence. By the time it was over there were tears running down Jess's cheeks, and Frank was white. They turned to each other and put out their hands, clasping each other's fingers tightly.

'I can't believe anyone could be so wicked,' Jess said shakily. 'Thousands of people starved to death or dying of horrible diseases, bodies like skeletons all piled up, and some poor souls still alive, nothing but bags of bones . . . And outside the fence they could see fields and farms, and Germans living as if there was nothing wrong at all. How could people *do* that to one another? How could the guards go home to their suppers at night? How could the people living near by let it happen?'

'It's what the war was all about,' Frank said soberly. 'Hitler running amok all over Europe, stamping out the Jews because he didn't like them. We were supposed to be stopping all that.'

'Well, I suppose we'll have stopped it happening from now on,' Jess answered, 'but that's not much consolation for those poor souls in Buchenwald. And how many others are there, Frank? How many more camps have they got like that one, with thousands of people rotting away from starvation and disease and just plain cruelty?'

They were soon to find out. Now that the Allies were in Germany itself, more camps were found and opened up. In Belsen, ten thousand dead were discovered, some scattered about the camp, some in grotesque piles. Like those in Buchenwald, they were emaciated beyond the point where the human body might be expected to survive, their sore-ridden and rotting skins clinging almost directly to the bones, with little flesh in between. Those who still lived were desperately ill with dysentery and typhus, their tortured bodies scarcely capable of healing. Some were children and babies, born in the camps, who had known no other life.

The tales went on, horror piled upon horror. Soldiers who had been all through the war, who had seen sights that no man should see – from the ordinary Tommy and the American GIs to great generals like Eisenhower, Patton and Bradley, who had led and orchestrated great battles – vomited and wept at the human devastation before them, and came away shaken and sobered by the suffering of those who had been treated worse than animals.

Buchenwald. Belsen. Dachau. Weimer. Auschwitz.

Their names would live for ever as symbols of the ultimate horror of the holocaust.

Towards the end of April, the final battle for Berlin began and ended. As May came in and people were waking each morning to the hope that it really was all over at last, the news came that the symbol, the perpetrator, of all this madness was gone at last.

328

Hitler had committed suicide.

Maureen Budd and Vera Baxter walked to school together. Jess took them, although there were no roads to cross on the quarter-mile walk, and then she went to collect them again at lunchtime.

Maureen was used to school now. She had already learned to read, astonishing Jess one teatime as she collected the *Evening News* from the doormat and came in announcing: 'Look, Mum, there's been a big raid on Berlin.' She spent hours poring over books and she had begun to set her own stories down on paper – large sheets of greaseproof paper which were the best Jess could find, which she covered with stick figures wearing either trousers or short, triangular skirts.

'I don't know why you waste money on that paper,' Rose said disapprovingly. 'She can't draw for toffee.'

Maureen heard her and looked at the pictures. She wanted to say that the drawings didn't matter, it was the story that was important – a long-running story which was represented in each little group of figures – but Rose wouldn't have understood, and in any case it was private. It didn't really matter what other people thought about them.

'It keeps her quiet,' Jess said, 'and she's getting too big to play with those bricks and marbles now.'

There were other interesting things at school, too. They were learning to write numbers and to add them up and take them away. They were given small pieces of chalk each morning with their small blackboards, and had to copy numbers and letters on them. Maureen would form hers as carefully as she could, her tongue protruding slightly from between her lips as she did so, but too often the curves and straight lines were wobbly, and Miss Jenkins told her off.

'The teachers might have something special to tell you today,' Jess said as she left the two girls at the school gates. Maureen looked at her hopefully, but her mother just smiled and kissed her goodbye. 'You'll be able to tell me at dinnertime.'

They went into the school. All the classes joined together in Miss Brown's big room for prayers. They said the Lord's Prayer – 'Our Father, whichart in Heaven, hollow be Thy name . . .' – and sang 'All People That on Earth Do Dwell'. Then Miss Brown rapped on her desk as if she were going to make a special announcement.

'Tomorrow,' she said in her most impressive voice, 'the war may come to an end.'

The children stared at her uncomprehendingly. The oldest amongst them had been only a year old when the war had begun. They had grown up to the wail of the air-raid siren, the nightly flight to the Anderson shelter, the rumble of tanks through the streets and the drone of aircraft above. Some of them had seen the flames of the Blitz and still remembered the crimson glow that had spread all over the sky. Many had not seen their fathers for years, if ever; some never would. Some of them had lost brothers and sisters, uncles and aunts, grandparents, even mothers.

They had no conception of life without war. They did not understand the word 'peace'.

Maureen looked at the head teacher with suspicion. How could anyone *know* that the war would end tomorrow? It was like saying it was going to snow tomorrow, or even that the world itself would end tomorrow. They were things that nobody knew. You woke up one morning and there was snow on the ground. You walked up the road one day and there were Army tanks biting into the kerbstones of September Street. The town was full of soldiers and sailors for weeks, and then suddenly they were gone.

Nobody knew those things had been going to happen. How could they know that something as big as the war, which she dimly understood went on all over the world, was going to end? How would everyone, all over the world, know it was time to stop? Who was going to tell them?

'If it does,' Miss Brown continued, her long necklace glittering on her broad black bosom, 'you'll all be allowed to go home early and you'll have all the next day as a holiday. You won't have to come back to school until Thursday.'

That seemed even more inexplicable. Nice though a holiday would be, the end of the war didn't seem to be any reason to have one. Maureen shrugged and went back to the classroom, dismissing the matter from her mind. It probably wouldn't happen anyway.

At home, she didn't even bother to mention it. In any case, nobody would have listened to her. They were all too busy. Frank was home early and went straight up through the little square hatchway that led to the roof space, where he could be heard rummaging about amongst the boxes that lived up there. He came down a bit later, covered in cobwebs, his arms full of coloured bunting.

'I knew we still had them.' He dropped the bundle in the middle of the floor and Tim pounced on them gleefully. 'Enough to decorate half the street, that is.'

Between them, Tim and Keith untangled the small coloured flags on their long tape. They strung them all round the back room and into the front room and up the stairs, and there were still a few piled up by the door. Frank and Jess sat down and laughed at them, while Maureen watched in amazement, wondering what it was all about.

They had tea, and for a special treat they all had an egg. A whole egg! Of course, they weren't really short of eggs, the hens kept them supplied, but Jess was still very careful with them and gave a lot to Annie. She hardly ever boiled six all in one go, so that they had one each.

Maureen dipped her bread into the yolk, trying to make sense of the talk going on over her head. What was a tandem? Frank was talking about having one, as if it were something really special. Perhaps it was a sort of dog, she thought hopefully, and missed the next bit. Now they were talking about street parties. That was something else she couldn't make head or tail of. For one thing, parties were something you had at Christmas, and you didn't have them in the street, you went up to Auntie Annie's, or she and Uncle Ted came down to number 14. She caught the word 'jelly' a couple of times and went off into another dream. Jelly was another thing you only had at Christmas or on special occasions. Maureen liked it, though she didn't like having to eat a slice of bread and butter with it: the crumbs didn't feel nice with the wobbly jelly, and she usually tried to leave that till last. (She'd tried eating it first, until Rose had noticed and made her have another slice.)

'Well, it'll be lovely not to have to think about all those horrible things any more,' Jess said, gathering up the plates and eggcups, 'but I don't suppose it'll all come right overnight. There's still Japan, you know. That Emperor of theirs won't give in. There's going to be plenty of people tomorrow like our Annie, still worrying about their boys in Japanese POW camps.'

Maureen went to bed soon after tea. It wasn't dark yet, and she could hear a lot of talk going on out in the street. It sounded as if people were clambering about on the walls of the houses. After a while she could bear it no longer, and got out of bed to creep to the window. Pulling the curtain aside very carefully, just in case either of her parents might be out there and see her, she peeped out.

There they all were: Frank and Jess, Bert Shaw, Annie and Ted, Tommy Vickers and his wife Freda, even Nancy Baxter and her mother. They had ladders and chairs and stools, and they were all climbing and standing on them, holding great festoons of coloured flags just like the ones her father had produced and stringing them up on pegs and nails hammered into the walls, tying them round drainpipes and guttering, fixing them to whatever they could find to fix them to. As they worked, they called out to each other and laughed, and now and then someone

331

would start singing – 'Roll Out the Barrel', or 'Pack Up Your Troubles In Your Old Kit Bag', and then everyone else would join in.

Mrs Sefton, who ran the little shop on the corner, turned her white head and Maureen ducked quickly back and let the curtain drop. She slipped back into bed and lay there, bewildered.

It must be to do with the war ending. She just hoped it would, because if it didn't after all this fuss, everyone was going to be so disappointed.

She didn't even have to wait for Miss Brown to tell them at school. When she got up next morning, her father was downstairs, just as if it were a Sunday, and Keith and Rose were at home too. Tim had had to go to the ferry, but he and Ted had gone off bearing another great swag of coloured flags, to dress the ferry-boat overall. It seemed as if Portsmouth was going to be a mass of red, white and blue, and Union Jacks were flying everywhere.

'The war's over!' Jess told her, catching her in her arms for a big hug. 'It's really over. No more air raids, no more bombs, no more rationing – well, there will be for a while, I suppose, but it won't be for long. We'll be able to go wherever we like, whenever we like.'

'Even more when we've got the tandem,' Frank put in. He was looking jollier than Maureen could ever remember, except at Christmas. He swept her up on to his knee, where she hardly ever sat, and jiggled her up and down. 'And then you'll see what the countryside's like. You'll be coming with us, in a little seat on the back.'

Jess took Maureen and Vera to school as usual, but the streets were different. There were flags everywhere, and more people out in the streets than Maureen had ever seen. They were all smiling and Jess stopped to talk to people so often that Maureen and Vera were very nearly late.

Not that it would have mattered all that much. They went into Miss Brown's room for prayers and the usual hymn, and Miss Brown called the register. Not much different there. Then she rapped on her desk, just as if someone had been making a noise, and looked around at them all. She was smiling, and so were all the rest of the teachers. Even, Maureen noticed with amazement, her own teacher, Miss Jenkins.

'I told you yesterday, children, that the war might be coming to an end today,' Miss Brown said. 'Well, I am very happy to tell you that it has.' Again, they stared back at her. They all knew this by now, and it still meant little more than it had yesterday, except that obviously everyone was getting ready for a party. 'There will be no more war,' she said impressively. 'This was the war to end all wars and from now on the whole world will live in peace.'

Well, that wasn't true for a start. Maureen's mother had said only last night that Japan was still fighting, and Auntie Annie still worried about Colin, but Miss Brown didn't seem to know about Japan, and all the other teachers were still smiling, so maybe Jess was wrong.

'Now you can all go home,' the head teacher told them. 'The rest of today and all day tomorrow is a holiday. Have a nice time, and be good children, and come back on Thursday morning.'

The children trudged out. It hardly seemed worth coming at all, just to say 'Our Father Which art' and sing a hymn and then go home again, but they were glad to have a holiday, and once they were out of the playground they began to whoop and run, playing tag and screaming with the excitement they had caught from the grown-ups and didn't know what else to do with.

Maureen and Vera Baxter walked home together. Maureen hadn't told her mother she might be coming home early, so Jess hadn't waited at the gate. They looked at the bunting that was being strung up everywhere, and at people with red, white and blue ribbons in their hats. One girl was dressed from head to foot in a big Union Jack, and everyone was laughing and happy.

'I still don't know how they knew it was going to happen,' Maureen said, mystified. 'How could they *tell*?'

But Vera knew no more than she, and after a while they gave up wondering and broke into a run. If there was going to be a party, they wanted to be there. What's more, someone had once told Maureen that when the war was over there would be bananas, and Maureen had never seen a real banana.

# CHAPTER TWENTY-FIVE

VE Day. That's what they were calling it – VE for Victory in Europe. It seemed as if the whole of Portsmouth, the whole of the country, and indeed most of the rest of the world, were slowly going mad with delight.

'Let's go down to the Guildhall Square,' Jess said. 'There's going to be a thanksgiving service there. All the bigwigs – the Lord Mayor and the Mayoress, and the Church people, and the Services – there's going to be a real parade. They say it'll be the biggest turnout since that one before the war, when Mr Chamberlain came back with his piece of paper.'

'And look what that led to!' Frank said, but he couldn't take the look of joy off Jess's face, and he was as eager as she to join in the celebrations. He went upstairs and put on his best suit, the one he'd got married in nearly eighteen years ago, and came down to find the rest of the family ready.

'It's a shame Tim's not here,' Jess said as they set off up the street, 'but I suppose someone's got to run the ferry. Not that our Tim runs it all by himself,' she added with a laugh, 'but you know what I mean.'

They caught a bus part of the way and then walked the last part down Commercial Road towards the Guildhall Square. It was very different from that other occasion, Jess thought. Then, everyone had been light headed with relief that there wasn't going to be any war after all, that Hitler wasn't the threat they'd thought. Now, after nearly six years of bitter conflict that had spread like a plague over the whole world, they were sadder and wiser. Their mood was of joy, but beneath it was a deep and abiding sorrow.

The city was different, too. On that day in October 1938, the buildings had been whole and solid, a reassuring bastion against all comers, but the enemy had come from the skies and beaten the proud city almost to a pulp. So many buildings had gone, so many streets been laid waste, and like a symbol that stood for them all, the Guildhall itself stood gutted, an empty and blackened shell, yet still dominating the square that was the heart of Portsmouth. Its tower still stood above the scarred and burnt-out walls, and the lions still rested at the top of its wide steps, but no one knew if it would ever be restored to the magnificence it had once enjoyed.

People were thronging from all over Portsmouth to join in the thanksgiving. They crowded into the big square, milling about to find the best places from which to see the procession. The police were there, clearing a large space in front of the Guildhall steps, and as Jess and Frank and the children arrived, they heard the first thumping sounds of the big drums of the Royal Marine band, and saw the first contingent march into view.

'Look at that. They're always the smartest, always have been.' Frank gazed proudly as the band strode into the square, trumpets and trombones gleaming as they played 'Land of Hope and Glory' and 'Rule, Britannia!'. At the sound of the patriotic tunes, the crowd cheered wildly and joined in, singing at the tops of their voices, so that the chorus rose in a great roar to fill the air and reverberate amongst the streets and buildings that still stood as marks of defiance to the enemy who had given them such a battering, but who now lay vanquished and abject.

The Marines were followed by soldiers, sailors and airmen – not only British, but French and American and Canadian, as if everyone who happened to be in Portsmouth at this time had been bidden to join in. The women were amongst them, ATS and Wrens, and WAAFs, and then there came the civilian services – the ATC, the WVS and Civil Defence. Even the staff of the local hospitals were on parade this morning, nurses and doctors who had served throughout the war, tending men and women and children who had been wounded by bombs or shrapnel or flying glass. They lined up in front of the broad sweep of steps, unintentionally patriotic in their blue uniforms covered by white aprons, and with their red capes slung loosely about their shoulders.

'Like a ribbon,' Rose said, pointing at them.

Last of all came the Lord Mayor and his entourage. It was a shame, Jess thought, that it couldn't have been the old Lord Mayor, Sir Denis Daley, who had seen them through almost all the war and who had worked so hard with his wife to keep Pompey going, even though a lot of people had grumbled at the time. The new Lord Mayor, Alderman Allaway, had been elected last November and he seemed a good sort. He was certainly looking forward to rebuilding Portsmouth, and that was what was needed now.

The service was taken by the Bishop of Portsmouth and the Provost of the Cathedral. It was moving but short – everyone had wanted to come, but everyone also wanted to get on with the rest of the celebrations. When it was over and the strains of the last hymn had died away, and the Bishop had raised his hand in blessing, there was a moment's silence as they all stood with bowed heads to remember those who had fallen.

The square was still and silent. Nobody moved. Nobody spoke. All had memories of friends and relatives who had gone to war and never returned, or who had been killed in the Blitz. There wasn't a person present in the square that morning who had not lost somebody dear to them during the past six, bitter years. Then, high above their heads, there was a flutter of movement, just enough to make every head turn and every eye look up.

At the top of the Guildhall Tower, proud and undefeated above the blackened walls, flew the White Ensign.

The flag of peace.

The silence continued for perhaps another ten or twenty seconds, and then Portsmouth erupted into the most glorious cacophony of rejoicing that it had ever known. Every ship in the harbour, from the greatest Naval vessel down to Ted Chapman's little ferry-boat, sounded its hooter or its siren. Bells rang from every church tower, and people found whatever instrument they could to make a noise with – from musical instruments like trumpets or fiddles, which were brought out and played in the street, to tin whistles, wooden rattles, bicycle bells and even saucepan lids which could be clashed together like cymbals. If they had nothing to bang or whistle or ring, they used their voices, laughing and shouting and singing, calling out words they could barely hear and knowing it didn't matter, the words didn't matter. All that mattered was to make a noise, as much noise as possible, to pour out their joy and relief and thankfulness that at last it was over and the world was safe, the skies were safe, that the lights could go on again all over Europe.

All the way home, the Budd family's ears were almost deafened by the din, and they found themselves caught up in party after party as people burst from their homes and linked arms to dance, singing, all the way down the street. We're never going to get home at this rate, Jess thought, but Frank's arm was around her waist and Maureen was safe on his shoulders, and the other two were big enough to look after themselves. Jess laughed and let herself go, singing and dancing with the best of them, all the way back to April Grove.

After that, the day flew by, with one excitement following swiftly on the heels of another. At three o'clock, everyone was indoors by their wireless sets, waiting for Mr Churchill's broadcast from 10 Downing Street. Maureen sat on the floor, cuddling her mother's knees. Tim was back home from the ferry, and he and Rose and Keith sat on dining-chairs, with Frank and Jess in their own armchairs by the fireplace.

Winston Churchill's voice was almost as familiar to them as their own. For years they had tuned in to hear his rolling tones, that always sounded as if he were halfway through his dinner, for it was his voice they trusted and in which they found inspiration. His choice of words, the phrases he put together, made a kind of fierce, determined poetry which spoke to their hearts, and which they could carry with them through the long dark days and nights.

'We shall fight on the beaches . . . we shall fight in the fields and in the streets, we shall fight in the hills; we shall never surrender . . .' And they never had, even though it had never come to the invasion they had feared then.

On another dark day in the summer of 1940, soon after the terror and the miracle of Dunkirk, he had exhorted them: 'Let us therefore brace ourselves to our duties and so bear ourselves that if the British Empire and its Commonwealth last for a thousand years, men will still say, "This was their finest hour".'

There had been his acknowledgement of the debt owed by the nation to the brave young pilots and airmen of the RAF during the Battle of Britain: 'The gratitude of every home in our island . . . goes out to the British airmen who . . . are turning the tide of the war. Never in the field of human conflict was so much owed by so many to so few.'

Yes, there was poetry there, poetry of the finest sort, that could appeal to all, from the humblest to the greatest in the land, and even telling the country that he had nothing to offer but 'blood, toil, tears and sweat' had been somehow an inspiration. You felt that whatever happened, he would be there with you, toiling and bleeding, with the sweat and the tears pouring down his own cheeks.

'He must be feeling so proud today,' Jess said softly as they waited. 'All this long time – he must have wondered at times if we'd ever get through it, but he never let anyone see his doubts. Now he can stand up and tell us it's over – and it's him that's got us through it. I feel really grateful to Mr Churchill.'

'Not everyone agrees with you,' Frank said. 'There's some that say he's made a few bad mistakes.'

'I daresay he has. So have we all. But it's the good things we've got to look at, not the mistakes.'

Frank turned the knob and the wireless crackled into life. The deep, measured voice of John Snagge came into the room, and everyone fell silent.

'This is London.'

Jess felt the tears prick at her eyes. She reached across the fireplace for Frank's hand and with her other hand she stroked Maureen's fair head.

Then came the voice they'd been waiting for, to tell them that the war was officially at an end, to tell them that in Europe at least, the fighting was over and peace had come.

'The German war is at an end. Advance Britannia! Long live the cause of freedom! God save the King!'

'God save the King!' Tim cried, and leaped from his chair to stand at attention, his hand raised in a salute. As the National Anthem was played, Keith followed suit, and then all the family, even Maureen. They sang with the tears wet on their faces, and when the anthem was over they hugged each other, crying unashamedly, even Frank, normally so serious, allowing his tears to flow, and Tim and Keith forgetting that tears were babyish and that boys didn't cry.

'I don't know what we're all doing,' Jess said at last, shakily, 'crying like a lot of babies. The war's *over*. You'd think to look at us that it was starting all over again.'

At that, they all laughed, though their laughter was still mingled with tears, and Jess went out to the scullery to put on the kettle. 'We need a cup of tea, and today we're going to forget what Lord Woolton says and have one for each person *and* one for the pot!'

Before she could make the tea there was a hammering on the door and a moment later Bert Shaw burst into the room. Behind him were his daughters, Gladys and Diane, and they were pink faced with excitement.

'Did you hear it? Did you hear Mr Churchill? It's really over, it really is,' said Diane. They were both in uniform, Diane in the slate-blue of the WAAFs, Gladys in navy, and they were both bubbling over with joy. They stood and looked at the Budd family, their lips pursed tight as if they were suppressing giggles, and then Diane gave her sister a sharp nudge in the ribs. 'Go on, Glad. Tell them.'

Gladys blushed and Jess, staring from one to the other, realised that their excitement came from something more than the war ending. She raised her eyebrows at Bert. 'Tell us what? What are they on about? They look as if they won the war all by themselves.'

'Too pleased with themselves by half,' Bert grunted. 'Only come home and told me they've got engaged – the pair of 'em! Never a by-your-leave or a thought of asking their father for permission, but that's what girls are like these days.'

'Engaged!' Jess exclaimed. 'But who to? I never even knew you had a young man.'

'Well, we have. Two, actually,' Diane giggled. 'One each, I mean. And we've had them for quite a while, and we're engaged and got rings to prove it.' She stuck out her left hand, and Jess saw the diamond gleaming on her finger.

Gladys held out her hand too. She had a five-stone ring. The diamonds were the size of pinheads, but they looked real enough, not that that was the important thing. It was the thought that counted, and the love behind it.

'But who . . . ?'

'Cliff,' Gladys said, blushing again. 'Cliff Weeks. You know, Tommy Vickers's nephew.' She giggled suddenly. 'I'll have to call him Uncle Tommy now!'

'Cliff Weeks? Well!' She didn't know quite what to say. She could understand Bert feeling a bit flummoxed. Girls just didn't go off and get engaged without their parents' approval – though Gladys was quite old enough, of course, and Diane had always been an independent miss. 'Well, congratulations. I hope you'll both be very happy.'

'Well, *I* won't be able to do much about it if they're not,' Bert said. '*This* young madam –' he indicated Diane – 'reckons she's going off to America, of all places. A Yankee pilot, that's who *she's* got herself hooked up to. Off to the other side of the world, that's where she's going, and I don't suppose I'll ever see her again.'

'An American?' Jess's eyes widened. 'But—'

She said no more. The front door had been left open and outside they could hear voices, laughing and shouting, calling to them to come out. Tim and Keith, bored with talk of engagements, dashed outside and the rest of the family followed.

April Grove was full of people. They were bringing furniture out into the street, setting up tables in the middle of the road and spreading them with cloths, standing chairs around. Piles of crockery, mostly the white utility sort, were being carried out and it was clear that the entire street was getting ready for a party. Even Carol Glaister was there, bringing out what was left of her mother's best tea set, her pale cheeks flushed and her eyes brighter than Jess had ever seen them. Perhaps the poor girl would come to life a bit now, Jess thought, though she still had her mother to look after.

'Leave the door open,' Jess said to Frank. 'We can hear the wireless out in the street if you turn it up loud enough.' Other people did this too and as they went back and forth, bringing out the cakes they'd made with sugar and fat hoarded for this day, and the bowls of jelly and blancmange, and the sandwiches so many of them had spent the morning and half the afternoon filling and cutting, they could hear the crackling voices coming to them from London.

Mr Churchill had gone straight from Broadcasting House to the House of Commons, to read his statement there. After that, he'd gone to Buckingham Palace to talk to King George and he'd actually appeared on the balcony with both the King and Queen Elizabeth. The crowds in front of the Palace had gone wild, cheering and shouting and calling for him over and over again. Together, they all sang 'Land of Hope and Glory' and 'Rule, Britannia!' and Mr Churchill told them, 'This is your victory. In all our long history we have never seen a greater day than this.'

The day seemed to last for ever. The sky was grey and there was some drizzle, but it didn't seem to matter. Nobody cared that they were having their tea in the street in the rain, and they just made jokes about the quality of the tea being better, now peace had come. Later, as darkness fell, Frank dragged Jess's piano out and she sat down and began to play songs that they could all sing – songs like 'Keep the Home Fires Burning', that had been popular during the First World War, and tunes that she'd learned quite recently, like 'Run, Rabbit, Run' and 'Smoke Gets In Your Eyes'.

Annie and Ted came down the street to join in. Properly, their house was part of March Street, but since their windows looked straight down April Grove and they had family there, they always felt more a part of the little cul-de-sac and it was only natural to want to be together on a day like this.

Beneath her smile, Annie was looking sad, and when Jess took one hand from the keys of the piano and laid it on hers, she saw tears in her sister's eyes.

'Annie! What is it?' As soon as the words were out of her mouth, she regretted them. 'I shouldn't ask. It's Colin, isn't it? Oh, Annie, I'm sure the war'll be over in Japan as well, soon.'

'I hope so.' Annie wiped her eyes. 'I hope so. I know I shouldn't let it get me down, Jess, specially today when everybody's so pleased and happy – but when I think of him out there in that prisoner-of-war camp, and when I think of the stories you hear about what goes on in them – well, I just can't help it. It's as if they've been forgotten. The war in Europe's the only thing that matters, and never mind the poor devils out in the Far East.'

'It's not like that really.' Jess was playing quite mechanically now, but she doubted if anyone noticed, they were all singing so loudly. 'People can't help letting off steam over VE Day. They're not thinking about

Japan just now, it's true, but they'll remember again, you'll see. Boys like your Colin aren't going to be forgotten.'

'I know. It just comes over me at times . . . and it's not just him, it's Olive as well.' Annie stepped back as Freda Vickers came up and offered to take over the piano-playing for a bit, to give Jess a break. 'I don't know what's the matter with her, Jess, I don't, honest. It's as if she's lost all interest in life. She's like Ted was when he had that breakdown. I tell you what, it frightens me at times.'

Jess got up from the piano and went to get herself a drink of lemonade. Someone had managed to get hold of a whole tin of lemonade crystals and made up a huge jug with water, a bit weak because it had to go a long way, but a treat all the same. 'When's she coming out of hospital?'

'In a couple of weeks, they think, and then she might be sent home for a bit, to recuperate. Mind, I reckon she'll be demobbed pretty well straight away. She's not needed on the ack-ack guns any more and they'll be looking to get rid of all the volunteers as soon as possible, now it's all over.' Annie sighed. 'I daresay Derek'll be home before long, as well.'

'Well, that'll be good, won't it? It's him she needs.' Jess sipped her lemonade and watched the dancers. 'Oh, Annie, isn't it lovely to think that people can do this sort of thing again – dance in the streets, let their lights shine out, and have a good time without being afraid of air-raid warnings and sirens and bombs.' Then her face saddened as she thought of all those who could not be here, to laugh and sing and enjoy the ending of their six years of fear and suffering. 'If only poor Peggy could see it. And Mum and Dad. And that young sailor, Graham Philpotts, that your Betty was keen on. And Mike and Kathy Simmons, and all the others . . .'

'I know,' Annie said. 'I know. It's a good day, Jess, and I'm glad we're here to be a part of it, but it isn't over, not by a long chalk. Sometimes, I wonder if it ever will be.'

# CHAPTER TWENTY-SIX

As Annie had prophesied, there was much still to be done before the war could be considered entirely over.

The bitter fighting continued in the Far East. The war in Europe had never been of much concern to the Japanese, who had merely taken advantage of it for their own ends. Only a few days after VE Day, Mr Churchill was broadcasting again with a warning that 'our troubles are not yet over' and a reminder to remember why the war was fought.

It was a shock to discover that the end of the war, which had somehow been expected to bring a miraculous change in everyone's daily lives, didn't seem to be making any improvements at all. In some areas, it was making them even worse.

'Rations being cut *again*!' Jess exclaimed as she listened to the news. 'But why? Only four ounces of bacon a week was bad enough, but three . . . And only an ounce of cooking fat per person, and soap being cut . . There ought to be more, not less.'

'It's because of Europe,' Cherry said. 'Now they're liberated we've got to help them. They're starving over there and we've got to share what we've got.'

'But Europe's huge. They've got much more room than we have to grow things, and we've had hardly anything coming into the country all these years.'

Frank shook his head. 'It's big, but look what's been going on there. All that fighting and bombing – crops ruined, animals killed, and troops overrunning the countryside. They've been feeding their armies too, and our POWs, I suppose,' he added as an afterthought.

'Not so as you'd notice,' Cherry observed. 'Gave 'em just enough to keep 'em alive and left it at that, by all accounts.'

'Well, they seem to be pretty well starving, anyway,' Frank said. 'I know we had a bad time of it, but it seems to me they've had worse. All that bombing – we hit 'em far harder than they hit us, especially in the last year or so. You felt sorry enough for them then, Jess.'

'I know.' She really didn't mind all that much, sharing what little there was with the people who had been so badly treated by the Germans. That was what the war was all about. But it did stick in her craw a bit, to have to give up a quarter of her bacon ration for the Nazis who had started it all and acted so evilly throughout the last six years.

However, the people of Portsmouth were too determined to recover from the war to let a little thing like a slice of bacon worry them for long. Less than a fortnight after VE Day, they were opening the first Navy Week for five summers. People poured through the dockyard gates for the traditional visits to the ships moored to the Southern Railway jetty, and Nelson's flagship, HMS *Victory*, was open again for the first time in six years. Tim and Keith were almost the first on board, laughing as they remembered how the Germans had claimed it had been destroyed in one of the earliest raids.

'That Lord Haw-Haw thought he could scare us silly with his daft broadcasts,' Tim said, and imitated the sneering, plummy accent. '"Jairmany Calling. Jairmany Calling". Huh! He could have saved his breath.'

'They'll catch him soon,' Keith agreed, 'and then I expect he'll be hanged or shot for being a traitor.'

Navy Week was a celebration that was special to Portsmouth. For years, these open weeks had been held and civilians welcomed aboard His Majesty's ships, and this time it was a chance for the citizens to say thank you in person to the sailors who so proudly showed them their vessels. Tim and Keith climbed all over the ships on display, imagining what it had been like only a few weeks ago, when the world was still at war. They stared at the gun turrets and climbed down vertical ladders to go below and look at the engines. Tim was especially interested in these.

'They're a lot bigger than the *Ferry King*'s, but I reckon I could work them all right. Tell you what, Keith, I'm going to join the Merchant Navy when I've finished being an apprentice. I'll go all over the world. I'll see Japan and China and Africa and Australia – everywhere. I'll get paid for it too!'

'I'd like to go to sea, too,' Keith said, 'but I'd rather be in the Royal Navy. I'd like to be on an aircraft carrier and look after the aeroplanes.'

There were events all over the city. Frank and Jess went to the concert at the King's Theatre and heard a fanfare of music composed especially for VE Day. The week came to an end with a grand finale in the Guildhall Square, with bands and community singing. Afterwards, people strolled home in the gathering dusk, still revelling in the novelty of lights that shone from windows without blackout, and the pools of yellow thrown on to the pavements by the gas lamps.

'I suppose the next thing will be the general election,' Jess said. Mr Churchill had resigned as Prime Minister of the coalition government and been asked by the King to lead a caretaker government while the election could be arranged. Now the parties were gathering together their resources just as if they hadn't worked together all these years. 'It seems a shame we've got to go back to party politics. I don't know why they have to be in such a hurry about it.'

'It's different now,' Frank said. 'They've been running a war. Now they've got to run a peace. I wouldn't be surprised if Labour gets in.'

'Oh, surely not! Not after all Mr Churchill's done.'

'Look at it this way. A lot of what's been done is more like Labour policies than Conservative ones, and people like a change. They don't want anyone in power for too long.'

The city was filling up now with returning Servicemen. Portsmouth's own Army unit, the 698s, were due to begin demob in July. That meant three men in the street coming home – Bob Shaw, Derek Harker and George Glaister – although nobody knew whether George Glaister would actually return to April Grove. He'd marched away nearly three years ago, swearing he never wanted to see Ethel again. Perhaps he wouldn't come back at all, but if he did he'd find things very different.

Ethel was still in bed, and Carol had to do everything for her. Her mother's body was thin and light now, so it was quite easy, but even so it took quite a lot of strength to heave her about in the bed. She'd had a second stroke, just after VE Day, and now she was completely paralysed. Only her eyes seemed alive, and they stared at Carol as she moved about the bedroom, giving her an uncanny feeling. She didn't know whether Ethel was really awake or not.

'It's creepy,' she said, and wrote to her aunt in Devon to ask if they could keep her sister Shirley there. Shirley was thirteen now and had been staying with her relatives since she'd come back from being torpedoed on the way to Canada. They were happy to keep her there; she was one of the family now and they'd been dreading having to part with her.

'You can come and stop here too, if you want,' her aunt wrote to Carol. 'We know about your trouble, but no one's going to hold it against you. We all make mistakes.'

Carol was touched, but she didn't want to go to Devon. If anything happened that meant she didn't have to look after Mum any more, she was going to Scotland. She still had the letter Roddy had written to his mother three years ago. When Roddy was let out of prison – as he must be soon – that's where he would go, and Carol wanted to be there for him.

She went upstairs to give her mother a wash. Gladys Shaw, who had been a nurse, had come in and explained to her what she must do, and Carol followed the instructions carefully. She'd helped the nurses at St James's too, with some of the worst patients, and knew how to lift and turn a helpless body, and how to prevent bedsores.

Carol's stay in St James's was something she tried not to think about too much. They hadn't been unkind to her in there, but they were firm and didn't take much account of people's unhappiness. Only one or two of the nurses had understood why she'd done what she'd done, and had looked after her with more gentleness when she'd first arrived, a weeping, crumbling heap of misery. They'd listened while she told them about Roddy and the baby and they'd understood her feelings of despair and the way her mind seemed to have just crumpled after she'd run out of the house the night Reg had attacked her. They didn't seem to think she was bad or criminal, and if it hadn't been for them, she thought she would have gone right round the bend, like some of the other poor souls in the wards.

Slowly, she had recovered her strength. She hadn't really thought they'd ever let her out again – there were a lot of old men and women there who had been in since they were young, for less reason than Carol – but always in her mind had been the idea that one day Roddy might find her and rescue her. She'd been determined that he would find her worth rescuing – a girl who hadn't, after all, let life beat her, who had kept her self-respect and could hold up her head.

She finished washing Ethel. It was strange, holding her mother's thin body and washing it as if it were a baby's, and she had to overcome a feeling of repugnance every time she touched the dry, flaky skin. Her mother's eyes looked up at her, and she stared into them, trying to see whether there was really any expression in them or if they were just blank. She felt a momentary pang of pity as she wondered what it must be like to be trapped in a helpless body, without any means of letting people know you were there.

It must be the worst prison on earth.

'Oh, Mum,' she said quietly, looking into the china-blue eyes, 'what happened to you? You must have loved Dad once. You must have loved Joe and Shirley, and even me. What happened to spoil it all? What made you change?'

To her surprise, there was an answering flicker in the doll-like face, a minute widening of the pupils. She stared as the blue eyes darkened and the still, frozen muscles of her mother's face suddenly changed. The mouth that used to be painted like a Cupid's bow twisted, and the whole of Ethel's face seemed to slip sideways and melt into a frightening blur.

'*Mum . . .*'

Ethel sucked in a great gulp of air. Her eyes were now completely black. Her nostrils flared and widened, her mouth opened in a ghastly grimace and she jerked in Carol's arms, then her body sagged and went still. Carol knew, without having to feel for her heart, without having to touch her face, that it was all over.

Ethel Glaister was dead.

The whole of April Grove came to her funeral, but everyone knew it was more for Carol's sake than out of respect for Ethel herself. Afterwards, a few of the nearest neighbours came into number 14 for a cup of tea and a sandwich or two. Carol sat in Jess's armchair, pale and quiet, looking dazed by the kindness she was being shown.

'I feel sorry now we never did more for her before,' Jess said to Annie. 'She's not a bad girl at all, when you get to know her. She's been a really good little nurse to Ethel.'

'I know. I've sometimes thought you couldn't really blame her for what she did – running off with that sailor. It couldn't have been much of a life for her after George joined up, especially when Joe went as well. And then having to give her baby away – well, I know it was all out of wedlock and that, but it was her baby, when all's said and done. I can't imagine ever giving one of mine away, can you?'

Jess shuddered at the thought. 'Well, maybe she'll be able to start fresh now. What with the war over and her mum gone, it sounds awful to say it, but she'll be better off. I wonder what she'll do now. Perhaps she'll go down to Devon to her auntie, or maybe she'll stop here for when her dad comes home.'

Carol had no intention of doing either of these things. She had made up her mind long ago what she would do, if ever she were free again, and when she went back into number 15, she went straight upstairs and opened the drawer of her dressing-table.

The letter that Roddy had written to his mother, before he had been arrested and taken away in Bournemouth, was still there, its envelope crumpled and the handwriting faded but still legible. Carol had never opened it. She knew just what he had said.

He had given it to her to take to his mother in Scotland, if ever she should need help. Carol had needed help very soon, although she hadn't thought then that his mother would have been willing to give it. Now,

346

though, she got out her own writing pad and sat down to compose her own letter.

'Dear Roddy . . .'

The bombing was still going on over Japan. Emperor Hirohito's palace had been bombed, but he and his family had escaped unhurt. The American Air Force carried out more firebomb attacks on the cities, and the Japanese responded with kamikaze attacks on their ships. These attacks were the most bewildering of all, for they were suicide missions, the pilots using their entire aircraft as a massive bomb and flying it straight into the target. A nation which was prepared to do that was never going to surrender.

'It isn't in their nature,' Tommy Vickers said. 'They lose face if they surrender, and they'd rather kill themselves than lose face.'

Tommy Vickers and his wife Freda had welcomed the news of their nephew Cliff's engagement to Gladys. They'd already started to prepare for the wedding, and Freda had told Gladys she would do everything for her that her own mother would have done. 'It's a dreadful shame she can't be here to see you, but I've done my best to be a mum to our Cliff since he lost his own, and I'll do as much for you too. I've always had a soft spot for you, Gladys.'

Even Bert Shaw couldn't find anything to grumble about in Gladys's engagement. She and Cliff wanted to stay in Portsmouth, she said, and although they refused to move in with Bert they wouldn't be too far away.

It wasn't the same with Diane. One of Chuck's commanding officers had had a long talk with her, to make sure she knew what she was doing in marrying an American – 'He did his best to put me off,' she reported later with some indignation – and they were going to be married as soon as Chuck was back with his squadron. Diane would have to wait for a while before she could actually go to America, but she was determined to leave at the first possible moment.

'America!' Bert snorted. 'I suppose she thinks she's going to be a film star. Always had her head in the clouds, our Diane has, not like her sister. My Glad's got a bit of sense, knows it's right to stop at home near her dad.'

'You can't keep them at home all your life, Bert,' Jess said, trying to comfort him, 'and your Bob'll be home soon. There's going to be a lot of changes and we've just got to get used to them. It's better than war, after all!'

The general election was held on 5 July, the day after Maureen Budd's sixth birthday. Because of the delay in gathering in the Service men and women's votes, the results were not announced until the end of July. It came as a shock to discover that, as Frank has prophesied, Labour had won and Clement Attlee was to be the new Prime Minister.

'It was a landslide,' Frank said, reading the results from the *Daily Express*. 'Three hundred and ninety-three Labour seats, against two hundred and thirteen Tory and "allies" – whatever they are – and thirty-four to Liberals and other parties. That gives them a huge majority – they'll be able to do just what they like.'

'Let's hope they don't get carried away by it,' Jess said, threading a needle. She and Frank had always voted Conservative, despite the fact that most of the people they knew were Labour. She felt sorry for Mr Churchill, who had worked so hard and now had to leave his home and his position to go into Opposition. 'He'll be back,' she said. 'People will soon realise what a jewel he is.'

The doorbell rang, making them jump. Frank went to answer it and came back a minute later with Carol Glaister. She looked pink and excited and a little scared.

'Carol!' Jess said in surprise, and laid down her needlework. 'What's the matter? You've not had bad news about your dad, have you? Or Shirley?'

'I haven't had bad news about anything,' Carol said breathlessly. She looked from one to the other. 'I – I just wanted to ask you if you'd look after my key for me. My front door key,' she added as they looked mystified. 'I'm going away and the landlord'll be wanting it back, only I haven't got time to go round with it myself. Would you mind?'

'Mind? No, of course not, but—' Jess hesitated. She didn't like to ask where Carol was going, but the girl was still young, after all, and it didn't seem right to let her go without someone knowing. Suppose her dad came back and nobody could tell him where his daughter was . . . 'I suppose you're going down to Devon, to your auntie's. Will you be bringing Shirley back with you? Are you going to be away long?'

'For ever,' Carol said without drama. 'I'm not going to Devon. Shirley wants to stay there and they want her.' She lifted her chin and looked at them, her eyes bright. 'I'm going to Scotland.'

'*Scotland?*'

'That's right. I'm going to be with my Roddy. We're going to get married, like we always wanted to.' Her eyes glittered with tears. 'You don't have to get permission once you're sixteen in Scotland, so we won't have to wait. I had a letter from him today.' She took an envelope out of her pocket and stared at it as if even now she couldn't quite believe it. 'He's out of prison and he wants me to go to him. He sent me the fare.'

The tears were slipping down her cheeks now and her voice trembled. 'He wants me. He still *wants* me, even after – after—' The quivering voice broke and she put both hands to her face and shook with sobs.

'Oh, Carol.' Jess got up and put both arms round the thin shoulders. 'Oh, Carol, I'm really glad. Everything'll be all right for you now, I know it will. He's the right boy for you. He must be, for both of you to still feel the same after all this time, and after all that's happened.' There was no pretence now that nobody knew that Carol had had a baby. 'I hope you'll be very happy.'

'I am happy,' Carol said simply. 'I was going to wait till Dad came home, but with Roddy's letter coming today – well, I can't, I just—' She looked at Jess, and Jess thought with surprise, why, the girl's really pretty. She had always seemed so nondescript before, but now her face was aflame with life and shone with a beauty Jess would never have guessed at. 'Will you explain to him? I've left him a letter, but I'd like someone to tell him, just in case he's disappointed. And I will come back to see him, some day. Only not to live here.' She shivered. 'I'll never live here again.'

I don't suppose George will want to either, Jess thought. Number 15 had never been a happy house – not like her own. She hugged Carol again. 'Of course I'll tell him. Now, what time's your train? Would you like Frank to come with you on the bus, help you with your things? Or Tim, he's upstairs.'

Carol shook her head, smiling. 'I'm not taking much. Just my clothes and a couple of knick-knacks that were mine. I don't care about anything else.' She handed Jess the key. 'I daresay Dad'll go down to Devon anyway. He's always hankered after going back there, and Shirley's settled. There's nothing for him here now.'

She gave them both a tremulous smile and hurried out of the door. Jess followed her and watched the slight figure walking rapidly up the street, a suitcase in each hand. She turned the corner and disappeared, without looking back.

So there she goes, Jess thought. That's an end to that story and a beginning to another. Let's hope it'll be a happier one for the poor girl.

April Grove was settling down to peace. The Anderson shelters were torn up or used as garden sheds. Jess planted some flowers in the back garden, where Frank had grown extra vegetables. They were still glad of the hens and their eggs, for it looked as if rationing was going to last for some time yet, but, like the war, they hoped it would be over by Christmas. All they wanted now was for the 'boys' to come home – the Servicemen who had gone away as boys and would come back as men who had fought for and saved their country – and, most of all, for the war to end finally with a victory over Japan.

However, this seemed as far away as ever. It didn't seem to matter what attacks were made against them, the Japanese refused to give in. Their cities firebombed, their people slaughtered, they still rejected all calls to capitulate. It was as if they too had heard that Churchillian call and determined that they would fight on the beaches, in the streets, on the oceans and in the jungles – they would never surrender.

And then, on the sixth of August, came news of the latest and most terrible weapon of them all.

The atom bomb.

Frank heard about it first and told Jess before she listened to the news herself. 'It was dropped on a place called Hiroshima –' his voice stumbled a little over the unfamiliar pronunciation – 'and they reckon it's caused more damage than any other bomb, even worse than those firestorms in Dresden and Berlin.'

'One bomb did that?' Jess said. 'But how could it? It must have been enormous – no plane could carry something that big.'

'It's not that big. It's a new sort of bomb. I don't understand all the ins and outs, but it's something to do with splitting the atom.'

'That's the tiniest thing there is,' Keith put in. He was doing science at school and had learned all about atoms and molecules. 'Everything's made up of atoms, and they're so tiny you've got to have a really good microscope to see them. I don't see how they can split one of those.'

'Well, they have,' Frank said. 'And when they do, it makes a huge explosion, don't ask me how.'

It was nine o'clock. He switched on the wireless so that they could all hear about it. They listened incredulously.

Almost a third of the city's three hundred thousand inhabitants died at once and it was believed that another hundred thousand could die within five years from its after-effects. It was a bomb that effectively wiped Hiroshima from the face of the earth.

'They'll have to give in now,' Jess whispered, but there was no word of surrender, and only three days later a second bomb was dropped, this time over Nagasaki. A huge orange fireball shot up into the sky from the seat of the explosion, and transformed itself into a ten-mile-high column of black, flame-shot smoke which could be seen as far as two hundred and fifty miles away. Again, the city was almost entirely devastated, again thousands of people died, and this time, beaten to their knees and unable to face more, the Japanese surrendered at last.

The war was finally over.

It was like VE Day all over again. VJ Day, they called it, and it began at midnight with a broadcast by Clement Attlee. It seemed funny that it should be him and not Winston Churchill, whose voice had become so well known during the past six years, but there was no time for nostalgia. The minute the broadcast had finished, Portsmouth burst into a frenzy of noisy celebration. For an hour, sirens and hooters sounded, fireworks were let off into the midnight sky, bells rang from the church towers and people poured into the streets for an orgy of singing and dancing. In the Guildhall Square, the crowd was delirious, and soldiers, sailors, airmen and civilians alike joined in a gigantic, boisterous party which went on until dawn. Above them, searchlights played on the drifting clouds, and for a climax and a symbol that Portsmouth was once more itself, someone climbed into the Guildhall Tower and set the chimes to play again.

The Pompey Chimes. The sound brought tears to the eyes of all who had known them so familiarly in the past.

Once again, the whole country was given two days' holiday. Maureen was home from school again and the street was decked with bunting, just as before. This time, she understood what was happening and helped to decorate the house with red, white and blue ribbon, and rosettes she and Rose had made with crêpe paper. The shops had managed to get supplies and everyone had spent the past few weeks preparing for the final victory. It was like a red, white and blue Christmas.

'We're going to get special mugs,' Tim said. 'They'll have pictures of the King and Queen on. I'm going to take mine on the ferry-boat.'

'You'll do no such thing,' Jess said. 'They're *special* mugs. You'll keep them at home, on the mantelpiece.'

Once again, it was a wet day, but nobody was going to let that spoil their pleasure. April Grove was fast becoming expert at holding street parties –they'd had a special VE party in July, with tables laid out all down the street covered with white sheets, and sandwiches, cakes and jelly for everyone. The children had sat at the tables, waited on by the grown-ups, and there had been games and races organised along the road, with prizes. Tim had won a bar of chocolate for running, and Keith had got a bag of toffees for leapfrog. Even Maureen had managed to grab quite a few boiled sweets when Granny Kinch had thrown handfuls over the heads of the crowd of youngsters.

Later on, as darkness fell, the grown-ups had had their own party. Jess had played the piano again and there'd been dancing, and a lot of the men had drunk beer and laughed very loudly. At that point, Frank and Jess had brought the children indoors.

351

Everyone had agreed that it had been a good party, though April Grove seemed unusually quiet next morning, and they'd been planning to hold another one as soon as the war was truly over. That was what the two days' holiday was for – to have a proper celebration, a VJ Day party. There had been just time since the last one to collect lots of tubs of fishpaste for sandwiches, and tins of Spam, and people like Jess who made their own jam had each given a jar. Once again bowls of jelly were made – Jess had found the Anderson shelter a good place to set it – and from early morning people were busy getting the street ready, from the bunting festooned all along the walls to the newly swept gutters, to the tables and chairs set out all along the street.

'We might as well keep this piano out in the street permanent,' Frank said as he and the boys struggled out through the front door with it yet again. He and Tommy Vickers had rigged up a tarpaulin shelter for it against the wall of the end house, so Jess and the music would be dry even if no one else was, but towards the afternoon, the rain eased off and the party went ahead with only a few dashes for shelter in between the games.

'Don't the kiddies love it all,' Annie said, watching as they raced up and down the street, their legs tied together for the three-legged race or wrapped in sacks for the sack race, potatoes wobbling in spoons for the egg-and-spoon and faces wet from bobbing for early apples off Mrs Ward's tree.

Jess smiled. Her sister looked much happier now, knowing that the war in Japan was at an end and nothing more could happen to Colin. It might be a while before they heard any real news of him, but surely the prisoners would be released and brought home as soon as possible now. There had already been quite a lot of men brought back from Germany, and every time one of them came home you saw the house decorated with the inevitable red, white and blue and big welcome banners hung outside.

Soon, she felt sure, there would be one for Colin.

'I'm going home for a minute or two,' Annie said suddenly. 'I want our Olive out here enjoying this. It's not right, skulking about indoors when everyone's having such a good time outside.'

She walked quickly up April Grove to the turret house. Olive had come home only a few days ago, and although the doctors had said she could do whatever she felt able to do, she didn't seem to want to do anything more than just lie in a chair, her eyes half-closed as if she couldn't bear to face the world. Even the news that the war was finally over didn't seem to be enough to rouse her – in fact, Annie had got the impression that it made her feel even worse.

Olive herself knew that it was doing her no good, but she just didn't seem to be able to muster the energy to lift herself out of her chair. It took all she'd got to get out of her bed in the morning and come downstairs at all. Even the news that the war had ended failed to touch her. She heard it with a sort of dull resignation and a wry twist of the lips. It was over, but it wouldn't bring anything back.

'It'll bring Derek back,' Annie said with exasperation. 'Isn't that what you've always wanted?'

Olive shrugged. Once, it had been all she wanted, but now . . . Everything was different now, and when Derek knew the truth, he might not want her. He almost certainly *wouldn't* want her.

I wish I'd died when Ray did, she thought. Or back in the Blitz, when Kathy was killed and I lost Derek's baby. It would have been better for everyone.

'You're just sorry for yourself,' her mother told her impatiently. 'Look, Olive, I know you've had a bad time, but so have a lot of others. There's girls and women out in that street now who've lost their own men, and they can still find a smile and a song. What makes you so different that you can't pull yourself together and see the good side? It's over. There won't be any more bombs. Derek's coming back. What is there to mope about?'

Olive could not even begin to tell her. What would her mother say if she tried? 'I've lost the man I loved, and lost our baby too.' She could imagine the shock and disgust on her mother's face, disgust that would last for the rest of her life. She would never be forgiven.

Perhaps she didn't deserve to be forgiven, but if anyone had the right to forgive, or withold that forgiveness, it wasn't her mother, it was Derek, and Olive still couldn't face the idea of telling him. Worse than the shock, worse than the disgust, would be the pain she would deal him. I can't hurt him like that, she thought, not after all we've been to each other. I can't.

'Don't keep nagging at me to come out, Mum,' she said, turning away. 'I just don't feel up to it. Anyway, nobody wants to see my long face.'

Annie stared at her, baffled. She couldn't believe that this sad, drooping figure could be her Olive, the girl who had always been so full of life and warmth and happiness. She remembered the wedding day, not long after Dunkirk, and Olive's glow as she and Derek had walked down the aisle of the little church. There had been a sparkle about her that day, almost as if she were on fire, a glitter of happiness, and every time Derek had come home, she had lit up in the same way, warmed by her love and warming everyone else around her.

Now her warmth had disappeared. Something – or someone – had taken it away.

'I'll make you a cup of tea,' she said at last, 'and then me and your dad are going back out to help celebrate. It's VJ Day, in case you haven't noticed. It's history. There'll never be another day like this, and I want to be able to remember it as something good for the rest of my life.'

After she and Ted had gone out again, Olive sat for a little while longer in her chair and then dragged herself to her feet. She went upstairs to the bedroom she used to share with Betty, and then with Derek. Her things were still there: the civvy clothes she'd hung in the cupboard when she'd joined the ATS, the wedding picture of her and Derek in its frame, the photo of him in his Army uniform, taken just before the first time he'd gone away, and the one of the two of them leaning on his little red sports car and laughing. She sat on the bed and looked at them.

Derek's face smiled out at her. It was the face of a boy, fresh, open and unlined. His hair – its dark auburn colour looking merely dark in the sepia photograph – was brushed back from his forehead and in the one of the two of them leaning on the car, he was wearing a Fair Isle pullover in six colours that Olive had knitted for him. It had been her first attempt at Fair Isle, and it had taken her some time to learn to keep the different balls of wool separate and untangled, but Derek had been thrilled with it.

I bet he looks different from that now, she thought. He'd been away two and a half years, and in that time he's been all over Europe, from Africa through Italy and France and Belgium and now he's in Germany itself. He'll never be able to tell me all the things he's seen, and he might not even want to. And even though I've been writing to him all this time, there are plenty of things I haven't mentioned – not just about Ray, but things at home, things that have happened in Pompey, that I've never told him about because the censor would cut them out, or they would only worry him, and what's the use? The doodlebugs, the V2s, the planes we've shot at on the ack-ack . . . Two and a half years of just too much happening. We'll never be able to catch up. We're different people, too. We're older, we've lived different lives. We never even had a home for me to keep for him. We'll have to start all over again, getting to know each other.

And we'll never be able to have a family.

That was the worst part of all. If she had just had a fling with another man, a passing affair, it could perhaps have been forgiven and forgotten. She could have forgiven herself. But the affair between her and Ray had gone much deeper, and its end had brought consequences that would follow her for life. Ray had been killed, and she would never be able to forget him, or forget those last few hours at the flat in Hampstead, the painful joy of lying in his arms. Their baby had been lost, only a few hours after she had felt its first butterfly movements deep within her, and there would never be another.

She could never give Derek a baby.

I can't go back to him, to our marriage, and not tell him the truth, she thought. He has a right to know that if he does want to go on being married to me, he'll never have any children, and I don't know how he'll feel about that. I don't know if he'll be able to tolerate it for the rest of his life. Seeing other men out with their families – seeing his friends with their babies and their children, their sons and daughters. Knowing what he's missing, and all because of me and Ray . . . How could any man live with that?

How can he live with me?

A sudden commotion outside brought her to her feet. She heard her name called and ran to the window, her heart thumping. Down below was a little knot of people. Her mother and father. Her uncle Frank. Gladys Shaw, with her fiancé Clifford Weeks and her father. And someone in Army uniform . . .

Derek! But no – it couldn't be. It couldn't be Derek.

Olive stood at the window, staring down. Her aunt had stopped playing the piano and joined the little crowd of people. The soldier was standing in the middle, talking and waving his arms, and all at once Olive realised who it was.

It was Bob Shaw. He was in the same unit as Derek, had been with him and George Glaister all through the war. He had been to Dunkirk, and to Africa and to Italy, and last of all to Germany, and now he had come home.

That meant that Derek must be coming home too. Suddenly, without warning, without even a telegram to prepare her. He might be walking down the street at this very moment.

Olive backed away from the window. Her body was trembling with shock. She sank down on the bed and looked at the photographs again.

Until today, she had not even been sure that she would be able to live with Derek again. Although all during her affair with Ray she had been aware of her feeling for Derek as a separate thing, something that could live in a different compartment of her mind and could not be touched, the explosion seemed to have changed that. It had burst open the locked door and her feelings had flooded out and leaked away, leaving her numb. She had welcomed that numbness, for without it she would not have been able to face the anguish that she knew dwelt in her heart.

But now the numbness was beginning to wear off, and she looked at the photographs and felt the anguish begin.

I deserve it, she thought, I deserve to feel it, all of it. I've got to take my part in the pain I've caused.

She felt her mind unlock the doors which it had tried so hard to keep closed, so that she could once more begin to feel, and she discovered that after all her emotions had not drained away in the explosion, that they still existed, that she could feel pain again, and love, and perhaps even – one day – joy. For the war was over, the killing had come to an end, and Derek – her Derek, whom she'd always loved – was coming home again, safe and unhurt. He had got through the war safely, and the dread of the little yellow envelope was past.

I love you, she thought, staring at the photographs. I love you. Oh, Derek, I love you so much. If you still want me when you know the truth, I want to start again, to try once more to be the wife you knew and loved. Even though we can never have our own children . . .

She gathered up the photographs, the three of them – the one of him in his Army uniform, the one of the two of them leaning on the little red car, the wedding photograph taken soon after he had come back from Dunkirk – and she pressed them against her face and kissed them.

She stood up and looked into the mirror that hung on the wall. Her face was pale and thin, her hair lank. Derek might have changed in the past two and a half years, but so had she. The photographs showed a laughing girl, a girl whose face glowed and sparkled, who was full of life and love and warmth.

I'll have to do something about that, she thought. I'll have to get back to the girl he remembers, the one he thinks he's coming home to. I'll have to be his Olive again.

Outside in the street, she could hear the strains of the piano. Auntie Jess would be playing it – she'd always loved her piano and even through the war the two families had often gathered together on Sunday nights to stand around it singing as she played. She was playing dance tunes now and Olive went to the window and looked down.

The street was brightly lit. Both the gas lamps were burning, and every house had its lights on and curtains drawn back. The piano had been carried up to the wider space in front of the Chapmans' house, where it stood against the end wall of the last house in March Street. Auntie Jess was sitting on a kitchen chair with her hands on the keys, and Uncle Frank was turning the pages of the music. The road itself was full of people dancing.

Olive watched and listened. Mum's right, she thought, we'll never see another day like this. We've been through history together, all of us, and this is a part of it. Nobody ought to be sitting indoors moping over the past when there's so much future ahead.

She turned away from the window and went to the cupboard to find a frock to put on. Her hands pulled out the red one she'd bought years ago, to go out with Derek the first time he took her to the pictures. Despite all that had happened, it still fitted her, and she pulled it on and brushed out her chestnut hair, then ran downstairs.

The front door stood ajar, light spilling out into the tiny front garden and on to the pavement beyond. She stood at the gate for a moment, drawing together all her courage, and then she heard the tune of the piano change.

> Moonlight and love songs, never out of date,
> Hearts full of passion, jealousy and hate,
> Woman needs man, and man must have his mate,
> That, no one can deny . . .

The melody stabbed at her heart, and as she listened, her eye was caught by a movement at the edge of the circle of light and she saw the tall, familiar figure stride out of the darkness and pause. For a few moments he stood there, unnoticed by anyone else, his eyes searching the throng as if seeking one particular person.

Oh Derek, please understand, she thought. Please, please understand.

And then she took a deep breath and walked forward, into the future.

# EPILOGUE

Repatriation of the German prisoners of war began some months later. They were kept for a while, for there was nowhere to go in their own ruined country, and their labour was useful while the complex task of demobbing the Services and beginning the rebuilding of Britain was being organised. Every now and then, though, a band of Germans was sent back home, to scrape together the remnants of their own lives.

Maureen and Vera were at school one day when a party of these men were marched through Portsmouth to the ship that would take them back to Hamburg. The playground was full of children, playing hopscotch, fivestones and skipping. Maureen and Vera were throwing a ball to one another, and Michael was 'piggy in the middle'.

The tramp of feet was almost unnoticed to begin with, but as it came closer, the children slowly stopped their games and turned to see what was happening. They ran to the railings and pressed their faces against the bars to watch. One of the older ones, who understood more of what had been happening, shouted out, 'It's Jerries! It's German prisoners of war,' and he began to boo.

The jeering was quickly taken up by the rest of the children. They hissed and called out names, the worst they could think of. They pulled their mouths into horrible grimaces and waggled their fingers beside their ears. Some of them bent and picked up gravel from the playground and threw it across the pavement.

Maureen watched, silent and unbelieving. All her life, she had heard about Germans. She had heard her parents and brothers and sister talking about them, she had heard about them on the wireless, she had seen her father stick little pins with black heads into his map to show where they were. She had known that the word itself meant something bad, the worst it was possible to be, and in her mind she had pictured these evil beings as being a kind of black goblin, with fat bodies like spiders and hideous faces. Somewhere along the line, she had associated them also with the word 'germ'.

However, these were not black goblins, nor were they anything like her mental picture of a germ. Instead, she saw a straggling group of ordinary men who looked tired and dirty and unshaven. Men in ordinary dark blue boiler-suits, with worn boots on their feet. Men who looked very like her own father when he came home from his day's heavy labouring in the dockyard. But when Frank Budd walked home from work, he walked upright and proud. No matter how tired he might be, his back was never bowed as these men's backs were, he never looked ashamed and sad and humiliated, as these men did. He had never, throughout the whole war, in all Maureen's knowledge of him, looked defeated.

They must be people's daddies too, she thought. They're not horrible at all. They're just the same as anybody else.

As the party trudged past and she heard the jeering and abuse of the other children's voices in her ears, she felt the tears come hot into her eyes. As she pressed her face against the railings and wished she could smile, to make up for the behaviour of her playmates, there was just one word repeating itself, over and over again, in her bewildered mind.

Why . . . ?